ASPERIA
FIRST LIGHT

MONIQUE ANGEL

Asperia, First Light

Copyright © 2025 by Monique Angel.

MILTON & HUGO L.L.C.
4407 Park Ave., Suite 5
Union City, NJ 07087, USA

Website: *www. miltonandhugo.com*
Hotline: *1- 888-778-0033*
Email: *info@miltonandhugo.com*

Ordering Information:
Quantity sales. Special discounts are granted to corporations, associations, and other organizations. For more information on these discounts, please reach out to the publisher using the contact information provided above.

Library of Congress Control Number: 2024926411
ISBN-13:   979-8-89285-345-3   [Paperback Edition]
                  979-8-89285-346-0   [Hardback Edition]
                  979-8-89285-347-7   [Digital Edition]

Rev. date: 02/21/2025

CONTENTS

THE APOTHECARY

He waited...and watched without the restraints of time, stoically maintaining an eternal vigilance, watching for anomalies and ripples left in the wake of decisions made by his children. It held that his strongest qualities were patience and forbearance. On the surface, everything was normal and predictable. Underneath, he could sense the interplay of fire and water and air. He waited for a day like any other.

EVA

Eva dutifully walked the perimeter of the apothecarist's estate at first light. Just like every other morning, her day started early. Every day she made a thorough daybreak check for fallen birds and other stricken wildlife that might have arrived overnight. Eva's duties as an apothecarist included caring for the injured and the ailing, mainly birds, cats, and dogs. She was on the lookout for sick animals drawn by the apothecary signal emitted by the estate. Eva was the only apothecarist in the town of Destin, and she was constantly on alert for animals in distress for fifty miles surrounding. Eva was inundated every week, almost daily, with calls from townsfolk to assist with an operation on a pet or to call for a lost stray pet.

No animals had arrived overnight. Now for her next service before lunch: crafting. She stopped by the herb garden to gather fresh herbs.

Picking bunches of savory herbs such as chervil, thyme, and oregano, Eva returned to the homestead and hung the herbs in the drawing room to dry. Eva then gathered armfuls of fragrant dry herbs from a nearby table and set to work, filling the bags of dried herbs that she gave away freely to the citizens of Destin. Eva finished bagging the latest batch of remedies and, briskly exiting the house, began to fill the baskets sitting outside the front gate beside a statue of St. Francis, which pertly overlooked the entry to the apothecary. From these baskets, passersby were able to help themselves to the bags of herbs. They usually left a donation in recognition of her gifts in the nearby mailbox. The herbal remedies she deposited in the baskets were labeled with the concerns they addressed. She was able to assist with all the usual maladies of the populace: insomnia, depression, anxiety, skin and lung problems, remedies for substance abuse.

Eva smiled as she put pink-and-yellow ribbon on some of the bags and tags on bottles of oils. She briskly set about decorating love potions and unguents to attract the object of heart's desire for giddy teenagers and relaxing and stimulating balms to stoke the ardor of older couples.

She quickly refilled the basket sitting at the feet of St. Francis. And as she turned to go, he was there! The puppy Albion was sitting at his feet.

"You gave me a heart attack!" yelled Eva.

St. Francis beamed back. His hooded eyes twinkled mischievously.

Eva sniffed. "I haven't got all day," she said, raising her chin to the grinning apparition. "Where's the location of the rescue?"

A location formed in her mind. Flowers. Earth. That was good. A heat map. St. Francis was showing her the animal that needed to be rescued, hadn't crawled underground, or had been locked in a cellar. Rescues from below ground didn't often have successful outcomes.

Tulips. Bells of Ireland. Mournful arrangements. Eva felt an influx of grief. St. Francis sent her an image of himself elbowing her. Eva was far too sensitive, which was, of course, an important trait of apothecarists.

But if Eva wasn't careful, she could get lost in her emotions, drift off into abstraction, and be no use to anyone—least of all to herself.

He sent Eva another feeling—peace…a vision…expanses of fields and stone pillars, headstones.

She tried to think where she had learned of this ancient term. It must have been part of her training.

"A ceme…tary," said Eva awkwardly. "But where?"

St. Francis touched his forefinger to his chin. He looked grave. Eva giggled as she received the word and the impression. But she was still stumped as to the exact location. It was the turn of St. Francis to look impatient.

"Grave, cemetery," said Eva, breaking down the pun.

He raised his eyebrows back at her.

"Look," said Eva. "I can't remember the last time there was a burial in Asperia. We usually cremate pets when they die. I don't think…

maybe outside Asperia? Her heart thumped. "You can't..." Her voice trailed away. "Oh *my*," she said.

Albion thumped his tail noiselessly.

A jogger looked at her quizzically as he ran past. She smiled back at him to show she was unperturbed at being caught talking to a statue. Eva looked back to St. Francis.

He was gone.

"Oh fuck," said Eva fruitlessly, with no audience.

Perturbed, she walked back indoors. She hoped she wouldn't have to go too far outside of the town boundaries for the rescue. She didn't like to leave the town limits, and it would be a hassle to cross the border into the unconsolidated territories, with its wild unmapped trails and disparate vagabonds. There was no suggestion she would have to go near one of the outlying bound cities? Guardians forbid. Eva shivered at the notion.

It was a depressing thought, the prospect of leaving Destin to travel through the unconsolidated territories. Of course, Eva could read during the journey. She could get quite a long way in her self-driving car before the map GPS dropped out and Eva had to take over. But it would be a constant battle to fight nausea, even with medication. And as an apothecarist, proximity sickness was stronger for Eva than for the general populace of Asperia, she reflected as she tidied away the remnants of the dried herbs.

There was a time when the repulsion didn't affect people: city outsiders, elderlies in ascension. Historians, like her first parents, Doug and May, indicated that the taint that bound or repelled was more widely dispersed previously. They said it had always been there, just at imperceptibly low levels. City states, collectively known as the bound cities, may have been merely wary of outsiders in centuries past. There had apparently been a lot of anti-Asperia sentiment dating right back prior to the year of the breaching though, with generations of shock and calamity following the breaching. Now only trading posts provided common ground for a freer flow of information and trade for those who could withstand any repulsion sickness. Implants and race immunity engendered such a tolerance.

It wasn't clear what the difference in cultures between the free states and the bound cities were like before the rise of the city repulsion fields. It was documented, but special training was needed to grasp the contextual differences by even the most high-browed Asperian academics.

Ugh, Eva had long given up book study for the more rewarding sides of her family's lineage: fighting and healing. She smiled as she thought of the upcoming annual karate contest she would adjudicate. She was due to give an opening demonstration of martial arts skills, and at the end of the competition, there would be a lot of cuts and bruises and wounded pride to salve. She thought again of the rescue.

Because Eva was an apothecarist, she was acquainted with the notion of burials. She observed how primates in the zoos, she sometimes attended for skills training, tried to dig into the ground in an attempt to bury their dead fellows. Eva had, had a brief introduction to the concept of burials during her training at the College of Mind. But modern humans had realization of ascension and had had divined such knowledge since the breaching. It was also useful to rise into ascension to communicate with crossed-over souls and loved ones.

Biology certainly made you foolish at times. And more than that, it made you susceptible! Eva mused as she heaped some coffee beans in the grinder, making herself a fresh cup of coffee. She considered what she needed to do to prepare for the upcoming rescue, before the appointed rescue was lost to death and time. Guardians forbid! It wouldn't be the end for the soul though. Oh no! Death was inevitable. Sad. An interruption. But one had to be pragmatic. One day a body was no longer needed. That was all. Nothing sentimental about passing over in Eva's eyes. Yet it was hard to let go. And the journey was not guaranteed to be discomfort free. The body aged. Attachment to life was pain and suffering and indescribable wonder all rolled into one.

Eva gathered her things together as she was thinking. It was helpful to know in advance to prepare your worldly affairs. Once a body was used, it was discarded. Was it necessary to ritualize a shell with a burial? Not in this day and age. Some did in the unconsolidated territories though. Curious. Eva crossed herself. She was blessed to be rebirthed in a position where she could help those who weren't so sophisticated and couldn't necessarily speak for themselves.

It was a thin layer that separated the dimensions of corporeal Earth and ascension. And at some point, in evolution, it was assumed, human minds wouldn't have been able to cross this layer. Eva crossed herself again.

Eva touched minds briefly with her parents currently in ascension. By the time Eva was in ascension, they'd be in a state of rebirth, just like Eva's other parents. It wouldn't be long now. Eva made an effort to keep in touch.

Doug and May were getting younger. After forty years in ascension, they looked to be about thirty-five years. Still in the drawing room, Eva drew down and occupied her incorporeal self.

Eva, Doug, and May flowed through ascension together. It was an experience reminiscent of walking the busy streets of modern-day Tokyo, Chicago, or Mexico City: scores of people all moving in the same direction—all with purpose and the connected consciousness opening for the passage of an individual here, allowing a connected group, like Eva's family, to shoot the gap there.

Eva, Doug, and May had the usual discussion about events in the corporeal world. Wordless, the pictures flowed between them. Eva became convinced May looked smug.

Finally, Eva told May to quit smirking. Eva guessed she must know of something about to occur in the corporeal world. May always did like being the first to know and loved lording it over others. Given her level of excitement, she must know of information that Eva didn't—typical historian.

An image of the front door of Eva's house opening and a huge broom sweeping Eva out was passed to her. At the same time, St. Francis flowed past. He winked at Eva.

"Hmmm," said Eva. She scowled. "You all think it's funny."

If May could have shrugged, she would have. A speech bubble: "It'll be good for you to get out of the house."

A moue of amusement followed.

Eva seethed. Parents!

Eva dropped out of ascension. Her other parents were too young to talk to, and if Doug and May were going to continue to withhold information, she couldn't be bothered. She was far too busy.

"Hannah! Terry!" called Eva. "I've got to go outside Asperia for a rescue."

Hannah walked in from gathering eggs. She was warm from cuddling hens. Wise but yielding, her round freckled face gave the observer the impression of a chocolate-speckled cupcake.

"Well, that sucks for the rest of us," she vouched as she padded though from the kitchen. "You will be missed, even for a short time."

Eva inspected her. "Can you look after the infirmary while I'm gone?" she asked, not expecting an enthusiastic response.

Hannah wrinkled her nose.

Eva could see a vein in her temple throbbing in her forehead.

"Can't Terry do it?" Hannah asked. "I don't want to go back and forth from the infirmary to the kitchen, particularly if I have to assist with an operation. It's insanitary."

Eva considered this. She cocked her head. "Hmm," she said. "So far he's been straight one day out of the last seven. What do you think?"

Hannah ignored the largely rhetorical question. "Let's go think in the infirmary," she volunteered.

Eva nodded, and they turned to walk down the hallway to the wing that housed the animals.

"Get off the ditch weed, Terry!" Hannah yelled at a closed door they passed in their procession to the infirmary.

The door opened.

"Ladies!" said Terry. "You called?" A cloud of smoke framed him in the doorway.

Hannah rolled her eyes.

A lizard ran along the hallway and scaled Terry's body, coming to rest in Terry's breast pocket with its little head poking out. Terry glanced at the lizard, then pushed his cap back and coughed.

Eva suppressed a giggle. "Oh, Terry," Eva said. "I worry it's ruining your motivation."

A parrot flew down the hallway and landed on Terry's shoulder.

"So motivate me, darling," he said, with an attempt at a roguish grin.

"I'm going away for a few days," said Eva. "I need someone to tend the animals in the infirmary while I'm gone."

"I'm your man," said Terry, and he turned and sauntered down the hallway toward the infirmary.

Eva opened the doors to the east wing of the house, and the trio passed through. A large bathroom lay off to the left. This was used to wash the animals. There were two other smaller rooms, one a store and laundry and the other an operating theater. To the right lay spacious quarters for the animals with wooden flooring and cages on the floor and hanging from the walls.

The racket started as the animals sensed the trio's presence. Chirps and whistles and the thumping of tails filled the infirmary with a raucous uproar. As Eva walked around, she opened up the doors of the cages of the animals that were well enough to come out and play. There were a few stricken animals in bandages, and Terry walked around the room, crooning in a low song to these others.

"Any operations scheduled for today?" asked Hannah. She took herself off to the laundry and busily set to work putting on rags and aprons to wash. Turning the sterilizer on, she turned to await Eva's response.

"Dr. Tan is going to be here at 10:00 a.m. to operate on Randy, the brown lab with a cone around his head," said Eva.

Randy regarded them both mournfully at the mention of his name.

"Randy has a benign lump just under his subcutaneous skin layer at the back of his neck," continued Eva. "He's been pawing at it and irritated the area around the lump, so we put the cone on him. Naturally, he's not a fan, but he should feel much better once the lump is excised and the wound dressed. And the Wilson cocker spaniels need their ears flushed. That's all for today."

"When will you be going away?" Hannah asked as she started folding the clean linen she had taken from the industrial dryer.

"Friday. I hope to be back Sunday," said Eva.

"I think I can manage the infirmary," Terry said, pretending to fall over and pass out.

Animals swarmed all over him. They nuzzled into his clothes. He rose to his feet and swayed toward the girls like a zombie, a weird human-shaped tree with birds, rodents, and one squirrel hanging off him. The girls squealed and then mock swatted at him. Swaying around the room for comic effect, he stopped in front of each cage and deposited a furry or feathered tenant in each home.

—⁂—

Dr. Tan arrived shortly after the animals were returned to their cages, and Eva prepped the operating theater. The operation on Randy went well, and the Wilson cocker spaniels had their ears cleaned without incident. They were checked for ticks and put into a holding kennel for pick up.

Dr. Tan was one of Eva's fathers. He was as old as Doug and May. Eva hoped he'd be corporeal for a while before his ascension. He was measured and pragmatic in his manner and not given to displays of emotion. He anchored Eva, who was more inclined to emotional peaks and troughs. She had just one other father who had just ascended. The words "Kumbi Salah" came to mind, and she wiped away a tear. He too, like Dr. Tan, had lived nearby, on the outskirts of Destin. He had made her many of the tools and weapons she fought and hunted with as well as the baskets that Eva used to display her herbal remedies. She missed him terribly, but immersing herself in African culture kept the connection to the values and knowledge he'd given her before he'd passed over.

ELIZA

It was hard to see what the point was anymore. Eliza kicked the ground despondently with her regulation leather camels. The most unattractive shoe imaginable, she brooded. Everyone in education or training wore them. They were standard issues from all college and technical faculties. So why not wear them? She stuck little embellishments on hers. Decorations from the kinder art classes she had helped out at for work experience and some of her own inventory: studs and shavings from working with her precious stones.

Maybe she would call it quits now on her dreams of being a jeweler? The day had been so disappointing. And now she had to make the effort to not show it. Eliza felt her heart hurting, and so was her stomach. She was going to projectile vomit from a combination of frustration and disillusionment. And the boredom! Life was a mind-numbing palindrome of sameness. All she wanted was a little beauty in her days. No, strike that! There was beauty enough in the streets of Diaspora. Gardens and water features and striking sculptures at the outbound trading posts and the Lambda, where the highest-level decisions were made. Diaspora was pretty enough if you liked stamped out sameness and predictability. Eliza wanted more. She wanted chaos and choice—delicious, frightening choice.

She kept this sentiment to herself, lest she be accused of illness or evil, though they were pretty much seen as one and the same. There was no way out of her life. Eliza was so sick of everyone intruding in her mind and every aspect of her life being decided for her. Wherever she went, the same phrases and emotions ran over and over in her head.

Right now at the jewelers' stands, all she could hear were feelings of elation and success from the throng of designers, after a successful city trade fair. Eliza shook her head, dislodging the braids she had plaited on the top of her head this morning. She had to make the effort not to let her repugnant, negative thoughts leak out. If she showed bland fawning appreciation of the designers, she might get an apprenticeship with a fashion house—anything to bypass college.

What a fool she was to even try merching her wares today. The direction of the day had been dictated out even before she got out of bed. There was no way she was going to get the longed-for breakthrough into the jewelry trade. Honestly, it's a wonder they were apparently allowed to choose their own job. Until they, the teenagers seeking employment, came up against blocks that forced them into an occupation they had no appetite for, it was meaningless choice. And what was the point of choice without meaning?

Eliza kicked the ground again. As a sixteen-year-old it was time she chose the direction of her college education, unless she chose a trade, of course. Eliza liked working with her hands. In her spare time, she oftentimes turned her hands to making jewelry, ordering gemstones and affixing them to chains.

The materials weren't too freely available, though they weren't quite luxury goods, the jewelry that the fashion houses produced was. And Eliza was dying to work as a jeweler and get picked up by a fashion house. She'd even gone so far as to establish a market price for her less-valuable jewelry and setting up at a trade fair, but the buyers hadn't given her a look. Eliza knew she was capable of working in a fashion house. She knew she could scale up her operation. She didn't know how. She just knew she could build up business. The gaunt, earnest Eliza could not, try as she might, make that connection with the buyers. And when she had approached a bigger house to see if they'd take her designs, they'd outright mocked her.

"Go away and play with your shiny stones," said one cold-faced representative.

"No one will ever buy that junk," said another.

Eliza packed up, smoldering with shame. This was the fourth year in a row. There were other small-scale operations like hers. But she couldn't see anyone new this year.

Job mobility was nonexistent in these parts, she thought scornfully and with a sense of shame and futility.

There was no such thing as job mobility in bound cities. The citizens had traded mobility for security. Once settling on their future career at the apprentice fairs at the age of sixteen, they stayed in their chosen career and largely with the same company that apprenticed or hired them until death or incapacity aged them out of the city workforce, only taking breaks for child-rearing or sickness. Eliza rolled a ball of spit on her tongue and spat on the dusty ground outside the convention hall.

The same old-fashioned houses dominated the trade show every year. It would be mostly their creations that entered the stores this year. And what was more, nobody seemed to take any risk. The puissant-sized stones that adorned the gold chains in the flagship collection from House Modesto were laughable.

"It was hard," reflected Eliza as she returned on the air train to her one-bedroom apartment. Everything was so extraordinarily predictable. She couldn't ruminate on the crowded train. She wished she could block all emotions, like the Asperians and the unconsolidated territories, she thought, as she stepped through her front door. There were just no fucking surprises here in Diaspora. And as for passion, it was a marvel anyone got around to having sex to procreate. She supposed it would be engendered by hormone treatment. But how boring it would be knowing exactly who was right for you and when you'd met the right one! A routine courtship with everything laid bare, the inevitable marriage, and no surprises from then on in. Eliza dumped her backpack on the tiled floor and checked in her backpack. Good. She still had a full bottle of whiskey. She could get high and fall asleep watching TV.

Eliza didn't really need much. The TV bored her, so she turned it off and started daydreaming. At least in her city-owned apartment, she didn't have to worry about guarding her thoughts. She imagined she was lying in a bed. There was a curtain that draped her, so she couldn't see below her breasts. Likewise, the procession of boys (men) walking past couldn't see her breasts or her face. She felt their touch. They looked and then touched her, quickly sampling her and then moved on. The next visitor did the same.

After ten minutes or so, Eliza allowed herself to climax. She brought her fingers back up to her face. Then she reached for the bottle of whisky. She rolled onto her elbow, unscrewed the top, and took a swig.

The bustling of the city street below her window pulled her back. She was hungry. She left her apartment to grab some dinner.

She turned left toward Chinatown and the best food stalls and saw a familiar face was walking toward her. Eliza's stomach clenched. An ex-classmate from Leviathan High walked past. Eliza startled, and her gaze slid away. Eliza felt anger and clenched herself to shield her thoughts.

The classmate, was it Bianca? thought Eliza. *Must be visiting the city.* Eliza wanted to yell, "Fuck you!" at the retreating back. Instead, she let Bianca dip and leave her mind.

Eliza's last year at Leviathan High had not been happy. Every succeeding generation hopes that bullying won't be an issue for adolescents, but people never change. Certain years are rife with exaggerated snubs to ready adolescents for adulthood. Eliza's class was no more or less punitive than others. Eliza tried to remember when it had started.

It was an unmonitored class party. Their teacher had left their classroom, and the support staff never arrived. After ten minutes, the horsing around turned into a game of spin the bottle. When the bottle had been spun by Shakira and landed on Eva, she had grabbed Shakira instead of the nearest boy. It had partly been a gag and partly something else. Pashing her fully on the lips had momentarily seemed like a riot to Eliza—until she felt the full weight of the class approbation land in her mind.

She recalled the feeling of the knife turning in her gut. Shakira did too, and she pulled away and never spoke to Eliza again. She'd been merciless in organizing anti-Eliza sentiment in her classmates.

When groups turn on an individual, it is all but impossible to reverse the tide. Fifty years ago, nearly one in fifty teenagers killed themselves each year. Eliza crossed herself, a gesture popular among the young. It comforted her though, and she turned and looked to make sure no one was watching. Religion wasn't banned in Leviathan. Young folks sometimes played religions. Anyone of Eliza's age might attract attention.

The rate of child death had since decreased dramatically. Public awareness campaigns had helped, but really, the main reason the suicides ceased was the enactment of shortened school years after the age of twelve.

She sniffed to herself. Fifth graders, friendly with all and sundry. Yet the moment they moved onto upper school, the knives came out.

Eliza had struggled to tell her parents about the incident. She'd had such a hard time at school that despite the public awareness campaign, she was contemplating the damage to her psyche if she took the ultimate measure: suicide and the complete breach of the relationship with Lana and Rob.

Eliza crossed Dover Street, where a few augments were milling around passing cigarettes and waiting for the night clubs to open. She could have joined them, but even to the augments, Eliza was a freak. So she continued mulling her college options and the request by her parents to visit Eliza in her new home city. Could she put on a happy face to Lena and Rob? Was she obliged to?

That Eliza had no other sets of parents made her suspicious that she had breached by suicide before, died by her own hand. Most people had two or three sets of parents. And this deep sense of uncertainty and rejection led Eliza to broach the topic of relocation with her parents.

Eliza had been vague when she approached her parents. Relocation had been taken up by three people already in her year, so the request wasn't unheard of.

It wouldn't do for the populace to think they didn't have a choice about anything, thought Eliza cynically, pulling a face to a passing child.

The child burst into tears. The mother bent over to soothe the crying infant, and Eliza farted in both of their perfectly primped faces.

Priuiip.

The mother looked appalled, and the child smiled.

Eva turned toward the bowling alley on Factotum Street. Sometimes she could have a late-night conversation with a housemaid or a mainto, a city maintenance worker. There was counseling available for the dislocated following the relocation. Copycat requests were not uncommon.

Eva stuck it out for the rest of the school year after the bullying episode, despite the emotional pain. Every morning she walked into that classroom, the knife twisted again. She only made it through the year by strengthening her mental defenses. It was the challenge that kept her alive: keeping everybody out every day. When they probed a weakness, she popped up a defense.

"Crazy survives," she told herself. A truth that had occurred to her one day.

You're so silly, silly teenagers would meet the intruders probing into her mind. Nobody was fooled. It was obvious when someone was no longer part of the pack. It was a game to everyone, and when they figured they couldn't break her, they left her alone. It was then she started enjoying the encounters and turned from prey into predator.

Callie had emptied the contents of her bladder while waiting in line at the school canteen. Eliza, now studying brain anatomy in her spare time, knew the many neural weaknesses of the human bladder. To this day, Callie felt embarrassed about "holding on too long." Like a child, her friends teased her as they covered her from stares with their cardigans. Callie, with her pink cheeks and blond bob, was well liked so didn't suffer the social stigma for too long. It was weird how some people were forgiven for anything. But if she, Eliza, had wet herself, she'd have been taken to hospital and deemed "unsafe," a catchall word for odd displays of behavior.

"Are you being bullied?" asked Lena and Rob.

"No," lied Eliza like a professional actor. "I love school. You know me. I just want to be sure I know what to do for the rest of my life. I'm a perfectionist."

Then she went to one of the bathrooms upstairs and made herself sick. Every night for the three months remaining in the school year, she did this.

Lena and Rob talked to the school, but the headmaster assured them Eliza was doing well academically and was well liked by her peers.

School ended, and usually, adult children stayed with their parents before entering a hostel at a university of their choice in the same city. But a small percentage like Eliza chose to leave home early. Some like

Eliza left their city. Eliza couldn't bear the thought of building a life in the city that housed her school.

Lena and Rob organized the relocation from Leviathan to Diaspora, a city located fifty miles to the north. They tried not to worry. They had five other children. But Eliza seemed to burn the brightest out of all of them.

It was a big deal to relocate even after school. Eliza had to speak with a counselor, and this time she was truthful. She knew she had to lance the boil of her memories and let all the pus out until it ran clean, even though she knew the counselors would disclose the truth to her parents.

She'd never forget the last visit with her parents. They looked so hurt and so worried.

Eliza gave Lena a big hug.

"I'm fine really," said Eliza.

Rob's eyes misted over. Lena stroked Eliza's hair. Rob put on a brave show.

"If the call comes, answer it," he said cryptically. "You were meant for pastures further afield."

Then Eliza cabbed to the hospital with a few possessions. Over the course of a few days, she'd be prepared for transfer, then lightly anesthetized and transferred to the gates of the other city.

The medical team in her new home would ensure she was brought round carefully to avoid boundary sickness. They'd also implant a small neurotransceiver to allow her to quickly join the consciousness of her new city. If she forewent this procedure, she'd have terrible communication problems.

It'd been three years now. She was exhausted thinking about it. Eliza was no longer hungry, so turning, she strode home and fell into a fitful sleep.

Eliza was walking home from morning calisthenics the next day and a puppy ran under her feet.

"Here, fella," Eliza called to the puppy, but it was improbably gone, fading into the gutter.

A man in a long coat walked past. He fell into step beside Eliza. Unwittingly, she assumed. Eliza felt a sharp surge of anger. She felt toward the man with her mind, attempting to edge a bit of discomfort in his. Just enough for him to realize he was invading her physical boundaries but not enough so that he would realize it was purposeful and take offense. Eliza had become quite skillful at this in her final months of school. It was useful when she came to the attention of her classmates. She'd choose the most vulnerable and sharpen her mind to get in without being caught. She'd insert a bit of fear or disgust, and the individual would usually leave the conversation after that. Only once had she nearly got caught throwing shade. She'd been summoned by the headmaster. She'd admitted only to an extreme anxiety attack but had been sent home for the day. There had been more talk the next morning and more stares, but the students were starting to give her a wide berth.

She couldn't get into the elderly gentleman's mind.

She was trying to send, "Do you like 'em young?" laced with shame.

He was a closed book. She recoiled. They both stopped their walking progress. The puppy ran up from behind him and jumped into the man's outstretched arms. A voice came into her head.

Look to the north, Eliza.

She took his words literally and swung around to look north. There was nothing unusual about the view. She swung back to give the old man a piece of her mind.

And he was gone. Both the old man and the puppy were nowhere to be seen. It was crazy making.

"Oh, phooey," said Eliza. But she was left discomforted. She must have been imagining things. Maybe the effect of hormones or the level of despair she had been feeling.

Look to the north, the figment of her imagination had said.

She couldn't physically go any further north as her apartment was in the outer ring of Diaspora. There were only a few commercial buildings and then the fields outside the city. No walls though there may as well be. A few roads led from Diaspora, built long ago, no longer maintained and host only to flocks of crows. Any traffic in and out of Diaspora came in from the airport in Diaspora south or one of the trading posts. Outside the city limits lay the unconsolidated territories: crows, bounty hunters, and disease.

BOUNTY HUNTERS

They roamed the unconsolidated territories. Technically, they were employed by the city proctors to return runaway citizens or loot nearby abandoned structures. They made most of their money from pillaging and looting dead bodies closer to Asperia and other city states. The lesser principled hunters stooped to mugging the poor idiots who deserted the city. Desertions happened only a handful of times a year. And when it did happen, it was high profile. Every other citizen was broadcast a profile of the escapee, along with a reminder that "Citizens are the power of the city." There weren't a lot of other crimes taken more seriously than self-exile. Wisdom had it that recovery was more effective and prevented copycat exiles if these individuals were recovered within the first forty-eight hours.

Alex, a slicer, was one of the best bounty hunters around. He'd come to it late. He was twenty years old once he left the orphanage that had been home since his parents died in a car crash when he was eight. There wasn't a lot else he could do once the firefighter's union crossed him off the intake due to his lingering limp and a deficiency with his vision, a blind spot in his periphery.

Alex had been crushed when he was rejected from the occupation he had chosen. Being a firefighter was all he had wanted to ever do. Alex shuffled at the unbidden memories. He finished restocking his week's supplies from the trading post depot just after daybreak. Turning to grab a coffee from the Bring 'Em In canteen before it got crowded with furriers and gem brokers and heading off to the baobab tree he passed late yesterday, he made a mental note to get a health checkup that week. Right now, he planned to sit under the baobab for his morning meditation. With his lifestyle, Alex didn't talk to many people, but he preferred it that way. If you started up a conversation, it could end up in what? He was unsure. Distraction perhaps. The life path he was on was pretty spartan, but he also preferred it that way. It was a dead-end going outside himself for answers. True knowledge could only be found within, through exploration of mind and spirit. Self-sufficiency and exploration of one's physical limits. Alex ruminated as he walked. The trauma of seeing his parents die before his eyes had been replaced over time by the memory of the firefighters and their bravery at extracting Alex from the burning wreck. It was the aspiration to be like them that had got him out of the wheelchair at age thirteen, to participate fully in school life, then to enter track and field and to compete with everyone else who wasn't an orphan, who hadn't suffered the crippling injuries Alex had. Every year he became more and more determined to become a firefighter like his heroes. But the medical requirements were rigid.

He'd passed every test. He'd been the fastest, strongest, leanest, and hungriest in the intake, in the strike. It was the final medical exam that he'd been medically evaluated and found wanting. The limp that he'd conquered and all but disappeared was discovered when they hit his knee with a hammer.

"Overactive reflexes," the doctors said.

It would betray him under stress, they'd said. He'd known then he wasn't going to make it. They didn't scan him; they just gave him a field vision test, which he just passed. But they used it as further ammunition.

"There are better options for you, Alex," they said. "With the level of endurance you have and your physical capabilities, you'd be great in management. Maybe even fire department administration."

He'd declined the job sheet they'd offered him and went away with his heart torn in two.

He left the orphanage the next day. It was his sixteenth birthday. He took only the clothes he was wearing and a couple of other items and went to the local justice. While they checked his credentials, he visited the bathroom. He tore up the photo of his parents. It went into the trash can along with the fireman's badge he'd been given by one of his former heroes.

Presenting himself back at the office, he swore he was of sound mind and body and signed up as a bounty hunter employed by the city of Diaspora.

The alarm honked, rousing Alex from his morning meditation. Someone was trying to exile the city of Diaspora. The information came in: sixteen, a girl, tall, brown hair. She'd left north of Diaspora.

Alex quickly showered while chewing some tobacco. Good ole faithful chew. Grabbing his tools of trade, he noted the time and the amount of money left to pay the bond debt to the city proctors. Eighty thousand dollars kronos showed the digital readout.

The bounty hunters were alerted as soon as it was established that a citizen had left the city without a legal transfer or paying the $100,000 exile bond. The city had paid Alex's for him when he took up the position of a bounty hunter and signed a contract with the city proctors for twenty years or $100,000, repaid by duties carried out as a bounty hunter. Most citizens could never expect to earn this amount of money in a lifetime. This bond amount was set on the average level of investment in each citizen.

Being "bound" wasn't so much of a burden to most citizens. It was more of a badge of pride Alex had noticed. It was a measure of your birthright. Free education. Free medical treatment. A simple tax system. You tithed some of what you earned to the city, choosing the amount, and kept the rest. Duty-bound citizens were content working away at their vocation during the week and filled the pools and parks during the weekends! What was not to love about the lifestyle once you found a suitable mate. Alex was a little skeptical at the predictable way of life that the city guaranteed. He was skeptical because he alone among his peers knew the grip of another man's hands around his throat. He knew the pain of straining for breath while looking directly back into that other man's eyes, beyond and into a chamber of desperation, animal instinct, and savagery and Alex almost died right there and then. The pulse of oxygen carrying blood that had given Alex the strength to push a knife through his opponent's rib cage and into his gut. Alex had walked away after, sucking back life-giving oxygen into his lungs while his assailant died writing in pain. One animal victorious. Another became carrion fodder. It had erased any thrill of hitting a small white ball around a manicured golf course as many Diasporan citizens did on the weekends. And he'd have to wrestle a woman to get to know her, so that limited opportunities for dates or true connection.

It was physically uncomfortable to leave the cities. Any adolescent knew that if they tested their limits by straying too far away from the city, they suffered boundary sickness. It only took one round of vomiting for teenagers to accept their welfare lay staying inside the city and discomfort lay outside. A lesson reinforced in school. On their own, individuals were vulnerable. City living kept them safe. The survival of the city and the individual meant the city needed citizens to stay duty bound. Boundary sickness was a strong deterrent for citizens to leave the city. He, Alex could come and go, thanks to the bounty hunter implant which made him immune to Boundary sickness and gave him relative freedom, he thought with satisfaction as he started jogging away from the city limits. Moving faster toward his prey.

EVA

Eva had left bright and early that Friday morning. Hailing a charged-up vehicle suitable for her needs from the town fleet, she climbed into the driver's seat and set out with her rescue kit. Technically, she wouldn't be doing any driving once she neurolinked with the vehicle. She would use the time to research her destination and visualize successful outcomes. The apothecary was on the outskirts of Destin, nowhere near the township proper, for which Eva was thankful. She had been able to avoid well-intentioned conversations and questions about where she was going. There were a few ranches and estates to pass on the outskirts, and then the car was driving through the rolling hills of territory. Currently, she was passing through Idlewild.

Eva watched the scenery for a few miles and then put her headgear on and entered a state some referred to as meditation and Eva thought of as listening to her inner ear or butter time. So nicknamed because time flowed around her like melted butter. She visualized herself sitting on the outer whorl of her own ear. Behind her and reaching into infinite distance lay empty space. She looked at her ear. It was beautiful: smooth, warm, and the color of nutmeg. She lay back in her ear and languorously stretched one leg down beside her. She heard the distant sound of the ocean washing up from her inner ear.

She let herself fall. A few moments of weightlessness, and then blue sky met the blue sea she was now bobbing in.

The waves talked, and she listened for one voice in particular. There were distractions, other voices. She wanted to help them, but she couldn't. She couched a reassuring message and sent a wave toward the voices, hoping that would offer solace, and listened again. A wave was forming on the horizon. Splashing lazily, she rotated onto her back and waited for the wave to lift her. She waited. She felt a tidal pull. It was getting stronger. Her stomach clenched. Bringing her out of her ear. Something was not right.

What was wrong? She had the motivation to go off-grid. It wasn't wholly unusual to go off the grid. For some couples, it was a rite of passage upon engagement. As if to dare the fates before their future were tied together for eternity. Thrill seekers sought the ultimate thrill of leaving all contact with the grid. Some people came out here mountain climbing or skydiving, and when accidents happened as they sometimes did, the repository withdrew the DNA, and the ascension process began prematurely. Eva glanced out of the window, watching the scenery change.

Wide boulevards gave way to snaking roads. The foliage started to change. Here the trees were shedding leaves, and the leaves littering the road and upturned like hands gave Eva goosebumps.

She pressed on for another twenty miles. She felt the tug from the small voice calling for assistance, the small brave voice, and focused her attention on it.

She first waves of nausea started. Eva pulled off the road and swallowed an antinausea pill. She was pretty much at the limits of most people's geographical tolerance of the bound cities, except, of course, the most extreme adventurer, scientist, or masochist.

Cupping her head in her hands, she surveyed the landscape. She'd pulled off at the apex of a hill, and it would have been quite pleasant if it wasn't for the boundary sickness. Hedgerow lined the ditch beside the road. It had bushed when the land was abandoned, but you could still see the evidence of it having been once upon a time maintained. Behind was a fence in disrepair. It wove its way down the hill and ended in some collapsed palings. She could sit on the nondescript rolling hill, if only she didn't. She swallowed. Boundary sickness. If it was just an off-putting odor or akin to motion sickness, she would be less revolted as well as physically sick. But the waves of nausea corresponding with emptiness threatened to overwhelm her.

Returning to the car, she drove until she could see the city silos on her maps. Putting herself closer would put her in bounty-hunter territory. She wasn't particularly bothered. They were a feckless lot, and physically, she should be more than a match for them. The physical training as a vet assistant and apothecary demanded that she be physically fit. She was a striking individual, with her lean-toned body, blonde tipped hair, and nutmeg skin. Though Eva could handle herself, she didn't want to attract unnecessary attention.

She didn't want to spend longer than necessary in the vicinity of a bound city. Diaspora, she thought this one was called, again swinging maps across her vision.

"Feck!"

A dark shape loomed too quickly for her to stop. The impact was brutal and sickening. Eva pulled over and slapped her forehead and immediately wished she hadn't. Retching, she opened the door and surveyed the male body lying on the ground beside the road. A small trickle of blood ran off the temple of her victim. He appeared to be in his early twenties. He looked to be older than Eva's usual associates back in Destin. Eva assessed him. He was breathing. It was quite labored but regular. His pulse was slow but not extraordinarily so. He was wearing a neck chain with a pendant on, a sharp-edged disc in motion. He was a bounty hunter then, a slicer.

Eva had no time for this. She rolled him onto his side so he wouldn't choke if he vomited. She'd check on him when she returned, she told herself.

Two miles further on and she could bear the boundary sickness no more. But she was close to her prey and was starting to get the usual ring of tinnitus that told her she was nearing the subject of the rescue. It was an educated and intuitive guess. She'd researched the middens surrounding Diaspora and artifacts and dropped a pin on what she thought might be harboring her rescue. The tinnitus would now only grow more as she approached her target.

TERRY

Eva had been gone for sixteen hours. In that time, the apothecary's menagerie had increased by a total of seven animals.

Dr. Tan was making his rounds of the apothecary. All the animals were faring well apart from one small rabbit. The rabbit's chest heaved, and its breathing was labored. Terry looked over the doctor's shoulder.

"Poor little guy," he commented. "Just as well, Eva's not here to see."

"Yeah, she takes any loss hard," agreed Terry.

Loss didn't affect Terry so much. And his own logic told him that if there was ascension for humans, there was a place for animals to pass through for animals.

COUNCIL MATTERS

The bang at the door pulled Hannah from her reverie. She answered the front door.

"What's the problem, Carlotta?"

"Where's Eva?" came the peremptory demand.

Hannah stared at the pent-up young woman.

"The apothecary is licensed to Eva," Carlotta, the town clerk, said tersely. "She's meant to file with the registrar if she goes off grid."

That was quick, thought Hannah. Eva had only been gone eighteen hours.

Hannah offered a large smile and stared at the young woman's chest. Hannah wasn't beyond middle-school tactics if it moved the unwelcome visitor off the front door mat.

Carlotta adjusted her top better to cover her exposed chest.

"And when is she back?" Carlotta demanded.

Hannah drew herself to her full five feet six and looked down at the younger woman.

"Get off your high horse, Carlotta," she said.

Carlotta swatted the air with her hand, not deigning to answer this. Instead, she glared at Hannah, and enunciating each word carefully, she stated, "You'll be sorry you received me in this manner." Then she turned her tongue over in her mouth, and Hannah watched astounded as Carlotta gobbed a spitball at Hannah's feet and then turned to take her leave.

ELIZA

Eliza sank to the floor of her apartment and cupped her head in her hands. It had been six hours since the incident with the old man in Central Park. She couldn't say what had come over her.

"Look to the north, Eliza," he'd said.

She'd sat by the window for hours, watching the sun sink and then threaten to rise again. And then she suddenly started to see the stark truth. She questioned the bonds that tethered her to Diaspora much as a planet is tethered to a star.

Family. She didn't have any other than Lena and Rob in Leviathan. They had five other children. Sure, they would grieve for her. But they wouldn't be pulled down with Eliza gone. They would know how to carry on with life. They lived for their kids and vocations, duty-bound.

Work. Despite her best efforts, there were no real employment or apprenticeship prospects on the horizon. She'd tried so hard to see where she might fit in professionally in Diaspora. She wanted to work with her hands.

She'd approached a number of guilds to this end with no success. She wasn't particularly academic and couldn't imagine herself in a union. And at sixteen, she was running out of options. The city would support her regardless. For every Eliza, there was a productive citizen. But there would go any chance of a normal life for Eliza. She couldn't imagine she'd attract a man to spend the days with, and sure, she could gain some extra baubles with prostitution or housekeeping but couldn't imagine herself doing so for much the same reason she was an inappropriate companion for marriage.

Friends. She'd never had any.

As she pulled each element of life out and examined it, she felt more and more alone and miniscule. Her despair grew. No one would miss her. Lena and Rob would grieve for sure. But no one else she had regular FaceTime with would miss her—not the lady at the bakery where she regularly swapped food stamps for bread, not the people she sometimes rode with in the Skyway to work and relief. She saw the same old faces each week. But they'd never know there was a loss to mourn. They'd lose from their lives the pang of recognition of her face. Having never known her, they'd never be aware of the lost element in their lives. She was, on one hand, so unremarkable and, on the other hand, a cause to attract gazes with her height and her long lolloping gait. Maybe her physical self was the reason behind her inability to make meaningful connections. It might be a relief for the fellow Skyway passengers to never have to be mocked by her ungainly presence again.

Eliza Cruikshank. Even her name was a travesty. It was so painfully apt. She knew full well she wasn't graceful. That if you put a giraffe on stilts, it would be a playoff as to whether she or the giraffe were the most physically plausible. As she sat and ruminated over her life, she began to feel as if she were suffocating. That, by virtue of her implausibly and unattractive self, she might forfeit the right to exist. Round and round she went in her head trying to find even one reason she shouldn't pursue the course of action her stomach was telling her she should.

The city. She wasn't remotely compelled to serve the city. If it was that wonderful, it wouldn't need to be sold to her hour of the day. Her stomach knotted.

Not the final solution?

She wasn't sickened by the idea of limbo. The message was pushed sometimes in the theaters. Don't suicide! Suicide is selfish and leaves grievous wounds on your immediate family. Your soul might never incarnate. Limbo is forever, and you'll never get a second chance.

Yeah, right, thought Eliza with a wry smile to herself in the midst of the emotional pain. Well, there's a thought. She might never incarnate, but she would never feel pain again.

Loyalty to the city. Right through school the message was pushed. That Diaspora had invested so much in you, you must invest in Diaspora. Diaspora had invested in Eliza, and she didn't feel the least bit of loyalty.

Eliza continued to sit, and the pain increased. She felt hot and cold in turns. She would do anything to throttle this pain that had taken on a life of itself. It was feeding in on itself like a white-hot sun. Eliza felt like she was going to implode. She pulled out the whiskey. Her supply was kept steady by swapping food stamps for alcohol with the prostitutes that made the streets of Diaspora their home at night. The other avenue for despairing women. No friends there.

The alcohol usually helped, but tonight it merely fueled her despair. She'd made her mind up. She would look north and take her life by jumping from the roof of her condominium. Capping the bottle, she resolutely put everything in her small apartment in order. It would take the city a minimum of effort to clean and relet it. Maybe the next occupant might even have a job.

Her apartment, hers for life. *If she'd had a life*, Eliza thought. She'd never had any real income to furnish it. She stood at the door what was not and what could have been and then let the door swing shut. She climbed the three floors to the roof, letting herself through the door she stood in the dawn light. A balmy seventy degrees. It was pretty typical of Diasporian outdoor space, utilitarian and token.

Where's the beauty? thought Eliza.

And then the pain in her spirit was so intense she doubled over.

She tooled herself. It wouldn't hurt for very long, less than the psychic pain she was experiencing. She'd get it over with—stand up and smash herself onto the pavement below. She wasn't a coward. And then something faint and distant rose in her consciousness. A faint voice. Great.

She was having visions. Now she was delusional and suicidal. Would she turn herself over to the city physicians for treatment? She knew there was a mental fix for every malady. But it couldn't cure her repulsiveness, she thought dispassionately, and nor could she bear the thought of turning into a zombie either through surgery or through long-term medication. She would take her life into her own hands and flush it into the sewer. She'd be found and cremated and her disgusting remains would be appropriately dispersed into the sewers of Diaspora. She stood, and her vision went watery. She was viewing the sterile rooftop through a sheet of water. Maybe she had a brain tumor. Something certainly felt as though it was sitting in the corner of her mind.

The door opened behind her. A figure clad in black walked through.

"No roof access before dawn," said the unwelcome intruder to her suicide attempt. He walked closer.

She was unable to fix on the figure due to the visual disturbances she was experiencing.

"Are you okay, miss," the figure asked of Eliza. He was pushing a cart of cleaning gear. A janitor or a mainto. Oh, the irony.

In what way wasn't she not okay spiritually, mentally, and now physically not okay? And she just failed at suicide.

She'd have to change her plans.

Perhaps she could let nature or the attentions of a bounty hunter take their course. Eliza left the roof and started walking north.

Every resident of Diaspora was routinely scanned. A retinal scanner was embedded in the entryway of all houses and apartments.

This allowed quick identification of incidents of illness or misfortune. It also incidentally allowed quick identification of any citizen who decided to defect. There was no wall around Diaspora or any of the bound cities. There was no need for a physical barrier.

Eliza thought back, what time had she left her apartment? She'd gone onto the roof at 6:00 p.m. It was now 9:00 a.m. She had nine hours to put as much distance between her and the city before the city was alerted to her absence, then maybe an hour before she was classed as a defection after they checked hospital records and the gate for any late-notified transfers. And she'd have to fight the boundary sickness first. Maybe this effort would cause whatever that was in her head to rupture and kill her. Passing the road that was notable only for a cluster of brothels, Eliza crossed the ring road that defined the borders of Diaspora. Then Eliza began to run.

To begin with, she loped along easily. It was so good to run. The only people who ran in Diaspora were trained gymnasts who competed in the annual games. At the two-mile mark, Eliza started to feel pressure in her head. Eliza ran for another thirty minutes. The pain increased, but she was able to disregard it. She talked her body through the pain, so it wouldn't betray her or stop Eliza from exiting Diaspora. It was hard but not impossible to convince her body to keep going.

Why not stop! Wait for a patrol to retrieve her. Give up her goal before she reached it. She fooled her mind to keep going. "It's nothing, just toothache."

Suddenly, despite Eliza's entreaties, her body betrayed her.

One arm stopped moving. The pain increased.

"I think I'm dying," she yelled at the woods she was passing.

She lumbered on. The pain grew unbearably. Her mind rebelled, and she collapsed.

She awoke moments but a world later. The sun had moved past its zenith and was in decline, Eliza guessed. And it was obscured by a halo of golden curls.

MEETING MINDS

Eva was lost for words, so she read some off the headstone the girl was propped against.

> Here Lies Ann Mann
> Who lived an old maid.
> But Died an old Mann.

"Ha!" said the dazed and confused apparition, its gaze sliding off Eva's.

"It's the epitaph on the gravestone," said Eva. "It's inscribed, 'England 2076.'"

"Am I dead?" asked both girls at the same time.

"Excuse me," said Eva. She turned and took two steps to vomit into a shrubbery beside another gravestone. Turning, she explained, "You must excuse me. I've never been this close to a bound city before. I'm quite affected by proximity sickness."

"What's that you're saying?" queried the girl in a husky voice. Her hair rolled and then settled in no particular style around her shoulders.

Eva wondered if the girl had ever seen a hairdresser in her life.

"You escaped from a bound city," said Eva.

The boundary is the repulsion field the city proctors maintain to keep us out and the citizens in.

"Is there any other type of city?" the girl sounded genuinely puzzled.

Eva extended a hand to the girl, who had slowly risen to her knees. She looked deathly pale. Eva put one hand out and the girl clasped it. Eva placed the shaking hand on her own shoulder to steady her.

"I estimate you passed through the boundary," said Eva.

"I did?" came the tremulous voice.

"Look," said Eva. "We've got to move. I'm jacked up on antinaus and steroids, and I have a field dampener in the car. But as soon as the medication wears off, I'm in trouble. The nausea might prevent me from driving. It's not unknown for people to seize and fit at this proximity to a bound city."

"You are?" came the husky voice shyly. Two brown eyes finally caught and held Eva's gaze.

"Yes," said Eva emphatically. "Whatever you just experienced when you pushed through will affect me one thousandfold."

The girl's gaze took Eva in. Then came a dramatic change in her manner—surprise mixed with confusion and some anger.

"I can't read you! But you're in my head! Is this some kind of wicked joke?" More anger.

"Relax," said Eva.

It was the worst thing she could have said.

The girl drew herself up to her full height and glared at Eva. Another tactic.

"I knocked out a bounty hunter on the way here. Care to stick around to be picked up and returned by the next mercenary on the scene?" queried Eva of the girl.

The girl bowed her head.

Eva put her hand on her shoulder.

"I'm Eva Ventura. Apothecary. I live in the town of Destin, in the province of Asperia. It seems you've self-exiled from the bound city of Diaspora. Few individuals leave bound cities. I was sent here to rescue you by a mischievous old saint," said Eva dryly.

The other girl's eyes looked shyly at Eva from beneath the fringe.

"Eliza Cruikshank," she said tersely, the mouth beneath the pert nose creasing into worry lines.

"Pleased to meet you," said Eva. "Now let's make like a tree and leave!"

"I guess," said the girl, confused.

"Is humor not common around your parts," asked Eva rhetorically.

"Have I really left Diaspora?" This in a faltering voice.

"You have. Right up to the point a bounty hunter finds us and hauls your sorry ass back to the city," said Eva. "I imagine if the reports of how the citizens are treated are true, a psychiatric hospital or prison time might be the outcome for you if you return. My car is this way." Eva turned and started walking.

"I'm really out?" Eliza asked of the air. Then she turned and followed Eva.

ALEX

Alex coughed. He caught a dribble of saliva with his tongue. He opened his eyes and found himself lying on the side of a dusty road under some bushes. He recalled events prior to losing consciousness. As soon as he had reached notification of the exile, he had hiked five miles from his cabin to the last-known position of the exile. He recalled he'd taken a leak in a bush and went to cross a long, disused road and heard the sound of an electric car accelerating before he was knocked off his feet and everything went dark. Where was the car from? Asperia, he guessed. What was it doing so far into Diaspora's catchment? The driver would have to know there were grave health risks of coming so close to the border of a bound city. Not to mention the risks to life and limb by the roaming mercenaries.

Bounty hunters being the least of anyone's worries unless that person had a bounty on their head. Though heavens knew, judging by the pain in his shoulder, he was no longer as much of a threat as he might have been. He winced as he felt the egg-shaped lump on his head. Checking on his maps that connected him to the Diaspora catchment, he could see two other bounty hunters converging on the flagged location. He was the closest still, by the looks. He winced as he got to his feet. He'd better get moving. Hobbling a few steps, he swung his backpack on and started jogging. Pain radiated from at least five locations in his body, but he'd learned long ago tricks to block out pain and push himself physically.

The drone of a vehicle started in the distance. It got louder quickly. Jogging toward a bend, he realized, "Oh shit!" Once again, there was a car coming straight at him. He tried to jump out of its path. The car slammed on its brakes, but both the driver and Alex realized at the last minute it was too late, and Alex again flew into the air.

The body landed and splayed awkwardly. Eva bit down on a scream and uttered a curse, "Shit, not again!"

Eliza barely noticed. She had been mute during the brief journey. The shock of being in a car had rendered her speechless. Her mind was documenting without emotion the details of which she would dissect later. When the car stopped, it seemed best just to sit mutely while Eva grabbed the door handle and raced to the side of the road where the body lay prone.

Alex probed his awareness and ascertained any damage to his body. Good. He was conscious. Pain screamed down his upper arm from his left shoulder, and he was fairly sure his right hand was badly sprained, if not broken. He blocked the biofeedback and checked his head with his other hand. It would appear he now had two egg-shaped bumps on his head diametrically positioned on his brow.

What were the odds of that, mused Alex.

Alex's training for the Fire Corps, though ultimately not leading to a career, served him well in this type of situation. In the evenings, Alex and his fellow apprentices had amused each other with stunt rolls and dives testing the limits of human ability to be the fastest, jump highest, land with the greatest impact and walk away unbroken. This off-duty recreation had culled more than a few apprentices from the ranks.

So once Alex had realized that impact was inevitable, he had both curled himself into a ball and launched upward and sideways. Time slowed, and Alex was able to gauge the car was driven by a blonde tipped hair female and a slightly younger dark-haired companion. After glancing off the windscreen of the vehicle, he heard the car pull to a stop. The occupants of the car didn't look particularly threatening, Alex decided the best move was to lie on the ground and wait to be approached. He prepared himself mentally for combat.

The blonde woman spoke. "Shit, not again!"

The words made their impact, and Alex rolled and jumped to his feet in one fluid motion as Eva approached.

A single breath escaping from Eva's mouth was the only sign that she had been surprised.

Eva settled into her heels into a defensive stance, and as she did so, Eva's eyes met Alex's.

Alex said, "What do you mean by 'Shit not again'?" Oh, so he'd heard her first shout of dismay and connected the dots. He followed up with, "When was the last time you hit someone on this particular stretch of road?"

Eva's mind worked furiously overtime. "Well, you know…" This she threw out while flexing and assessing her physical fitness for combat after the long, arduous journey. She'd have to finish this quickly as the rising nausea would take its toll in a prolonged altercation. Truthfully, she was more suited to endurance fights and wasn't wholly sure she could take this one. But Eva thought she hadn't come this far to rescue her charge, to fail on the homestretch.

Alex looked at the other occupant of the car: tall, female, brown hair. This fitted the description of the exile. Perfect. She was there for the taking. He just had to get through the blonde first. The attractive blonde was waiting for him to make a move. He sighed.

"You have something that I want."

Eva replied, "If you can take her back, she's yours."

Alex took her words literally and approached the car. And suddenly, the blonde was between him and the car again. He reflexively tried the same maneuver and got a clip across the head for his efforts. Anger and then interest rose inside of him. She easily blocked his right hook and held his gaze fiercely. He parried for a while, gauging the blonde's strengths and weaknesses. She was slightly quicker than him but not as strong in her upper body. He stood back. This earned him another clip across the head. Alex suddenly lost interest in recovering the exile as he felt the fortunes shift, in her favor and self-preservation became more important.

"Enough already," said Alex. "She's yours." He extended his hand. "Alex, slicer."

"Eva Ventura," said Eva, and she glared at Alex until he felt his face scorch.

"Seen this?" asked Alex. He drew a screen in the air and pulled up his maps. "In about fifteen minutes, three other bounty hunters are going to converge at this point, and as fit as you are, Eva, you'll be overwhelmed by sheer numbers. And the girl will be going back to Diaspora. You, Eva, may be too bruised and broken by the encounter to drive home. Then the other bounty hunters will steal your car and leave you for the crows on the side of the road."

Alex had let his voice harden. He'd heard in her voice discipline and strength. For some reason this angered him. He didn't want her to overestimate her abilities and end up skeeter fodder. Alex knew wasn't going to make any kronos today by returning the exile, but he was going to get the tough chick to take him in a new direction instead. Here a little bluff was called for. She looked exhausted.

"Eva, either you take me to wherever it is you are going, or we're going to reenact that tableau, and this time I'll win."

Eva's eyes filled with a mixture of anger and defeat. She drew herself to her full height, which Alex noticed matched his.

"Discretion can be the better part of valor," she answered.

Alex smiled and relaxed. "Here let me." He opened the driver's door for Eva and then climbed into the back of the car beside Eliza.

RAVENNA

Ravenna laughed in what she thought was a queen-like manner.

Cackled more like it, thought her lady-in-waiting, Brynn.

Not short and more than a little plump, Ravenna was an impressive and sturdy sight to behold. She dripped from head to toe with jewelry, from her father's forays into the mines of Arcadia. Ravenna, replete with jeweled decoration, radiated light, reflecting and scattering the candlelight and light from the carefully placed lamps. The effect was to exaggerate rather than diminish her stature.

"How do I look?" Ravenna demanded of her steadfast lady-in-waiting, Brynn. She pointed one taloned finger at the girl, waiting hungrily for an answer.

"You look beautiful," assured Brynn, trying to keep the truth from her eyes.

"Liar!" said Ravenna. "I'm fat, aren't I?"

"There's no one quite like you, Ravenna," came the discrete, measured answer.

"Whatevs," answered Ravenna, looking Brynn over coolly. "Help me with my corset," she demanded.

"Sure," said her lady-in-waiting, coming closer to assist Ravenna with the oversized bejeweled undergarment.

What was her name again? wondered Ravenna of her lady-in-waiting. *That's right, Brynn. What a strange, sexless moniker.* She herself might be tall and lumpy but her name, "Ravenna," was befitting of a princess. She was ever grateful that her father, the king, had named her so even as her mother had died in the throes of labor forcing out Ravenna.

Brynn helped Ravenna stuff handfuls of flesh into Ravenna's intricate, bejeweled corset. She pushed the lower bulges down into Ravenna's jodhpurs. Then Brynn selected a riding smock from Ravenna's dressing room.

Ravenna puffed as she stretched her arms toward Brynn.

"Careful," said Brynn as she dodged the talons threatening to tear her cheeks.

"Sorry," said Ravenna as she swayed into the smock. "Let's go see Daddy. And please don't leave me alone with the captain of the guards."

"Who should I leave you alone with, Ravenna?" asked Brynn wryly.

There's a little bit of life in this one, Ravenna thought. Most of her previous ladies-in-waiting had been intimidated by Ravenna. They hadn't lasted long. If they ever tried to stand up to her, Ravenna found subtle ways to hurt them, hurt their pride and their person until more often than not they quit before they were fired by Ravenna for some made-up transgression.

But not this one. Ravenna regarded the thin wary girl with a smidgeon of admiration. Ravenna filled every new lady in waiting's jodphurs with stinging midges in the first week that she harvested from the chicken coops and duck ponds that supplied the castle. She intercepted a new girl's clothes from the Palace's Washerwomen, who was in on Ravenna's antics. Gladys the charlady, being low down on the palace pecking order as she was; lower even than the cook, roared with laughter when any new frightened and offended girl shot past the scullery as if the hounds of hell were after her, in a mad bid to escape Ravenna's craftily devised punishments. But not this one. "Brynn". Ravenna rolled the name around in her mouth. Tasting it. She had popped the midge infested jodphurs on and gone about the day's duties not showing any discomfort. 'And", remembered Ravenna ruefully. Gifted a couple of the midges back to her by depositing then in her slippers. Ravenna had welts on her feet for three days and Brynn had none. And there was the time Ravenna ordered Brynn to play the childhood game; William Tell. Stood her against a Castle wall with an apple on her head while Ravenna threw knives with the aim of cleaving the apple in two. She would have used a bow and arrow but hers had mysteriously disappeard after she went target practicing in the duck ponds.She thought knives would work as well but the blades all fell out of the handles before getting anywhere near the apple! One had sliced Ravenna's toe; "Gosh Darn it". Ravenna had given up provoking Brynn after that. The girl had obviously learned the first rule of Palace life. Trust none and be one step ahead of everyone. "Or was that two rules", Ravenna mused.

RETURNING

"We're back on the town grid," Eva said brightly. She established a neural link to a screen on the back of her seat so her hostages could follow her travel dialogue.

Both Eva and Alex stared vacantly ahead, totally displaced and seemingly unable to get a fix on the interior of the car, let alone the screen or indeed, Eva herself as she chatted to the pair, regardless of their lack of response.

I'll have to get a physician to give them a complete physical exam, she thought.

Eva was in her element. Okay, so she was hauling humans back to the apothecary instead of animals, but the rescue mission was successful. She had the target, and a plus one!

Eva ran through several possible ways the pair could be accommodated at the apothecary.

When they were a couple of miles from the estate, she offered them refreshments.

They accepted the nuts and juice pouches gratefully, and within minutes, the passengers fell asleep.

TERRY'S NOT IMPRESSED
WITH THE GUESTS.

Exhausted, Eva drove the last few miles to the apothecary, and much relieved, she pulled the car into her garage. She made a nonchalant entrance into the house, her face not reflecting the turmoil in her mind.

"Well, look what the cat dragged in," said Terry.

Eva smiled back. It was lunchtime on Sunday. Forty-eight hours after her impromptu departure from the apothecary. Delicious smells were wafting in from Hannah's kitchen. Suddenly, Eva felt weak. She couldn't remember the last time she had eaten, and she'd been without sleep since Friday. And even then, she'd only dozed off on the outbound trip from Destin. It felt like a lifetime had passed. Eva let her shoulders droop. She swayed and felt her knees buckle.

Before she hit the ground, Terry was behind her, one strong arm behind her back. His other arm encircled her around her shoulders, and he drew her to him and gave her a firm hug.

Eva hugged Terry back, drawing strength from him. She regained her footing.

They heard a clatter from the kitchen, and Hannah rushed in, pulling off her oven gloves.

"You're back!" she squealed. She rushed in to hug both Terry and Eva.

Eva took a deep breath. She looked at each of them in turn with a measured gaze.

"Spit it out, old girl," said Terry. "Are you okay? If anyone tried to harm you, I'll fucking kill them," he boldly declared.

Hannah made some comforting sounds. "I'll put a pot of tea on." She whirled to go back to the kitchen.

"What is that delicious smell?" Eva asked.

"Roast chicken with tarragon butter," replied Hannah. "Tan and Nicoletta are coming over for dinner. We were all so worried about you. I can't believe you're, you're just standing there. 'What is that delicious smell?'" Hannah raised one eyebrow. She bustled off to the kitchen.

"I'll kill 'em," Terry repeated. "I'll put 'em in my pipe and smoke 'em." He executed a series of clumsy martial arts moves for the benefit of Eva and Hannah, who had returned to the dining room with a steaming pot of tea and three ceramic mugs.

"What would we do without you to mother us, Hannah?" Eva gratefully accepted a mug and stretched her legs out, arching her back against the slate leather sofa.

All three spoke at once.

"Oh, good," said Hannah

"What the...?" asked Terry, trailing off. "Did you complete the rescue?" This also from Terry.

"We have guests", said Eva but the others seemed not to hear her.

Eva checked her wristwatch. Technically, watches were redundant and had been ever since neural links to the grid became commonplace two centuries ago. An evolutionary brain structure in the orbitofrontal cortex, the part of the brain responsible for sensory integration could be tasked by any Panacean to download and render maps, time, and calendar functions overlaying a person's vision. But some things had never changed over the millennia, and Panaceans kept watches as status symbols or heirlooms. For some it was a statement of style or level of affluence. Eva's watch was a gift from Tan and Nicoletta on her sixteenth birthday and had sentimental value.

"Hey, guys," said Eva, flicking her eyes from the titanium watch face studded with gold stones and red beryls to Hannah and Terry's questioning eyes. "There's no easy way to explain it—we've got guests!"

"Guests!" exclaimed Hannah, throwing her hands in the air dramatically. "Whatever shall we do? Where shall we put them?"

Eva laughed, suddenly feeling lighthearted. "They're not guests of the furry four-legged variety. We can't just cage them and board them in the animal quarters. This is a large estate. I am sure we have room. Now, it's time to bring them inside. I sedated them, but the quixonine is due to wear off," explained Eva.

"Them?" queried Hannah. She put a hand out to the house fox, her ever-present companion for the last forty-eight hours, who quickly pushed its nose into the palm of Hannah's hand.

"Terry, Hannah," said Eva. "I've got two people in the car. One a female, our age. I think she escaped from the bound city of Diaspora."

Hannah didn't miss a beat, though a vertical line deepened on her forehead. "Who's the other?" Hannah queried lightly as though refugees were an everyday occurrence at the apothecary.

Terry stood up. As always, when feeling confronted, he had to move. He patrolled the drawing room, pulling his shoulders forward and back.

"Eva, I thought you were in the business of rescuing animals!" Terry said, eventually. "Not exiles!" This too was said with a furrowed brow.

"I think the other person is a bounty hunter," Eva offered.

"'I think!'" Hannah also got to her feet.

The room and Terry and Eva were doing a strange dance. Hannah took a deep breath. She started fussing, winding a woven friendship bracelet around her wrist.

Eva gave her friends a moment for the news to sink in.

"Yes. The hunter was on the way to return the girl to the city. Okay, guys," she said vehemently. "It's an odd couple. But this is the thing. This girl escaped a bound city despite the physical discomfort and potential harm. That is significant. That I was called to rescue her is unheard of. It's the first time I have been called to rescue another human. It may be an evolution in the apothecary role. A phenomenon for later consideration. It's unheard of for an apothecary to bond directly with another human. And then I ran over her bounty hunter! Twice. It seemed to be only fair I bought him back for a bit of medical attention!"

Eva gave an abridged account of the previous thirty-six hours. She left out the part where she consented to bring Alex only after he indirectly threatened her. Terry guessed she was leaving details out from the way she shifted from one foot to another. This was Eva's usual tell that she was anxious, maybe not comfortable retelling all the events of her travels and he scowled down at the fox who was nibbling at Terry's shoelaces. Foxy obliviously nuzzled into Terry's calf.

Eva finished. Terry's eyes were stormy. He stared at Eva, willing her to say more, but she wouldn't field his gaze and could not be drawn further.

Hannah kept fussing. She twisted a dishcloth in her hands. "Guests?" She sounded distressed. "Wherever shall we put them? What do we tell the town council? We are not licensed for additional services other than healing animals. Certainly not two-legged ones!"

Eva ignored her. "Fifteen minutes!" Eva said, slapping her hands on her leather-clad thighs. "That's how long we've got until they wake up."

Terry was momentarily distracted, and his mood lightened. Eva had disheveled hair, and her black leather pants had that creased look of having obviously been slept in. One sole was falling off one of her riding boots.

But still, thought Terry, *a warm-blooded man couldn't blame himself for looking at an attractive woman. Could he?*

Eva followed his gaze neutrally, neither flattered nor perturbed.

"It's not for sale," she said, crooking her fingers and leaning forward. "Terry!" she said sharply.

He lifted his gaze from her chest and winked.

"Can you help me carry them in?" asked Eva brusquely. "Hannah! Make up a bed in Terry's room for the bounty hunter. Use a stretcher from the infirmary."

"What shall we do with the girl?" asked Hannah.

"The little room at the back of the infirmary perhaps," Eva said. "Yes. Hannah, take the armoire from your room and move it to the laundry. Our supplies can go into that for the moment. Any overflow can go into shelves into the laundry." Eva was more confident now that she had a plan.

"I...I..." Hannah twisted her dishcloth, seemingly unable to move.

The fox darted between Eva's ankles, and Eva felt irritated and mystified by Hannah's fussing. The unbidden thought came to mind: *I am the one who should be feeling distressed right now, after all I've been through!*

Terry snapped his fingers, thankfully disturbing Eva from her train of thought. "Panacea to Eva," he said.

Eva breathed out all the tension sitting in her chest.

"We'll all fit in here, Hannah, darling," she said.

Hannah nodded and met Eva's eyes, dropping the dishcloth on the table.

Terry whispered to Eva as they walked into the garage, "Hannah just struggles with change."

Eva nodded.

Terry whistled as he saw the contents of the car. "The girl first," he said.

Eva nodded again and helped Terry lift Eliza into the fireman's lift position across Terry's shoulders. She followed him into the infirmary.

Hannah had been into the room before them and placed the guest chaise lounge under the small window. The dry scrubs had been removed from the hangers, leaving a clean environment. Hannah had also put a small vase of flowers on a night table in the corner. They laid out the newest resident of the apothecary on the chaise lounge and returned to the garage for Alex, who still lay prone in the back of the car. Terry lifted Alex by the shoulders while Eva lifted his legs onto her hips. They carried him in this fashion to Terry's bedroom. Hannah was just finishing pulling blankets up over the stretcher. Terry and Eva lay Alex onto the stretcher, and as they turned to go, Terry jolted to a halt as Alex's hand snapped out and took hold of Terry's wrist in one fluid movement. Pain shot up Alex's wrist, but he held a strong grip. Terry glared at Alex with a strong measure of enmity. Alex held his gaze and then released Terry's wrist to slump back onto the stretcher.

Hannah finished fluffing the pillows and composed herself. "You need to sleep," she told the bounty hunter. Hannah took Alex's wrist to check his pulse, and she motioned her head, directing Terry to leave the room.

He raised one eyebrow and did so, instinctively heading toward the infirmary to check on the least troublesome of the pair. He looked in on the occupant in the small laundry and storage room that was now a bedroom. There was no one on the chaise lounge. Terry looked around.

Eliza had woken and was now crouched behind the door looking agitated.

"Hey, old girl," said Terry calmly. "One of the intermediate term side effects of being tranked with quixonine is short-term anxiety."

Eliza didn't raise her head to meet his eyes, but she did bob her head slightly in a nod and gripped her ankles.

Terry thought what undemanding company she was. Personally, he couldn't abide seeing a wild animal in distress. Whistling a popular folk tune, he crossed to the chaise lounge and swung his feet up. Other than a slight hunching of her shoulders, Eliza appeared not to be affected by his presence. Without talking, Terry reached out one hand. He inched his fingers along the floor to hers. She peeped up at him shyly. He winked at her. His incongruous wink, together with the collapse of his cheek as he dimpled at her, got through. Accepting the outstretched hand with her own, she came back up to sit beside him.

NICOLETTA

Later, there was a bang on the front door. Terry raised his eyebrows to Hannah. Hannah stepped from the fire over to the front door and unlocked it, stepping well out of the way of the entry. Moments later, Nicoletta sprung through, hovering in the doorway and then landing in the foyer, swinging a pair of nunchakas. Tan followed at a quieter pace, merely modestly a cane decorated with two eagles and his everpresent medical briefcase.

Nicoletta drew herself up to her full height. "Is Eva okay?" she quizzed Terry.

He bounced on his heels and his eyes slid away from her piercing gaze. "S'far as I can tell," he said. "You know Eva. She's a tough cookie!" He fist-bumped Tan. "Hey, Doc. S'up? Held the fort well, didn't we?"

Nicoletta droned tonelessly, looking unseeingly into the distance. "I saw trouble when I was farseeing."

"Trouble is six foot one by my estimation," said Terry.

Eva isn't saying much about the whole experience.

"Trouble is six foot?" asked Nicoletta. "Whatever do you mean?"

"Follow me," said Terry.

They went to Terry's room. Alex was turning to look at his visitors when Nicoletta landed the pointed toe of her boot inches away from the stretcher frame. Alex's eyes blinked, and he stared at the knife she suddenly wielded a mere three inches away from his nose.

A hand dropped on Nicoletta's shoulder. Eva grinned as the older Asian woman turned to meet her eyes.

"Are you planning on tickling his tonsils?" asked Eva of the other woman. "Poor guy," Eva said with mock sympathy. "He's already been subjected to a couple of unreported hit and runs!"

Alex glared at Eva.

"I saw him fighting you in my farseeing stone," said Nicoletta. "Are you sure he can be trusted?"

"He's as trustworthy as any bounty hunter," said Eva. "Maybe more so as he seems to know how to bargain." She winked at Alex, who returned her gaze with a stony glare.

Eva and Nicoletta slung their arms around each other's shoulders.

"Give it another half an hour until you're all right to stand. Then come through to the dining room," Eva sent back over her shoulder to Alex.

The two women walked back to the dining room. Nicoletta threw a piercing look at Eva.

In the dining room, Hannah was busily serving dishes onto the long table. Terry was engaged in mixing up a jug of something with what looked like several measures of spirits. He added pomegranate juice and crushed a selection of herbs. They sat—Tan, Nicoletta, Terry, Hannah. Terry had a drink in front of him in a ceramic bowl with a handle. The fox nuzzled into Hannah's knee.

"First, let's talk between ourselves," said Eva finally. "Then we can get the girl and the bounty hunter to see what they know." Eva asked of the group, "Who wants to start? repeated Hannah.. It might be quicker to explain in ascension, but anyone who is family will delay us." Eva had stated the obvious.

The others nodded.

The group sat in silence.

"Oh, for goodness sake," said Eva. "Hasn't anyone got anything to say or any questions about the events of the last few days?"

"We know. It's just!" Hannah said in frustration. "We know everything and nothing." This last said with more than a hint of frustration. "You left on a rescue. It took you close to a bound city, and you return with two strangers. And now nothing will ever be the same again!"

Terry poured himself a second cocktail.

"Careful," said Eva, noticing Terry pouring himself out a measure. "No more than two when you're under stress."

Terry nodded to Eva. He smirked and made a mental note to return to the drinks cabinet when everyone was asleep.

"Did anything unusual happen here in my absence?" asked Eva, adeptly changing the subject. She noticed Tan and Nicoletta dart sidelong glances at each other.

Hannah spoke up. "The bureaucrats are back." Hanna related the details of Carlotta's visit.

"Hmm," said Eva. "I might pay a visit over to the county halls tomorrow to find out the motivation behind her coming here. That wasn't just a social visit!"

"Tan, Nicoletta?" Eva looked to her feisty stepmom. "How are the animals? What have you seen?"

"I saw fire," said Nicoletta. Her pupils shrank, and she adopted a purring monotone. "A circle of fire. I looked through it. I saw the fight with the bounty hunter. What I saw had a different outcome. I saw that two other hunters joined you." She flicked her eyes toward the sleeping quarters. "He! He bargained with the other hunters to share the proceeds of returning the girl. You tried to fight them, but they took the girl and left you on the ground injured. Your arm bent up behind your back. They did not despoil you. We were just on our way to get equipped to come and find you when we were notified you had rejoined the grid. I saw inaccurately!" She finished with, "I mean, I am very glad you have arrived back safely, but you can't trust him."

Tan put his hand on Eva's. "I'm glad you are home safe, daughter," he said. "Everything has changed, but we'll weather any adversity. You'll see."

Eva preferred action to endless empty words. If nobody had any questions or insights into the events that had bought the two strangers into the house, then she wasn't interested in small talk. Terry, Tan, and Nicoletta could banter endlessly in humor, concern, and in anger.

After another fifteen minutes, Eva jumped to her feet.

"Let's get our visitors," said Eva. "Tan, you get the hunter. Nicoletta, you go too." Eva smirked at Terry. "Go on. Have one more."

Terry reached lazily for the jug and refilled his glass. Eva walked back and collected Eliza from the dressing room and noted the prone

Alex was as sound asleep as anyone with a suspected concussion (or two), she sniggered, might be. Ignoring Eliza's inertia, she frog-marched the girl toward the dining room. Nicoletta passed her in the hallway to assist Tan wake Alex.

The group regathered.

"Okay," said Eva. "For better or worse, we've been pulled together by circumstance, the Fates if you will."

Alex examined his nails sullenly.

"Cruickshank!" snapped Eva.

The daydreaming Eliza was startled. A flood of emotions washed through her, and she retreated into herself, posting a vacant look onto her face.

"You're the key!" said Eva. She pulled the seat out for Eliza. "Sit! Eliza, you called me. In this part of the world, we keep our minds separate. It's unprecedented that you were able to link to me, call me to rescue, draw me toward you."

"Where do you imagine we go from here, Eliza? I'd like to hear your thoughts. What were you thinking when you left Diaspora?"

Eliza considered Eva's words. She'd never imagined her miserable life could take this sudden change in direction.

"I...I wasn't thinking. I just couldn't stand it anymore. Everyone listening into your thoughts all the time and the city aware of your every move. The Blind Eye directing your life path." Eliza exclaimed, "I can't go back!"

"The city will be looking for you," said Tan. "That is not good. There'll be communications by Diaspora to the incorporated territories. The towns and the bound cities mostly keep their affairs separate, but everyone will want to keep the natural order of things preserved. There will be government communications." He put his thumb on his chin. "We'll have to organize you an identity, maybe an apprentice. You can be my locum. You don't have a birth certificate, but I could always say I treated your mother in one of my clinics in the unincorporated territories, that she wanted a better future for her child before she died."

"My mother isn't dead," exclaimed Eliza. "It's far worse than that. I fear she and my father are slaves to the city."

DIASPORA

"Latest exile not recovered," droned the shabbily dressed man to proctor Herbert in the generous sized but dimly lit office.

"Have you notified the outlying districts," the proctor cast back to the man, who was stepping uneasily from one foot to the other. "It would have to escape into the unconsolidated territories before getting to Asperia."

"There's no way she could have traversed the boundary sickness border—"

"Damn it, Horace." Lines drew across the elder man's face as he prepared to dress down the unfortunate adjudicant hovering uneasily behind him. "Damn it to perdition and back. If we lose anyone to the unbound, they're as good as dead—permanently."

"Yes, of course," said Horace listlessly to the air. He raised an eyebrow at the proctor and droned the familiar dogma instilled in Diaspora citizens in all schools and institutions. "Each citizen is an important part of Diaspora society. Our collective will maintains the unitary safety and the integrity of the Blind Eye, who protects us and keeps us safe from all the dangers that surround our fair city."

MONDAY AT THE APOTHECARY

A sharp rap on the front door pulled Hannah's attention away from the pot of jam she was stirring on a low boil. The one plum tree in the yard fruited prodigiously, and every year Hannah preserved the forty pounds of plums as sauces and jam. Pushing back the sleeves of her apron and turning the gas to low, she went to answer the peremptory knock at the door.

An engineer of the town council, an aging man with a salt-and-pepper quaff, stood there on the doorstep.

"Thirty-day notice of eviction and council possession of underutilized property," he said emotionlessly. Meeting her eyes to ensure she had heard him, he transferred the bound and wax sealed legal document to Hannah. Taking a sidestep, he closed his satchel and retreated from the doorstep.

Hannah had caught a glimpse inside the satchel and seen other similarly bound documents.

Hannah's voice quivered as she called out, "Eva, Terry!"

"What, what!" asked Eva, hurrying from the drawing room, alarmed at the urgency in Hannah's voice.

"We just got served an eviction notice by a town official," said Hannah miserably.

"What?" Terry was there.

A shadow moved in the corner of the room, Alex noiselessly moving his weight from one foot to another.

Eva slipped a letter knife through the wax and unrolled the embossed document.

"Planning Department," in boldface at the top.

Your residence at Formosa Way is being reacquired as part of new zoning rules.

We are excited to announce new zoning rules for the town of Destin. Due to higher commercial traffic in part coming from surrounding towns and threats from the unconsolidated territories, The town of Destin seeks to reacquire certain properties that do not meet regulation and regularly fail standards. Also, we require additional housing due to a natural increase in the birth rate.

BIRTH RATE

At this, the air sucked out of the room. As the three apothecarists struggled to process the information, their knees trembled and, attempting to draw on reserves of strength each of them in turn, lost their balance; and they fell to the floor.

Alex watched from the corner of the room as the three bodies collapsed to the floor. Involuntary passage into ascension was rare, but it occasionally happened if a person was in shock.

"Or in this case, three people," mused Alex.

He wasn't a fan of ascension himself, after seeing his parents burn to death in the flames of the wreckage of their car. Intellectually, he knew it was a way of staying in touch with the deceased. But his heart wouldn't let him ascend. He just felt that sense of betrayal that had never passed.

Still if the healers could get something out of the process, he thought, stretching out his calves one by one. *Then bully for them.*

Remembering back to what he had learned about ascension in firefighter school, he concluded there was a neural link bridging their consciousnesses and maintaining a link with their physical selves. Their breath had slowed and was imperceptible but was fully capable of sustaining life in the short term. But Alex instinctively knew they couldn't stay in this state forever. He set an alarm for eight minutes time to wake them.

The consciousnesses of Hannah, Eva, and Terry experienced the weightless flow of ascension. Midway between worlds of rebirth and the living, faces and voices carried them.

"It doesn't feel quite right," whispered Terry. "Usually, someone meets us on the cusp. Is anyone able to give us guidance?"

The Smiling Saint became apparent.

"Her presence indicates fortitude through lightness of being," said Doug to Eva; there on her shoulder as she regained her equilibrium.

The Smiling Saint was joined by St. Augustine, the patron saint of brewers and printers, and St. Francis, the patron saint of animals and the environment. He letter looked weary, and Albion was nowhere to be seen.

Direct thought transference from the saints was unavailable. The saints had ascended so long ago that the mimicking of human speech in ascension was well in the past. That they had achieved sainthood meant they would not be reborn but would remain saintly caretakers. Unlike humans who were in the constant cycle of rebirth, the sainthood were granted eternal life, or presence, and could move through all three states of existence. They could invigorate statues or appear in the dreams of humans, come together with and separate from Eternal Source, and be a nonverbal source of guidance in ascension. If not through mental image transference, their bond with the elders in ascension was generally enough to provide insight.

"Doug, May!" called Eva.

Suddenly, the elders were there with the saints. It wasn't essential, but sometimes it helped to imagine human conventions. So they all perceived themselves in a circle holding hands. A deep thrum set up in the distance. At first, irregular, it settled into a steady cadence and deepened.

Eva and Hannah kept their focus narrow. Terry was solely focused on St. Francis, who had materialized by St. Augustine. The thrum became a drumming. Eva couldn't confirm, but she could sense other older saints in ascension, with an aura of gold and intense impossible light.

Was time going faster or slowing down? Eva couldn't tell. Her senses were contrary to her consciousness. The impact of the sound! All her senses were drawn on. The thrumming took up everything to the point of pain. Every emotion rushed through the trio, and then left them leaving behind a sense of conviction that, through this ceremony and the support of the saints, they would be able to face whatever lay in front of them. The trio felt also the presence of another contrary compulsion: dirty, brown, and malignant.

In the physical realm, the bodies of the three apothecarists were motionless, slumped in an awkward triangle. Alex circled them, padding like the extinct big cat, the panther. He moved, hypervigilant. He kept an eye on their vital signs. He watched the pulses in their necks. The rise and fall of their chests with each shallow breath.

The consciousness of Eva, Hannah, and Terry in ascension brushed each other. The saints jitterbugged among them. The reassuring presence of May also helped, her aura shining with a yellow fire. Doug was as angry as Eva had ever perceived him. His aura was pumped up with fury, white hot, and he was unable to communicate effectively. Such was the level of his anger.

So May verbalized for the group.

"There is some evidence that the balance between the physical world and ascension has changed. Tragically, souls are perishing and not ascending. The rebirth rate is too high. Souls are spending less time in ascension to gain wisdom and guidance before rebirthing."

May continued in her measured way, "This is of import as less mature souls are rebirthing and affecting the incarnate timeline with poor judgment and selfish desires. Oh, it's not their fault, the poor things. They must feel an underlying sense of abandonment and isolation. All we can assume is that at this stage of history our evolutionary progression has ceased. Some of our scientists are suggesting DNA markers are regressing. Five hundred years ago, marked the start of the latest evolutionary epoch. Before this, telomeres eventually shortened leading to senescence and death. Physical death that was often painful and miserable. There was no spell between bodies in ascension, just a vague concept of an afterlife. This is what we call the Source, the wellspring of all including ascension. A shift in balance between the elements is okay, but given the malignancy you feel here in ascension and the change in rebirth rate, the Source in turn could be repolluted. There is a very real danger to the Source."

No one commented. All were trying to conceive the inconceivable. May, in her role as a historian, was touching on the nature of creation itself. Concepts of source and rebirth—they were well acquainted with in their everyday lives, but no one had ever raised the possibility of a threat to the Source.

An alarm went off in the physical world. The connection held strong long enough for Doug to impart the following:

"Lives for the most part are led peacefully. Generations and towns live and die never knowing strife. Other societies in other times must bear the brunt of cataclysmic strife. I fear the world may be on the brink of war."

Now fully incarnate, the trio slowly opened their eyes and pushed themselves up from the floor. The "beep-beep" of Alex's alarm persistent in awaking them.

Tan and Eva spoke over each other.

"First things first. We've got a threat to the apothecary that's blindsided us."

Tan said, "But it's not happening today. We can appeal at the town meeting. We can call in experts to put our case forward as the rightful tenants of the apothecary".

THEY'RE PUTTING UP WALLS

"What the hell." Eva cast a glance as Tan stormed into the infirmary. Eva was surprised. She rarely heard Tan this emotional, let alone raise his voice.

"I was driving over and over by the library and the town hall. They're doing some quite extensive construction work. They've bulldozed over a children's playground and put down foundations. I dropped into the council buildings anyway, to lodge the notification challenging the acquisition of the estate." Tan's voice shook as he related his observations to Eva.

"I wasn't the only one lodging an appeal. There was a queue of us. And there is some serious construction work in the pipeline."

Lily, Tan's sister, worked in the Council Planning Department; so he had informally popped into her office.

Lily looked defeated. Putting her chin on her hands, she looked at him without surprise that he was there.

"Where to begin?" she said, guessing the reason for his impromptu visit. "All external consents had been put on hold."

Lily would normally open or further along at least five new consents a week. She would consent the occasional new dwelling for a family or estate for a council-approved profession. The population didn't tend to wane or flux overly, so new building consents weren't a large part of her job. Mostly, she prepared consents for minor additions like Nicoletta's horse stable or a request for perpetuity for a dwelling that also served a humanitarian purpose like the apothecary, now threatened by requisition. Usually in these case, like the Ventura apothecary, generations of families had performed the same role over the years for the town; and the council generally kept out of their business.

Lily opened a file. "Look at this! The council has issued a hundred reacquisition notices. They're in no particular part of Destin. What they have in common is that they are multibedroomed. All have been in perpetuity for at least five hundred years. All are imbued just like Eva's apothecary—"where purpose had been associated with a building for so long it emitted a distinctive psychic signal". Tan knew this but it beggared belief why the council would act against the best iterests of Destin and reaquire the dwellings that kept their very citizens healthy and vigorous. Lily continued: All have well-kept gardens, their caretakers take pride in maintenance, and there is no reason for the council to look askance at their operations," she said while twirling a strand of hair as she gazed into the distance.

"How many objections to reacquisition?" asked Tan.

"One hundred percent objection rate," said Lily opening another drawer. "The letters are here. There is construction though. It looks to be motivated by council agencies. Rather than citizens at large. These still need to be consented, but the mayor and his staff are referring external consents to unrelated third parties so they can't be accused of cronyism. Much of the recent legislation being passed is related to this. The consents have been outsourced mostly to towns other than Destin, asking for third-party clearance. It's bizarre."

She continued, "And I'm effectively being asked to rubber-stamp internal consents. The nature of my job has completely changed."

Tan wished Lily the best and proceeded onto the council chambers.

The stenographer, the interfering Carlota, was busily typing the mayor's fast-paced patter.

"I move we continue to outsource the external consents for construction projects."

"Aye, aye" came the voices of the twenty councilors.

Tan listened from the gallery. At first in puzzlement, then in shock.

"I move to amend the perpetuity concessions to limit broad perpetuity to businesses, excluding any and all medical services. The town of Destin will provide all these henceforth."

Eva had heard more of Tan's experience than she could take.

"Stop, stop!" she begged him.

Tan turned his face to hers. "We were going to appeal on the basis we are providing a humanitarian need. But that's another commonality between all the notified reacquisitions? We are not safe because we are healing professionals?" We healers appear to be specifically targeted.

HANNAH CLEMIRA

"We can't do anything until Monday!" lamented Hannah as she and Eliza washed up the lunch dishes. "A week ago there was no Eliza and no Alex!" Hannah said in wonder.

Eva walked up to the two girls and slung her arm around Hannah's shoulders.

Hannah raised her eyebrow. "Can you believe it's only been a week? Hopefully, they're not still bickering this time next week." The frustration was evident in her tone of voice. She could hear Terry and Alex duking it out over a minor issue in the treatment rooms.

The two guys had not warmed to each other on their initial acquaintance and had made poor bunkmates. Terry's rakish façade and "could care less" approach to living was anathema to the brooding Alex who expected nothing but complete discipline and neatness from his bunkmate. Minor annoyances had escalated to a full-on screaming match the previous night when Alex had confiscated all of Terry's medical marijuana.

"I need it for my mental health," shouted Terry. "I'm fine at the moment, but I get anxious, depressed."

"It's no wonder you're depressed," Alex yelled, glaring at Terry and jabbing his finger at him. "I bet you've never exercised in your life!"

Terry considered this point and couldn't deny the truth of it.

And truth be told, he was more bothered by Alex's arrogance and less bothered by the missing marijuana. There were greater concerns in the offing, but it annoyed him no end that a total newcomer to the apothecary had blatantly confiscated his private property. Following this, Alex commenced to arrange his toiletries in Terry's bathroom and rearrange Terry's things. Terry muttered, "Fucken' idiot," sotto voce and left the room.

—◊—

Eliza and Hannah made a much better match as roommates. Eliza had lasted two nights in the infirmary closet before the combination of feeling confined and curiosity about the fox that lived with Hannah got the better of her. She pushed away her natural feelings of shyness and asked if she could sleep in Hannah's room. It was across the way and a mirror image of Terry's and Alex's room. A single set of bunks and a bathroom. Nicoletta and Tan dropped off a mattress for the lower of the bunk beds and a table and lamp. Hannah politely ignored the muted sobbing from the lower bunk bed until the fourth night when she was woken by a piercing scream.

"Eliza!" She tugged at the petrified girl's shoulder. "Eliza, it's all right! You're just having a nightmare. Here, sit up!"

Eliza sat up, her wild hair framing her pale face and centered by her dripping nose.

"It was awful," she muttered as she pulled the thick wool blankets around her. "I dreamed the bounty hunters got me. They took me from here back to Diaspora and took me to work in a factory. And no one could understand me. I was everywhere, and I was on all the screens, and everyone was mocking me. Why would they take me back after I had unplugged? They made an example of me!" This with her shoulder's heaving. "Do you think they will want to take me back?" she asked.

"I'm sorry you had a nightmare," Hannah said to comfort the sobbing girl. "That's all it was, a nightmare." She and chased the unwanted word "premonition" from the back of her mind. "I'll make us some hot cocoa and we can talk further." She cooed at the shadows, and an orange streak darted into the room. "Here have some company."

Hannah left the room, and Eliza dried her tears on the fox's silky mane. After ten minutes, she felt a lot calmer.

"Thank you," she said, pressing her nose against that of the fox's.

The fox's eyes coolly regarded her, and she heard a shadow thought in her brain, *You're welcome*, followed by an image of a cooked chicken leg.

Eliza chuckled. "Foxy, I will get you some delicious nonsentient fowl," she promised the raised nose.

An image came of Foxy rolling over to get his tummy tickled. Eliza laughed.

"Shoo, Foxy," said Hannah, returning. "The girls need to talk."

The little beast did a fair imitation of a canter out of the room with nose raised proudly. It was plain to see he almost knew he had been of comfort to the disturbed girl. They heard the click of his entry flap into the exercise yard.

"It's so different here," said Eliza, looking questioningly at Hannah. "Here you can hear the animal's thoughts, but nobody can get into my mind in the apothecary!"

"No," said Hannah. "Not like in Diaspora and the other bound cities." She pretended to gag, and Eliza smiled. It was the first smile Hannah could recall seeing from Eliza.

Hannah continued, "I believe in the bound cities, from what I understand, latent psychic power is realized in the group think you experience in being a citizen of the bound city. You're all used to your minds being open, so you tend not to have a lot of individual thoughts, good. bad or otherwise. We in the incorporated territories respect there is strength in that, that you're stronger collectively, networked, and linked in with the city mind." She leaned forward. "Some of us."

And by "us," Eliza guessed she meant most of the people who lived or visited the apothecary around Destin.

"Some of us train to put our psychic energy into specialized areas. Eva's family line, which I am a member of BTW, have a honed affinity with animals. And in some cases, members of the family line have combined this with fighting prowess. Eva is trained in most of the ancient orders of martial arts. She attained yogi status at the age of fourteen. At this stage, she was deemed to be worthy to hold the license for this ancient estate by the last four generations of Venturas."

Eliza took this all onboard without questioning. Her reality had been knocked, nay, blown clean out of the water. With a clean slate, it was easier for Eliza to suspend belief entirely rather than casting her mind back to her previous life and raising points of contention about the way the Asperians lived.

Hannah's green eye winked at her.

Eliza pushed her bangs off her forehead and leaned forward. "What can Terry do?" she asked.

Hannah answered, "He's a dear and very good with distressed animals. Otherwise, he has not proved much more use than party entertainment, but he can control smoke with his mind. Kind of like balloon animals."

Eliza laughed at this. She had seen enough of the way the trio interacted over the week to relate to the humor underlying.

"And he's got that magnetism with the animals?" she ventured.

"They do love him," said Hannah.

Eliza pushed her hair aside. "And you?"

"Well," said Hannah, her eyes glinting. "That cocoa in your hand?"

Eva looked down.

Hannah continued, "If I didn't like you, in about half an hour, you might experience a mild bout of indigestion at the very least." A smirk moved across the warm cherubic face. "And at the worst? Well..." She languidly leaned out and tapped Eliza on the forearm with her two-inch-long nails. "Carlotta, the city clerk, was bugging the heck out of us last summer to agree to three monthly council regulation visits. She quit after she got laid up with a case of boils on a rather sensitive part of her anatomy. She spent a week in bed. I'd just seen her at the local tea and coffee house. Muffin in time!"

Eliza looked down at the nails. She glanced back at Hannah and startled. "I never noticed, you have one green eye and one blue eye."

Hannah motioned back to the cup. The remains of Eliza's cocoa were forming a funnel. It swirled into a mini maelstrom. Just when Eliza thought the contents were going to rise clear out of the mug, the liquids settled back. Eliza looked back at Hannah, amazed.

Hannah gazed back at Eliza with, now, two caramel brown eyes! Eliza jumped as goosebumps raced down her arms.

"I'm Hannah Clemira." She tapped her long nails on her ankle, and her dressing gown dropped away to reveal body-hugging nightwear that proclaimed the slogan "Asp Woman." This was inked in black on white with a border of red roses and vines. Hannah the Merciful; of the family Woodhead, part of the Ventura lineage. "I'm good in the kitchen,"

Hannah said once more with a wry smile. "I'm practically invisible, out of it. Oh, and I can act a little."

At this, Hannah stood and drew herself to her full height, which was all of a sudden shorter than when she had been previously sitting next to Eva. She shrugged back on the dressing gown, which had bunched to the floor. She turned her back to Eva, then looked back mischievously.

"At one moment you can be a child in any situation."

As she turned to Eva, the years fell off, and Eliza could have sworn Hannah had previously been wearing a bun instead of the pigtails she now sported. Hannah's face dimpled, and she shrugged the hood of the dressing gown on. Suddenly, she was a veritable cherub. Eliza was not prone to maternalism, but she unexpectedly wanted to scoop Hannah up and protect her.

The voice from within the dressing gown muttered some incomprehensible syllables, and the voice lost its mellifluous tone and wore thin.

"The next you are a crone," Hannah intoned and shrugged the hood off.

Eliza gasped. The hair was gray. The eyes turned sepulchral. Hannah's cheeks were now gaunt, and liver spots speckled her arms. As Eliza watched amazed, the cheeks filled out, and once again Eliza found herself looking at the sweet middle-aged dumpling face of the Hannah she had met only days earlier.

Her persona restored to normal, Hannah held Eliza's gaze. "Poisons, weather control, and shapeshifting." She named her skills matter of factly. Little balls of cocoa languidly rose out of the cup and then plopped back in. Matronly, Hannah patted Eliza's shoulders. "Go to sleep now," she said. "We can talk more tomorrow."

And obliging, Eliza did so, replaying what she had just seen in her mind while she drifted off to sleep.

—⟋⟍—

Hannah related her tête-à-tête with Eliza to Eva the next day following the recount of Terry and Alex's latest fight.

Eva smiled. "Mom," she said, "one day the wind will change, and you'll stay as an old woman instead of your current age."

Hannah chuckled. "That's not going to happen." She waved her hand over an open pot bubbling on the range. The soup popped up a carrot for a nose, spaghetti for hair, and the unmistakable shape of a face with a tongue poking out took shape.

"Nice, Mom, nice."

Hannah winked a blue eye at Eva.

"I'll go get Eliza," she said. "It's time she got a makeover."

TOWN HALL

The townspeople sitting in the gallery seating overlooking the mayor's table heckled the councilors as they filed in. Bruno Stewart, the councilor for the suburb of Timsdale, glared up at the seated townspeople as he took his seat at the large oval debating table. Sue McLaren, the councilor for Amberwoods, peered shyly out from under her bangs. A paper airplane launched from the seats at the end of the oval table and stopped mid-trajectory, then turned and flew over Carlotta, the stenographer's shoulder, who was sitting to the right of the mayor. Just as it passed over her shoulder, it neatly pooped out bird guano, which landed on her yellow-and-black polka-dot blouse, entangling in her hair as it did so. Two burly lads in the middle seats high-fived each other to the accompaniment of sniggers from the audience. The mayor banged his gavel.

"There will be no more of that kind of disruption, or I will clear the council chambers," he trumpeted.

The audience shifted in their seats and quietened. The mayor banged one more time with his gavel and continued.

"We are here today to pass Ordinance 510, where external consents for new construction and new dwellings are outsourced to external third-party engineers for the foreseeable future. We just don't have the expertise in house, and we have many applications sitting in the pipeline."

Terry sat in the gallery watching forlornly. He knew Lily would be watching via Sati Link and would be chastened and bruised by the passing of the ordinance. He and Lily had dated last spring, and to be honest he was still a little sweet on her. She had given him a lock of her hair in an amulet he kept around his neck when she sweetly broke it off with him.

She was too young to be in a serious relationship she had said. He in turn had given her a dried rabbit's foot in an aged leather pouch.

"Oh, gross." She had giggled at the sight of it, but he was pretty sure she had kept it as Tan had wondered out loud about the appearance of the leather accessory one day in the infirmary.

Terry refocused on the proceedings. The councilors were debating animatedly. Wendy Bighorn, Sarragrasso, had the floor.

"Why have we so much new construction?" she demanded of the mayor.

"We have an influx of militia, and we need to garrison them and also provide training camps," answered the mayor coolly, dismissing Wendy with a wave of his hand.

"Excuse me, Mayor. Excuse me," said Wendy. "That's not good enough. We have never been a town that has required a lot of military protection. Why is there a shift toward militarization?"

"Shut up, Wendy," shouted Bruno. "Your background is as a café manager. No wonder you don't understand why Destin needs to beef up its protection."

A couple of the other councilors murmured in agreement.

Wendy refused to back down and stood up proudly, her chest heaving deep breaths over the table. "I want to see some statistics. How many soldiers and how much new construction."

Sue murmured, "Aye aye," at this.

Wendy caught her eye gratefully. "I demand we take a vote on that first."

The mayor glared daggers at her and moved to hijack her momentum.

"Our sole business today is to cast a vote on Ordinance 510. All those in favor say aye."

Most of the table said "Aye" and stuck up their hands.

Carlotta was busily scribbling on iPad, typing into a screen. A spitball flew from Bruno aimed at Wendy. Terry couldn't believe it. Along with wasting the town's resources, they were all acting like children and completely disrespecting the audience. He pursed his lips. Sighting the air-conditioning vents around the council chambers, he sensed some movement within, in the narrow ducts that connected the intake with the rows of pipes. He called with his mind.

"Come on me, pretties," he said. "Come for a day out. Come to play in the light." He whistled, and a few people turned to look at him, amused by his spikey hair and his insouciant grin. It didn't take very long, and then suddenly, there they were—rows and rows of marching cockroaches streaming out of the vents.

Sue was the first to notice. Normally quiet and self-effacing, she started to scream. Louder and louder her screams rang around the chamber walls. Marvin, the councilor next to her, slapped her on the right cheek; and she stopped and started sobbing. The rest of the councilors looked on fascinated as the small army of cockroaches marched determinedly toward the mayor's table and started climbing the legs. A few councilors vacated the room while others half-heartedly tried to stomp on the cockroaches but found to their disbelief they could not be flattened. Terry followed the cockroach army up with some physical chemistry. He reversed the process of the evaporator coil in the air-conditioning unit, causing warm air to come off the unit. He bought it through the vents, and as it recondensed, he painted it white and elbowed the man next to him.

The man yelled out, "Fire," and all of a sudden, there was a stampede from the council chambers. The cockroaches and the vote were both largely forgotten. Terry waited until the last person had exited. He idly picked his nose and flicked the proceeds onto the back of the nearest cockroach. He pulled down his sunglasses and sauntered out of the council chambers, turning to take one last look at the thousands of cockroaches sunning themselves under the UV light lamps. Sniggering, he adjusted his shades as he stepped onto the sidewalk. Technically, he didn't need sunglasses at this time of the year in late fall. Nobody did since 50AB, or the year of the Asteroid Belt that appeared after the breaching and sheltered Panacea from the sun. They lost a few weeks of sun each year, but they sure did get a lightshow each night, mused Terry as he walked back to the apothecary.

NEW BEGINNINGS

Brynn was pissed off. Not so you could tell. Brynn's icy composure never faltered or failed to stand her in good stead with the mostly male work force of the stable, and even when she'd just been subjected to a rather boorish attempt by one of the groomsmen, Ted, who tried to pinch Brynn on the hip. He protested when she swatted his shoulder with the lunge line she was holding. The whip end caused a trickle of blood to start down his chin.

"Aww, Brynn," he said. "What will it take?"

"More than you've got to offer," Brynn told the sheepish groomsman. Then she gave the unfortunate lad a break and changed her tone to a more jovial banter. "But I can offer up my boss lady in in my place! She hasn't had any loving in a while."

Ted rolled his eyes. "You know what they say about the last guy from the stables who went with Ravenna!"

"How is Mitch?" asked Brynn, lifting the saddles up to the high shelves as she spoke. "Has he stopped peeing blood? I did warn him not to play doctors and nurses with Ravenna!"

Brynn was mostly joking to cover up her natural shyness and to put them both on an equal footing. After all, they all lived in close quarters and had to rub along together, or the horses' welfare would be the worse off for it, and they might eventually be unceremoniously turned out into the Steppes if the horses suffered. The King was not generous and neither was he harsh but he wouldn't stand for a poorly run stables.

Brynn mixed as easily with the stable hands as she did with the self-appointed new "royalty" at Castle Ridich. It wasn't really a castle in the historical sense, but the closest you could get in these parts where the inhabitants of the lands outside the king's lands referred to themselves as either the Wretched or the Wrenched. If you were unfortunate enough just to be born in the Steppes, you were known as the Wretched. If you were mad, to boot, you were the Wrenched and doomed to scavenging or being used as target practice by bounty hunters and vagabonds and those merely with brutal tendencies, which was nearly everyone. Castle Ridich was a wooden and concrete homestead with several other structures surrounding including the stable and a bunkhouse where she mostly resided.

Brynn and the other stable hands finished mucking out the stables. They each grabbed a cigarette from their duffel bags and, after a final check, left for the bunkhouse to play dice and talk in the final light of the evening. Brynn was the only girl in the stables, but it didn't bother her bunking down with lads for company. In fact, it suited her well. She'd be up before first light to go hunting, for rabbits. Partridge were surprisingly speedy, though they only flew short distances close to the ground. Unusual species: small, feathered mammals that were said to have appeared in the decades directly following the breaching. They had little quills and stubby front legs with a more powerful hind. Usually, they would travel in groups rooting out mushrooms truffles and acorns that they would barter among themselves. At the first sign of trouble, they would vie to find shelter by kicking a littermate and crawling under others. It was known as a Judas pig.

Brynn finished joshing with the guys. The talk had been fairly predictable, revolving around eunuchs and bodily functions.

Ferg, one of the portlier grooms of the stables, elbowed Brynn on the way to the latrine. Short of temper, Brynn unleashed a string of invective at the disappearing back of fat Ferg.

This made the youngest groom of the stables, Ninepin Nico, blush and regard Brynn with wary eyes.

"It's all right, Nico," Brynn said to the shrinking groomsman. "I probably couldn't surgically remove that particular organ from Ferg. No one's sharpened their minds or knives enough to help me catch butcher a chicken let alone a pig or similar, around these parts for weeks!"

Nico had recently been acquired by the Ridich musterers less than two weeks ago. Like every new recruit by the Ridich musterers, he had been assessed for his potential as a soldier, a farmhand, stable hand, or carpenter. If the recruits weren't suitable for any of these, they were either given the tasking of providing entertainment or were used as practice range fodder as runners. The girls, however, were merely housed until they were old enough to be useful. Their only real use was to breed more boys for Castle Ridich. Brynn had been lucky or devious or both. She had pretended to be a boy until it became obvious to the musterers, she was every bit as good with horses and strong and wiry as any of the boys. The muster who alerted her that they were onto her game had clapped her on the back; told her to keep dressing like a boy; and if she was to continue to get board and an apprenticeship at Ridich, that she had better outride, outrun, outhunt, and outwit all the other stable hands. Then he had said, "Good job, lass."

A knock at the door jerked Brynn from her thoughts. It was House, the castle runner.

"Ravenna wants you up at the main house," he said tersely, jerking his head in the direction he had come from. House turned and ran toward the homestead, and ruefully, Brynn turned to follow. She threw her moccasins on and strode after him.

"Brynn!" shrieked Ravenna Ridich as Brynn climbed the stairs to the self-appointed princesses's quarters.

"Sleep with me tonight," said Ravenna.

"Do I have to?" groaned Brynn. "I want to go hunting in the morning."

"Please," said the querulous voice from behind the glossy auburn tresses. "I really want you to."

It had started as an order as part of her maidservant duties that Brynn was to sleep with Ravenna to keep her company. They both had been surprised to find they enjoyed the overnight jaunts. Brynn shrugged at Ravenna's response.

"Okay then, fine," she said.

Ravenna was a fairly solitary person. She couldn't abide small talk or the simpering of commoners. However, she did need stimulus from the company of others, so her encounters with others were mainly sadistic. The only pleasure Ravenna enjoyed in dealing with others was in relishing other's pain. But once Ravenna figured she couldn't break Brynn's spirit, that she had met a form of equal, she had infrequently started asking Brynn to stay over instead of with the other stable hands.

Ravenna nodded and turned to light the fire.

"Here, let me do that for you," Brynn said, taking the lighter.

Ravenna went to sit at her armoire and selecting a boar bristled brush languidly started to drag it through her hair.

"Did you hear what I did to the last stable boy?" sniggered Ravenna to the mirror.

"I did," replied Brynn, climbing out of her jodhpurs and grabbing herself a silk dressing gown. "I mean really, Ravenna! What did he ever do to you?"

Ravenna smirked. "It was what he wouldn't do to me. Limper than spaghetti!" She slammed her hand on her palm for emphasis. "So I got out my toolbox. He enjoyed the first part. I was just starting to enjoy the proceedings, and he started squealing like a pig! He had no tolerance for pain." Ravenna sighed, climbing into the ornate bed under the upturned duvet.

Brynn shrugged off her dressing gown and climbed in after her.

"I heard he is still in the infirmary," said Brynn, her lips making a moue of amusement.

Ravenna cupped Brynn's breasts with her hands, and they both rolled on their sides to watch the flickering flames in the fireplace.

"How is your father?" asked Brynn"

"Much the same," replied Ravenna. "The king wishes I was a boy and speaks to me like one. He tells me about his hunts and his pillaging forays, how many men he kills and how he brings about their deaths. Yet he won't let me assume any responsibilities other than running the household affairs."

Brynn considered this but didn't comment. They chatted further and drifted off while the fire flickered low in the hearth.

NICOLETTA FARSEES

Nicoletta was stretching after her workout. All the horse riding she did tended to knot her muscles a lot, she reflected. Taking her feet wide, she cupped her hands and pushed them to the ceiling. Then rolling her shoulders out, she dropped into the sumo wrestler's pose. Pushing her heels to the floor, Nicoletta held for ninety seconds. It had taken a lot of stretching today to release the knots and tensions she had accumulated over the last few days. Today she'd ridden Blake, her sire of the stables for an hour and a half, before she left him with fresh water, carrots, and sweet chestnuts.

The most impressive dwelling on Nicoletta's parcel of land was the stable itself. Her cottage sat to one side furthest away from the road. The cottage itself was fairly humble. Two bedrooms, one for guests, which was more often than not Tan, and one for herself. The lounge, rather unusually, was at the back of the house. Nicoletta preferred it this way. The layout wasn't as welcoming as others in the wooded enclave on the northern border of the town of Destin. Nicoletta wasn't much fussed with visitors. She preferred not to be surprised by unexpected callers, and she had ways and means of viewing any stranger's approach other than merely looking out of a window.

Her time was largely her own, and she spent it either with her horses or in the lounge toward the rear. Her divination room, Nicoletta thought fondly.

Long ago, Nicoletta had removed the doors to the room and replaced them with sheets of hanging glass beads and cut crystal. As she approached the divination room, the beads caught and moved on the wake of her movement.

"For once I have visitors," commented Nicoletta.

The much-loved Albion wound around her ankles and dashed in front of Nicoletta as she pushed aside and into her divination room. Albion was familiar with the room and ran over to Nicoletta's working bench and rolled on his back as though expecting his noncorporeal tummy to be tickled. Albion then looked at Nicoletta adoringly with limpid brown eyes, this as she laughed and blew a kiss at him.

Then Nicoletta let her eyes relax and drift around the room until she saw him.

He was in his painting, humble and weathered but at the same time youthful and fresh. St. Francis lent on his stick and raised an eyebrow and cupped his hand in his ear, cocking his ear toward Nicoletta.

"Oh, Francis," said Nicoletta, turning and curtseying to the painting. "To what do I owe the honor?" She looked pointedly at St. Francis, who gazed back at Nicoletta with a deadpan expression.

The water in the cauldron quickly started steaming, and words took their shape.

"Sister of Shadows, we part before we meet."

As was indicated at this stage of the ritual, she dropped a handful of white sage into the cauldron and turned to the painting. She could see the tears forming in his eyes and drop into the cauldron below the painting. A flurry of words formed from steam:

"Farsee!"

"Look south and west. In the madness, darkness and light. Excess, want and might."

"A new ruling tribe!" A daughter to travel and lead the fight. Three souls torn apart by fate. Your charges must leave and travel far and if they follow true to their hearts. In the shadow of the Bleakness, they will reunite."

Another last string of words: "They must challenge that which seeks to corrupt the Source."

Nicoletta's fists clenched, and she held the gaze of the saint without dropping it. Then she let the old man go. Albion ran through the painting from one side of the frame, and by the time he reached the other, he was gone. Nicoletta let her tears slide into the cauldron, and the surface of the water settled.

EVA: MARTIAL ARTS TRAINING

Eva liked to fight. She was a regular at the martial arts complex. With all the events of the past eight days, it had been longer than usual since her last visit. Proficient in five other martial arts, Eva was currently practicing the African martial art of Dambe. She wrapped her right hand in rope and walked up to meet her opponent. The aim was to subdue her opponent in three rounds.

Official fights with professional boxers could be quite brutal and were fought outside on sand. Though there were frequent injuries, there were rarely head injuries. And there was substantial mana accorded to the winner of a Dambe match in the incorporated towns. Boxing matches tended to attract a large audience of professionals, tired housewives, and giggling teenagers who would all imagine themselves heroes inside the ring.

Eva noticed her opponent was lefthanded as this was the hand he had wrapped. That meant she would have to both strike and block with her dominant hand. She was the first to strike. He parried this easily with his right hand, but Eva had already launched herself into the air and was sweeping her feet and legs under him. He fell to the ground clearly frustrated, and Eva acknowledged a pang of satisfaction. She had taken the first round. The pair continued to parry and strike, both clearly relishing the even match and the chance to work out.

CARLOTTA

It was a lot of work, thought Carlotta, *a lot of work running a town the size of Destin.*

Carlotta raised a perfectly arched eyebrow at the mayor while she waited for the mayor to speak. Her pen was poised ready to capture the mayor's every thoughts to assist him in writing his weekly address to the town. Today the mayor was taking a long time to get his thoughts in order, probably because he couldn't drag his eyes away from Carlotta's ample bosom, she noted with grim satisfaction. The mayor was a fool. And there was no fool like an old amorous fool. His ascension was long overdue, but she'd bet he'd die of natural causes before he ascended instead of ascending first. Mind you, she smirked wryly, with her network of ne'er-do-wells and criminals, she was sure she could arrange a not-so-natural passing.

She prompted him, "We are used to times of relative peace and prosperity on Panacea. But it is emerging that we have clear and present threats to the security of our and others in the unconsolidated territories, right?"

"Right," he stuttered. "The bound cities are adopting a hawkish relationship with us and numerous other towns. This due to the latest incidences of self-exiles. And also, we note increasing levels of violence south and to the west. So it is pleasing that work to convert the compulsorily acquired properties in the event of a military draft is proceeding at a fast pace."

It's too slow, thought Carlotta angrily. She heaved her chest.

The mayor faltered. "What was I saying?" he asked hesitantly.

"You were saying we need to increase the rate of conversion of buildings to barracks," she said.

"Yes!" said the mayor, striking his hand forcefully on the chair.

Carlotta smiled to herself. It was all too easy. Had it only been two years since she'd started working in the council chambers? She'd actually started in the council reception. It had taken only three visits to the mayor's desk with spurious reasons—outright made-up reasons, Carlotta admitted to herself proudly—before the mayor decided that his longtime friend elderly male assistant Cecil would be better deployed in the operational side of the council. *It was perfect*, thought Carlotta. Cecil made a wonderful head of planning. He took any order the mayor made without question. And he was completely oblivious to the reality that it was Carlotta that was deciding the council policies. Her official title was council stenographer, but she was much more than that.

Though Carlotta got the feeling Cecil didn't entirely trust her, he was unable to put his finger on what effect she was having on the mayor.

Nobody really realized the power that Carlotta held at her fingertips, and certainly not those twerps at the apothecary. Carlotta despised them. Helping animals and the weak with their herbal woo-woo. They could have a normal veterinary practice in the town center. That estate was a waste of a building that would be far better to be utilized by the council. And tomorrow it would be taken over by the council, and they'd be powerless to do anything.

KING RIDICH

Ravenna climbed the stairs of the turret her father had just added to his quarters. Ravenna was sick of the constant building activity as the king constantly enlarged the original building to impress his subjects. But his castle was starting to look reasonably formidable, allowed Ravenna. The king had recently hired artisans and craftsmen to decorate the exterior, and the castle looked quite established. Looking out over the steppes, Ravenna could see Brynn in the foothills of Craggy Peak. Hunting, no doubt, with a makeshift bow.

She must see if she couldn't source some more impressive weapons for Brynn, thought Ravenna. The girl had softened her up, she mused. And the affection seemed to be returned. When Brynn left this morning, she advised Ravenna that she would bringing her some rabbit stew for dinner.

"Mmmm," breathed Ravenna heavily at the thought. Other than inflicting pain on some unfortunate individual, her next favorite pastime was eating, preferably game.

Ravenna's father came into view: King Ridich, surrounded by eight of his burly Polynesian henchmen. Ravenna thrilled at the thought of one day traveling to the near mythical islands of Polynesia. All she knew was the Arcadian Steppes, born of the chaos of the wrenching following the breaching. Scientists posited that it would still take decades before psychic madness was low enough in the population to allow easy travel. Her father's generation had the most impact on establishing order. They had set about uniting cities and villages and killing the unfortunate mad. The Polynesian men would suit Ravenna better than the poor, puerile individuals her father bought into the fold, she mused.

Her father wasn't aware, but sometimes Ravenna would sneak into the latrines of the barracks in pants and a work shirt, disguised as a man. Her bulk made it easy to do so. She'd busy herself in a stall and soak up the smell of blood, piss, and sweat. She'd hear the occasional story of how someone's mother and father crossed the Seas of Pangaea to land on the shores of the New mainland, with Arcadia proper being the closest landing point to the Warm Island Seas, and more hospitable than the tundra and ice continent that lay south near King Ridich's castle. No one in generations had heard fresh tales of Polynesia. After the global manifestation of psychic energy and the resultant wrenching, the taste for air travel had subsided and the range of planes was limited. The Earth was liable to emit unpredictable electromagnetic radiation, dropping planes from the skies. It was almost impossible to believe that once upon a time air travel had been the safest form of travel, mused Ravenna. While Ravenna was scanning the horizon, her father crossed to stand beside her on the balcony.

"What do you think, Rav?" asked the king, folding his arms across his burly chest. Watching Ravenna shrewdly, he awaited her response.

"I think we need to concentrate on increasing the size of the stable," she replied. "We know we've captured and cleared south to the tundra. Now we need to go west, where the land bridge is infested by the psychic mad, the violent psychic Wrenched. But there are reports of some with powers that can be controlled. Maybe if we have more horses and men, we can start building outposts on the land bridge. It will be hard to bring order to the chaos though."

"Wretched lands," agreed the burliest bodyguard flanking the king.

The king chucked Ravenna under the chin. He regarded her shrewdly.

"If only you were a son, Rav," he said. "We could ride out together and clear the Wretched lands."

Ravenna's heart sunk.

"But you are a daughter, and I cannot risk losing a male heir through you. However, I can promise to stretcher back a few unfortunate souls for you to torture in your private chambers. Tank here"—he gestured to the bodyguard—"and his friends can pick the poor souls out especially!"

The king opened his mouth and laughed, the booming hateful sound ringing about Ravenna's ears and enmeshing her to the castle walls.

Her ears ringing, she suddenly lost her taste for torture and felt a flicker of fury at the lack of the king's understanding of her wants and abilities.

He is as mad as any of the Wrenched, Ravenna thought miserably. She would have to come up with another plan to get some taste of life outside Castle Ridich.

EVA SMELLS TROUBLE

Eva stepped out of the apothecary at first light to do her usual rounds—and then froze when every sense told her that things weren't right. She could hear a rattle of coins, or metal pellets being poured from one hand to the other. A faint smell of cigarette smoke. Others were nearby, and the cigarette smoke and metal were signs of aberrant behavior.

No part of Destin could be described as ghettoized, but no matter how mature the society was, there was bound to be vagrancy to be found, reflected Eva.

Not wanting to draw attention to her presence, she withdrew back into the apothecary. Drawing the blinds in the lounge, she saw three hulking off-road vehicles parked alongside the narrow curb. A man dressed in black cooling his heels and smoking a cigarette while leaning of the fender of one. The hair on Eva's neck stood up, and she retreated to the infirmary to find solace in the company of animals and wait for Dr. Tan.

CARLOTTA MOBILISES

Carlotta kicked the leg of the mayor's chair. "Fuck!" she cursed the dead air. She straightened the scowl from her face as the mayor returned from his lengthy trip to the bathroom. He looked at her. She returned his gaze levelly, tapping her fingernails of her right hand on the glass overlay of the mayoral desk. He looked back blankly. In recent weeks, this was much the pattern of their interactions, and the mayor often waited for Carlotta to make the opening statement in their conversations.

"You know it's imperative we have adequate room to house the units coming out of the training barracks this quarter, Mayor," said Carlotta, noticing a spot on her right thumbnail where the varnish had worn. She felt a surge of ire.

He looked at her rheumily. Then he blinked and pushed his back his glasses.

"Remind me again how many troops we have to station this quarter?"

"One hundred thousand soldiers," said Carlotta.

"And how many do we intend to have in total?" asked the mayor as though his mind was on something else.

"Two hundred fifty thousand," responded Carlotta with steel in her voice.

"Two hundred fifty thousand," said the mayor, sounding genuinely surprised. "That's an increase of 1000 percent! From ten years ago. The armed forces are not intended to be a fulltime offensive guard, Carlotta. They're merely a deterrent for the mutants and the horsemen from the Arcadian Steppes who occasionally banded together and tried to loot the houses on the outskirts of Asperia."

With three land borders, Asperia was surprisingly self-regulating as far as defense against any want-to-be intruders. And commerce dominated the sea border. It was far more lucrative to trade with Africa, Arcadia, and Polynesia, the other continents with big seaports than it was to earn a living pirating. The pirates were more interested in expanding their floating islands, though the odd abduction did prove problematic for the more notable families of Arcadia.

The mayor pulled his attention back to Carlotta, framed by the window that looked over the town square. A crow alighted on the ledge, and the mayor imagined for a moment it winked. He refocused and turned his attention back to Carlotta. He really hoped he wasn't going dotty. Perhaps he'd better pay more attention to Carlotta's actual words and intent in the future.

She seemed so competent, and he could find no detail to fault her on, but it really was odd the army was building up to two hundred fifty thousand troops? Of troops?

PART 2

It was 2:00 p.m. Proctor Herbert glanced at the adjutant, fifteen-year-old tow-headed male who had proved himself proficient as an assistant. Even more so than the usual fawning specimens that the wardens of the city regularly threw up for his consumption. Herbert wasn't sure he liked his hair, which seemed to glow from within and caught Herbert's attention out of the corner of his eye at inopportune times when Herbert was trying to work on his files. Herbert almost wished he had anyone else as his assistant.

The boy was just so lubricious, thought the proctor.

But Herbert did not get a say on who was put in his employment. The Blind Eye selected suitable candidates, and the wardens interviewed and selected an appropriate individual based on academic performance and personality traits such as biddability and servility. Annoyingly, this young man was here to stay until the Blind Eye moved him on. Herbert touched his in tray and got a static shock, which reminded him he had better be careful with his thoughts. His assistant was too low in status to read him, and the Blind Eye didn't scan while the proctors were working, but it wouldn't pay to have anomalous thinking on the air train or in a meeting!

"What's your badge number again?" asked Proctor Herbert.

"It's 2758," responded the boy. "My name is Tom. Tom Torn." He cast his eyes down to the proctor's shoes.

"You can go," said the proctor, ignoring the boy and absent-mindedly turning the pages in a large plaid ring-bound folder in front of him.

"But...but," stammered 2758, "if I don't get a full day's work, I won't be able to give my mom board."

It was common for older teenagers to pay board to their parents. "It encouraged self-responsibility," declared some of the info screens in the city supermarkets.

"Enough," said Proctor Herbert. "Stop mewling! You're only here to do as much work as there is available. There is no more work for today. Come back at 10:00 a.m. tomorrow and do not be insubordinate again, or I will request a transfer from the city wardens based on your misconduct."

The boy cast his eyes upward to the proctor. He was sweating and noticed the lines creased around the proctor's mouth. The boy wished he had said nothing.

Mom, he thought piteously. *My first placement is not what I expected.*

His mom, Joy, had made him a packed lunch of tomatillo and ham pie, and Tom had eaten it quickly and tried to anticipate the proctor's every instruction. But the proctor was clearly unhappy and looking to discipline Tom. The proctor was wet under the arms and disturbed at how little self-control he had had this early in the day. If the boy didn't leave soon, he wouldn't be responsible for his actions. As the thought came into his mind, a loud crash echoed through the room.

A rather top-heavy decorative urn bearing an elephant ear plant had toppled over; and before he could stop himself, a surprised and shocked, Herbert, reached out, grabbed the boy's right ear and twisted it sharply.

The boy didn't make any noise other than letting out a sigh at the sudden onset of pain. He drew back and darted out of the proctor's reach as Herbert let the unfortunate adjudicant's ear go.

Then a concerned tender expression washed over the proctor's face, replacing the mask of ferocity he had previously worn. Incongruously, he smiled and moved past 2758 to open the door for him with a caring backward look.

In the strange dimly lit of the office, Tom moved toward the door confusedly and haphazardly. He walked out miserably, cradling his right ear with his right hand, a single tear tracing its way down his red and cheek.

"See you in the morning," said Proctor Herbert brightly.

He closed the door behind the unfortunate boy and breathed a sigh of relief. He had his office to himself. Moving back toward a bookcase lining one entire wall of the spacious room, he deftly moved aside a photo of a barn owl in an engraved frame. A stunning image of the barn owl in flight, claws extended. It was about to grab its unfortunate prey: a shivering, terrified mouse. He really was quite distracted this morning reflected Herbert. Boils had raised on his buttocks. He was running a quiet fever, and it stung when he passed urine. It was nearly two weeks since his last infusion. It was not surprising he was suffering. He had been warned by his mentor about the possible physical side effects of missing transfusions once the process had started. But, damn, it was uncomfortable. And today? Barely tolerable. There was now a discreet but deep cavity in the back of the bookshelf level with his shoulders. It could have been for display purposes.

"But," assured his mentor, "it had been built decades before for the very endeavor he was about to undertake.

Reaching his hands up into the cavity, he felt a sharp painful prick just below his thumb on his right hand as a needle was inserted.

Pain was a not unpleasant sensation if you knew what to expect, Herbert thought.

He knew blood was going from his radial artery into the collection bowl below that had appeared under a thin shelf that slid sideways into the bookcase.

Radial artery, thought Herbert appreciatively. *All those thousands of miles of blood vessels were like snakes. And they could be milked with a single mechanical butterfly needle at any spot!*

It was a very sterile and neat process without a human to jab and prod and make messes, observed Herbert. He appreciated this parchment and filler in it. Rivulets of blood trickled down his wrist, and he withdrew his hand. Wiping his wrist with a square of linen from his breast pocket, he listened for the sound of plastic on metal as anticoagulant tipped into the bowl.

The window opened behind him, and a rush of feathers announced the arrival of a visitor Herbert had been eagerly expecting.

"Do you like my new wings?" came a gravelly voice spoke from the shadows.

Again, feathers brushed through the air, accompanied by a slow-beating thrum, air moving slowly around the expense of the study.

"They are several inches longer than the last set," said Herbert tensely, new lines forming around his mouth. Somewhere in the pit of his stomach, he felt his colon crawl and retreat, pulling on his sphincter and testicles.

"Twenty-four inches long," rasped the course voice. "I want to augment with twenty-nine-inch wings eventually."

"LaVey, I feel sick," started Herbert. "I need an infusion."

"Stop!" said the figure. "Don't grovel. The infusion is just one part of becoming. It's time for you to take the initiation ritual and investiture. Remember what I said. Once you commence down this path, there is no returning to your shell of a life. Your spirit becomes interwoven with the group energy. The more we number, the hungrier we are as a group. We are more powerful, but we must eat more often to maintain the firmament. If you don't hunt and supply, you don't get the benefits of membership."

Herbert nodded miserably. He didn't enjoy being inferior in this power dynamic. And what could she mean by hunt? He'd only consented initially to biweekly life-extension serum transfusions at a general practitioner's office. LaVey had been the nurse on duty. Afterward, she had met him in the parking lot of the medical buildings and explained to him that because he was in the upper echelons of city management, the Blind Eye had selected him for a special version of the serum instead of just vitamins. Herbert had been startled when she unfolded her wings and changed into nonhuman before his eyes.

Amazed and convinced, he spat out, "Please hurry, b——. I have boils on my buttocks, and the tinnitus from withdrawal is driving me crazy."

LaVey reached into the leather satchel she was carrying. She handed Herbert a richly decorated carafe.

"Take this receptacle. We have an orientation and an initiation scheduled for tonight. Have you got your entry offering? The party starts at 8:00 p.m. It's 4:00 p.m. now. The orientation and infusion will come before the party. Of course, if you have boils on your ass, there won't be any pre-infusion action, if you know what I mean." The woman, if that's what she still was, snorted.

Herbert no longer thought of LaVey as a woman. Technically, she had been born a woman, but following augmentation, she was now devoid of any of the usual feminine characteristics. Her hair, Herbert knew to be all transplants. (He had tugged on it one night coupling in his office.) A mistake as afterward, she became less like the meek nurse he had met and preferred and more dominant and authoritative. But how she had gripped him when he was inside her. It had been almost worth it, and he had cried out to the Guardians as he climaxed. She had not offered herself again; and Herbert, though miffed at being ignored in this respect, had not sought another sexual encounter from her. LaVey's hair was a sleek brown cap with a few orange streaks as an attempt at a more natural look when she circulated among the everyday residents of the city. She was often mistaken for a creative and would get asked for her autograph, and LaVey would oblige; changing her signature every time. Sometimes she scribbled in the name of famous creatives she resembled. Others mistook her for a lady of the night, and the men would make amorous approaches. Some would regret this and wake up in nearby alleyways with punctures on their toes and the balls and soles of the feet rubbed raw and left bleeding. LaVey's chest was equally smooth as her back and her shoulders bulky.

I wonder what happened to her breasts, thought Herbert.

"I had to lose them when I got my wings," said LaVey amused.

"How did you—?" asked Herbert querulously.

"Read you?" said LaVey. "Just assume I can perform all the same functions as the Blind Eye, including erasure and compulsion. I did after all start off as a humanoid extension of the Blind Eye."

Herbert shrugged reached into the cavity of the bookcase, where previously he had placed his hand, and grabbed the blood-stained pad of linen and the bowl of blood from its innards. The silent winged augment moved another photo of a bird this time a vulture and pressed a button and directly behind it came a grinding sound informing Herbert that the next stage of proceedings were about to commence.

A panel in the bookshelf to the left moved sideways, exposing a stainless-steel metal door. Momentarily,it moved sideways, exposing its function as an elevator, and the proctor and LaVey stepped into the open cavity. Herbert was breathing laboriously.

"The investiture is on level B5, but we'll go to B11 first and triage you. You obviously need to have an infusion prior to investiture. You really are suffering, old man," said LaVey, her ivory wings barely managing to fit in the elevator as she kept them unfurled.

"Oh, please!" entreated Herbert, new lines forming around his mouth.

The elevator went sideways, then down. It sped up and then stopped, coming to a halt, and the door opened. It tilted forward, expelling its occupants onto a concrete slab in a white hall with a large open room at one end. A white-coated physician greeted them as they regained their balance on the concrete slab. It was the very doctor Proctor Herbert had seen on his first visit to an infusion clinic, except his hair was longer, tied up in a ponytail. Not effeminately, decided the proctor, more to display the picture of glowing health. Presumably he too was the recipient of infusion treatment.

"Please sit. Sit." The doctor gestured to a chaise lounge in the large area he had deftly started walking them toward.

The pair set on the chaise lounge, LaVey idly inspecting her nails. The walls of the room were adorned with shelves containing jars what appeared to be embalmed small animals and parts of dead animals.

A young man in green scrubs and a white medical overcoat walked up to them with an IV tower and a trundler of medical devices.

"I'm Wesley," he said. He also looked the picture of health and had his hair tied back in a ponytail. "Here, sniff this. It's a mild sedative in a salt." He passed Herbert an old-fashioned handkerchief knotted at the top.

Herbert took a sniff of the smelling salt and felt slightly less lightheaded. The handkerchief had bees on it and a honeycomb pattern, he noticed.

Herbert relaxed. The aide bustled around Herbert, taking his vitals and making comments, sotto voce, into a mouthpiece. He was being instructed remotely, presumed Herbert, as he acknowledged and responded to what sounded like instructions in response to his comments. Unfortunately, the sedative started to wear off, and Herbert became more aware of his surroundings.

Herbert's heart pounded. He perspired and the skin on his back crawled. LaVey appeared to be enjoying his discomfort. Herbert stared around the room for relief, but the masonic jars lining the walls with the grizzly contents of pickled and named animal body parts gave him no reassurance.

"Here you go," the doctor glided up to Herbert, affecting an upbeat tone in his voice.

Herbert saw he carried a cage with a rabbit and side, also pushing a stand with a white box and bag of fluids and a tray of instruments and needles attached to it.

"Oh, thank the Guardians," said Herbert weakly.

"Left or right?" asked the aide of the doctor.

"Just give me the infusion, by the love of Erythros," grumbled Herbert under his breath.

And in one fluid movement, the doctor pushed a needle with plastic tubing attached into Herbert's neck. At the same time, the rabbit went limp as a red fluid flushed into the tubing that ran into the bag of fluid connecting both Herbert and the rabbit.

"No bubbles in the tubing," commented the doctor to the aide. He turned to Herbert. "You should start feeling better almost immediately. In about fifteen minutes, you will feel much better, and there is a small amount of synthetic adrenaline added to the saline in the IV in addition to the that from the animal, from the offering."

"You can join the main party in thirty minutes," interrupted LaVey. The voice glittery, and she was visibly excited. "Can I leave him here?" she questioned of the doctor. Her eyes widened, and her pupils shrank. "I have some business to take care of on B15," she purred. Without waiting for an answer from the doctor, who had nodded to the affirmative, she glided out of the room, and Herbert once again relaxed.

NICOLETTA'S FALCONS

Nicoletta stood in her closet. She donned some leather chaps and falcon-handling gloves and wondered for a moment where else her life might have led her if the eternal Guardians had not watered her with grace and trusted her with the care of all the souls of Destin, and perhaps even Asperia. She had been entrusted with care of the welfare of the souls of Destin after graduating from the Advanced School of Theology and Martial Arts, particularly those of her family.

First, Nicoletta needed to see what was happening at the apothecary. Taking three deep breaths, she turned, walked out of the closet, and exited to the rear of the kitchen to the falconry. A cacophony started up. All the birds knew when Nicoletta was approaching and showed their love for her with loud trills. They loved Nicoletta, and she loved them all back equally. People can be surprised to find that birds of prey have individual natures. Birds had relatively small brains, so you wouldn't think they have personalities. Nicoletta had cared for her falcons long enough to know which of them liked racing, which liked culling the field mice population, which liked delivering her personal missives of guidance, and which liked being companion birds to the other alone and suffering birds. Nicoletta clicked her fingers and called out three names.

"Come, Farrow."

"Come, Ice Breaker."

"Come, Trillow."

Three birds hopped forward and jumped on to her outstretched arm and moved up her arm to make room, beady eye looking to the sky, then turning to face Nicoletta. They drew their feathers in to themselves. Nicoletta walked to the launching zone and held her left hand over her brow, readying looking toward the apothecary and readying herself to instruct the falcons.

SERVED

The hair went up on Terry's neck. He was in the kitchen, grabbing a handful of nuts, and he sensed someone that was approaching the front door. Just as he sensed the visitor, the doorknocker fell, the heavy thud on the oak. A frown furrowed Terry's brow.

He placed the fistfuls of nuts in a glass bowl. Off guard and startled, he turned and opened the door, his level of bewilderment rising by the minute. A guardsman stood there with a sheaf of papers. He thrust them at Terry.

"You've been served," pronounced the guardsman.

"What the hell does that mean?" asked Terry alarmed.

"You're all being evicted," the guardsman said tersely. "All the people on the premises must leave by Friday, and all the animals will be rehomed by the town council to a council facility."

Terry drew himself up to himself to his full five feet six and stared at the guardsman's Adams apple.

"We'll see about that," he choked. "I am going to take this up with the Ventura's, the rightful license holders of this residence in perpetuity."

The guardsman ignored Terry. He took the sheaf of papers with one hand and held it to the door, swung back with his left hand with a short blunt metal object, pounding a seal and a nail onto the bundle of papers, driving the nail through and into the door and compressing the wax seal onto the papers.

Terry stared blindly at the guards back as the guy turned and walked to the metal visitor gates to the streets. He felt a tightness in his chest, and his breathing became shallow. Drawing on a measure of strength, despite his difficulty catching his breath, he yelled out, "Eva, Hannah, something terrible is about to happen."

Before any noise came from the rest of the house, the tightness in his chest intensified. His breathing became more labored, and a pain pierced through his temples. Strangely, he smelt the scent of cinnamon in the air, and as he tried to turn and move inside the house, his knees buckled.

"Oh, he, no," he groaned and slumped to the floor, clutching his temples and breathing shallowly.

Hearing a crash at the front door, Eva rushed to the entrance way to see Terry lying prone on the floor with his head at a forty-five-degree angle.

"Terry!" she shouted.

As she dropped to her knees, she put her ear over Terry's mouth to feel his breath, and she reached for his wrist with her other hand to feel for his pulse. It was faint, but it was there.

"Hannah!" yelled Eva.

Hannah appeared out of nowhere. She gasped at the sight of Terry's prone body and straight away took up a position beside Eva. She felt Terry's forehead for a temperature, then gently palpitated his abdomen. She bounced back on her heels, perturbed.

"What on Panacea could have caused poor Terry to collapse? He was so well and out of the blue—"

"I can't imagine, but right now let's concern ourselves with stabilizing him," said Eva, cutting her sentence short.

Hannah looked around and noticed the bundle of papers sealed and nailed to the open door.

She read, "Notice of termination of lease."

A whisper of smoke trailed its way up the door.

Instinctively, Hannah backed off. "I smell cinnamon," she mused.

Eva looked away, pausing momentarily from monitoring Terry's vitals.

"That seal looks skeezy," she said. "Suspicious. Even if it's official, it may have been tampered with. I wouldn't risk touching it right now." She got up and shut the door. "Help me with Terry."

Disturbed and bemused, the two women lifted Terry by the knees and shoulders, Hannah propping one knee on each of her hips. His breathing had resumed a more normal pace. Eva lifted his shoulders; Hannah, his legs. They moved him down the hallway and laid him on his bed. Foxy skeetered to the door, jumped up on the bed, and lay down at Terry's feet. Raising his head, he looked at the two girls mournfully.

"I wonder…," said Eva thoughtfully, and "I am thinking…," said Hannah at the same time. "Poison," they both said at the same time.

They left the room to walk down to the infirmary. Eva grabbed a manual from the bookshelf and started leafing through it.

"I recall," said Hannah, "making a spice dish called dhansak, and it advised avoiding a certain strain of cinnamon as it was neurotoxic in larger quantities and can do a number on the liver. I smelled cinnamon outside."

A broken keening came from the rear of the infirmary. The girls looked around and saw through the glass wall-to-wall window three falcons swooping down out of the sky and then flying directly toward the apothecary. The "kikkikkik" noise came from the first of the three birds of prey.

Eva sighed thoughtfully while flipping through the section on poisons in the *Everything Medical* manual.

"Those look like Nicoletta's falcons, three of them anyway. I recognize Trillow."

The three falcons passed over the skylight and the roof of the apothecary, and the girls continued looking for answers as to Terry's sudden life-threatening illness.

Hannah was the first to speak. "I believe I have found the answer," she said. "The smell of cinnamon corresponds with an easily obtained poison that could have been pressed into the seal that was used to attach the council documents to the door. When heated even by the warmth of body temperature or warm metal, it disperses into the air."

Eva looked at her, alarmed.

"We have enemies!" Hannah cried out. "There is nothing in the history of our family as caretakers of the apothecary that indicates our family has had dealings with adversaries before. So we know the council is intent on acquiring our premises despite the Ventura family line holding it in perpetuity. There is no precedent for acquisition of any humanitarian practice, scrolling through the written history of the last one hundred years. This is unprecedented. Something is deeply wrong." Hannah held her hands upturned to the ceiling and touched her thumbs to her forefingers. A tear traced its way down her left cheek.

Eva reached out and cupped Hannah's upturned hand.

"It's very unnerving," she said. "We have an enemy. But we can't assume the entire council is directly out to target us and harm us directly, although their approach and intent has changed over the decade. It's baffling. It's sickening. We don't yet know all the facts. What is going on inside the council, and who stands for what? That brazen Carlotta certainly seems to have more influence than she should. She appeared to have an incredible sway over the mayor."

Hannah scowled. Eva plucked another book from the shelf and ruminated how Carlotta had gained more influence than even than the entire body of elected councilors. She must have gained the mayor's ear, although historically he was never known for giving credence to anyone else's views. He was a grumpy old sod by anyone's measure. He was inclined to take the moral high ground, but people knew where they stood with him, thought Eva, as she brushed her fair hair from her brow deep in thought. The mayor's position was always defensible, and he was pragmatic and had the best interests of Destin at heart. Everyone knew that even if not everyone agreed with him. Eva would have said he was totally incorruptible but for the change in pace of development in the town and the sinister way the council was taking over people's property and livelihoods!

"Hannah!" said Eva.

Hannah was lost in thought and didn't respond. Eva clicked her fingers to get Hannah's attention. Then she purled a thread of thought into ascension to get May to help her bring Hannah back to the present.

Two of them in la-la land, thought Eva. *Why am I always the one who has to take charge?*

Hannah stared in amazement, then chuckled as a miniature May danced down the crease of the book, then made to tap Hannah's nose. Hannah received an unpleasant static shock on her nose.

"Ow!" she cried and looked up at Eva, who stared back seriously, then winked and continued speaking to the room and Hannah, who was poking at the miniature dancing May.

"The guardsman was just the messenger, enforcing council policies. But if he relished being the bearer of bad news, the changes coming from the mayor's office are having an unneighborly effect on the town culture! Who or what caused the council to turn against their townspeople?" Eva asked herself quietly. "For decades, centuries even, small business owners and professionals such as herself went about their days freely, offering some services and advice, helping others and carving out a niche and celebrating the victories. Precious life fought for and won. Holidays celebrated with communities and family. We never made a profit. Never taken out a loan. We've always fed and clothed ourselves and donated any surplus. We feed others if we have visitors but saw off the profiteers. And then as we grow older, people take care of us in turn. They give us care. We give them secrets, knowledge, and insights of the healing arts. And they get handed on to our sons and daughters. The cycle repeat—rebirth, regrowth, ascension, regeneration. This is wrong, aberrant, the happenings threatening the apothecary! We must fight back! I can't imagine disbanding the healing profession that feeds the Source!" Here Eva finished. There was no use talking it over any further.

An animated Hannah clapped her hands.

"I've got it," she said. "The council seal was contaminated by a poison harvested from a specific variety of cinnamon plant. It's advised not to consume this variety in large quantities because it's a known carcinogen. It's also found in rat poison though nobody poisons rats these days, now they can be led away by music. And who knows? Maybe something else was added to irritate the lungs and slow Terry's breathing. The substance must have been added to the seal wax with a chemical that turned it from inert at room temperature to a gas when heated and the sun activated it. And then Terry must have breathed it in." Her words were tumbling out all in a rush.

"Well, that explains it!" said Eva. "Well done! Let's go check on Terry."

The two girls walked back to Terry's bedroom. Terry was sitting up in bed, idly cleaning his ears with a used cotton bud and his fingers.

Blinking his eyes miserably, he offered, "The last thing I remember was the guardsman nailing something to our front door."

Hannah cut in, "You were poisoned. It looks like some people really don't want us to be living here anymore and got all bent out of shape about it."

Terry clapped his hand upside of his chin. "Oh my goodness, guardians," he said. "What about all the animals? Who will take care of them and heal them?"

NICOLETTA WAITS FOR TAN

The sun was high in the sky when the three returning falcons circled once again above Nicoletta. She chucked each of them on the beak and let them nuzzle up to her to show her their love. As she returned them to the cage exhausted but content, she gave them each a seedless apple core.

"Good work, my lovely girls," she said to the falcons.

They were all female as female falcons were the toughest of the sexes and had the greatest endurance for the task she had set for that day.

The visions she had received from the falcon's foray had disturbed Nicoletta. She had seen that there was trouble at the apothecary. Hannah and Eva had looked perturbed, and it seemed one of the healers was sick as she reviewed Terry lying slumped on the floor in her mind for details she might have missed. Then she ruminated over the increased construction and outsize growth in the numbers of the armed forces around. It was all unprecedented.

A near vision of Tan on a bike hurrying her way came to mind. Nicoletta felt he would be there in fifteen minutes. She knew they were both of the same mind. The safety of the children was paramount.

"Grown children." She caught herself with a rueful smile. She couldn't fight their battles for her stepchildren when they already dealt with life and death every day at the apothecary. There was limited time to prepare Eva, Hannah, and Terry; but if he thought there was going to be trouble at the apothecary, the first task to hand was to get the three off to a safe place. Perhaps it wouldn't be so bad. Perhaps it could be couched as a much-needed vacation. It would be better in the interim than having a confrontation with the council if the council was that hostile to healers. Perhaps the three could put forward the case for continued ownership of the apothecary in a neighboring city instead of keeping themselves in harm's way.

Nicoletta was not happy, but by the time Tan bustled in to see her, she was absentmindedly removing her falcon handling gloves. She was resolute.

"Tan, they must leave today!"

Tan's eyes widened at the urgency in Nicoletta's voice.

"Nothing good can come. Nothing good can come of delaying their departure. When they sent a guardsman to deliver the eviction document, they sent a warning. They poisoned Terry". "Who knows what the council might do, if they come to take over the apothecary. "Say they stay here overnight…" And she trailed off, and despite her conviction that the indomitable healers must leave before disaster befell the crew, she had not put much thought on the situation might play out.

Tan picked up her train of thought.

"They could go by sea or horseback to Stigiformes and head to the mountains from there," said Tan. "At least, in the mountains, they could conduct research with the Fellows Bran. Rekindle the relationship between the Fellows Bran and the humanitarian professions of the towns of Destin and the town of Trove. Open up the lines of communication."

"Maybe the other towns are suffering a similar phenomenon of council overzealousness?" Nicoletta mused on this. "No, I haven't heard any word from other apothecarists or any of my guild healers with regards to overstringent zoning rules or evictions out of hand. But who knows what could be happening to other towns and vulnerable populations. The children will need transport. Horses, they can go on horseback. I'll prepare five of my most reliable mounts."

She left for the stables to begin preparations and had them riding out when the healers arrived.

It hadn't taken much to convince the apothecarists to spend the night at Nicoletta's and agree to depart Destin temporarily. None of them wanted a repeat of what happened to Terry. Or worse. The following day they'd had a good breakfast and saddled up five of Nicoletta's finest steeds. All of them were enjoying the sensation of riding out. All of them, that is, except for Eliza. "Why do I feel like I'm missing things that other people get naturally?" asked Eliza of herself. Right now, she was falling behind her companions.

Eva, Alex, and Terry all rode three abreast, and Eliza had fallen behind, plodding on Zillow.

"I'm so f—— hopeless," she said to herself, but with no audience, it made her feel worse, not better; and she fell a couple more strides behind. Rain drizzled inside her mole-skin coat. Really, she couldn't have felt more miserable. Zillow started whining as if to try and soothe her fitful companion.

Eliza tapped the neck of Zillow. "I'm sorry, old girl," she said. "I'm a brand-new rider and not very good company either, but it's just me and you boy." Slowly, Eliza's spirits started to lift.

The fivesome stopped in a clearing. Zillow almost stopped too quickly, causing the mare behind to stumble and a surprised Terry to slide off!

Terry shook himself and fished out half a bar of chocolate in his pocket and sat on the ground good-naturedly, but Eliza burst into tears.

She said, "I feel like I'm holding you up!"

Eva said, "Chill out, Eliza, you'd never been on a horse until three days ago. You, my dear, you need to give yourself a break—or life will break you."

Eliza knew that Eva was talking sense, but that gnawing import of dread in the part of her stomach was such an ever-present companion that she couldn't close it off entirely.

"If you say so," she said.

The fivesome finished up the meals picked for them carefully by Nicoletta: beef jerky, crispy apples, cherry pie, and a hot mug of pea and ham soup. The group mounted their steeds and pointed south toward Stigiformes. Mountains started to rise on the right.

Eliza, now riding alongside Alex, asked, "What are those mountains?"

Alex replied, "They are gathering grounds for rare spices. The Stigiformis Before the breaching, they were mined for metals. The leachate from the process of mining left an awful stain on the lands around. So much so the mountains crumbled and fell away somewhat, it is thought. And then the breaching happened. Goats and all sorts of exotic animals made it their home, eventually carrying organic material that led to reforestation.

"Now five hundred years later, and as you see, it's lush and green. And the Fellows Bran are tasked with caring for all strains of plants on the surrounding slopes. The mountains are Asperia's seed repository. A natural feature of the landscape now holds all the plants that have ever lived. The history books say we used to have silos of seeds in case anything happened, and it did in the Breaching. Imagine that instead of all these hills with everything growing and reseeding year after year, just a warehouse of seeds, a seed bank, and a plant genome library in case something happened."

"What is a bank? A seed bank?" asked Eliza.

"That's right. I forget that you come from that vastly different culture. You seem so normal," said Alex. He stopped when he realized he had hurt Eliza's feelings.

Eliza tugged one brown curl absentmindedly. "I must say I've had a sick feeling every day since I came out of Diaspora, but it is not unlike the sickness when I left. Oh, Alex, the history books at the apothecary, they called it culture shock!"

Eliza smiled and Alex noticed how she lit up when she did. She was quite a pretty girl under that mess of hair she hid under.

"What a funny concept," she said. "Is that because the culture is so different here from where I lived and grew up. But coming here everything *is* so different. That is so funny." She almost giggled, and then she grew serious. "I was born into the bound city life," she said. "But I never fit in. As long as I can remember from as long as I can remember, I was miserable.

"It's the strangest thing. I grew up in a c-cul...ture. That's a new word, 'culture.' For me, it was just the way it was. I grew up in a family in a city with no walls but no real concept of outside the City. We knew there were alternatives, but there was no such thing as travel. Occasionally, people left, and I became one of them. I hated city life so much; the blind eye of the city tracking your whereabouts and your thoughts. Anybody who knew this made fun of me. They said their health care was wonderful, and they couldn't fix the way I felt if I wouldn't make any effort. I didn't think like them. I like to learn new things, facts and information from books. I like to make things with my hands. It seemed that they never liked to make things new or work better. Everything was allocated, returned, and reused."

Alex said, "It sounds like you wouldn't have a lot of fun." He reached out and chucked her cheek reflexively. "Don't be too…don't be thinking about it too hard, your past. You're here now. I can't remember much of my childhood either."

Hackles raised on the neck of Alex's horse. It was only midafternoon. And they expected to travel for two more hours before looking for a place to stay for the evening. It was possible that they would meet trouble in the way of rogue wanderers down on their luck, bondsman and bounty hunters who were looking for an easy mark. But it wasn't likely. There were sparse pickings in this part of the land avoided by traders and any persons of note, and the small satchel each of the five carried didn't look as though it was attractive booty for thieves. It was more likely the company would have to seek shelter from the weather or have their time wasted by pods of dust devils. The five weren't overly well dressed for the weather by any stretch of the imagination. The oilskins Nicoletta had provided them with would give them some protection just in case the weather became inclement. The path narrowed ahead. The light started to turn golden, and the pattern of leaves dappled over the despondent company. More than one of them felt a little woeful at the events that had caused them to flee the apothecary, although Hannah was considering if she might have room enough in her satchel to store some sheaves of lavender that lined the path. So they were moving quietly and reflectively and were completely unprepared when a loud whooping and wailing, traveled toward them from the path in front of them.

Shortly following the unexpected outburst, they heard, "Oh, guardians!" exclaimed Hannah.

Alex got his disc ready for what trouble might befall them; and as they moved toward the noise, around the next corner of the path, unexpected crashed an imperious sight. A squad of tall black females dressed in hardly anything were approaching them hurriedly without any attempt to minimize any noise their approach made. Despite the warlike cries, the women wore no leggings, tunics, or mail. Nothing. And what they *were* dressed in was the barest makeshift armor leather coverings comprised of leather, kite feathers, and bone spikes. The women had also embellished themselves with a mix of resin and paint, making an imposing sight. Once again came the unnerving whooping from the approaching squad. The quintet divided; and Eva, Alex, and Hannah spread themselves across the path defensively. Terry dragged Eliza off to one side. The tallest of the warriors stopped as her forehead came level with Eva's, and they eyeballed each other, with Hannah and Alex lining up behind Eva. And likewise, all of the rest of the painted warriors lined up behind the woman who was head to head with Eva.

Finally, the black woman spoke.

"Spies and threats! Beware, girls!" she said.

Completely confused, Eva took a step back and spoke.

"Calm down, we weren't the ones hooting and hollering in and making a loud entrance on a group of strangers just quietly making their way through a forest."

The woman smirked. "We were just having fun, and lo, we find traffic is going busier on this path than we expected. We find that those who run, generally have something to hide. Those who go like you do, head to head are a little more trustable, and we're just making sure nothing threatens Momma Mountain, the mountain you just passed." The woman's voice got serious. "One of you is a genuine threat. One of you is new to your group."

Eliza shifted uneasily. Alex darted her a warning glance.

Terry stepped forward and spoke up.

"Ain't none of us a threat to anything, except a meal at the end of the day. Could you be clear on your words?"

The head woman stared Terry up and down, and Eliza got the feeling she was less than impressed with her evaluation, but she offered, "You can call me Sonia. I mean what I said, one of your party is the threat, and that one will have to come with us."

The weary but formidable quintet sprung into the air, arranged their backs inward and formed into a circle.

"We're taking her," repeated the embellished female warrior.

Eva was not intimidated. She snapped her fingers, not taking her eyes from her opponent. Unnoticed, Terry fell back a couple of steps. The women dismissed him, eyes sliding off him one by one. The warriors were clearly only interested in the women, and Alex as worthy opponents. Terry was not worthy of their attention for more than a fleeting glance.

Eva considered her options to keep her party safe.

"Can we discuss this further over a meal," she requested, drawing on all her composure not to knock the opposing woman on her smug visage.

"No talk can change matters," came a quick reply. "Your member threatens our civilization if she is not instructed by our kind. Our time will pass, and we cannot allow that to happen! We've fought for too many ages, too many centuries and lost too many women to allow that outcome to happen."

Eva barked in the woman's face," How do you know the threat is female. How do you know it's one of us, and what's the threat?"

"No more talk!" said Sonia.

The "Amazon," the word coming to Eliza from the recesses of her mind.

Eva launched out of the way, and the others closed around her and moved into defensive mode. Eva landed off to the side, and Terry finished what he was doing to the other side of the path. Fighting started up. Knees and elbows and fists started flying.

That is, thought Eva. Hannah's and Alex's fists and elbows were flying—and landing blows.

Eliza seemed to have frozen in a state of shock, a mere few paces from the frazzled action.

"Terry, what was Terry doing?"

And then it became obvious as a putrid smell of sulfur, eggs, and fish enveloped the fray. Eyes started watering, and a couple of coughs disturbed the ear as a breeze sprung up.

Tendrils of smoke drifted into the fray.

"Oof," said Sonia, immediately looking furious at having let even a murmur slip. She redoubled her efforts to land blows on Alex. Alex himself was coughing as he fought off attacks from various directions.

Terry had dropped to the ground, stretched himself out and propped himself up on one arm. He was blowing toward the action, his eyebrows full of dirt. The path turned into dust, obscuring the fighters, and all of a sudden the fight was taking place in a dust bowl.

Eva dove into a roll and going through the fray, landed beside Eliza on the other side of the path. She elbowed her pack off and fished out some handkerchiefs. Knotting them together, she said to Eliza, "Pass your fellows a bandanna and join the fray," and although Eva's party was outnumbered, they appeared to be winning against the tall Amazonian woman, and Hannah and Alex then redoubled their efforts with vigor.

Eliza was sneaking a peak here and there from behind her fingers as she dropped the makeshift mask over her face. She had more than a sneaking suspicion that she was the person the Amazon woman were talking about. How was she a danger? Other than the occasional schoolyard scuffle, she had never had any formal combat training. And it wasn't that she didn't want to fight. Guardians! She wanted to walk in and clap their opponent's heads. She felt like a complete idiot standing back, but what if she made their chances worse if she got into the fighting? She was just a new addition to their fellowship, and it was also new to her, Eliza to have friends. And with that thought came relief as her thinking changed. She, Eliza Cruikshank, a nobody of Diaspora, an exile, was one of them. Then came that insidious self-doubt again. Okay, she needed to help her friends, but what if she looked stupid fighting?

For whatever reason, she couldn't get companionship from anyone in school, but her new friends offered it freely. But what if she looked stupid coming to their defense?

Some dust was blowing into her eyes as tears flowed out.

Think, she heard a voice inside her head, maybe more than one voice. They said, *It's done.*

"What's done?" she said to herself, while the fight went on in front of her. Momentarily, she was transfixed by the fighting action and distracted by the voices talking to her. Her noisy subconscious, she presumed.

It doesn't matter what you look like, as you are fighting, came to her finally. *It's that you're actually fighting. Go! Join them in the dust bowl!*

Suddenly, her body was buzzing with energy radiating up and down her body starting from her midriff and going down to her toes and back up to her head. Her shoulder blades were giving off sparks, Eliza felt, and her head buzzed with heat. If she didn't find a way to cool her head, she would explode. The energy coursed from her head to her toes. Reaching her hands to the sky, she stumbled toward the dusty melee, and without warning, "Clap!" then "Boom," came a sound from the heavens.

Sonia and Eva were knocked off their feet to the ground, with Eva landing with one foot in Sonia's mouth, then Eva yanked her foot back to her person and rolled to the side, out of the path of Sonia's quizzical, hostile glance. Just seconds later, lightning speared down from the sky and pierced the ground where Eva had landed. The lightning had missed everybody; but one of the forks had stabbed a tree trunk, causing it to smolder, noticed Eva, and a startled skunk scampered away. Terry made as if to go after it.

Someone breathed, "Stop it! Stop, stop it!"

Were they talking to her? wondered Eliza. *Was she responsible for the lightning?* Eliza couldn't tell. She was fizzing. She could feel the energy filling up inside her. *Like water,* she thought, and as she shook her hands out into the wind, she felt her legs buckle a little and was totally unprepared when a blow came to the side of her head and someone threw a sack or something material over her head. Suddenly, she could no longer see. Eliza felt herself scooped up, her feet gone from under her. She could hear noises, a commotion, sense the energy turning; and she knew what she was. It was what she had feared. She was hostage, not to the bound cities but to an unknown third party, these ferocious semiclad women. And who knew, they might well barter her back to Diaspora, especially when they discovered she was nothing. The misdirected lightning discharge had unfortunately worked against Eliza's companions, knocking Alex, Eva, and Hannah off their feet. As they scrambled to their knees, the remaining foursome saw Sonia dance around as one of the other woman drew a symbol in the air. A mist rose up and temporarily blocked Eva's vision. When it cleared, she saw Terry frantically trying to draw wind to assist the mist to disperse. From the direction of the mountain ranges, she saw five horses that weren't theirs canter into the assorted grouping of women.

That's it, they've beaten us and taken Eliza, Eva thought dully, anticipating the women's intent.

As a gentle rain started to fall, the party could only watch, with ears ringing and blood oozing from the blows landed in the fighting, as the barbarian woman propped their stolen companion behind another of the warrior women on a sturdy gelding. The other four horses each took a woman, who mounted effortlessly on their steeds, and then forming a unit around Eliza's horse, the group moved off down the path. Hannah sank back to her knees.

"Guardians! What the hell just happened?" she prayed up to the sky.

Eva was equally bewildered. "All I know is we were winning, and then something knocked us off our feet."

"It was lightning," said Terry.

Alex was pacing and thinking how fond he had grown fond of Eliza in the short time he had known her.

"Tracking," he said. "We can track her".

The shock of the unexpected loss reducing him to curt, abrupt sentences.

"The sooner we start tracking her, the better our chances are of finding her." Alex cupped his temples in his hands, suffering at the thought of not seeing her again.

"So how...?" Hannah said.

"So how do we know which way they have taken Eliza? They have horses, but that doesn't mean anything," said Terry. "If the horses get tired, they could change them out at a stable or town forge. Oh, I wish we had Nicoletta and Tan here to advise us. Let's go into ascension."

Hannah chucked her tongue. "Tsk, tsk. It's not safe," she said. "It was always possible at the apothecary because it was imbued and protected. Here we're out in the open, and there's nothing to stop us untethering from our bodies."

Terry started whistling.

Alex cleared his throat. "Terry," he snapped.

Terry and his whistle got more strident. He whistled a popular folk tune, and the two girls and Alex walked away.

"He's having one of his moments," said Eva.

"The timing couldn't be better," fretted Alex, letting off steam.

Spotting a patch of angle berries and mint, Hannah went to collect a snack for them. They were all low on blood sugar, and they may as well eat while they were waiting for ideas.

"Eechup, eechup," came the sound of a response to Terry's incessant whistles.

Hannah looked back to see a heavy-set falcon chirruping and circling above Terry's head. The falcon circled once more and landed on Terry's shoulder, nuzzling against Terry's temple. Terry bent his arm, and the falcon hopped around on to Terry's oilskin-clad shoulder to rest. The falcon nuzzled its head against Terry's head as Hannah watched and realized it was one of Nicoletta's falcons. She watched as a two-way exchange of information took place. The falcon nuzzled and blinked. Terry stood still. The whole entire exchange took a long five minutes. The falcon blinked once more, and then as Terry stretched out his hand, the falcon launched into the sky. A shuddery sigh came from Terry, not enough that Hannah could hear it over the distance, but she saw him shake. And gathering together the edges of her moleskin jacket, she walked slowly back, giving Terry enough time to amalgamate the visions and the information passed on by the falcon.

Terry looked jazzed, thought Hannah.

Terry looked dazedly at Hannah grunted and said, "Nicoletta's instructions were quite clear. She knows that Eliza is no longer with us, and we're not to follow her. We're to water the horses at Hampshire and carry on to the city of Trove. We are to carry on to the city far north of the mountains, and she'll let us know when it's safe to return."

Hannah said, puzzled, "They can't be thinking straight. Where goes one of us, all follow. Well, yes, you would assume the natural healer laws apply" said Terry. But later, she saw that disaster would happen if we went after Eliza. "This is too much," cried Hannah. "Eva!" she called, and Eva appeared by her side.

She'd been listening but waited to interject until Terry had collected himself, gathering his thoughts. "Okay, well, our horses need to be stabled. We're going to need somewhere to stay and a plan."

Alex said, "We have to make this decision over Nicoletta, and we have to make it on the basis of whether we think harm will come to Eliza."

Physical, mental, or emotional harm, Hannah thought. "You're right, Alex. On one hand, we run the risk of interfering with the Source if we go against what Nicoletta says. On the other hand, this is a whole new scenario. Screw this, Terry. I say we take the horses, we call the birds, and we go look for Eliza. We could find her by morning. That lightning was bad luck, but we could take those women if we go fast and surprise them."

Eva hadn't spoken until now. She was the most authoritative when it came to strategy and how it affected the cure and protection of the apothecary. It passed through her mind that they weren't even at the apothecary, but still, they were a gang, and at the end of the day, she was responsible for all their well-being—the Ventura line; Terry; and poor, beleaguered kidnapped Eliza.

"It's unfortunate," said Eva finally. "But I don't see any alternative but to carry on to the Hamphire stables. We can lodge our horses. Talk to somebody in the humanitarian professions who has an ear to the underground. Get in contact with Nicoletta and Tan. Maybe we could enlist one of the night watch.

"Trove has a night watch or retired guardsman. A hired hand could be a good thing at the stage of the game. And Eliza just got carried off by a group of big-breasted unclothed savages," said Alex exasperatedly.

Terry said, "Well, they were hardly unclothed."

Alex said, "You know what I mean. There wasn't much left to the imagination, and I just fought like they fought, like their skin was made of leather, and the softest thing about them was their teeth." He stopped.

Eva said quickly, "I thought about this. I don't think we can assume at the stage that they mean her any physical harm. While we were fighting, they didn't land one blow on Eliza."

"They kept landing blows on us," said Terry.

"Blows that hurt," Alex said hastily. "You ain't got no blows landed on you, mister, because you were nowhere near the fighting!"

Terry said, "I'm flabbergasted at your insinuations, Alex. I was assisting us in the more arcane arts of combat. And I did get an injury."

"What?" snapped back Alex. "Someone stepped on your toes while you were going, 'I'll huff and huff till you blow the house down'?"

"My toes are bleeding." Terry glowered back at Alex. "And I lost a nail off my big toe."

Hannah intervened, "Enough, boys, stop your scrapping. We were outnumbered. It was looking bad for us until Terry's kinetic wind put the odds back on our side. They fought around Eliza, and the lightning charge seemed to come at her instruction somehow. That's what knocked us out of the fight. Now let's move on. Where to from here?"

Eva tugged a curl absent-mindedly and stuck her thumb into her top of her oilskins. She began thinking.

"It's a complication on our journey. One we didn't need," she said. "We could veer off and track the women, their settlement, and find Eliza. But given that Nicoletta sent the peregrines out to warn us specifically, we will not go after Eliza. We have to put it in the unsolvable for now basket. Four hours and we'll be on the outskirts of the town of Hampshire, and we can water the horses."

Alex was miserable as hell. Silently, he pledged to go along with Eva's plan, but if there was no firm decision on tracking Eliza or no knowledge about where and who could have taken her, he was going to set out on his own and come hell or high water bring her back. It was one tenet he was and would live by if he was chief guardsman: no one left behind.

And so the diminished gang mounted the horses and trekked on toward the town of Hampshire.

"Walla walla walla walla. Oh, poos," came a husky female voice.

Eliza canvassed the situation dejectedly. She had against all odds fallen asleep after being thrown over the back of a horse and presumably tied on somehow. Though she was unable to feel where exactly she was bound to her mount, edging sideways to feel for the give in the ropes, she gauged that she was for all intents and purposes glued to the back of the horse—and a guest to the inside of a potato sack, by the musty smell of the canvas.

Close to her head a hand slapped the neck of the horse.

"Almost there, old girl," came the husky voice, directing her speech not at Eliza, but at the horse itself.

Eliza maintained her stoic resolve to endure and said nothing.

A song started up spontaneously as the travelling warrior pack started to sing tunelessly but boisterously.

Ugh, thought Eliza as the women sang a disharmonious song.

It went like this.

"Fifty-one pairs of male ears on the wall. Fifty-one pairs of male ears. Fifty-one pairs of male ears on the wall. Staple them up! Take one down, pass it around. Fifty-one pairs of male ears on the wall. Fifty-one pairs of male ears on the wall. Fifty pairs of mail ears. Take a pair down, pass it around, forty-nine pairs of male ears on the wall."

Eliza raised her eyebrows in the darkness.

"These women were not fans of male company then—that was clear. What was the historical term for this type of behavior? That's right, *feminism*," Eliza recalled.

The horses went a little faster, and Eliza bumped and rocked on the back of hers. The women hollering tunelessly finally got down to "Twenty pairs of ears on the wall" and despite her predicament, Eliza relaxed a little more. She'd calmed down once she realized she had sustained no physical harm.

Evidently, she was with an all-female war party. They may not have her best interests at heart, but they probably weren't going to swap out one of their own to a bounty hunter to return her to Diaspora. It was awkward to be removed from the fledgling party she had just started to get to know, but she was used to awkward, and she was used to being alone. It didn't take long before the emotions of awkwardness crossed with anxiety changed to become a mild excitement around having a new adventure. And that ever-present relief she was no longer in a bound city was there. And so, she bumped along on the back of the steadfast horse as content as could be in the circumstances, vaguely hoping the apothecarists weren't too worried about her.

—꘡—

Eliza dozed and then realized that that the level of light was waning and that it was nearing dark. The noises the war party made while traveling changed from the more expansive sound of hooves on grass while cantering through the wide open plains with only a few dotted trees. The horses diverted around these, causing Eliza's head to lol from side to side, and then came sounds of hooves striking firm ground in unison, that indicated narrow paths and more vegetation to each side. The air got more rarefied; and as Eliza heard the sound of a river in the distance, the horses slowed, bunched together, and finally stopped traveling.

Someone squeezed Eliza's toe firmly.

"Ow!" she said.

"Well, our booty is alive and well enough to squeal," said the individual responsible for pinching Eliza's toe.

Somebody else tugged at the sack but moved in front of her head, preventing Eliza from seeing what was happening, and then all of a sudden, Eliza was spilled off her mount onto the ground in front of the horses. Eliza looked up to stare at the woman in front of her.

"Well, well," said Sonia. "You traveled well. You're not a puker. That's a good sign."

"Where are you taking me?" said Eliza, emboldened but nervous now she was all on her own. "And where are my friends?"

"They will be deciding right about now," said Sonia, "whether to come after you. I would imagine they have top-notch tracking skills or to follow whatever your plans were before we abducted you."

Eliza couldn't believe how brazen the woman was about their intentions, but then she also couldn't believe that she was a no longer in a bound city. Anywhere, even having been taken hostage, had to be better than that. Having seen how the women comported themselves, nay glorified themselves in battle, she ceased her line of questioning before she wound up her abductors. Sometimes discretion was the better part of valor.

Sonia filled the gap in conversation by asking the question for Eliza.

"Where are we going? Oh, in about twenty minutes, a barge will come around the corner. And you, us, and the horses are going to get on the barge. And we're going to Themystrichyr, okay?" Sonia looked expectantly at Eliza, obviously waiting for the girl to respond.

"Where are we going?" asked Eliza woefully.

"Themystrichyr," the barbarian woman replied. "Or Mystrichyr for short." "The Myst Islands"

The Myst Islands. Eliza looked around, but she couldn't see a body of water, much less a barge to accommodate the pack of barbarian woman and the horses. It was grassland as far as her eyes could see.

"Soon you will see," said Sonia. "We'll build a fire first."

Overhearing Sonia, several of the woman started bustling around pulling out kindling wood from their packs.

They were in a little clearing with some trees between them and the path, and presumably, they were far enough away from the woods they had just passed through to start a fire without incident.

Eliza started chewing her nails. One of the younger women plopped herself down beside Eliza.

She looked friendly enough, thought Eliza, seeing she had smile lines under her eyes and a thick braid of auburn hair swinging behind her.

"You're amazing," the older girl said to Eliza as she sat to rest beside her.

Eliza looked at the girl and said, "Hello!" She continued bluntly, a little fed up from being lugged to the current location like a sack of potatoes, "You all told me I was a threat. How do I go from being hunted down, seemingly as I am a threat, to being yoked to a horse and taken hostage, to adulation? Pray, tell me." Having come forth with what was on her mind, Eliza limply finished with, "Well, here we are." She was out of breath and not able to make head or tails of this next turn of events that had befallen her.

The girl said. "Well, you're amazing. All that energy you unleashed from the skies. I wish I had half your energy, and *boom*, I'll tell you what! If we could harness your energy, there'd be no battle in the world that we couldn't win."

Eliza wondered which of them was the crazy person in this conversation and then concluded that just because one of them was crazy didn't mean the other one wasn't as well. Briefly, she pined for the waters of her native bound city that were dosed up with vitamins; nutrients, antidepressants and anything that anyone needed to remain calm and level and keep the populace under control.

The girl reached forward and hugged Eliza.

"I know it's crazy making," she said. "Wait till you hear! Just wait to hear where we are going and what's in store for you."

Sonia came over.

"Despoina," she said, "don't fill the new girl's head up with rubbish." Sonia said to Eliza. "Come, dear. Come sit by the fire. Have yourself some venison kebabs. We're going to travel to the islands overnight, and it's going to be cold. You'll need the energy."

Despoina pulled Eliza to her feet.

"There's a problem," said Eliza snarkily, regaining her composure. "We're in the middle of nowhere, and by nowhere, I mean I no see no boat or river."

"Tsk, tsk,"said Sonia. "Do come and eat up."

The smells from the fire were so alluring that Eliza found herself happily complying. She helped herself to kebabs of meat and spoonful's of yoghurt dressing from flat wood pottles that were being passed around.

The meal took about thirty minutes and included lots of backslapping and lip-smacking, with some of the more boisterous women telling rude jokes and breaking wind. They were all braggarts, as far as Eliza could tell. Occasionally, she tried to get a word in edgewise, and someone would always start up right at the very moment she tried to talk. And then when Sonia spoke, all their heads swung to look at her.

"Okay," interjected Sonia when all the kebabs had been devoured and crows had appeared overhead waiting for their chance to have at any uneaten morsels. "It's time to board."

Eliza thought at this stage she must be hallucinating as everybody stood to their feet and looked in the same direction of grassland— moving as one. Eliza followed along, standing behind the nearest woman as everybody formed a line led by a big-breasted woman in a brown dress with red-and-gold braids. Eliza looked beyond the row of freshly brushed horses and gasped. Shimmering above the fields of grass bordered by the walls of brush was a large moving object: a flat-bottomed barge.

"The grass is an illusion," said Despoina, noticing Eliza's look of shock. "It's actually shallow water."

"But we just walked over it," said Eliza disbelievingly.

"Yeah, well, if you walked over it now, you'd get your feet wet," said Despoina. "And if you do dip your toes in the water, Skeeters will bite your toes off." She giggled, and then she elbowed Eliza as again Eliza looked concerned. "I'm just joking. That's what Mom's tell their children to get them to go to sleep, 'Skeeters will get you.' She looks a little sad at this. We don't have very many children in the Myst. It's woman only on the island. And now most of the women are past childbearing age. It's mostly old woman on the island."

The barge drew closer to the all-female war party, and then it put out a plank from the stern, and then another starboard. A figure came to the bow to greet the women.

"All aboard," they said. "All aboard for Mystrichyr, the Myst Iles, where woman reign supreme."

"Rains bless us, with female offspring," the women replied.

Eliza was tugged up to the front, pulled onto the barge, and then suddenly, the boat was moving. The captain—or whoever, whatever they were—pushed off an invisible bank with a massive barge pole, and although it appeared that the boat as moving along fields of grain, the audible lapping sound informed Eliza they were waterborne. She turned toward the prow, seeing a cliff to the right, hazy skies beyond. And now they were travelling along an obvious body of water, a river that widened as it rushed toward the cliff.

AFTER THE SEA JOURNEY

"You saved me!" said the pantaloon-clad barbarian atop the pyre. "You saved me! And now, macramé," the barbarian said despairingly.

Sonia found this hysterically funny. Tears rolled down her cheeks as she bent forward in fits of laughter. Two dark-brown-skinned girls of approximately ten years ran up with lit kindling and touched it to the stack of wood. Eliza watched nervously. She didn't like the barbarians particularly, but neither did she want to see an impromptu barbarian barbecue.

The woman on the stake chuckled. As the flames licked the pile of wood, she slipped free of the chains. One moment she was affixed to the central pole; the next, freed. She skipped up to Eliza and stretched out her hand.

"How do you do?" she said. "Pleased to make your acquaintance." Black hair stuck out around her head like a halo. Strikingly, two gold teeth twinkled as Eliza discerned her predicament as being the following: She had somehow wandered into a gag, a production, an elaborate scheme designed to embarrass her. Her throat felt hot, and tears welled in her eyes.

"Why are you doing this to me?" Eliza asked falteringly.

Spikey Halo blinked slowly as she took the full measure of Eliza, running a calculating glance over her.

"Oh, boo-hoo, sucker," she said finally, staring directly into Eliza's eyes and holding her gaze for a minute. Then she turned and walked away.

Something ruptured inside of Eliza. She missed her new and only friends from the apothecary. She hadn't known them for long, but they had a promise of something to give, ahead of her relationship with her birth family: kinship, true family. And now this disheveled barbarian was accusing her of cowardice? A charge crackled along Eliza's calves. The energy traveled up her thighs. She reached within and, with a throw of her hand, an almighty thunderclap was released, and she shook the ground.

"You will not call me afraid!" Eliza roared at the top of her lungs. "Turn around! Turn around and face me!" Spittle ejected itself from the corner of Eliza's mouth. She was so furious she thought her eyes might launch from their sockets.

Even though two of the women had fallen to the ground following the thunderclap, the haloed savage kept walking. She called back, "I can't hear anything, little kitten." She taunted, "Run home to your littermates."

A now-familiar sensation traveled Eliza's body. Buzzing energy rushed up and down her body starting from her head running to her toes. Eliza reached her hands skyward.

"Clap," then "Boom" came sounds from the heavens. Seconds later, lightning speared down from the sky and struck the pyre. The pyre flamed alight. Torched alight, it reached for the sky wholly ablaze, and flames danced and tripped energetically in front of the astonished women.

Energy drained from Eliza's skyward-reaching fingers, but as though sourcing from an inexhaustible supply, the tingle in her fingers told her she had more of the strange power.

She concentrated on the walking figure in front of her, and her resentment grew, and she mentally snapped her fingers. "Crackle" came a noise, and oh, Eliza got tweaked on the temple by a stray electrical charge. She grabbed her calves and dropped to her knees and rolled.

"And the princess," the words came to Eliza swiveled on her heels, commencing to walk back to her side, and just as Eliza moved, she smirked. "Well, well, the kitten has some fighting spirit. You must be wondering if you have lost your mind."

"I did wonder if you were making fun of me," admitted Eliza cautiously.

The woman reached out a hand. "Here let me help you out and let me get some cream for that burn."

Sure enough, Eliza's head was tender to the touch. She shuddered as the other women assessed the burn with a deft touch.

"I know you tried to lightning-strike me." The woman laughed.

Eliza blinked sheepishly. "I didn't mean to," Eliza ventured.

Acknowledging this with a nod and then a shake of her head, the woman put her hands on her hips. "Allow me to introduce myself. I'm Kat the Skull Crusher. Kat, short for Katalanta." She shook her head again. "You wouldn't hurt me because we're not enemies, dummy."

This last mild insult was so out of place that Eliza again felt crazy.

"Take notice that's your first lesson from all of this wing stretching," said Kat. "If you try and discharge friendly fire, it'll come back and hit you, if you are not careful." She let out a hoarse laugh. "Hopefully, that will be a lesson that you'll only make once or twice for yourself! But anyway, what do you think your name is?"

"What do I think my name is? Eliza! My name is Eliza Cruikshank."

The woman looked quizzical. She said to Eliza, "We've been looking for you for generations. Your name's not Eliza and most definitely not Cruikshank. But anyway, I'm getting ahead of myself. Are you hungry?"

Eliza blinked and looked down at her feet. "No," she said.

"And what about the lightning?" asked Kat. "Is the fire still ablaze in you? It'll burn out."

Eliza doubted it was fully ablaze, and sparks were jumping toward the forest from the pyre. Seeing as things were way out of her control and had been for a few weeks now, she demurred to the slightly older woman. All of a sudden, a wave of emotion rushed over Eliza, and she burst into tears.

"Oh, hey now, there's no need for that. Big girls don't cry. Big cats don't cry," said Kat gruffly. She squeezed Eliza's shoulder. "Just through the forest there, we've got a hut for you to rest up in, honey, and there'll be plenty of time." She let out a peel of laughter. "You may not feel like that's the case. But for now, you need to rest and get your strength back. And there's no rush. We'll talk again. There's plenty of time. There's always plenty of time. They said I was dangerous to civilization too and wanted to cage and control me. But out here, I live free. You'll see. And you will learn to control your gifts," she said to Eliza, who collapsed against Kat's shoulder gratefully.

"Kahretsin," cussed Despoina, "what curses bought rain to dance on our celebrations."

A light rain started falling, and the last of the sparks danced their merry dance on the pyre and they smoldered off into oblivion.

THE GREAT TALENT QUEST

Brynn choked back a peel of laughter. The three stable hands stood in front of her in oversize skirts and cotton blouses. That the garb was oversized added to the comedy of the scene presented to her. Brynn clapped her hands to her ears and said to the stable hands, "If Ravenna sees you, one, she'll cut your rations; two, she'll give you cause to regret this; but three, this is the funniest thing I've seen all week."

The tallest and skinniest of the trio stepped forward.

"Hi, I'm Colonia," said Curt. "And I'm sick of riding out with horses. I want to be an actor." This he said in his highest pitched voice.

"Oh, you're practicing for the talent quest," said Brynn rhetorically.

"What do you think?" said the middle chap.

"What does a dress like this do for me on any other given day? Troy here talked me into the talent quest. Apparently, there's a purse of five hundred gold coins to be given to the winners of the talent quest. You know it's not real good gold. It's not pure gold, but we should be able to melt it down in the foundry, you see," said the last one, scratching his head.

"Have you got an actual dance or a skit?" asked Brynn.

The tall guy said, "We're acting out the legend of Harry and Hermione. I'm Hermione and fat Tucker here is Harry, and well, we're not too clear on the actual legend, so Colonia is playing an owl, and Hermione and I catch him attacking the town with skeeters (leeches with legs) who drink blood. We have magical powers, and we fight Charis the Owl with these magical powers, and we're almost overcome by the Skeeters, who suck our blood." Tucker was relishing the words "suck our blood."

"But we prevail, and we kick his ass, and then because we're so funny and mighty, we win the competition. And we win the five hundred gold, and then after we melt the gold down and sell it, I can get my own horse."

"Sounds like a plan," said Brynn. "You do realize that Ravenna will be watching the talent quest, and she might notice you are wearing her clothes."

"She's got so many clothes," said Colonia, "surely, she won't recognize a few nondescript skirts."

Brynn said, "It's pretty funny."

"Two more nights, and then we're going to win," said Tucker lasciviously.

"Two more nights," echoed Brynn.

She had plans of her own. She had quite enough of the lifestyle here and King Ridich's stables. While the talent quest was underway, she was planning to steal a horse and head toward freedom and the land bridge to the west. Brynn had a taste for adventure so bad she could taste it. All she needed was a rough set of the few knives that she put away, and she'd head off when the time was right to see the sights and wonders to the west. Tales had been told in the stables about people who could draw pictures in the air that looked real, of objects that became real; modes of transport that were not just horses, that moved in the air without spitting out smoking fire and did not just fall to the ground like the Panacean post-breaching modes of transport; air cars that glided rather than jerkily spitting smoke and fire. Come what may, it was time for Brynn to leave, and one thing she knew, there were horses for the taking. Horses were everywhere. Horses and dogs and handlers she'd have to avoid.

I have the old-age thirst for adventure, Brynn mused. *I have never been on the sea.*

Amused as the three youths cavorted some more, Brynn made her plans to escape the stables.

NICOLETTA AND TAN

"It's a bad day," said Tan.

"It's a bad day, true," said Nicoletta. "And we've still got a job to do."

"Oh, look at all this," said Tan. "There're at least one hundred animals that we can't re-home in time. We only have forty-eight hours. The sick ones can't be left with anyone else. This is just cruel to them. What happened at the council? Maybe there's new blood on the council. Oh, Syd!"

A lizard had bitten into Tan's thumb, drawing blood.

"Oh my, now the animals are losing it."

"Tan, you sound like a teenager," said Nicoletta. She reached out and pushed a lock of black hair back behind his ear. "You're in shock. I am in shock. Our kids are gone, Guardians knows where."

"Yes, I'm well aware of the facts. I'm not seeing where Eliza is. It's like she just dropped off the radar."

A movement out of the corner of Nicoletta's eye caught her attention. Black figures walked past the big window the full-length window.

Tan frowned. "What the heck have we got here?" he said.

Nicoletta said, "Two guesses."

"Goons from the council," said Tan.

"You got it in one," said Nicoletta.

Tan took a defensive pose as the black figures moved toward the doorway and in the room.

"You've got to leave now," came a dispassionate voice from the lead figure. "Your property has been acquired in the interests of the council and the wider interests of the town of Destin as per the notice served PW 25301."

Nicoletta drew herself up and said indignantly, "Is that right? We don't know for sure. We have to find homes for all the animals."

Tan moved over to the goon. "And besides," he said, "you have some up dog on your shoulder."

The goon stared at him blankly.

"Whussup, dog?" said Tan.

Glancing his upturned hand off the Goon's bemused shoulder, the goon realized what he was doing and pulled back his hand just as Tan was about to high-five him. The goon looked at the gang behind him.

"I don't think these people realize we're from the Department of Interior Security, and this is not a laughing matter." His voice turned glassy, and his lips pulled back slightly. He made a gesture and clicked his fingers behind him.

Three men stepped forward, and Nicoletta turned from what she was doing, depositing a brown lizard into a carry case, to see the lead goon slap Tan across the face.

"Coesus! What the hell are you doing?" cried a stunned Tan.

The goons proceeded to stomp past him and show Nicoletta and Tan exactly what they were doing.

As cages came down from walls, doors were unlatched, and little creatures were tipped out, it became obvious that the men were intent on causing merry harm and had no concern for the well-being of any of the animals. Nicoletta felt her heart start to ache. She stood in front of a cage housing a dachshund with a bandage on its poor stop.

She said to the man advancing to her, "I swear to Coesus I can get that dog out and put you in there unless you stand away."

The man gave her a black look and spat out, "Maybe you are the dog."

Nicoletta had had enough. Confused animals were pulling at her and backing into a corner, looking for a way out. The ignorant twit she was facing narrowly missed standing on Blackie, the cat. Nicoletta had truly had enough.

She unsleeved the knife she had on her on her person at all time from her cowl, and executing a series of defense movements, Nicoletta jumped like a cat and landed in front of one of the goons with a knife at his throat with one hand and another knife, which appeared from nowhere in her other hand, at another man's waist.

The third man gasped.

"Just move," she said. "Just move."

The fourth man found himself with Tan's arm squeezing around his neck around the region of his Adam's apple. The four men were suddenly neutralized, and it happened so quickly there was no time for blustering, no time for more threats. Nicoletta felt no sense of relief at having neutralized the men as the animals were all now thronging in the infirmary looking for a way outside.

"I think we understand each other," Nicoletta said to her captives.

With a knife to the abdomen of the man to the rear and the tip of the knife to the shoulder of the man in front of her, she pushed them together in the direction of the third man. They made a crestfallen party of four, together with Tan's captive.

"I know who sent you," said Nicoletta. "You go back and tell your boss Carlotta to shove it where the sun don't shine and come back Monday." She pushed the men in the direction of the door.

The men left. In a rush to be the one to open the door handle, the men jostled, then fell outside.

"Well then, that just made it all a lot harder," said Tan.

"Let's think outside the square, we need help," said Nicoletta. "Open the front doors. Open the gates and see if anybody's passing. We can ask them for help to take any of the animals. By now somebody's got to know that something's up at the council."

Tan nodded soberly, and they set about making makeshift leashes to tether the startled animals.

STUBBY THE POSTMAN

The gates swung open and hit Stubby, the postman.

"Hey, I was here!" said a startled Stubby as Tan with a pony with a dappled stomach charged past him. "Tan, what the hell. All the animals are outside."

"We're being evicted," said Tan tersely.

"Where's Eva?" asked Stubby.

Nicoletta replied to Stubby, "She and Hannah and Terry left, with a young lady called Eliza rescued from a bound city. Things got bizarre in the last few weeks. The council took measures to evict us. We just got called upon by four dummkopfs who sacked the infirmary. They let out all the overnighters. All the animals are running wild. Just as well we didn't have any exotics. The last time we had a baby tiger and it got out, we just about had our license suspended."

MAVEN

Maven stood beneath the trees. In the vast forest that stretched in every direction she observed trees: spruce and birch and cherry and oak. Trumpet trees comingled with tulip trees and beech trees shielded maples from the full glare of the midday sun.

It was her favorite place, her only place she could hear their communication with her feet, the subtle electrical pulses massaging her toes, the impulses registering in her brain, and the branches caressing her hair. She squeezed her toes in appreciation and felt in her pockets for her divining rods.

It's dry for this time of year. It's dry this year, Maven thought. She thought she heard an affirmative response to her observation. *Why?* she thought rhetorically. *Has there been so little rainfall, yet the sky is perpetually cloudy and has been so for the past three reawakenings?*

She sent out a tendril of thought query to interlock with the tree's growth pattern where it kept its memories. She read that the individual tree had seen many reawakenings and hadn't experienced pain. Neither had its family trees, but there was disquiet within the forest. Things were not okay. The mycelium (the upside down underground forest wasn't happy either), the big communicator of the forest, the mushroom undergrowth, searched Maven for reassurance. She searched.

I love you, she thought back.

A younger Bran came to rest beside her. "Boo! I bought your tea," he said.

"Well, thank you, River. And thank you for scaring me." She smiled. "I wasn't expecting you to drop in just like that."

"You were lost in thought. You were far away," said River.

"I was inside this big fella's interfamilial memory," said Maven, gesturing to the nearest trumpet tree. "She's not happy," and Maven shivered. "There's something just not quite right."

"There's always something affecting the trees with the seasons," said River.

"You're young, sweet River. You don't have the memory that we older Bran's have. With or without tree perpetuation and symbiosis, our trees have even longer memories. It may seem like there's always something, but that's seasonal microclimate variations or a bug infestation. That's day-to-day life. The variations that the seasons bring. The recent changes the trees speak of is perturbing."

"Meidhbhín," River asked, using her formal name, "have you eaten today?"

"No, I'm trying to get as much information as I can from the trees," said Maven. But she dutifully sipped on the flask of tea and nibbled a buttermilk crumpet smeared with plumberry jam. She finished her tea and nodded appreciation to River. Her body buzzed with the need to move. Her fingers curled around the branches of the acacia tree, and she suddenly sprung into the air. A large horse fly buzzed past her ear, and she swatted it absentmindedly.

"Can you pass me my tools?" she asked River.

"Here," said River, passing to her, her divining tools.

"Am I bleeding?" she asked. "The horse fly got me on my tail."

"The most blood rich part of your body," said River. "No, but see, there's more flies around than usual."

Maven was swinging gently back and forth on the lower limb of the tree.

"Yes," she concurred. "You're right. More horseflies mean more horses. More horses mean more bounty hunters. More travelers from the land bridge between the Steppes in the western reaches and Asperia."

As Maven and River hovered above the ground, over a large branch above them, a throng of spider monkeys gathered; and a smaller member of the throng threw a peanut at River. It bounced off his head, and Maven asked, sending pictures, "Where is the spider king?"

An image of the spider monkey king stretched out on a hammock of acacia tree branches with a baby and a group of female spider monkeys surrounding him came to Maven, and she tsked in disapproval. The occasional peanut thrown at the pair was becoming a hail of nuts, so she jumped from the acacia tree to a baobab tree and took refuge behind its thicker trunk. She caught her breathe and concentrated. In her mind's eye the spider king sat up and took hold of a hookah pipe.

Oh, Maven thought, *the spider king is young, and everybody loved him, but he definitely was prey to the more sybaritic influences in the low mountain territories. I'm digging deep today.*

Maven searched for any negative influence that might be threatening the forest communities. Where the combination of the Turtle Mountain volcanic plateaus met the rivers there were great growing conditions for all intoxicating species of plants that humans, halflings, and some members of the Fellows Bran like to indulge in.

Not all of them, thought Meidhbhín. She preferred her mind clear, not cloudy.

River looked after her with uncertainty.

"How should we travel back to Hearthstone, River?" said Maven in a reassuring voice. "Treeborne?"

"Yes!" replied River enthusiastically.

The trees nearby also moved perceptibly, low boughs reaching closer to the pair.

Maven smiled. "Hold on," she said.

River curled his tail, sprung, and landed on Maven's wiry, strong shoulders.

"Use your toe for balancing, River, and curl your tail around mine," shouted Maven.

"I'm on it!" shouted River.

Maven reached out and grabbed a branch, and spotting the next branch, she launched, and off she sailed, foot to branch and arm to reach the next branch and stretching a foot to the next branch and the next branch, and just out of reach, the spider monkeys chatted excitedly, and Maven and River had collected quite a following by the time she had gone half a mile through the forest. The peanuts had stopped sailing toward the pair as they flew through the trees. Now it had become a race between the larger more agile Fellows Bran and the smaller skittish spider monkeys, and it was neck and neck between them by the time they reached Hearthstone on the canopy floor.

"Wheee!" called River, enjoying the race, knowing he was perfectly safe balancing on Maven's back.

The canopy became thinner at the forest center.

"Look! There's Hearthstone!" called River over Maven's shoulder.

"Have you got your flint?" Maven asked River as they drew closer.

"Absolutely."

"I'm coming over your shoulder." Maven launched River, who did a somersault in the air and struck his flint on the Hearthstone. A blue flame leapt from the Hearthstone, and a rock rolled sideways, exposing a door in a nearby baobab tree trunk.

Maven hugged River. "You're going to make a great Fellow one day. You're so agile!"

They knocked at the door and, without waiting for an answer, turned the indented knob and entered the baobab trunk interior, to find dinner set out for them by Maven's parents.

IF TREES COULD TALK

Bridget rustled, vexed. The large acacia tree off gassed a message to another Guardian, Greta. Following their communications, the mother trees sent alerts through large mycorrhizal networks to the whole forest.

"Generations ago, my mother spoke to your mother who had it passed down from her mother that there would be a time come to pass when chaos transmogrified the landscapes, and our people shall be wrenched from the ground. Our friends who rely on us for shade, for food, and for sustenance; their very existence will be imperiled. Yet though some of them betray us, we must protect them to the last so that we may once again rise from the land through their actions. The landscape will change in coming years. The very factors that make us impregnable and invulnerable. Our strong dense hearts and fast rate of growth will count against us when the forest becomes dry and fire draws near. At the mention of the dreaded element fire, the whole forest shuddered. Guardians grant us eternal life. We must change to meet these threats in the coming days. Our allies, the monkey folk, are our friends. They are not fighters. Our values we must hold to. To fight means betrayal of the peace. It means choices. It means weapons. We must not let the monkey folk know of the pending war. They must remain pure of heart because they are the future. We are Hardwood. We are Heartwood. We are their shelter. They are the future. Better Hardwood than Deadwood." Bridget chuckled. "Lastly, we shall have the ability to fight, and we will have many weapons." Bridget chuckled. Her breast, her central branches, rustled; and she finished with good humor. "Afterall, there were many ways a man could die, and only one way a tree could fall. And even then, trees could stay alive

135

indefinitely. There lay mighty roots hosting new communities. We have the advantage of surprise." She rustled. "And all the poisons known to mankind or monkeykind."

This was quite a long speech for the swarthy acacia tree, calling on the mycorrhizal network for phosphorus, magnesium, and other nutrients, she reflected:

"Let the monkey men stay innocent for a little longer. The war will consume many, and for God's sake, on a related note. Since the new spider king took the throne, the spider monkey population is getting out of hand. I have a graft for a pheromone fruit that will take on their favorite fruit trees. They will love that, and it will lengthen their cycle by two weeks."

Greta signaled she had understood all the subject material, and the Old Guardians cast long shadows as the earth turned, and hyenas laughed at life in the distance.

HERBERT

"It hurts. Should it have?" The line into Herbert's carotid artery didn't feel as benign as usual. He looked down and could see a thin red line indicating infection spiking away from the incision point.

LaVey clamped her hand on his shoulder. "No pain, no gain. It's time you showed me where you live, Herbert. We shall go there after your infusion."

"I can't take you there," replied Herbert anxiously. "My mother is there."

"Why not? She is lovely, your mother," said LaVey as though she knew her intimately.

"My mother is awake most of the time," said Herbert.

"That shouldn't matter," said LaVey. She smiled a thin, bone-chilling smile that sent shivers running up and down Herbert's spine. "How old did you say she was? Isn't she eighty something."

"She's sixty-five!" said Herbert, daring to be cross with LaVey for once.

"Whatever," LaVey dismissed Herbert with a sweep of her hand. "Let's just hope she needs a rest while we are there, so we can poke around properly. I'd like to have a look at your house. We've known each other for some time now. It's time we got familiar with each other's dwellings." Her voice lowered into a snarl, and her incisors penetrated out of her mouth as she suddenly appeared to grow taller; and pushing Herbert to the floor with one hand, she removed the infusion tubing from his neck with the other, disrobing and snarling to get Herbert's attention.

Herbert beheld the beast that now stood shaved and naked beside him with a measure of alarm.

Suddenly, she leaned down and slapped him across the chin.

"Wake up, Herbert! Where's the downside here? I just want to pay a social visit and see where you come from!"

Herbert whimpered.

"You know where you're going, Herbert? You're going up in the world. You're meeting more and more influential people. You're getting younger every day from the infusions. Stick with me, kid! The sky's the limit!" LaVey snorted.

Finding herself hilarious, she reached down and patted Herbert's crotch, which was now a hard lump. Climbing off Herbert, she adjusted her wings and put on her pants, a smoking jacket, and leather boots while Herbert regarded her cautiously.

—⧖—

Leaving the office, Herbert asked the adjutant to hold calls and appointments.

A female adjutant today, a little older than usual, he thought with displeasure. *The younger and better looking they are, the better for my image. Besides, it's a two-way street. They get ahead of the other grads, and I've softened them up for the exchanges come drafting time. I lost my looks a long time ago. Not that I'm bad-looking, but youth certainly is wasted on the young. It's a pity that my hairline isn't quite as defined as it was when I was twenty-five, thirty, fifty-five. But the thickness is coming back, thanks to regular infusions. It's better than eating steak for dinner. It's amazing how raw infusions invigorate and bring back your libido.* He smiled. *I wonder if that young thing in the office will stay behind and eat with me tomorrow? Oh, where is she going?*

Herbert watched LaVey pick up the pace along the sidewalk and turn up a pathway.

"Harrumph! Oh, LaVey!" Herbert rushed to catch up with LaVey before he she got to the front door, but he was too late. Resignedly, he entered through the front door that the Beast held open.

"Hello, Mom," he said without much color, his voice trembling.

"Oh, hello, dear, who is your friend with the big shoulders."

LaVey bared her teeth in a semblance of a smile. "I work with Herbert, Gladys. He really is a great boss and a wonderful human."

Herbert tittered and then felt like a complete dork. All at once he wished he was back in the safety of his office with the attractive slightly older-than-desirable but model assistant outside his office, ready and waiting to do his bidding. He wondered how LaVey knew his mom's name.

"Oh, Mom, it's so good to see you," he lied.

Gladys adjusted the faded red gingham tablecloth.

"I'm tired, son. Perhaps I'll sit on the couch in the drawing room. You're both welcome to stay. I'm sure I'll just nap for a short while."

LaVey looked absolutely delighted. "We'd love to stay," she said enthusiastically. "Herbert was telling me how much he was looking forward to seeing you. Such a shame we hadn't met! You have a nap we'll be right here making plans for dinner." She smiled and chuckled.

Soon gentle snores from the drawing room punctuated the air. LaVey looked absolutely transported with glee.

Herbert regarded her. "You're up to something," he said, and for the first time, he spoke with confidence.

"If you love yourself, you can do anything." LaVey smiled.

Herbert felt a little wary. "What do you mean?" he asked. He peered at her over his bifocals and flicked a piece of fluff from his linen pants.

"Have you got a small bowl?" asked LaVey.

"Yes!" Herbert grabbed one from the cupboard and handed it to the she-beast.

LaVey bent and rocked on her heels and regarded the sleeping woman. Herbert barely had time to wonder what was going to happen next when LaVey dropped to her knees, covered her mouth over the woman's ear, and bit right through!

"Hey!" said Herbert.

LaVey ignored him, drawing back from Gladys, blood dripping from her mouth.

"Oh, she's not going to wake up. Now it's your turn," said LaVey said gleefully.

"I'm not going to do that!" Herbert said outraged. "That's disgusting, and we need to leave right now!"

"Oh, I thought you were, wel…Oh, you're not going to? I thought you were one of us. I thought you were able to graduate up in rank. She's not going to wake up. If you can't do this, you can't be one of us," LaVey said in grave tones to the shocked proctor.

Herbert pushed back. "This is low-rent stupid bullying, and I haven't even met anyone else. I haven't even met anyone, just some medical staff and you, and you are the weirdest creature I had the misfortune to come across, to ever meet. Why am I here?"

LaVey's tone grew conciliatory. "You're right, it's about time you met the others. But there's a point to this activity. Your mom's not waking up. Did you wonder why? Did you stop to think, why not even a murmur?"

LaVey added, "Right now she should be choking in pain, yelling at you like she always did when you were a little boy, blaming you for the world's ills and even calling the police, but she's perfectly comfortable."

LaVey held the bowl under the woman's ear; smiling all the while and the blood the blood pooled and dropped, dripped, and pooled.

"Well," said Herbert, now more intrigued than disgusted. "You have me there." Herbert was bemused. "I am wondering why she is not reacting. Probably she's taken a pill. Maybe had some wine. She always was partial to a lunchtime glass. Who knows?"

"You're such a dumbass for someone with such potential," LaVey doled out with a smirk. "I like you, Herbert, so I'll spell it out for you. People like you and I have latent abilities. I haven't actually caused your mom any pain. I found her seat of consciousness as soon as we came in the door, and doing that allowed me to prevent the motor neuronal transmission of pain to her central nervous system. What I'm doing is practically painless, practically." She threw her head back and guffawed.

Herbert motioned for her to shut up.

"She'll have a dream before she wakes and wake to think she's scratched her ear in her sleep."

"Now it's your turn, you schmuck. Your turn to practice." With a loud "Pfft," LaVey flipped the sleeping woman onto her other side.

Herbert was, to say the least, flabbergasted. His vision filled with a haze.

"That's part of it," said LaVey, somehow knowing what he was thinking. "You're seeing what she is dreaming."

"Oh fuck," said Herbert. "Even if I was to accept what you said, that you can 'hold' someone else's consciousness, it's my mom, dude." Shocked, he found himself back-chatting for the second time since he'd met the feathered half woman/half creature. He recalled when he met her as his vision settled.

He had been checking out one of the few places you could mingle with other adults outside of work, mingling between officials and laypeople, or carrots, was not really condoned; but officials turned a blind eye to anyone from the Correctional and Research Department because they could say they were there under the guise of research.

"If you were in the Correctional and Research Department, you got away with a lot," Herbert said to himself.

He'd found himself in a recruitment kitchen after hours and had turned his badge to Blind Eye mode and found himself with a mix of fellow proctors and strange half human, oddly augmented specimens that he'd never encountered before.

He'd expected more carrots, unspecialized workers without rank, but if any drifted in, they left immediately with another guest more senior. LaVey had approached him with a meal of protein and rice, and his pride wouldn't allow him to ask questions or react though he noticed her wings straight away. He just snapped his fingers to order a drink and fielded the questions that LaVey had presented him with. When he finished eating, they bypassed the dancefloor and went upstairs and had sex. God knows he wasn't looking for sex. He preferred work to physical release or the occasional vague, anonymous encounter usually initiated by the other person. LaVey had come on strong and entangled him with a sense that he was unique and offers to show him strange and wonderful phenomenon. This all flashed through his mind in an instant.

LaVey, sitting on the floor, was watching him with a smirk of her mouth, as though she knew exactly what he was thinking, her hands on his mom's ankles.

"We haven't got all day, dearie," she said. "Well, actually we have. Ready when you are."

Tilting his head, he wondered why he'd been of interest to LaVey. And now he was wondering what to do next. Comply with her directions? Flee and hope she lost interest in his mom? He couldn't do that. Gladys irritated him at times, with her anxious displays of affection, but her well-being was his responsibility.

He looked down at his mom, her head hanging sideways endearingly. He looked over at LaVey who looked back unconcerned. The two of them made an odd tableau. How was he to find the seat of consciousness. His vision was too fuzzy! He looked through the haze at his mom, and then he saw it. A purple marble shape; and past that, through her head, he saw the couch.

"Just look," said LaVey. "You don't have to do anything else at this stage."

Herbert looked and fixed on the purple marble.

"Now I'll guide you," said LaVey.

And then he felt so f—— hot. He felt LaVey's mind inside his. At first, he tried to move against her. Then he felt meat in his mouth and a warm trickle coursing down his chin. Gross! He came too and felt bloodlust unlike anything he'd ever felt before. Then the feeling faded as the meaty lobe slipped from his mouth. His mom winked back into existence in front of him. A red crescent scar marked the ear closest to him. Suddenly, he too was whole in his body again, the hazy overlay gone from his vision. A wave of anger rushed over him.

"You b——," he yelled at LaVey.

She was unperturbed and caught his swinging hand as he went to slap her. His mom snored on, her sleep undisturbed.

"You drew blood. You've got your revenge. Now you'll be unstoppable," said LaVey jauntily. "You're one of us now."

"I don't know what you mean. My revenge?" questioned Herbert.

"Are you happy with where you are in life?" LaVey queried quizzically. "You're a glorified pencil pusher who started as one of those poor creatures who sits outside your door waiting for you to dole out crumbs of appreciation. Everything is preordained. The city knows if you have an independent thought, do they not? And there is no real alternative."

"Well…," said Herbert, wondering. "Well, no, I wear my Blind Eye proudly."

"Then why were you so happy when I dampened your Blind Eye field the first time?" snickered LaVey. "Do you remember?"

Herbert said, "Of course, I remember."

He'd been glad to see LaVey again so soon after the initial encounter. Though it had perturbed him, she hadn't left his mind. He'd been careful to keep his thoughts around her nebulous, so the city wasn't aware of the singular attraction. She had requested a meeting in his offices. Herbert asked the adjutant to buzz her in. He was puzzled about why he felt pleasure and hoping that he wasn't broadcasting it. He explored the intensity of the feeling.

"And your name is…?" he said quickly to the augmented woman.

"My name is LaVey," she answered at leisure. "And if you're interested, we could go somewhere. Or we could couple here."

"I don't understand," Herbert had said.

LaVey reached across the desk and inverted his Blind Eye badge.

"Hey!" Herbert protested at the time.

LaVey spoke to him in a reassuring tone as though speaking to a child. "It's okay. This doesn't work for everybody, but I have a field dampener and turning your badge inside-out prevents every thought that you have going to the neural net of the city. You're now off the grid, off the city network. You won't even be missed. A ghost of yours is transmitting in your place."

She smiled, her incisors punctuating the information as Herbert struggled to make meaning of the information.

"Now, I'm going to take you with me for lunch, somewhere you can start to get used to the in-between places that my folk are able to relax away from the bound."

And they had gone for a most peculiar lunch in a sewer. A tunnel where whatever Herbert had imbibed had left him mildly intoxicated and suggestable. He had eaten a dish of what resembled glands in a broth and answered all LaVey's intrusive questions about his sexual history. He wasn't sure if he ever wanted to repeat the experience, or he couldn't wait to see her (it) again.

"And what was this?" asked Herbert, coming back to the present day.

LaVey answered brightly, "This was part one of your investiture. You've exceeded our expectations beyond our wildest dreams. We are excited to have you number among us."

"And who is we?" asked Herbert giddily.

He was really getting more comfortable with this creature. This, well, friend, he guessed she was, he hadn't met any of her other friends; but the culture in bound cities wasn't conducive to friendships. In the bowels of the city perhaps, where the night denizens traded with only minimum oversight.

Perhaps, thought Herbert, *he should just let the latest turn of events unfold and be guided by LaVey, because the alternative was fighting irrelevancy into deep, cushioned obscurity, like his mom here.*

He looked down at his mom's ears. That was bizarre. They were healing over. He could have sworn he had seen blood dripping from a fresh wound just moments ago, and he felt a momentary pang of guilt. This was a new emotion to him. Perhaps it was what caused him to feel so angry. He wasn't angry anymore. He was just curious how his mom's ears appeared to have healed up. Well, that took care of any awkward explanations. He breathed a sigh of relief.

LaVey looked at him curiously, and he thought he felt a warm bloom in his heart. She really was quite a curious creature with her maroon nails and the aforementioned lipstick and those wings. That had taken some getting used to, but by three or four visits in it hadn't shocked him nearly as so much, there had been a multitude of evolutionary lines of animals inhabiting Panacea before the breaching. Some were many millions of years old. Some brought to life by scientists. It was entirely possible some of the resurrected DNA had got mixed up with human DNA.

LaVey smiled and said, "Come on, silly, let's go meet your friends. Your mom will be just fine." And she chucked Herbert's sleeping mom under the chin, grabbed his arm, and shunted him out the front door.

HERDSMAN GRAHAM

Herdsman Graham stood in the cavernous ballroom. A makeshift stage had been thrown together. Hand planed mismatched wood lengths, laid over wooden crates glued together with wattle and daub. He thundered instructions for the talent quest, held to celebrate this year's reawakening.

"As a testament to man's eternal driving optimism and also as testament to our place and the universe as the greatest civilization that ever lived, we hold the celebration annually to commemorate the survival of the greatest disaster that ever befell mankind. We celebrate what we have today. What we learned, and we show our appreciation to King Ridich. We are eternally grateful for our king. A king for eternity—the first, the last, and the only King Ridich of Arcadia."

HAMPSHIRE

"Look at those mushrooms!" Hannah said.

The brightly colored fungi lay everywhere between the outlying houses of Hampshire and the spruce-covered mountains.

"Yes, look at them," said Alex grumpily.

Terry whistled. "It sure is a picture."

"So what do we do now, Terry?"

And the four intrepid exiles looked at each other. It was bizarre not having Nicoletta and Tan to lean on or their other parents out here in the open. Between the four of them, they had to come up with a plan, and they had to come up with a plan fast.

"Here's our current situation," said Eva. "Eliza got kidnapped by a band of warrior women who say they were looking for her. After Nicoletta conveyed what she knew, we assumed that she was physically and mentally unharmed. The bandits want her for a purpose not to hurt her. To have her in their ranks perhaps."

At this, Hannah jumped in. "Maybe she had latent abilities we weren't aware of," she said. "I hope she's safe. It could be dangerous if she fell into the wrong hands."

This last comment didn't improve Alex's mood any.

"For whom?" he muttered.

Eva continued, "Chatting to the townspeople might shed some light on the nature of the women who captured her. But our priority is finding out if there is anything we can do to get back into the apothecary."

The other three nodded pensively. Terry kicked the top off a mushroom in thought.

The horses snickered as the four moved around them adjusting the tack, and they remounted and pensively made a single file and trekked onward the town of Hampshire, remarkable only for its staging post that fed and watered the regions horses and their riders. Conveniently, it was next to the largest tavern in the region, the Bolton and Bury, which catered to families all during the day and into the early hours of the night.

The four weary exiles tied their horse to a water trough and, upon entering the tavern, took an orange lavishly decorated menu from the tavern's proprietor, Mellie and set about dickering over choosing starters and sides. Eva joggled the coins she had in her money pouch. They would have to be careful once they got to Trove, but they could afford to eat well tonight and take the leftovers for the remainder of the ride to Trove tomorrow.

TROVE

The four companions rose early. Before the sun lightened the sky above the mountain ranges and throwing off the hay and woolen blankets, they returned the much-appreciated supplies to the tavern. Mellie, the only other denizen of the town to be awake at this time, gave them all a kiss on one cheek and slapped the boys and Eva soundly on their backs.

"You get a free meal on the return journey, ladies" she said, belly jiggling, all humor and hospitality, even at this predawn hour. "And please repeat the impersonations of your council staff! Hilarious." She chuckled and returned inside with her lantern and the woolen blankets.

"Ladies," sniffed Terry, but he was smiling as much as the other three.

They untethered their steeds and rode off.

—ɱ—

Four hours passed without incident, just the trees of Hampshire receding behind them and brush and acacia trees rising to replace them.

Though there was a woods on the west of the city, noted Terry with satisfaction.

Entering the outskirts of the city of Trove, the riders trotted toward the center, where a large forge anchored the city as an informal assembly point and meeting house travelers' horses were shod and the blacksmithing needs of the city were satisfied.

"Oh, I don't know," said Basil, the forge's chief blacksmith after the travelers had arrived with their horses. "I generally keep to myself. Come to think of it. Recently, there was a traveler who came through.

A salesman from the desert bazaars who takes local wares through the region. He commented how some of the inns or businesses he used to frequent in Destin were just no longer there. Instead, they had been converted into soldier's barracks."

"Yes, that's exactly what happened to us," said Eva. "We were going about our day-to-day business at our apothecary as healers of animals, and then we were issued with a notice of compulsory acquisition of the premises by the council. And it's an imbued dwelling. Over generations a healing imbuement has infused the building. Carlotta, the town secretary, said it was to be acquired as a barracks. An army barracks! And there's been no militants, no uprising, no threats to for generations! It's all so sudden and pernicious and baffling!

"One day everything was normal, the next thing we know we got notice from the council that our premises were being acquired, and we barely had time to turn around and think. So we're here to try and find answers to see if there's anything similar happening in any of the surrounding towns and cities. Can you tell us where we might find these people who have traveled from the outer regions and the desert? Starting with your traveler?"

"That would be Jason, and he's not here at the moment. He got a lead on some dried mushrooms, some spices over in the desert."

"Let us know if anybody comes by," said Eva wearily. "We will go call on our council contacts tomorrow."

"Aye," said Basil, looking Eva squarely in the eye and passing a tempered spear from hand to hand. "Aye, I will."

Later that day, at sunset, Terry headed back to the forest. The mushrooms were even more colorful, red with white spots. They carpeted the ground underneath the forest. Terry was a little weary. Though he didn't show as much as his housemates, it was so depressing losing a home, their connection with parents, and then Eliza to the barbarians.

A small white mouse poked its head out of his breast pocket, and he patted it absentmindedly.

"Hey, Falcon," he said. "It's going to be all right."

The mouse squeaked and popped back down into Terry's pocket.

Having walked just a short distance from the town, he reached a great sprawling tree with roots that he could sit on, and sitting down, he pulled out his flint and a stick of Palo Santo. Laying the incense in the ceramic crucible he carried, he tipped the flint to the incense and lent back on the big tree and touched the smoke with his mind. Horses, falcons, lizards, and mice took shape in the smoke. He sent a lizard chasing after a mouse and heard a squeak from his breast pocket. He smiled. He got the falcon to pick up the mouse and landed them both on the horse's back. It was a wonderful way to relax, even if his pet mouse was the only witness.

He made a hot-air balloon and sent it up into the sky until it dissolved. He made a pair of pigeons fighting and then flew them down to land on the back of a tiger. Having impressed himself mightily, he put the tiger in a cage and flew the pigeons off into the sunset. Doing all that smoke conjuring had made him hungry. He had some fruit and nuts on him, and with the mushrooms all around, he had the makings of a rudimentary dinner. Picking some brightly colored mushrooms, he snacked away on apple slices, nuts, and the meaty mushrooms.

"Careful," came a voice from just above his right ear.

"I knew you were there, you know," Terry said nonchalantly. "I didn't have any extra fruit or nuts, and I would have felt rude had I invited you down without offering you any food. Plus, your tail! There is not enough room for your tail, so how's about I come up there." Terry laughed and went from lying down and leaning on his arm to executing a perfect somersault and landing on the branch beside River. "Whussup, Tree Dweller?" Terry laughed gregariously.

River warmed to this stranger immediately. "Well, you know? I'm trying to avoid parental oversight. Trying to hang with the movers and the shakers, the usual, and then I came across an interloper who can move from ground to tree without a tail, but I'm a little worried," he said with a slight frown.

Terry goosed his shoulder. "Kid, you're a bit young to worry."

River said, "You munching out on those mushrooms, and well, do you know what you ate?"

"Oh, you mean the fly agaric, otherwise known as amanita muscaria," said Terry proudly. "A very mild poison, but genetically, I'm a super metabolizer of ingested poisons. I'm immune to most poisons. I'm immune to anything that attacks the nervous system, i.e., animal venom. I produce antibodies to bacterial poisons. My liver will regrow if anything gets past these first lines of defense."

"Way cool," said River. "Way cool," he said again. "I've heard of poison immunity. It's called innate immunity, and it's not uncommon in the Fellows. But it's unusual for full humans to have a nice immunity unless you dose yourself over time and you're young." Then he frowned again. "But let me explain. There's something you're not understanding. These mushrooms are different."

"I know the difference," said Terry proudly. "But I'm immune to poison, and it was a yummy snack. I'm hungry, and I'm a vegetarian, and I'm a mushroom connoisseur." At this, he picked up a piece of straw from the ground. "There's always a straw to chew on," he said to himself. "No hay within miles and still this straw to chew on. La dee da, la dee da," he said idly, and out shot an arrow of flame as he blew out.

The piece of straw went on fire. He quickly dropped it as it burned his fingertips.

"I tried to…I tried to warn you!" said River. "And then you lit it! Didn't know that was going to happen, didya, ha! You should have seen your eyes." Then River mimicked Terry. "Furthermore, I don't get poisoned. I don't lose my liver," he mimicked. "But I almost lost my fingertips!"

Terry was dumbfounded. "This has never happened to me before whenever I've eaten mushrooms," he said. "Would you please stop laughing at my misfortunes and explain, please."

"Well, that's what I was trying to say. These mushrooms are suffused with a mineral called iridium." River was now dangling by his tail from the bottommost branch of the baobab tree. "They're iridium-suffused mushrooms. You know about the symbiotic relationship that mushrooms have with trees? I believe it's common knowledge in Asperia," said River conversationally.

"Oh yes, sir," said Terry. "The mycorrhizae network. Nutrients and knowledge and transferred between plants and large underground fungal networks."

"I believe we've got company," said River, hearing leaves crunching and turning to look.

"Oh, that's just Foxy," said Terry, and he clicked his fingers.

Foxy came running up and lay down beside Terry with his head in Terry's lap. Two brown fox eyes peered mournfully up at River.

"So anyway," said River. "The trees have been talking, and they believe there is a threat coming from another civilization further outside Asperia. They don't want us to worry. They want to protect us and keep us unaware of any danger. They think that we don't know that they are worried. But, well, kids are good at figuring stuff out. Part of the trees protecting us is altering the forest. Some might say for the better. In the outer rings of mushrooms under the spruce trees are a variant of mushrooms. When we eat these mushrooms, we find that a few of us individuals breathe fire. Not all of us do. There's no way of knowing who breathes fire and obviously it's not just isolated to us Fellows Bran!" River laughed. "You should have seen your face."

Terry said cautiously, "That sounds like a defense mechanism. Are the trees really expecting an attack?"

"It would seem so," said River, then he swung around the branch on his tail, dove into the air, turned a somersault. "Can't catch me you're a Christmas tree."

Terry looked down at Foxy. "Well, that's a turn up for the books. That sure will come in handy tonight for my pyromaniac tricks, Foxy."

Foxy licked Terry's nose, and they stood, Terry carefully picking a couple of the fire mushrooms so he could demonstrate what he had learned from River about the forest.

HERDSMAN GRAHAM

Herdsman Graham called for the next act. A boorish-looking youth lumbered out onto a makeshift stage.

"I am Magellan, the greatest explorer that ever lived!" Proclaiming this in a monotone, he deftly dodged an apple core thrown at his head.

Somebody threw an entire bag of trash at him, and it landed on the floor at the front of the stage.

Magellan glared in the direction of where the missiles had launched. With a nimbleness belying his size, he danced out of the way of the next missile sent as a token of appreciation.

Known as Robert ordinarily and not one bit fazed, Magellan quickly continued, "Around the world I sailed and spoke with many people. I was the greatest explorer ever. Fish and fowl were named after me. The tallest of my people discovered the greatest inventions, and we built cities in all the unknown parts of the world, and for a time there was peace and prosperity."

Magellan was quite convincing, and the audience was quiet as he sailed around the stage, continuing his monologue.

"Such inventions as flying cars or airplanes flew in the sky, and autonomous machinery was common."

The audience gasped.

"You might think it was better than now, but it wasn't," he said.

Members of the audience stamped their feet in appreciation.

"People were too busy to talk to their neighbors and then bad people took the greatest inventions, and a terrible thing happened."

The audience gasped.

153

"You know the mini suns that power the city?" He looked directly at the audience.

"Yes, Magellan!" the audience shouted.

"A bad man stole one," he said. Then Magellan paused and continued, "From the greatest city on Panacea, Patagonia."

"Is it still there?"

"No!" Magellan dropped his voice. "Because the man who stole the mini sun couldn't control the power, and what happened? Disaster! Patagonia went beneath the sea. The sun radiated too much energy, and all the sky cars fell from the sky. The orb that once circled the Earth…"

Here, the crowd went silent.

"Fell out of the sky and broke into pieces. And now there is no orb, no sky cars. But now there is peace on Panacea," finished up Magellan.

The crowd heartily clapped.

Magellan took a bow turned back into Robert and left the stage.

A young woman, his daughter, handed him a small bouquet of flowers; and the next performer took the stage.

Brynn received an elbow to her ribs. She looked left to see a figure with a hood sitting there. a plump bearded figure in a hood. Princess Ravenna!

"What the hell are you playing at, sitting here in the audience with us commoners?"

Brynn hadn't seen or heard much of Ravenna for two or three days, which suited Brynn being as she was making plans to run away from the household. She liked Ravenna well enough, but it was time to leave, and Brynn couldn't allow sentiment to alter her plans.

Unfortunately, Ravenna had turned up right as Brynn was about to exit stage left.

"I just wanted to have some fun theater, clearly I wanted to have some fun," said Ravenna coyly.

"What do you mean fun?" asked Brynn suspiciously.

"Fighting fun," said Ravenna sotto voce. She leaned toward Brynn, and Brynn smelt whiskey on her breath.

"How much have you had to drink?" Brynn asked disapprovingly.

"Not much," slurred Ravenna. "A pint of beer and a tumbler of whiskey. The king's finest, ha-ha." Ravenna laughed. "And I took a knife from his armory." She pointed to a sheath sticking out of her boot. The markings on it say it was made in Brunswick. It's not just a kitchen knife. It's one of his finest weapons. Ravenna raised her eyebrows. "He wishes he had a son, but I'm sure I can fight just as good as any boy."

The latest skit had come to an end up on the makeshift stage, and Brynn thought carefully before making a suggestion.

"Ravenna, no one will notice you if you leave between skits, and even though it seems like a good idea now to come and hang with us, if anybody knows you're here, there's going to be trouble!"

Ravenna said, "Yeah, that's what I'm here for—to start a stir and slip away."

Brynn was dumbfounded. She said under cover of the loud noises coming from the stage, "It's not a game, Ravenna, it's not a f—— game. Half the people that work for your dad, the king, think you mistreat them. The other half would f—— you for a favor. Either way, you have no friends here. No one to watch your back. You could get your dignity compromised."

Ravenna raised her eyebrows at this.

"Okay," said Brynn, "your dignity is not at stake. You can't compromise what you don't have."

Ravenna snorted.

Brynn continued, "What I mean is, at the very least, you'll be set upon by the crowd. And anyone who wants a piece of you, and at the very worst, you'll get kidnapped, Ravenna! Do you understand me? It's not about you. It's about the s—— show that's unleashed from your unthinking actions. Have you got no shame?"

Ravenna looked a little subdued at this, though Brynn suspected that was because the alcohol was wearing off a smidgeon.

The stable hands around them were starting to shush them as the next tableau started up.

"Oh, for f—— sake," said Brynn back to them. "Just give me a moment."

And then a burly guardsman noticed Ravenna, tapped his nose, and bawled, "It's the king's daughter!"

Brynn thought quickly. She attempted to shield Ravenna and herself from the stares that started coming their way. Some of the gazes had dropped off as people were far more interested in what was going onstage.

Ravenna started to get childish and stuck her tongue out at the man and barked at him.

She wasn't lying about wanting some action, thought Brynn.

A stubby man in a trench coat turned around and said, "Quiet, wench."

Ravenna said sotto voce, "Wench? Surely, that's a cliché these days." She flushed him a glimpse of her cleavage, proving the man's claims in part and then gobbed a spitball at his feet.

"Oh, fer fuck's sake, Ravenna," Brynn despaired, pushing Ravenna aside, who promptly overbalanced and fell off the bench backward. Her legs went up and so did her skirt, showing her a petticoat and the king's insignia of a crown and sword, the knife hilt sticking out of her boot.

"The king sent his daughter down to spy on us," said the ruddy-faced man.

Everybody stopped jeering at the participants onstage and turned to look at Ravenna trying to get up off the floor, legs akimbo, skirts around her neck.

"Let's go," said Brynn tiredly. She extended her hand to help Ravenna up.

All of a sudden Colonia was there, and behind him, Tucker and Troy.

"Not so fast," said Colonia. He skirted Brynn. And while Ravenna was grunting, trying to twist onto her knees, he stretched out one boot, placed it on her chest, and pushed her back.

Ravenna's eyes widened surprise. "Oww," she said in pain.

Tucker and Troy linked arms behind Colonia.

It was actually Curt, Brynn reminded herself, but it was hard to think of him as anything but a well-dressed female, dressed as he was in a woman's costume with one foot still on Ravenna's chest. Brynn, two feet away from Colonia, was casing the situation.

"Where's the $500 for first prize for the talent quest, Princess Ravenna! I don't think we've got that in the bag," asked Colonia/Curt with a mildly aggressive tone.

Troy reached behind him and grabbed a ten-year-old boy. "Lads, here we go!" Troy dragged the confused boy in front of him. "Here's the star of the show so far. Our William here. Oy! He only juggled two balls and dropped one!" said Tucker.

"Yes, but he can be guaranteed to split the proceeds with us!" said Colonia.

"We got something a little more valuable here though, the king's daughter. What word am I thinking of?" finished Colonia. "Steak?" asked Tucker.

The crowd had fallen quiet, just as any crowd does when they sense it's all about to start.

"No chucklehead," said Colonia. "The word I'm thinking of is 'ransom.' If the wrong persons came around, the princess could get kidnapped! So to prevent this, we take out the kingdom's heir, buy her some dinner. How I feel like a burger or half a chicken! And we send the king a message saying that she'll come back unharmed, and we'll have prevented any harm to her by taking her out, because there's all sorts of nefarious folk around after the annual reawakening ceremonies, and then maybe King Ridich will be grateful enough to reward us for keeping his daughter safe!"

Troy and Tucker's eyes widened.

"Otherwise, anyone could kidnap her," finished Colonia.

"Oh, I see. You're not going to kidnap here because that would be wrong, but you're going to expect that the king will give you money because you'll keep her safe from being kidnapped and that's different from a ransom," said Tucker.

With one hand, Curt ripped off his dress, exposing mail trousers underneath and drew a sword from a bronze scabbard and pointed it in front of him to let everyone know in no uncertain terms that he actually meant business—the business of keeping everybody safe and walking away a little financially better off than he was, prior to the engagement.

Herdsman Graham turned to the crowd. "What's all the fuss about back there," he called. He looked penetratingly at Brynn.

Troy and Tucker joined arms to provide cover for Curt, who had not taken his boot off Ravenna's chest. Until now, only a small circle of interested onlookers had surrounded the skirmish.

"Here, it looks like you've got your foot on someone. A thief?" asked Herdsman Graham. "Is someone interrupting tonight's proceedings? Who could be so precious to interrupt our fine annual talent show? It looks like we have one final act in the crowd, or maybe we have more than one act. Bring out the Headless Horseman."

The Herdsman drifted to the back of the stage. The crowd gasped, and then there was a deadly silence as two of the king's leather-clad blind assassins carried out the torso of the body of a man on a makeshift chair with his head in his lap. The head was the head of a second Herdsman Graham! The confusion in the audience was palpable as blood dripped from the man's waist to the floor. The two blind assassins' eyes were oblivious to the crowd's distress. Their eyes had been removed specifically for the purpose of blind fighting as teenagers, and they were also oblivious to the sound of crowds shouting after years of fighting in arenas and cages.

The standing Herdsman Graham scanned the crowd. Then he reached behind his back with one hand, drew a sword, turned to the chair, poked the head of his double, and hoisted the sword in the air. The head groaned loudly, and the crowd went, "Ohhh!" Herdsman Graham waved at the crowd with the other hand, and the crowd waved back.

Brynn watched in disbelief as he reached over to the neck of his double and fumbled under the hairline, cracking open a layer of plastic, and then smoothly as a snake shedding skin, the head shed a layer of makeup and some prosthetics from below the neck fell away, exposing a live head and upper body. To everybody's dismay, the crowd realized it was King Ridich himself who promptly unfolded himself and sat up straight on the makeshift chair. Herdsman Graham handed him his sword and stood down. The two blind assassins took a step back and to the side of the king, flanking him. It was a formidable sight.

"Who's going to leave me a finger as a token of appreciation," asked the king. "But, first, my fatso daughter can leave intact."

Ravenna slid out from under Curt's foot, who left his foot hanging in midair, mouth agape. She popped herself to her feet, curtseyed to her father, and darted behind her father with the agility of a thousand elk knowing that they're going to get eaten by a lion.

"This is not satisfactory!" shouted the king. Suddenly, he pointed the sword at in Brynn's direction. "This is your fault," the elegant king said in icy, controlled tones. He smiled. The king beckoned Brynn forward.

She calculated her chances of making it to the banquet hall door before she was caught by the king's guardsmen. She decided that it was probably in her best interest to meet the king on his ground as she had no reason to fear the king's wrath. She had been a model groom and stable hand, and she had tried to protect Ravenna tonight. With a thwack, the sword flied through the air as she stepped forward to the king. Appalled, Brynn noticed the tip of her ring finger on her right hand down to the first knuckle come off her hand, fly up into the air, then fall down and bounce off her boot.

"You wretched handmaiden," thundered King Ridich. "How dare you put my daughter in danger?"

Ravenna stuck her head out from behind the king and spoke up.

"Father, can you not mutilate my people? I'm worried you'll start taking off heads. I have to look at them every day, and I don't want to look at headless fungi woman."

"I'm not going to demand anymore offerings. If she was doing her job, you wouldn't have been in the danger that you would seem to be in," said King Ridich.

"I'm not a child, Father!" Ravenna protested. "I am a woman."

Brynn's finger was throbbing and already quite painful. The tip lay on the floor. In a smooth fluid movement, the blind assassin stepped in front of Brynn, picked up the fingertip, and handed it back to her. The assassin moved back into place and resumed a stiff posture.

"You three," roared the king.

Curt, Troy, and Tucker looked at each other and made the same calculation that Brynn had done. Realizing there was little choice but to go up to the stage, they moved to the front of the crowd. Tucker made gurgling noises, and up onstage a dark stain started spreading on the front of Troy's trousers. They froze in front of the king.

"What the ever-loving turnip!" said the king. "Is there not an ounce of courage among any of you apart from this wench."

His eyes flickered toward Brynn, who was ignoring her pain and irritation with reserves of courage and energy she had not been aware that she had. Now that Brynn thought about it, she was more than slightly irritated. The king had stopped talking, so she rated her anger. She was actually furious the king had disparaged her ability to care for his daughter. She had done nothing but look out for Ravenna's interests since joining n his household. Although Ravenna might be a princess by bloodline and by name, she was nothing but a tramp, a hoochie, and a doxie by nature. Since Brynn had known her, Ravenna had tried to bed everyone and everything in that order. Brynn had even caught her examining the kitchen dog for its potential for sexual gratification. Brynn had actually slapped Ravenna to bring her to her senses at that time. Brynn hadn't worried about the mutt so much as she told Ravenna, "You cross a line, and there is no coming back." The slap hadn't curbed Ravenna's wanton behavior. Just like any overgrown malicious kid, she was preoccupied with her own wants and needs.

Ravenna wanted to feel good and to see people suffer, and it filled a need to make them uncomfortable and squirm in a similar but more chaotic manner to her father. She enjoyed wielding power over people, but whereas the king would balance the suffering with a lesson, Ravenna got pleasure out of other people's misery and degradation. Now Brynn had lost her fingertip to protect this shrewish, royal Jezebel.

"You three," roared the king again. He pointed to Curt, Tucker, and Troy. "Dance." He motioned for the crowd to make room for the trio. "Dance said I!" said King Ridich. "Curtsy to the kingdom boys. Dance, and the rest of you shut up and watch, and after, it's your turn. We're here to celebrate the reawakening. Celebrate and drink. Don't lose your heads though!" He waved the sword.

Over his words and the boys awkward shuffling, something propelled through the air and smacked an elderly gentleman in the head. Brynn's eyes saw the impact. She knew where the missile had come from. That little b—— Ravenna. The king frowned, and Brynn had never noticed this before; but the king was, to all intense and purposes, standing tall looking cruel but purposeful. He appeared to be wondering what his next move should be to keep control of the crowd. The crowd was still somewhat stupefied, but it was looking for a release.

Ravenna was standing a little bit left and behind the king, grimacing like she was possessed. Curt, Tucker, and Troy were still nervously shuffling; and then Tucker got a hold of himself and started doing a reasonable two-step. The crowd breathed out, and the king beamed.

Brynn got angrier. She felt the anger building in her chest and her stomach hurt. The king beckoned to a scullery maid. Nervously, she approached the stage. A cook reached into their apron, then something sailed through the ear over Brynn's head. The tension between Brynn's shoulder blades grew. A stable hand wolf whistled at the trio dancing onstage, and now the king doing the grapevine with the young maid. An egg got thrown at the stage but fell short. Brynn got angrier. A vibration started low in her stomach.

"Stop!" she yelled.

Half a cut melon flew past her head, fell out of midair, hit the ground, and smashed.

Brynn wheeled around to face the offender, who darted out of sight.

"Have you no respect," she roared.

The unruly crowd started gabbing at anything that could be thrown across the hall. First to be grabbed by the crowd and pulled apart were the pot plants dotted around the hall, used to decorate the occasion. Brandon, a youth from the stables grabbed a branch, stuck it behind his ear and threw another at Brynn. The branch seemed to freeze in the air before it fell to the ground. Brynn could feel vibration go right through her body. She yelled, "Stop!" and then the whole room exploded.

Kids thrust other kids out of the way, neighbors jumped on neighbors, and the king who had no bodyguard other than the two still on the stage waited for a pause in the fighting. Curt, Tucker, and Troy two-stepped their way to the side to hide behind the largest of the pot plants.

"Find the king," yelled somebody else.

But the stage was empty. Brynn felt an arm around her waist as she was guided off to the side.

RAVENNA

Ravenna was in the stables breathing hard. The alcohol had left her system, but the bravado hadn't. She was hungry. She wasn't sure exactly what she was hungry for, but it felt like the start of a hunt, so she lifted her nose to the air and started sniffing. She could smell a horse who was as hot to ride as she was. Maybe they could be friends. She needed one friend in the world to stay disguised, hidden from the kingdom at large. The kings' guardsmen might already be looking for her. She stopped at the stall of a dappled seal-brown horse called Percheron. He was approximately sixteen hands high and ready to ride out. She noticed a pile of hay in the back of the stall. She pulled off the hay and found a bag with clothes and basic supplies like someone was thinking of riding out and staying away for a few nights or leaving.

"Hey, girl, what have we got here?" She slapped one of her own meaty thighs. "Hey, baby," she crooned to the horse: "Hey, baby," she crooned again. "Show me you love me and keep me from harm, and you and I will go ride for a ways, all right?"

The stable door was open. Ravenna opened the stall door, threw the backpack on her back, and mounted Percheron.

"Well, let's go."

She wasn't sure where she was going, but she had a fair idea she was leaving her dad's castle tonight. She had the warmth of a horse to keep warm. She had enough food in the rucksack to eat until she could use her wits to get more food. Hell, she'd sell her body if she needed to. She smiled bleakly.

THE MYST OF THEMYSTRICHYR

Eliza was lying on the bed of stuffed pillows atop a bamboo frame. Beside her a lamp glowed in its glass and bamboo frame. She had been dozing off and on quite deliciously, she thought. She could hear water in the distance. Eliza didn't know where she was. She had stepped into the pages of a book apparently, and unless she woke up from a dream within a dream, she would assume that this was maybe what life was like traveling outside the city. It wasn't just leaving somewhere intolerable and arriving somewhere unknown, it was more like a series of linked adventures. Strike that. This was not linked to her brief stay in at the apothecary at all. Her abduction by the warrior women was way out of left field, whatever left field was. Must be a sporting term, maybe a team sport. *We didn't really have those in Diaspora*, Eliza mused. A hard wood door pushed open into the room as Eliza reconstructed her memory of the evening.

"It's all good," said Despoina, walking into the room and looking at the expression on Eliza's face. "It was a big day, and well, you had a little bit too much kava to drink." She giggled.

"What's kava?" asked Eliza.

"It's a mild relaxant," said Despoina. "It's not completely intoxicating, but for some people who are predisposed, it can induce a mild euphoric effect. Do you remember the 'butterflies'?"

And then a memory came back to Eliza. Butterflies! She didn't think she'd ever seen a butterfly apart from in drawings and books, which could be borrowed from the library, which presumably had pictures of them. It was just another of those extinct species.

She wondered if perhaps there was other worlds that had butterflies but didn't have horses! Or maybe had horses with horns!

"You're still a little stoned!" Despoina laughed. She sat down on the bed and rubbed Eliza's head.

The sensation was not unpleasant. Eliza marveled how people were nice to have touch her hang on that sentence was the wrong way around. How nice it was to have people touch her.

"You are all very nice," she said to Despoina. "Frustratingly, my words don't describe the nice touch."

"It's wonderful to have you here with us," said Despoina. "You must be starved for affection. You don't need to choose your words with us. They'll come. I understand you grew up in an intolerant patriarchal society."

"I don't think so," said Eliza. "Men and women were quite equal where I grew up. We grew up in loving homes. With two parents. Sometimes one. There were incompatibilities, of course. My mom and dad lived together. We all were educated. Everyone got to work in a job they enjoyed."

Despoina raised her left eyebrow. "You enjoyed? Did they choose their work? True freedom is doing what you love. Tell me, did you fight alongside each other?"

"Fight?" said Eliza. "What do you mean fight?"

"You know!" said Despoina, although it was obvious Eliza didn't. "If there was a threat to your town, did you rise up and meet it together. We're lucky here. We only have one land boundary. There's plenty of warning if we get approached by sea. But it happens, especially when the Mysts come in, in spring."

"Well, no," said Eliza. "Boundary sickness stops any other city coming near us." She stopped, lost for words. There really were no words to describe her experience growing up compared to the absolute—

"Freedom," interjected Despoina.

"Stop it!" said Eliza. "I feel like you're reading my mind."

"Hmm," said Despoina, choosing her words carefully. "I could tell you were comparing the lifestyle you grew up to what you're seeing here. I didn't mean to invade your boundaries."

Eliza rubbed her eyebrow, remembering how her thoughts had been open in Diaspora to the city. How was she to explain that to Despoina? But Despoina was more interested in Eliza's orientation to her new surroundings.

"Have you noticed anything else that's very different from other places you have been, including the city you grew up in?" asked Despoina.

Eliza asked, puzzled, "Where are the men?"

"They're not living here," she said. "And to be honest, we don't really miss them. At least, we don't miss living with them. It was frightening going to high school and reading about the treatment of woman before the reawakening. Women were treated as inferior to men, and they were routinely beaten and abused unless they found a protector. It seems to be the case worldwide. Woman were a lesser species like monkeys in a zoo."

"What's a zoo?" asked Eliza.

"It's an enclosure where certain types of animals were kept, and they didn't go outside the walls. And people could pay money to go look at them. Their only purpose in life was to reproduce, essentially to keep the species going, but also for entertainment."

"How dire," said Eliza, and unbidden into her mind crept the thought: *Gosh, that sounds a lot like Diaspora*. "Actually it sounds nothing like Diaspora," she said out loud.

Despoina was watching her, tapping her chin with one finger.

"So we don't live with men. We see them. We feast with them. We need to mate. Just like in your culture.

"Oh, goody," said Eliza with forced bravado.

"You never desired a man?" asked Despoina.

She didn't sound like she had any particular judgment on the question.

"What about a woman?"

Eliza shook your head despondently.

"How old are you?" asked Despoina.

"Me I turned sixteen in April."

"All of our women have chosen by your age. By the first blade and the first fight, I took my first mate, Katalanta. We were mates for two years. We fought together, We ate together. We sheltered together. We fought in the war of Himenloch. Giants came down from the north, a great big wave of them. They had been passive for so long we had grown to think of them as not a threat, but they had grown more aggressive over the generations. They came in five great waves, and we were outnumbered three to one. We sharpened arrows day and night and charged in horses. We held them back. We shot them with bows and arrows. We killed them, and we tortured them with our beauty."

Eliza looked at Despoina with her weathered face.

"Oh, yes." Despoina nodded. "They begged us to keep them for playthings."

"Despoina!" came a loud call from outside the room. "Stop with the vagfaronade."

Eliza looked questioningly.

"Vagging. Crowing," said Despoina, handing Eliza some purple silk leisure pants and a matching top. "I took three of the Himenloch giants as lovers for a time. Two of them at once." She winked at Eliza. "This is a black star sapphire," she said, placing an agate choker with a central stone around Eliza's neck.

As Eliza looked at the sapphire as she placed it, it played with the light, and Eliza could swear it appeared as though there was a star trapped inside.

Kat walked in. "Come with us to the labyrinth," she said. "I will explain. By the way, it was lovely, your description of the butterflies that you saw while we were sharing kava together last night. Tell me, do you often have her visions of long-gone species?"

"I have," said Eliza, looking from Kat to Despoina. She was in a permanent state of puzzlement by this stage, and it seemed natural to suspend reality. She was safe. She was unharmed. She knew that her friends from the apothecary would be fairly pragmatic, and they would come for her when they could. At least, that's what she would do if that she was in their place. She was intrigued by these women. Kat and Despoina flanked her and moved her out of the room.

"No men?" commented Eliza. "How do you have babies without men?"

"There's plenty of babies, but we only keep the girls," Despoina ventured.

"We turn the boys into fish food," said Kat, smiling. "We even have a nursery rhyme that we teach the girls—'One sprat, two sprat, into the grinder goes young Jack.'"

"No way!" exclaimed Eliza, shocked.

Kat laughed. "Ha-ha, you're so gullible. We're fairly civilized. It's true we don't live with men. The boys go to families in the villages of Asperia and will meet their sisters and mothers twice a year for family days. Everyone seems content. Most boys would rather live with other boys, though a handful do return to live among us as a woman. You will see. Come now and meet the rest of the women of Themystrichyr."

They were hurrying through the corridors of a maze-like adobe fortress structure. The mudbrick walls smelt pungent in the rising heat of the day but not unpleasant.

"What is this?" asked Eliza breathlessly.

"It's the Myst's citadel," replied Kat. "It serves as our seat of governance. We quarter our soldiers here."

"At the center is a labyrinth," said Despoina, "It is where we observe ceremony, where we take blood and choose bloodlines. The spirits can take form here as the veil of the Myst is very thin here. Don't follow the spirits if they ask you to. Sometimes they will beseech, beg, and entreat you to follow them through the gates.

What gates? Eliza was thinking that she really must rethink this approach of suspending disbelief. Spirits taking form? I mean, of course, it was possible to communicate ideas with your loved ones who had passed. But you could no more take form as a spirit than you could unscramble an egg and have it become a yolk, right?

"New girl, new girl, new girl," chanted someone sitting on rows of seat that came into view as they turned a corner and walked into a rotunda.

Eliza could see a circular stone walking labyrinth laid out at the center. It was expansive. The labyrinth wound around as far as the eye could see with rows of seating surrounding. Kat, Despoina, and Eliza were walking onto the entrance of the structure. It appeared to provide seating for the crowd of women coming into Eliza's vision, and through a window in the distance, Eliza could see the sea from whence they had arrived the day or two previous. She supposed the barge had returned to the mainland of the unconsolidated territories. There were statues of carved stones on a promontory overlooking. Of giant figures with prominent foreheads and only one breast. Odd.

"Everybody's here to see you," said Kat. "We're going to walk through to the center. We're going to walk the labyrinth slowly, and you will have questions by the end."

To sounds of cheering and hooting, they started walking at the entry of the labyrinth, and as Eliza took one foot onto the labyrinth, she heard a whisper around her head.

"Lost to us!" the voice said. "Lost woman. Lost in time."

Kat moved in front of Eliza. Another voice spoke, and something took shape in the air. Eliza glanced at the diaphanous form as she moved past. The voice came just in front of her face.

"You have no parents in between," said another. "An orphan, how curious. Queen Mab will get you. My boys, the queen is here. Queen Mab brings you in. Queen Mab always brings you in. Sometimes she's late, but better late than poorly dressed."

"Queen Mab, bringer of songs and souls," another voice, rich and resonant. "We love you. Once bitten thrice shy."

Yet another voice caressed her with a promise. "He's out there, remember? He loved you. He loves you from the bottom of his heart, and you thought he was lost to you. There was a dispute between families. Forced into an arranged marriage to knit two warring guilds. Ha ha ha ha! Interfering fairy godmothers! They made you sleep for one thousand years, and then set you free! Money wasn't enough, was it? When you awoke from your slumber and gave up all your money and you left your children behind." The voice was quite magnetic.

Eliza knew it was one voice, like that of a narrator but with different intonations and modulation. Each time it spoke, it had a new personality. The speaker was always female. Eliza wondered who on Panacea they were talking about. She'd never had any money so to speak of. Her needs had always been met by her parents and the city of Diaspora. Her children? She didn't have any. So it wasn't her they were talking about. Who could possibly abandon their children?

The voice read her mind.

"You left for love," said a voice in song. "You left for life and your love, Atlas, and to see if he would meet you. You were to meet by an old oak tree, and he would take you away. He had family enough for you. He had sky cars to take you to see the world. He had only left you for a short time to go to a far-off land to get a cure because you were sick."

Now the voices were in melodic, storytelling mode.

"You both knew you were going to die. He couldn't accept this. Acute radiation sickness."

Another voice took up the thread. "Royalty. Betrayal. A cousin, Phani. This cousin did not want to see you throwing your life away to leave the clan. He meant well."

Eliza was getting closer to the middle of the circle, but there seemed to be a little bit more of the story she was hearing. Maybe everybody heard the story as they walked the walking labyrinth. Maybe it was some kind of imbuement. That was cool. In the libraries, the two libraries she knew of in Diaspora, they had legends and tales and books and stories of the times before the reawakening. It was funny, curious that there never seemed to be enough time to get books out of the libraries. This oral retelling was as good an introduction as any to her stay with the women of Themystrichyr.

A voice interrupted her thoughts.

"Atlas loved Talia so deeply. He couldn't think clearly. He received a message from Phani that Talia had taken sick and wouldn't live to see the week. Atlas left a lizard in a suit in charge and readied a sky plane. The sky plane was sabotaged. Atlas flew into a mountain that rose out of a land of fire and ice."

The voice spoke of more mischief.

"The lizard told Talia, Atlas died knowing that she did not care if she lived or died too. So she went to the old oak tree and hung herself with a rope made out of hemp and gold thread so that people would be sorry. Before she died, the heavens sent down a bolt of lightning and thunder, and an earthquake triggered the land asunder. Atlas recovered, to find his beloved Talia buried and the people of both clans mourning. He vowed never to love again and devoted all his time to making a weapon so powerful, so bright, and so heavy that it is said that you could hang orbs in the sky with it."

The two older women and Eliza had reached the center of the labyrinth. Eliza gasped. She hadn't realized while walking in that she had been walking up a gently sloping hill, and now she was in the middle, she was looking down at these concentric circles radiating out and all the woman on rows of seats looking up at her. It was like being on a stage with circular seating all around it. She thought she was walking onto a smallish space, but it was rather a large plateau. She looked out over the sea of heads. Kat gathered up Eliza and gave her a warm hug. Despoina smiled, looking at the crowd. And that was another realization Eliza had: she was looking down and around at one of the largest crowds she had ever seen. Despoina lifted her arms up on high and pointed at one section of the crowd and then moved around in a circle rotating, and as she did, so the crowd raise their voices in a loud cheer. Despoina kept on rotating, and as she did so, the crowd got louder and louder until it was roaring.

Kat said, "The bringer of souls has bought her to us!"

The crowd roared appreciatively. "Hip hooray to Queen Mab! Hip hooray," said the crowd.

Eliza was chewing her lip nervously. She side-eyed Despoina, who winked at her. Kat gave a first pump, and the crowd barked and howled!

"Oh my God," commented Eliza, sotto voce. Now she was freaking out, and she just wanted to remove herself from this orientation/introduction, whatever it was they put visitors through.

Eliza canvased her memories. These women had kidnapped her from her friends. But they hadn't harmed her; rather, they had fed her. And she had a fairly decent two or three nights sleep. But it was all so disconcerting, and she needed some answers. The barking and the howling had turned into cat-calling and black slapping.

"I see you," said Kat finally, turning Eliza around and eyeballing her, woman to woman. "I was waiting for you to settle back into yourself."

Eliza was irritated. She hated feeling being seen, and these barbarians had no right to expose her.

"Why are you making an example of me," she whispered over the caterwauling.

Kat looked somewhat chastened. "I never thought that you would think of it like that," she said. "You are being celebrated. Listen! The women are celebrating your arrival here."

Eliza was feeling quite lightheaded, woozy, and dissociated from her physical self. She felt like she was losing her grasp on reality. Something within her gave way. She wasn't impressed in the light of all she had been through that these women thought it was fine to carry on a conversation in front of hundreds of tub-thumping women.

The floodgates opened, and she started with, "You don't know me. You didn't know me before you carried me off from my friends. Oh yes, let's return to that. Why did you separate me from my friends. We were posing no threat, and you swooped in and attacked our group. I feel like I'm a lot friendlier with you than I really should be, given that you left several of my friends with injuries. Injuries to slow them down and distract them from our mission. They'll be worried about me!"

Kat waved her hand as if to dismiss this detail.

"Furthermore," said Elisa, gathering momentum without regard for the audience, as oblivious as if she was in a bubble instead of feeling self-conscious. She knew that at least some of the rows of woman could hear her. Regardless, she felt like she was due some goddamn answers. "You don't even know me, yet you sniffed me out and said that I was a danger."

Kat met her gaze and calmly asked, "Have you finished, dearie?" And she raised her hands and put them on her hips.

"Do you call yourself barbarians?" Eliza asked.

Kat thought this was the funniest thing she had ever heard. She clapped her hands on her hips threw her head back and laughed like a lunatic, then turned to the crowd and said, "Hey, women. Hey, women. Are we barbarians?" She laughed and moved around what Eliza that come to think of as the arena, as the open-aired arena.

The reply wasn't as loud, but it was definitely tinged with amusement.

"What do we call ourselves, ladies?" hollered Kat to the crowd.

"Termagants," called the women back.

"And?" called Kat to the crowd.

"Hellcats," called the crowd.

"We avoid male-oriented phrasing and names here, Eliza," Kat continued. "Eliza is not a very pretty name. It's strong, but it's not pretty, not like mine or Despoina's or Athena's or Cressida's."

The woman as they were named waved and hollered to Eliza.

"Hang on," Eliza said. "You can't sledge my name and expect to win me over."

"Who said that was your real name!" said Kat. "You're displaying moxie. You're quite a fighter, yet you were saying you weren't raised to fight."

The crowd cheered at the mention of the word "fight."

"Yes, you are a threat if without instruction, your gifts will go unrestrained, but that's not why we bought you here," Kat continued. "We bought you here because you're one of us, and we bought you here for your own safety. There are several spies looking for you. The city you left sent them out looking for you, ostensibly for your own safety. But they will kill you if they capture you."

The crowd grew quiet.

"This will be news to you. You didn't fit into society, did you? We wouldn't either if we weren't born here. We are not docile like city dwellers. We like to question. We like to craft. We seek the truth. We like our own company and have few friends. We don't like to be caged or live behind walls. We must have our freedom. We don't accept the status quo. We don't accept the societal norms. The rules that have been passed down from generation to generation. Generations that may have been duped by the parents' generation.

"Most of us were born here. A few of us wandered here by accident. Maybe took a boat ride looking for a meal or a salary, looking for a quick wage, some made it through the Mysts and stayed."

Eliza was thinking, *Well, this is all very well. I deserve the full story seeing as I was snatched away, and it really is quite compelling but will I be able to sit down soon.*

"Listen to me," said Kat. "Really listen and give what I have to say a chance to resonate. You were meant to be born here Eliza on Themystrichyr. You were a soul adrift. You started this life instead in the womb of a mom who was grieving a son who had previously passed.

Her grief pulled your soul to her. It was not meant to be because you are one of a handful in a generation of the defenders of Earth's heart."

Eliza scoffed internally. *Oh, spare me*, she thought, feeling like someone was going to pull her off stage with a crook. *Exit stage left*.

"Your previous life was much like a play. What is a play? It's a performance kind of like this, but this is not written and rehearsed. Well, it was written. It was written that you came here, and hear this, you were called here."

Eliza felt tremulous as she said, "I was my oldest child and I had no other parents."

Kat shook her head. "They were offered money not to tell you. Even the person who offered the money thought they were doing them a service. Doing you a service, they didn't really know the details. There was an incentive for the city fathers, the agency who offered the person who offered your parents money (a proctor) were aware that you were to be born, and they wanted to ensure your gifts would not come to light and could not be harnessed by yourself or anybody else. Do you have any other parents that you can remember other than your current carnate parents?"

"Well, no," said Eliza. "I assumed it was because I had breached, suicided, and my memory had been scrubbed. The city fathers said it is the only crime you have your memory scrubbed. It's the ultimate crime. Every other crime is forgiven via penance, but if you take your own life you take your connection from the city mind, and if you are reborn, you should be lucky consider yourself lucky that the city mind thinks you are redeemable. And precious enough to rebirth. But having rejected the city and your lineage, you lose your parents and ancestral memory forever. So I had wondered as everybody else has their parents their grandparents and access to varying degrees of ancestors."

"Boring," shouted somebody.

Eliza glared. "Well, excuse me," she said. "Have I just walked into cliché city?"

Kat asked, "What's that?"

"It's like when somebody's an outsider," said Eliza begrudgingly. "They are someone who's a misfit. They look like a misfit, and their clothes hang off them wrong. Even if people aren't outright mean to them, they never get to become part of the in group. Until one day somebody goes a little bit too far and does something that scares everybody so to make up for the kind of group trauma. They make the nerd the group leader, and the group leader turns into a real swan, which is why we talk about butterflies." She trailed with, "It's called metamorphosis, transformation between states. But here is the thing, that one, the old Chosen One has just become one of the pack. And the next time someone nerdy comes along, the first one becomes normal and a normal old bully. So there is no Chosen One. You stole me. But I'm still a nerd with no talents to speak of. I'll stay as long as it's interesting though." She brightened with Kat's thoughtful and the teensiest bit sad eyes on her.

"You had a rough time," Kat said, eventually in response to Eliza's faltering monologue. "No, you didn't breach. And you do have talents, at least if you consider fighting a talent. That lightning bolt strike you have some mastery of is quite impressive. Want to be called Elecktra?"

Eliza shuffled. She surveyed the audience of woman. Nervously, she looked back at Kat, and then feeling surprised at how warm and suddenly valued she felt. She smiled, looking ahead. One of the woman cheered Eliza, beamed at her, turned, rotating and smiling. More of the women started cheering all of a sudden.

Before she knew what she was doing, Eliza pumped her fists into the air, and the whole crowd responded by pumping by fist pumping and bumping hips and standing up and shouting her appreciation.

Suddenly, Kat pushed Eliza in the chest and knocked her off balance.

"Hey," said Eliza, a rush of fear rushing through her as she fell backward and landed in the waiting arms of Despoina and Cressida, who had jumped up to the stage to catch her.

"All hail to the Sun Queen!" praised Kat.

Eliza watched in disbelief as the women raised and lowered their arms in worship. All of a sudden, Eliza felt calm, and any resistance drained away as she felt relief and thought, *Whatever these women were doing and whatever they were playing at, they had to be crazier than Eliza was.* For the first time in her life, she felt totally at home in the manner of an explorer who had stumbled on an unsophisticated but wise tribe. Eliza felt herself being hoisted in the air, and all of a sudden, she was being passed woman to woman across the crowd, and they all were singing quite a catchy song:

"In times of doubt, in times of war you light the way, with your feminine flame, and in times of peace and times of plenty, you sow seed on the Earth, from your one bright ovary. Oh Mother Flame, take us home, take us home to the stars from whence we came."

Eliza smiled at the childish rhyme as she jostled and bounced in the cradle of the women's arms. She found herself having sleepy thoughts, and as she was deposited back in her bamboo bed, she had one last thought before she drifted off. *Fuck? Am I a princess? Am I the SunQueen?*

HERBERT TAKES A BATH

LaVey had given Herbert explicit instructions for the ceremony that evening.

"Will there be animal blood there?" Herbert asked thirstily, hungry for the satiation he had become accustomed to, the administration of a libation whereby he felt younger by morning, ebullient, indeed, larger than life.

"Of course," said LaVey. "Now if you want to know how to fit in right from the start. There really is no way to act wrong once you got to this level of acceptance. They know about you. I told them how intelligent you were and how eager you were to learn about your biological processes. You really are one of the most intelligent men I have ever met."

Herbert glanced at her. Was she teasing him? It's not that she didn't seem the kind to grease or ingratiate herself with him. That was part of her attraction. She seemed to keep on coming around because she wanted to be with him, despite him feeling like he didn't have much to offer. Maybe that was what genuine friendship was, and now she was complimenting him. Well, he wasn't unintelligent. At vocational school following high school, he had been one of the best in his class. He liked accounting and administration. He'd picked it up quickly. Some people had stumbled over basic concepts like accounting ledgers and the concept of taking something away in one column and adding it back in the other column. He sniffed at the thought that the concept was so basic.

LaVey carried on talking. "So you'll be fine, it's just a small gathering of humans. Five hundred or so. You'll see other proctors there, and there will be a handful of younger people."

Herbert interrupted, "Five hundred people!"

This was much larger than he imagined, and LaVey confirmed his fears.

"Five hundred people to welcome you, Herbert. To welcome little old you." She rustled her feathers and sat back on her heels. "It's a big deal, Herbert. You're in the inner circle. Normal people would judge us. It's unreasonable. We are just drinking animal blood. Animals that would end up basically on the dinner plate anyway, and this way it's refined to benefit us, and we can benefit them. I discussed this with you, Herbert, to make you feel comfortable. Because of our contacts and a combined expertise, we really are the Elect. Now you're going to be one of us here. How did we do it? We were able to take these animals for dinner and divert them between farm and plate for our humanitarian purposes. We had our scientists figure out, through amazing bioengineering processes, which animals and which breeds gave us access to the ability to stave off senescence. It's the f—— fountain of youth, Herbert! And it's just common old chicken blood, Herbert. Chicken blood! I can't wait for you to meet the scientists who bioengineered the fountain of youth from chicken blood and rabbit blood. And not just any rabbits. It's generally the same breed of rabbits that have the best wool, angora." She breathed.

"And why do we not share the benefits of the animal blood with the public?"

"Well, now there would be competition for resources. And, Herbert, fear of innovation is just a few of the reasons why we don't talk about this with the wider public."

"But how does the city not know?" asked Herbert.

"Too many questions," said LaVey.

Herbert bit back a retort. It was just the one question compared to LaVey's lecture.

"What shall I wear again?" asked Herbert, changing tactics.

"I've bought you some footwear. Just black slides. I usually wear leather lace-ups, but slides are a little more comfortable for meet and greets. In this backpack are some black trousers, a white shirt with a collar, and black vest with no arms. Now go take a bath," directed LaVey. "Drink this while you're bathing."

"What is it is?" asked Herbert.

"It's a drink known as kava, from traders immune to boundary sickness. They've travelled between the desert bazaars, the unconsolidated territories, and the bound cities. It'll relax you, nothing more, love. I'll be right back in an hour and a half."

And so Herbert was left to lol in the bath thinking as he so often did at times when he was alone with himself of how he presented to the world, how he was aging and of the new distractions that had taken him from the boredom of his life prior, to a routine that was still wallpaper, drab, and gray; but there were some delectable fruits of his secret life that he was privy to. These made his work and encounters with other people more exotic, made his encounters with his staff a little more fetching. He was smiled at by an adjutant working for him this morning.

Lubriciously, Herbert thought. *Had they done it deliberately? If they had, what were they playing it. What were they expecting?* Herbert looks down at his punchy paunch. He laughed at what he had thought. *I have a paunchy paunch*, he thought again. And then he fell silent. Why did he have a tubby midriff? He would do something about it. Then the next time the adjutant played their games of flirting baselessly with him, he would show them that he was not someone to be dallied with lightly. By then he would be initiated into this in a circle, this society. Every man had his ways and means of staying youthful. He probably wouldn't go around crowing about their activities. He laughed, "Crowing." But he could use a few inches off his waist, and all it took was the occasional preparation. Getting out of the bath, he felt quite relaxed. It must have been the effect of the kava. By Guardians, he'd see if he could obtain more of that as long as he didn't feel muddy in the morning. Not being a drinker, he was used to waking clearheaded, but he didn't have anything that took away the stress of his job. The main stress was how he had to correct adjutants, and he really was quite fearful and excited around them at the same time.

Where was LaVey?

Just as the thought came to him, the front door opened, and LaVey reentered. She was wearing barely anything. A diaphanous slip dress and the same slides he was wearing. She looked excited.

"Let's go. I'll chat," she said.

No kidding, thought Herbert as he walked toward the door.

She barely let him speak.

"Where are we going? How are we getting there?"

LaVey smiled coyly. "I'll tell you as we're moving."

They walked out of the door and started walking, or in the case of LaVey, hovering. Herbert for a moment was puzzled and then followed dutifully.

With nothing much to say, he said tentatively, "Well, LaVey, I was expecting a car." He was referring to one of the hop-on/hop-off electric vehicles that you scheduled and sent back to the vehicle bank as needed.

LaVey responded tersely, "You would think that, wouldn't you? We're just going to walk for a bit."

The funniest thing was as they walked, Herbert could have sworn the road started to curve the slightest.

"Did you notice that?" He turned to LaVey to ask her, but she was staring straight ahead.

They crossed an intersection. He was quite used to this circuit, but her pace was faster than usual.

"Careful, my lovely, you don't want to take a tumble," she cast back.

They started up a slight incline. Herbert was getting tired.

"Where are we going?" Herbert questioned wearily.

"We're almost there," replied LaVey enigmatically.

As they approached a neighborhood park, Herbert was absolutely positive the road appeared to be curving and did not reflect reality of the straight line they were walking. He was confused. Did he walk straight, or did he follow the curve? At first, he tried to walk straight, but that felt wrong, so he contemplated following the curve.

He thought, *Well, maybe it's the kava. Maybe I think I'm walking straight, and I'm actually walking curved, so maybe if I follow the curve, I'll be walking straight.*

So feeling quite relaxed and not actually able to walk fast due to the effects of the kava, he comfortably followed the curve. LaVey, seeming quite relaxed and not at all in a hurry herself now, stuck to a uniform pace. And so they walked, and he followed the curve, and then he heard the thunk of a horn followed by an impact. And the last thing he saw before going unconscious was LaVey's face looking down at him with a lascivious grin. Then he was on his back, lying in the back of a car or some mode of transport. He was hurt. He felt a trickle of liquid from his ears. He was passed a wad of cotton, and he pressed it to the trickle. Pulling it away and examining it, Herbert realized it was blood.

"You won't feel pain," Herbert heard from LaVey. "You've had a combination of the kava to relax you, and we've given you a small amount of morphine as a spinal block to prevent any pain anywhere. It will wear off in about two hours, and you'll be good as new."

"Where are we driving to?" asked Herbert sleepily, scratching his nose.

LaVey, who was sitting in the front of whatever they were driving in, shot him a quizzical look in the rearview mirror. "Driving?" she said, framed as a question.

Herbert looked in the mirror and quickly realizing it was an angle and they were suspended off the ground. "What the hell!" he said.

"Well, there's an ancient cuss," said LaVey. "You just wait. You'll be amazed what technology has come back from the past." She was being mysterious. "I can't be more specific just yet. Sorry. And sorry about the hit and fly, it was necessary to get you off the city grid. It's only necessary for the first time we bring you in. And you might want to feel sympathy for the poor idiot who had to knock you down in such a way as not to kill you or knock you out for so long that we couldn't unplug you."

"What do you mean unplug me?" asked Herbert.

The swarthy man driving turned and said, "Unplugged you from the city mind for good. Now you are open source."

"Did you get something out of me?" asked Herbert, feeling around his body. At least, the parts that were socially acceptable to feel around.

"Nah, mate," said the driver. "It wasn't what we got out, it was what we put in."

"I'm just going to wonder about that," Herbert said cautiously. He felt half hopeful, half bemused, half frightened.

"That's three halves," said LaVey.

How did she know what he was thinking?

"The same way the city knew what you were thinking, or at least what your intentions were. And from thereon could issue subliminal directions and direct your actions," said LaVey.

"You said you put something in me. What are you talking about?" asked Herbert. "Like is it a wire? A transmitter?"

LaVey teased her words out carefully. "You really have got to start thinking a little more high-tech, Herbert," she said slowly. "It's not a clumsy wire or mechanism. At least, nothing you could see with the naked eye. No. Animals are your friend here, darling. It's an engineered poison that went in with the morphine block. The poison reacted with the cerebrospinal fluid in your central nervous system. Then the poison reacted with an enzyme in all your cells via a lock-and-key mechanism. One side effect is that it extends the life of every cell in your body. The other side effect—you can block and receive short range thoughts. Block the city mind. Send instructions. Manipulate people." She was watching him closely.

The jocular man in the front of the car snapped his fingers. "What do you think about that, mate?" he said to the air. "F—— witchcraft, isn't it?"

Herbert didn't know what to think, so like any of his lowly stupid adjutants, he asked the next obvious question: "Why doesn't this car fall out of the sky?"

"Oh, that," said LaVey. "Ha ha ha, get used to finding out you've been lied to all your life. 'Liar, liar, badge on fire,' as we say. After the reawakening, the Earth was a literal hell. Whoever got their hands on the ability to recreate the energy of the sun triggered a series of events that led to cataclysmic electromagnetic pulsing from the sun and also from other sources, including deep within the Earth. Civilizations collapsed and went feudal. Parts of it stayed feudal. Where we are, people were herded into cities and were told what was good for them, for us, which happened to benefit the city fathers and secretaries. The city fathers and secretaries have access to more technology than you would think. And now so do we augmented. In some cities, we are the fathers. The actual fathers are proxies. We are in charge. And you can be too. You can be young forever and have power beyond your wildest dreams!

You've seen what we do. It's harmless. We take waste products and repurpose them. We're very good at what we do, and we want you to join us. During the day nothing changes. You're a very good accountant."

Herbert preened as well as he could lying supine.

"We will need people like you to run the cities, to set a good example. To set the best example to the youth so they know that the way things are done are for the benefit of everyone. Set the direction for the future.

"You'll have permanent access to the fountain of youth. Imagine staying young just by injecting and imbibing a hormone derived from animal blood, with no unpleasant side effects other than the discomfort you've experienced from withdrawal. Not everybody has access to this, only the best—the smartest, the brightest, and, excuse the joke, the fastest people, or shall we say those who are discreet in their activities and may have had to make a hasty exit on occasion."

The driver laughed. "She's being silly. It makes you feel young again this whole business, and you don't want to get caught with your neighbor's wife, do you, mate?" He threw back his head and laughed.

Listening to them, Herbert concluded it all sounded like a combination of camaraderie, science, and whatever he'd been involved in so far, which while almost certainly illegal didn't bother him one bit. He wondered if…he pushed the thought to the back of his head, but it popped forward. Maybe he could date again instead of just going to see his mom for company. Maybe one of those nice young adjutants would look at him differently. Knowing what he did now would surely change the effect he had on them. Knowledge was power after all. He was sure with this knowledge he could persuade them on a date. All the sudden his head was buzzing.

"Oh," he said. "What did you do that for?" Startled, he looked at LaVey, genuinely puzzled as to why he had dropped off to sleep and woken to the unpleasant physical effect.

"We're here, sugar," she said. "That was to activate the potions some more." She turned into the driver.

"Oh, okay," stammered Herbert weakly. "I see. Can we not do anything that gives me any more physical distress today?" Damn! He should sound more authoritative than he did, the puny weakling he still was.

"Certainly," LaVey said with the touch of steel Herbert was familiar with in her voice.

The car touched down, and the driver gave a hand to Herbert to sit up. Through the window, he saw a throng of people disembarking from electric vehicles. Why didn't the city know they were here?

"You can hop out now," instructed LaVey, exiting from the car. "What a dullard," she whispered loudly to the driver.

Inside, shiny glowing people were talking to each other.

"This way," said LaVey, and she pulled Herbert past the tables of food and past the bronze faces some of whom he recognized.

First of all, he recognized Proctor Casio.

"Hi," Herbert said.

Casio shrugged.

Then Herbert saw a popular singer at wedding events. He hurriedly walked behind LaVey, a young man opened a door for them. LaVey guided Herbert inside. She passed him a knife.

"It's your turn," she said.

On an assortment of tables inside the room, he saw cages and, in the cages, animals: chickens, a rabbit, a poorly looking hamster, some larger animals that stared dolefully into the distance.

LaVey gave him a push. "You know what to do," she said.

He looked down at the knife and his hand, then he looked back at the cages. Surely, she couldn't mean him to? He looked back at her. Her eyes narrowed, and she tapped her wrist. Herbert hopped from foot to foot. This was disgusting. He could smell fecal matter. When he had had an imbibement before and partaken of an infusion, it had been in spotlessly clean medical rooms with doctors administering the serum and facilitators in scrubs. This room just grossed him out. Perhaps he'd go back to the party and think about it and maybe review his association with LaVey. Herbert turned toward the door.

LaVey put her strong arms on him and chucked him under the chin. "I can't let you go!"

Herbert looked at her. "What on Panacea do you mean, LaVey? I'll go if I want to!"

With a swift leathery motion, she reached down and had his balls on her hand, squeezing and testing.

"Are you sure about that, Herbert?"

It felt like he had a tooth in his groin. His anger turned into alarm, and the desire to crawl away from the pain led him in the direction of the cages.

"You forgot this, sweetie," said LaVey. She handed him another different knife with pulls on the handle.

He made the mistake of catching it with the wrist of his watchband, and it bounced off and schicked a cut in the fat of his thumb.

Some of the animals smelt blood and started up with restless barks and groans and moans and grunts.

"Mmmm," said LaVey. "They can smell you. Now go hurry and make your choice and do what you have to do. Finish the investiture. There is a bowl under each cage. Don't be too long. There's a party in your honor. Go right to the back and look in every cage. Take your time to walk around and see what's on offer."

Weirdly hearing this, Herbert had stopped feeling afraid. She had just contradicted herself, he noticed. She told him to hurry up and then take his time. He was feeling relaxed again. He supposed he would have to go through with this. Remotely, he felt some hot pain. He felt some pain in his groin ebbing away. They really were quite serious about this. What had he to lose from participating in a ritual? And so far, he had gained health and cell renewal. If he could bring himself to act, he still had much to gain. Herbert paced and stopped at a cage. There was a young kitten, a black kitten with a bandage on one paw. It looked ill, and it blinked and shut its eyes. He moved on to a rabbit, then another rabbit, a noisy cockerel, then a lizard that wasn't worth his while. Another a large tiger lizard, a spider monkey. Moving back to a cage with a black hen, he grabbed it by his neck, held it upside down, and sliced the knife across its neck. It went still, and blood poured from the gash.

"Well, hurry up," said LaVey, and suddenly, there were three men beside him. One bled the chicken, one handed him wipes, and another one high-fived him and led him past the line of cages. The last cage he looked at, then he blinked in the half light.

The monkey looks amazingly like a little child, Herbert thought.

Now the door was opening, and he was thrown into pulsing music.

"Sit here," someone said, and they pushed them into a leather seat. Somebody else grabbed his slides and removed them. Then all of a sudden, he was getting a foot massage by a comely young woman no older than one of the adjutants. Again, he blinked his eyes as the figure came into focus. Was that the girl from his office? Really, he was so tired though he did still feel funny about parts of tonight he couldn't be worrying about things. So that was the investiture. Herbert closed his eyes and lay back.

TROVE

During the first few days of the apothecarists' stay, the city of Trove revealed a host of children who enthusiastically enlisted the trio of Alex, Hannah, and Eliza in their games. Mostly in the dusty main street of Trove. They rolled hoops of birch together down the street and hurled the same hoops at pegs outside Basil's forge. Basil came outside and shook his fist in the air as shopkeepers had done at children since the dawn of time. The bravest children snuck past him and put magnetite into his coffee grounds, which he didn't realize until he pooped out heavy black leavings.

It was a symbiotic relationship more than anything, mused Eva, as she dodged past a ruddy- cheeked redhead brandishing a bow and a quiver of hopefully blunt arrows.

"They're quite helpful, really," said Basil. "They help me separate the silica sand from the magnetite. Even if some of it does end up in my coffee." He laughed.

"I pulled the same kind of pranks when I was their age. I'm wondering…" Eva said to Basil. A thought came to her. "I wonder if they are here so often because they see you as a role model?"

Basil stood there in his great coat, his thoughts impenetrable, as she looked him up and down.

It didn't do a person any harm to work with metals and horses. The thought came to her unbidden. She noted he was quite muscular. "Good," she said, thinking out loud. "You're… you're a good role model for the kids. Some of them might follow in your footsteps."

A rather brassy Eva that observed her reaction to attractive men popped up and said, *Ooh a good role model for the kids that sounds like a pick-up line, Eva. One classy pick-up line.* She told the cheeky Eva to "settle down" and stop nagging at her with her outrageous observations. Levelheaded Eva had problems to solve.

Basil watched her curiously. "Their latent psychic abilities are even more developed than our generation," he said after a pause.

"Really, how so?" asked Eva curiously. "They're able to manipulate solid objects with their minds more than we ever could at that age. It was always a curiosity if we could move a knife or a fork over the table or hover a ball a little." said Basil.

Eva watched as the boy with the quiver of arrows cast the bow aside and, with his mind, sent each arrow into the air to come raining down on a range of targets: a breastplate on a mannequin waiting to be polished, a chicken that squawked and ran under a trough, a silver urn, a friend. Eva was pleased to see the arrows were indeed blunt.

Basil continued, "All these kids are actually quite useful at manipulation of solids and matter. They can't move big objects or use things as missiles to cause serious damage though that might be the first thing that comes to mind. Their most useful ability is sorting the metal sands. They reach in and have an affinity with one particular element and convince it to gather the same grains together. It's hard to explain. It's just unusual, but every generation is a little more gifted telepathically than the previous generations, so I guess it's not so surprising. I just know that our most sophisticated gift was farsight, and our intuition was quite developed. More highly developed gifts could be quite daunting, I guess is what I'm saying."

He wasn't the nimblest with expressing sophisticated ideas, and an audience made him anxious. And on top of that, he felt the urge to impress Eva, one of the smartest women he had ever met.

Eva put him out of his misery. "The term for it is 'tara kinesis.' 'Tara' means Earth. 'Kinesis' means movement. The ability to move earth metals with thought. It's not at all prevalent in Destin, so I wonder why it has manifested here in Trove."

Suddenly, they heard shouting and yelling from outside. Eva hurried outside, pushing the swing door open. In front of her eyes, a skirmish was taking place. About seven boys were pushing another boy into the ground and punching him.

"Take that, lizard," said the biggest to the boy. "Take that for dropping rocks on my little sister. Take that you turd."

"What on earth are you doing?" Eva demanded of the group.

The youth on the ground signaled help to Eva as the other boys warily moved back, throwing one last punch his way.

The boy looked up at Eva with a bruised lip and a cut above his eye. Putting his weight on his hands, he formed a bridge and said as best as he could, "I didn't mean any harm."

Eva put one arm in front of the boy and the other on his shoulder to try and get him to relax, then turned to address the rest of the group.

"Can we work it out with words? Guys, how old are you? Twelve? Your mom told me your age, David Conley. And what's your name? Thomas? And what's his name?" She gestured to the boy who had been receiving the blows.

"Oh, he doesn't have a name," said one boy.

"Bad Luck's his name," said another.

"And what's your name, Robert?" asked Eva, unfazed, addressing another of the group.

The boys started assembling themselves into a more formal line, and Eva could feel the weight of information about to burst forth from then.

Thomas spoke first. "My sister was panning for gold in the river. We occasionally still get small gems. It's nothing valuable, but we occasionally get gold and amazonite. She was having fun. And then this idiot picked up rock—a veritable boulder—threw it and it hit her on the head and now they said"—the boy crumpled into a heap—"and now they say she might lose her eye or go blind."

Oh dear, Eva thought. "Okay here's what we're going to do. Thomas and David and No Name, you boys stay here. The rest of you, the sun is getting low so you go off home and see if you can annoy your parents until they feed you."

The other five boys jostled a little and kicked the ground and some stones with their toes, but they eventually headed off down a lane bordered with hyacinths, threading past houses with smoke coming out of chimneys.

"Thomas, turn and look at No Name and shake hands. And, David, I want you to witness this," said Eva.

The two boys did as they were told and having diffused the energy between the two boys with this interaction, Eva touched Thomas on the shoulder and turned him to look at her.

Lifting his chin, she said, "I understand you're worried about your sister. Where is she?"

Thomas replied, "She's in the infirmary."

"Can I visit? Can we visit?" requested Eva.

Thomas glanced at No Name, scowled, and glanced at David. Finally, he replied, "I guess he"—and by "he," he meant No Name— "can come if David comes."

Eva responded carefully. "David's job can be to lead the way." Then she said to Thomas, "And, honey, I'm sure it's not as bad as you fear." She smiled at the bruised boy hopping from foot to foot on the side of the road. "Things got a bit out of hand, didn't they? And I haven't forgotten your name from when you were all friends. It's Corey."

The boy nodded, and the four of them walked down the road to the infirmary.

Sure enough, when they got there, Thomas's sister was sitting up in bed eating sherbet quite happily.

"This is my sister, Ashley," said Thomas.

"What are you eating, honey?" asked Eva.

"Waterfall sherbet," said Ashley, smiling. She had a bandage on her head, but she looked quite well otherwise.

The sherbet arranged itself in the air between Ashley and Eva, then tipped itself into the bowl. Ashley leaned forward and used a little metal spoon to collect and eat some and laughed as the sherbet evaded her to rise into the air and tip into the bowl again.

"Would you like some?" she said.

Eva laughed. "No, my days of eating sherbet are far behind me," she said. "That is some fancy candy you have. Is it imbued?"

Ashley shrugged. "I guess."

"Tell me why you are here," said Eva "I'll try and help you if I can. I'm a medic, an apothecarist."

"Oh, we were just playing around," said Ashley. "We were moving stones in the river to play frogger. A game that people played based on an extinct animal called frogs. They hopped in water. So we were moving rocks because we can't hop or walk on water, and then our new friend, he pushed it with his mind, and it hurt me. And Thomas, well, he's very protective. He panicked."

Eva thanked Ashley and stood to chat with the doctor who had just come in to check on Ashley and consented to Eva's use of herbs to hasten Ashley's recovery. They shook hands, and Eva gathered up the boys, and they left.

ALEX

It is quite comfortable in the stables, thought Alex. Compared to the terrain he was used to sleeping as a bounty hunter, on bare ground or, worse, rock or shale and piled up leaves, this was luxury. He noticed that sleeping in a bed for the few nights he'd been sleeping at the apothecary in Destin had made him soft. Glancing over at Terry, he saw one eye open looking back at him. It blinked and shut again. Alex groaned.

A white mouse hat shot out from under the blanket and ran over to a pile of straw where it retrieved a chunk of straw that was almost its size and dragged it back to the blanket.

Terry reached one hand out, scooped both the mouse and the straw up without opening his eyes, popped it in his breast pocket, idly selecting one piece of straw upon which he started chewing.

ALEX AND TERRY TALK

"It's morning," said Alex pointedly.

A hand pulled the blanket over Terry's head, and the blankets snored.

Mock snored, Alex thought.

Alex thought about his options: He could poke the blanket, he could yell at the blanket, or he could ignore the blanket. He discarded those options and decided to entreat to the blanket's better nature.

"Hey, Terry. Hey, how are you after the journey?"

The blanket snored on.

And Alex continued, "Well, you know, you just left your home. And here we are, and these horses are in good condition, so we've got a moment. Are we going to talk?"

With an audible groan, the blankets got thrown to the side, and Terry sat up into a cross-legged position. He slapped his left thigh and said, "You talk too much."

Alex was startled. Terry seemed anything but the happy-go-lucky Asperian he'd come to know and quite frankly despise.

Terry continued as though he could read Alex's mind. "You arrived here, took over, we moved on, and you got in everyone's face and talked so f—— much. It's time to give it a rest."

Foxy ran in and sat on his haunches beside Terry and eyeballed Alex with hostility.

Terry continued, "What's my name, Alex? It's Terry. It's not 'Hey You.' It's been a string of orders. 'Hey you, do this.' 'Hey you, do that.' You treat me like a pawn, Alex! I'm not a f—— pawn. I'm a person, and just because I pick up the rear doesn't mean I'm not fighting as hard as you, you arrogant prick."

Foxy growled. He yipped like he was calling to something; and two exotic-looking cats, white with brownish bibs, made the way elegantly through the stable and came to sit by side Foxy, one on each side.

Alex was now confronted with four animals—a rather testy Terry, a fox, and two cats. Alex made a consolatory gesture to Terry and leaned into one leg.

"It's hella hard for me," he said. "I'd only been at the apothecary a matter of days, not even a month. I'm worried as hell about Eliza. I guess the urge to control the situation turned me into somewhat of a tyrant. I'm sorry."

The cats purred, and Foxy snickered.

Terry regarded Alex coolly and stuck out his hand. "I think we can forget about going back to Destin for now. It's heartbreaking, but let's see what good we can bring about around here."

RAVENNA

Ravenna crouched low on the horses back and galloped across the plains. She didn't care how far she went; she was just focused on riding, on putting distance between her and Castle Ridich. The horse too, picking up her mood, was intent on gaining ground. To please his mistress, to hot breathe through the night, hooves pounded the earth relentlessly as his heritage and breeding demanded. With every bit of resolve and putting everything into the gallop and the receding day, Ravenna hunted without prey and held and called the horse to fly across the land. Its immensely strong four-chambered heart pounded its way across the plains and gave everything. For a moment, Ravenna was scared that an obstacle night rise up from the plains and trip Percheron, and a terrible fate might befall the horse and its mistress, but then she remembered from riding out a short distance from the castle that there were no real hazards, least within the estate walls because of poverty and the aftereffects of the breaching. There were no rivers. There were no jumps. Nothing grew really here. Nothing had grown for generations. What was worth having had been gathered up and given to her father by his vassals, by those who swore fealty and passed up any precious metals and livestock. They got his protection and lands to eke out a living, and there was enough to eat. But out here, there was no plenitude, no wealth, just a seeping misery and the bad that afflicted many.

Merchants that came by every weekend told tales of far-off lands and towns with commerce and taverns, but there were no real towns in these outlying lands and definitely no taverns.

Ravenna smiled with a moue of amusement even while every muscle measured the horses every stride. How she would love to sit in a tavern, in a bawdy atmosphere full of life and joke with townspeople instead of stagnating in her father's protected castle. Now she had nothing and everything to make a fresh start. She had a horse, and she would ride and see what the day brought. She kept her head down low on the cob's neck. The tireless Percheron pounded on, shoulders over hocks. Arrowing through the dusk, the sun set, but Percheron kept riding tirelessly into the night, into uncertainty, into the wide open plains.

What had her history teacher called them? The Steppes. She would go and see what the future held. Strike and rise and strike and rise and strike went Percheron's hooves in a regular pattern. The turf was impacted enough to speed their passage somewhat.

"I think you're gorgeous, boy," said Ravenna to her steed, gulping in oxygen. "We'll find a home, a stable for you, and you'll have your fill of carrots and straw. Maybe I'll find a stable hand to have some fun with."

At that point, pounding along on the horse with a wide open future, a blissful feeling started in her toes and coursed through her body. She was not just a person whose future was dictated by biological drives and who was at the mercy of other people. She was traveling into a new future, and though she felt older after her struggles to escape the confines of the castle, she was also eternal, and she was one with this magnificent beast carrying her. Their lives depended on each other, and the magnificence of the partnership lay in this treaty.

"I can hear the thunder of other hooves," she whispered into the horse's neck.

Strike and rise, strike and rise, they thundered across the plains.

"I feel we're not alone," she whispered again into the horse's flowing mane as they traveled along a gentle slope. Then she definitely heard the thundering of other hooves and now a whinny in the wind and the smell of horse leather and their honeyed sweat in the wind. Strike and rise, they still ran tentatively.

Relieved of the burden of thinking, the next time Ravenna heard a whinny, she lifted her head, and a line of black shapes boiled in front of her to cut her off.

She had no choice but to slow and pull around. Her trusty gallant Percheron rounded as she pulled on the reins. So she hadn't been alone after all. She hadn't been alone in how much...how much time had passed? Maybe three to five hours at least? Three of those she had been running and galloping, quite a tiring endeavor for both horse and rider. How long had she been followed? A prickle of fear started in her throat. She slowed to a trot. The black figures from the U shape bowed out around her to give her enough room for locomotion while horse and rider caught their breath and slowed. One of the figures cut off in front and then circled back to ride beside her. Ravenna wasn't one to follow anyone else's lead, and she certainly wasn't going to start now, so she kept trotting. The ground was flat, the turf was good, her horse was not tuckered out, and she needed to make ground. But all of a sudden, Percheron was coming to a halt. The other rider had a hand on his bridle, and his horse was snickering to Percheron. And now she, Ravenna, looked like she was about to make the acquaintance of her stalker on horseback with an entourage.

"Well, this is flattering. Why do you keep a simple stable hand company while they get some fresh air and learn the limits of their contumacious cob?" Ravenna questioned the hooded shape on the brown gelding.

The hooded shape drew back the cowl, and Ravenna made out an oval shape of a head, two eyes, but no more distinct features than that. The eyes were looking past her, then one hand drew the cowl back, and Ravenna noticed some symbols drawn on the inside of the cowl.

"We are yours to command," said the shadowed figure.

He still had no defining features that would allow Ravenna to place him. Nothing.

The forty other mounted riders flanking the spokesperson made no movement, and the air was still.

Ravenna was absolutely flummoxed as to the nature and intent of the riders.

"I have no idea. I have not any understanding of what you talk about," she said, trying to sound authoritative rather than petulant. But not having much success. "I am riding out on my day off from my master's stables." She ran out of words and thought it best to be quiet.

Her horse harrumphed.

The figure replied, "The shapes you make with your words indicate you are not simple. We have been searching for you for some time. Many in numbers are we. You are high-born Ravenna of Castle Ridich and have made many mistakes."

At this, Ravenna bristled. She didn't think she'd made many mistakes. She had made some mistakes, sure, but who didn't make mistakes? She had been a bit rough on servants and stable hands at the castle, but now here she was impersonating a stable hand. She was all too ready to get down and be one of the commoners and take anything life meted out to her because palace life was killing her.

The figure on the horse watched the expressions on her face motionlessly as she moved thoughts through her head. He only spoke again when she looked at them pleadingly.

"We know that you seek plain living, Ravenna. Quite and quietude. Common life. The minimum of comforts in your surroundings where your body does not betray you from over indulgence. Solitude and magnificence. The life of a horsewomen or horseman. This is commendable."

The figure dropped their riding robes completely. The very leftmost and rightmost riders flanking him held up lanterns lit, as far as Ravenna could make out, with fireflies. Ravenna was staring at a tall man, on horseback, now naked, though certainly his manhood and nipples were obscured by a saddle and tack. She felt more exposed than he was. Flushing warmly, she tried to brazen it out.

"What did you mean by 'you're mine to command'? I demand you tell me!"

He looked at her piercingly in the half-light thrown by the lanterns. Ravenna held his gaze, determined not to be the first to look away. The man's horse was still. Percheron sniffed and let out a hot warm breath; and Ravenna, transfixed, forgot there was an audience. She tried to think of the next clever thing to say.

"I really must be getting home to my master," she said, forgetting the man had already called her Ravenna of Castle Ridich and almost certainly knew who she was. It wasn't a random guess.

One lip curled up slightly on the opposition's visage. Ravenna was trying to get control of the situation, but oh Guardians! She realized was not in control. She was alone and not in control. No servants to call out to or Daddy to run to. Where the heck was Brynn to save her from herself or from this…this be-straddled knave on horseback? And could she be aroused! She was excited by the encounter. Egad!

All of a sudden the man grabbed the pommel of his saddle and…

Oh, what was he doing?

He was bringing his feet underneath him, momentarily he was staring straight at her. And then he somersaulted over her head, all skin and hot manhood, and all of a sudden, he was behind her. His arms reached around her waist, hot breath in her ear.

Ravenna squeaked.

The intruder to her person and her peace of mind spoke.

"We are yours to command when your mind is disciplined enough to will it."

Ravenna made no move to wriggle free. How could she? She was grounded to her horse, and though held loosely, she had effectively been captured from behind by the stronger individual.

Still with one arm loosely around her waist, he spoke one more word, her name.

"Ravenna."

Then leaning forward, he took one side of her neck between his teeth and then the other applying a gentle pressure. Letting go of her waist, he somersaulted back to his horse. He sat there looking at her directly.

Presently, he said, "Ride three hours in that direction. You will find a kolkhoz. They have your bed waiting. They will turn your horse out. Get ready to work for your dinner. We will meet again, but first, you must learn to control your mind—and your body." He run his eyes over her figure, not without appreciation.

He spun his horse around, and the rest of the riders fell in behind him. They peeled off in six spokes in a pinwheel formation and stopped waiting for instruction.

Ravenna, sitting straight up, realized she must have been riding for longer than she had thought. She could see the riders clearly as they moved off. It was the very beginning of dawn. Behind her, from where she had ridden, all she could see was straight plains in the early dawn light. In the direction the hooded stranger had pointed, she could see a copse of trees and, in the far distance, a table-topped mountain. A feature of the terrain she did not recollect having knowledge of.

The horses and their riders were waiting for instruction. They all had those mysterious hoods with strange symbols adorning them covering their heads fully. Only the man who had accosted Ravenna had cutouts with where eyes should be. It was an eerie sight. Finally, the man gave the instruction to leave, and they rode off into the direction from where Ravenna had ridden. She was weary now, having ridden all night and then having that strange interaction with the rider. She found she could do nothing but turn right in the direction he had sent her.

Clip-clop, clip-clippity, clop. And with a slow trot, she took Percheron, who was tiring like his mistress, along the plains, toward the trees.

MAGDA

"It's time," said Magda Heartwood. "Now centuries past the reawakening, the Guardians' disquiet had grown. We must show the humans and the Fellows the evil unleashed."

The mighty walnut tree submitted this to the vast forest canopy. Branches rustled. The dart frogs sensed the shift in frequency of the mighty Guardians' creaks and groans and hopped in agitation.

Magda emitted a series of olfactory, visual, and electrical signals that Bridget and Greta received and amplified. The Guardians called the forest into sederunt.

SEDERUNT

Hearing something out of place, Maven went outside and looked up at the stars.

River was passing by and stopped to see what had caught her attention.

"Why is it so quiet?" River asked Maven. "You can't hear any of the usual chirping and croaking. The forest is silent all of a sudden."

Maven replied jovially to the earnest little upturned face, "The forest has closed shop, River! It's a once in a lifetime experience. Why did you come past right now?"

"I guess I wanted to see what you were doing, Maven," said River.

"Let's go over and sit on the park bench near the clearing," Maven said. "I'm going to show you something."

Together they walked over to the park bench. They sat together— the older Bran who was about to complete her apprenticeship and the younger inquisitive boy who was eager to learn anything he could from the elder Bran. Fireflies drifted past. The shudder and screaming and screeching of dead, dry wooden branches, audible in the night, made for an uncharacteristically noisy backdrop. Though nothing living was audible.

"It's noisy even though there is no wind," said River eventually.

A bat flew overhead. In the far distance, two ringed eyes peered out from the underbrush watching them. Dark nocturnal eyes cautiously looking for an opportunity to cadge food scraps.

River elbowed Maven. "Look, a raccoon," he said. "It's not moving though."

"It's not moving, no," said Maven. "Nor are the fireflies! They are just hanging in the air."

River said, "Maven, what are we here for?"

"See those fireflies," said Maven.

Eventually, River gasped. "They're just hanging there, like a picture, aren't they?"

Maven chucked him on the chin. "Now look up. In this same fashion, the stars won't move."

"Oh, that's impossible. We're not at the center of the universe. So therefore, they can't stop." River was pleased with his logic. He said, "Panacea is the one that's rotating, and I wish I had bought food because I'm going to be hungry if we're going to be out here for a while. And why are those fireflies still hanging in the air?"

Maven said mischievously, "Now you know why. You just spoke of the reason why it's impossible for them not to move just like the stars. Therefore, we're rotating around them." She chuckled.

"Hey!" said River. He elbowed her, and the pair laughed.

"The forest is talking," said Maven to her interested charge, who was drawing circles in the air around the fireflies with a piece of straw.

"I know," said River. "I know the forest talks. It's in constant communication. I learned about the electrical, visual, and scent signals." He bounced on the seat excitedly. "Trees are immune to the electromagnetic earth pulses, and everything would be dead if they weren't! Oh my Guardians, This is so fun being up so late." He bounced. "So what's happening?" River asked. "What's happening?"

The firefly sparkled and hung in the air, and the raccoon gazed at them with bleary eyes.

Maven put her head on one hand and responded thoughtfully, "We're in a dampening effect so that the Guardians of the forest can communicate widely with the whole forest. The older forest with the newer growth and sometimes the animals. It's a vast auditorium of trees and mushrooms, the mycorrhizal network that stretches underground and other assorted forest denizens. Do you get what I mean? When they're in normal time, the electrical impulses they transmit go very slowly, but over the generations, the great forest brain managed to slow down everything else so that the trees can communicate in tree time in a psionic field. The Guardian trees, the oldest trees of the forest, call it sitting in sederunt. They sit rooted to pass on information. It's a little complicated. We're talking college horticulture and chromo kinesis."

River's jaw dropped open at the unfamiliar words, and he hung on to Maven's arm.

Maven continued, "We are right in the altered temporal field, so we don't move as fast as everything outside. The fireflies are so little, so they just hang there. Aren't they pretty? And everything so far, far away. Well, that just looks as though that doesn't move either. I've only seen it once before, and that was when I was little, and it was before a short war that swept past us, the War of Himenloch. The giants from the northeast came through. It didn't affect us very much as we didn't come to their attention. This is far more serious. The trees are very worried about something."

River thought of a question. "How will we know when it's finished," he asked.

Maven answered, "Something unusual will happen. The discussion will happen in tree time, and generally the first part of the discussion happens out of human and fellow hearing. It's going on under our feet. If you dig your toes in, you'll feel the communication. You can catch some of the thoughts that are carried by the mycorrhizal network. You might see a picture in your mind's eye. But it won't be the big picture that they are drawing. The way that trees think in sederunt is faster than the way that we think, so they share information at the individual tree level via the mycelium, and all the spirits that have passed are invited as well."

"Wait, the spirits!" said River excitedly. "You mean ghosts."

"Well, technically," said Maven, "ghosts are an old wives' tale from before we knew of rebirth and could come in and out of ascension. No, these are tree spirits. The life force of trees that have passed. Or the life force of trees that can move in and out of trees that are so old and vastly great hearted that they can for a short time become corporal. The name for these spirits is druids. And you won't find that in high school biology, young man. That is High Magic 101 and Advanced Forest Care."

"Have we always had tails?" asked River of Maven.

"Pretty much," said Maven. "But you know this. Are you bored?"

"No," said River thoughtfully. "I was out picking berries one night near the edge of the forest a week ago, and I was just hanging out, and I ended up kicking it with a human. I wondered why would you leave the forest and lose your tail and go and live on the plains. It just doesn't make any sense to me."

Maven nodded. She chucked him under the chin. "I know, sweetie. You're about the age I was when I was asking those questions, after interacting with different species. How come they live the way that they do, all awkwardness and overconsumption?"

Maven tried to think how she would explain it in language suited to his age.

"I don't think they're unhappy, and many of them are able to bond with animals and have farsight and other psionic abilities, so really, there isn't that much of a difference between humans and we Fellows Bran. It's just that they're missing a tail, and they've forsaken forest living. And instead of living in trees, they live in dead materials for dwellings when we live as one with the forest."

They'd been sitting for quite a while, but Maven and River weren't tired. It almost felt like a slumber party to River. And Maven wasn't so old that she couldn't resist the temptation to tell River a scary tall tale.

"The trees move," she said, "when no one's watching."

"Oh, I know that," said River "Mostly just around the riverbanks where the soil is wet."

"Oh, you're one step ahead of me," said Maven. "I can't scare you! You're quite the grown-up Fellow. But did you know this? They say that humans caused the reawakening because of a curse! A curse passed down through the generations."

River gasped theatrically. "Does it affect Fellows too?" he asked.

"Just humans," replied Maven. "It's one of those curses where humans are doomed to repeat the same mistakes until the curse is broken! Like the bedtime stories told to babies, where princesses are put to sleep for a thousand years by wicked stepmothers until the prince comes along and frees them of the curse. After the reawakening, the Earth was renamed Panacea. Wise people, the Guardians, were put in charge initially. But humans went forth and split into tribes.

"Basically, they were mean to each other and built hierarchies even though there were lots of resources for all of the Guardians' peoples. They were warned not to build hierarchies by the Guardians who sent floods and winged messengers from the skies. And even though the saints gave them clues to find the way to more gracious principled living, the cursed humans ignored the saints."

"How does that work?" asked River.

"I don't know for sure," replied Maven. "But I believe if a queen or someone elevated to rule over other people got too uppity, a saint would appear and do good works and life would get good for the people again.

"But time and history proved again and again that when most people had climbed down from the trees, they turned to making so many structures out of dead things and were mainly concerned with acquiring new stuff to show off to their neighbors. They were so busy building hierarchies that they stopped talking to each other and just made war on each other, making war across borders and across vast seas. Most people wanted to be left alone to have children and pray to a Guardian of their choice, but some bad people constantly wanted to make war and take all the money and all the dead stuff, and eventually, they made a machine so powerful it caused the reawakening and the Earth's sister, the Orb, to tumble out of the sky and fall into the sea. All the marvelous inventions that man found along the way no longer worked because the Earth was so angry it stopped some of the machines from working. The end." Maven hopped off the bench and curtseyed with a dramatic flourish.

"You're a good storyteller, Maven," said River, cuddling up to her as she sat back down on the bench beside him.

The raccoon was still peering out from the park bench opposite, only now there was a skunk with five little babies lined up beside the racoon.

River noticed and gasped. "Don't move quickly," joked River. "We've got company."

The aroma came to Maven over the air, and she said, "I don't think we'll get skunked. They usually save it for the humans and their nosy pets." Maven nudged River with her elbow. "That we can smell mommy skunk with her baby skunks means the field has been altered, so the trees must have finished sitting in sederunt."

"Why is it called sitting?" asked River.

"There is a universal agreement that the trees stay rooted," replied Maven, winking at River.

"I thought they didn't have a choice," said River.

"Remember what you've seen down by the river, River," said Maven.

"Yes, but those are willow trees, and I assumed that it was just by the river, and willow trees are the celebrity of trees, and their moods are quite changeable," said River, laughing.

"Ha ha." Maven laughed with him. "After sederunt, things might get a little interesting. From what I remember afterward, they like to stretch their roots. During sederunt, due to the universal agreement of trees, they stay rooted. But at the end of sederunt, some of them have a boost of energy. And with no mortals around to witness them, no time flow to disturb them, they can get around as nimbly as you or I. Just watch!"

A mighty creak came from the cedar tree behind the park bench that River and Maven were sitting on.

River jumped off excitedly. "Do you think they're moving, walking?" he asked, and he shot his head around to check he hadn't scared the skunks into inadvertently drenching him and Maven. But they were still just watching the pair, and the raccoon was sleeping.

"Come and sit, River," said Maven. "We're not going to see a performance. Imagine, wouldn't it be something—all the trees cavorting in front of us. Big old walnut trees like Magda Heartwood or Cindy Cedarwood."

At that moment, they heard Cindy Cedarwood scrape and chirr.

"Tree speak," said Maven abstractedly.

"Cederunt," said River gleefully.

"We'll wait a little longer and go home if nothing else happens," declared Maven. *Fellows*, thought Magda, *slower than humans but still too quick to move.*

With any luck, they would get drowsy, and Cindy could talk directly with them via druid sight. She would call on those trees with headier scents to start releasing their pheromones. Magda messaged the Flowering Quince and Hawthorne, and the air was soon pungent with a sweet aroma.

River put his head on Marvin's shoulder, and she was surprised to find herself drowsy.

I should be more used to this, I'm older, she thought.

She followed the example of the raccoon and the skunks.

I'll just lie down for a minute, she thought, and shutting her eyes, her breathing soon matched River's, and they breathed in the pungent, sweet smell of flowering plants of hawthorn and jasmine. And so the animals and the Fellows Bran slumbered. And not long after, the dreams and visions started.

NICOLETTA AND TAN

"Ow," said Nicoletta. "You kicked me!"

"Can you not yell in my ear?" said Tan. "I was having a nice dream."

"How can you dream at a time like this?" quizzed Nicoletta. "Our kids, including the extra ones we picked up along the way, need us!"

"Didn't you say that Eliza is currently with a tribe of warrior woman?" said Tan.

"Yes, as for Eva, Terry, and Hannah, they are in Trove waiting for us!" said Nicoletta.

"Well, we better get on the road, honey," said Tan, amused at her surly tone.

"Don't you 'honey' me," replied Nicoletta, rolling over and tugging his ear.

They were lying on a futon in Nicoletta's sleeping quarters, which was also the office, which was also the kitchen.

A piece of chalk lazily picked itself up in the air and moved over to the blackboard on the wall and started drawing.

Nicoletta and Tan watched as it drew a picture of a dog and a cat fighting and then an exclamation mark and then it signed itself off with the letters *M. A. Y.* and an underscore.

"We're being watched," said Nicoletta, laughing.

"Well," said Tan. "I guess we had better get on the road! That's May and Doug's way of saying, 'It's time for the family reunion.' It's sad that we need to put Destin behind us. But we must go where we must go."

Nicoletta demurred, "I'm not so sure! We still have two goats, five chickens, a rabbit and Ruby's kittens to home. Shouldn't we wait another day or so?"

Tan brushed a stray lock of hair from Nicoletta's eyes and said, "Doug and May were quite clear. The apothecary has been seized. It's empty. We don't know if we could have prevented it, but it's no use crying over spilled milk, Nicoletta. We have to forge our way forward toward Trove. We know from our own two eyes and Doug and May that darkness could come again to Panacea. What happened here at the apothecary is only a shadow of what is happening in our entire world if ascension is being affected.

"Let's drop the animals to Ruby. She'll love the chance to gossip with Stubby and who knows, they may form the nexus of a counter to the forces being deployed against us. Then we will group with Eva and Hannah and Terry. And come what may, things will come right if we stick together."

"I do hope you're right," said Nicoletta. "It just seems like a rather abrupt ending. And who will feed my horses and my falcons, my lovely falcons?"

"Stubby will," said Tan. "And he's here in the lane every day delivering mail." Tan sat up on the edge of the bed and clapped his hands on his legs. "Right. Let's pack!"

"I'm taking one falcon with me," said Nicoletta. "And that's all there is to it. My fastest, strongest, darling Maleficent."

CARLOTTA

"Cecil, the mayor has ordered fifty thousand troops to mobilize leeward of the Arcadian Steppes," Carlotta commanded peremptorily.

"*Leeward* is a seafaring term, ma'am," said Cecil.

"Oh, you know what I mean, Cecil. I mean, downwind of Destin," said Carlotta. She wouldn't let that old fool joust with her and get away thinking he was so smart. She had attained her first self-appointed mission, which was to barrack a whole lot of troops. Who would have thought Destin could have housed that many servicemen? She did. She'd been keeping an eye on real estate for the past five years, and it was surprising how many empty buildings there were. It was as though people had stopped having so many children. She didn't hate children. She wished she could have a baby. A baby would be a fantastic accessory to her ambitions! But a baby was for those who believed in the cycle of life and thereafter and who were committed to help the next generation by moving through ascension and taking the passover vow. That sounded like mediocrity. Screw that. She was going to accumulate as much power and wealth as possible in this life, by hard work and now by brute force! She would bypass Ascension, and she would dock herself elsewhere and come back when she was good and ready. In this life, all she was concerned about was gaining power and influence. And what she could gain in the way of favors! Favors were what made the world go round.

"Stella," she called to the girl in the next office, "you have children, don't you?"

"Yes, and I'm a grandmother," Stella said proudly. She came in and stood upright and still, rounding out her shoulders. "I have three girls, and I just found out I'm pregnant with my fourth—a boy and a new soul. So we're going to have a big celebration on New Souls Day next month. Three children already, but you wouldn't know, I'm hardly showing!"

"Actually, Stella, I'm quite sad," said Carlotta. "I can't have children, and I have no one to contact in ascension. Perhaps my ancestors are freshly borns. Anyway, I didn't want to make anyone else melancholy about my woes."

"A trouble shared is a trouble quartered," said Stella.

"Quite," said Carlotta.

"Maybe I could babysit your kids one day," said Carlotta, thinking it wouldn't hurt her own image, and she would be able to call on Stella for a favor. Stella had no idea of her motives, the poor simple creature.

"I should think that might be okay," said Stella. Then she squealed, "There is a large hairy spider crawling its way to me. Oh, where did that come from?"

"I have no idea. Where is it?" lied Carlotta, who had enticed it with thoughts of a meal to just above Stella and then removed its suction, so it dropped just so in front of her. It was the small things that gave Carlotta pleasure. She smirked. "Here let me take the spider. I think it's a tarantula! It's meant to be in the Resurrection laboratories. How get in here? Maybe it came in on some papers." Carlotta lied as easily as she breathed. "It's a real mystery," she said, knowing full well it had come from a council lab tasked with restoring a tarantula population. And who needed babies when one had spiders and snakes and venom and crawlies galore to play with?

Dismissing Stella, Carlotta turned herself to her next task. It was time Carlotta got rid of her good-hearted stragglers who were challenging her. She opened her desk drawer and pulled out the comms advisor she had convinced the mayor she needed for when he was "away," and donning it brought up comms and allocated maps to the left of her vision and the module she called War Room to the right of her vision. She really was quite pleased with herself as she had done the module development and linking herself. She had little stylized figures for each of the individuals who were in place ready to carry out her orders.

"Hey, guys," she said to her grunts, the soldiers who were going to carry out her goals.

"Hey, Carlotta. We're ready to take out any trash or do any town surveillance as we discussed," said one.

"Absolutely," she said to the War Room mirror. "The mayor asked that you go on a reconnaissance mission to see if there are any threats to Destin, and he said he has received intelligence that anyone who is traveling in pairs or alone are a potential threat and should be neutralized and bought in. These were his words, guys." She intentionally sounded like a deputy dippy.

"We got your words loud and clear, miss," said a teenage boy of about nineteen who was taking his deployment very seriously, she was glad to see.

LEAVING TOWN

Tan and Nicoletta trudged along the dusty road, looking to hitch a ride with one of the trucks of fruit or animals that traveled between the outskirts of Destin and Trove. Stubby cycled up.

"It's no use you know," he said. "Carlotta won't let you get away. She has soldiers looking for you." He chewed his great grubby thumb. "They have orders to comb the surrounds for troublemakers, for loners or pairs of travelers. A platoon of fifty soldiers is heading this way!"

Maleficent stretched one wing lazily and combed underneath it, sitting contentedly underneath a tree while the trio talked. Stubby could tell he wasn't being taken seriously, so he talked with more urgency.

"Perhaps hundreds of soldiers are on the way behind me. You will get hurt," he said.

Nicoletta considered the options. She'd suspected the council was going to use force to evict them, but she hadn't thought it would be directed against them on the road. She chucked at her bird. "Tsk, tsk."

Communication passed between them wordlessly. Then Maleficent took flight, and Nicoletta turned back to Stubby for clarification.

"The soldiers are all Carlotta's doing," commented Stubby. "She's running the show at the council. The mayor is just a puppet and a figurehead. What are you doing, Nicoletta?"

"I'm pacing. It helps me think," said Nicoletta.

"Oh dear, I really don't know what you should do," said Stubby. "I think you have maybe half an hour before you'll be in the path of the soldiers. How I happen to know? I overheard her talking about sending soldiers out after she wouldn't pay me, and I told her, 'That's not very nice,' and she made me sick, so something funny is going on there. She has more power than she should."

"How do you mean, made you sick?" asked Nicoletta.

"When I collected her mail, I came up with a rash, and I think she put something on the mail," replied Stubby.

"What kind of rash?" asked Nicoletta.

"I got boils and a nasty cough," said Stubby.

"Hmm," Nicoletta said, "I think I know what that might be. Poison willow and lizard gizzard. What a nasty piece of work indeed."

"What are you going to do?" asked Stubby. "I'm really worried, and you're just pacing."

"I can tell," said Nicoletta thoughtfully. She made the sign of a figure eight in the air above her head.

"Why is it getting dark? And where's Tan? He was just here. There's no trees for him to hide under," Stubby said to the air, puzzled.

"I'm just here with your mail sack," Tan said to Stubby, appearing beside him. "Mind you, it does seem to be somewhat fuller now than when you passed it to me."

"I didn't pass it to you!" said Stubby. "Hey, give me that." As he reached for the mail sack, it dropped on the ground between them, and as Stubby went to pick it up, it emptied its contents onto the ground.

"Oh," said Tan, staring. "I was just expecting plain ole mail. "Where did all those bird feathers come from, Stubby? That's a very interesting collection of bird feathers you have." Tan reached down to collect the assortment of feathers, naming each one as he picked it up.

"Those are not my feathers," said Stubby.

"What the heck, what the finickety heck?" Tan was not fazed. "Tall Grasse, Slender Taupe, Bette Monday, Tishe Breast, Spruce Lover, Little Sparrow, Big Sparrow, Twizzle Hawk…"

"Stop," said Stubby with his hands over his ears. "You're making names up."

Tan winked at him. "Names have to come from somewhere," he said deliberately. "It's not like they just appear unformed. Thought has to be put into them. Names are thought forms that could do mischief if not correctly attached or are mislabeled. This feather is very rare." He held up a purple and scarlet quill.

"What is it?" asked Stubby, wondering if he would wish he hadn't asked.

"A hippogryph feather," Tan replied. "Isn't it curious? It's unmistakable, and its existence contravenes all the laws of the Guardians and evolution. It's an amalgamation of several different animals. It appeared after the reawakening. Legend says that when the world was broken and made anew, these animals appear to shepherd us into a time of peace. Fortunate really, seeing as some animals that you and I know of, that were quite common before the Breaching, like bees and butterflies, became extinct after."

"What else?" asked Stubby.

"Well, there were these birds that were like bees. I know, you're going to think this is a story but seeing as we're waiting for Nicholetta to finish…there were these birds that were the same size as the biggest bees that would hang in the air. Their wings would make a humming sound, hummingbirds," finished Tan.

"You're telling me tall stories," said Stubby. "Bees are extinct."

"Butterflies and hummingbirds, just some of the big losses of the breaching," said Tan glumly.

"But where did all these feathers come from?" said Stubby, scratching his head.

"They were posted, obviously!" said Tan. "The question is, who is the addressee? Hmmmm."

A swirling vortex of clouds had gathered overhead. Lightning was streaking through the clouds. Nicoletta had finished what she had been doing and approached the two men.

"Stubby," she called, "how far away is the first platoon?"

"About five minutes. What are you going to do? They're going to harass you and take you in," said Stubby.

"Fear not, my dear aardvark," said Nicoletta, looking unconcerned.

Just then the trio heard the sound of boots and electric vehicles in the distance. And into their view, perhaps forty men on foot appeared with a couple of armored vehicles taking up the rear. Nicoletta dropped back behind and as she gestured at the sky. Maleficent flew from her hand, and a lightning bolt struck the ground in front of the men, leading the foray toward them.

Tan waved at the men. "How's it going, brothers? I hear we have some rogues around and bad men. Are you searching for them?"

The first soldier, a stocky redhead by the name of Vince, who Tan had known since he was five replied, "The council told us to take in people who are out on their own as there are one or two people they suspect of creating a disturbance and not adhering to council policies. You are to come with us for bag searches."

"Well, blow me down," said Tan. "I just searched this young man's bag right here."

Confused, the officer said, "And why would you search the postman's bag?"

Tan said, "I was looking for the vortex."

The officer asked, "What vortex?"

"The vortex that started the cyclone," said Tan, smiling and thinking the officer was walking into the trap nicely.

"What cyclone?" said the officer.

"The cyclone that gathered together all these feathers," said Tan, and he held the plume of feathers out in front of his face.

Stubby said helpfully, "Those feathers just appeared in my mail bag."

The officer was thrown completely off track and said angrily, "There is no—"

As he spoke, another man pointed and said, "Look, birds! Look, a cyclone!"

And indeed, the angry sky had sent down a column of furious air that was twisting closer as they watched. It circled and circled and came closer and closer. The sky was getting darker.

Tan leaned over to Stubby and said, "I don't want to want to ruin it for you, but it's a trick. Cheap theatrics, but not for those guys. It will seem like a threat to them. And the birds are real."

Stubby replied forlornly, "I just want to be left alone and not find strange stuff in my mail bag."

The owners of the feathers that had landed in poor old Stubby's mailbag took a bearing toward the soldiers, and the officers jumped and hopped from foot to foot as the cyclone funneled closer.

Nicoletta was quite preoccupied now with her runes as she placed them in the sand behind Tan and Stubby.

One officer noticed, "Hey, old lady, stop what you're doing. You must come with us. There's a direct order from the mayor under Section 2578."

The officer walked around behind Tan and Stubby and kicked Nicoletta's runes. There was a flurry of feathers; and a bird shot out of the sky like an arrow, straight for the officer, piercing the surprised guardsman on the forehead. Then a mass of birds flew out of the sky and dispersed among the squad, snapping and piercing and attacking the men the while the cyclone hovered over a cornfield off to the left.

It looked, Stubby noticed, for all the world like a windstorm. But there was no actual wind pulling at them.

"It's an illusion," said Tan.

The men stumbled and bumbled around in complete disarray. Maleficent flew to Nicoletta's outstretched hand, and the two travelers relaxed.

"The horses will be along in a minute," she said to Tan.

The soldiers gathered themselves and, completely undone, fled from whence they had come.

Nicoletta sent a swarm of mini cyclones after them, and as the soldiers paused to look back, they saw the cyclones and redoubled their efforts to race away. Tan doubled over laughing.

"Did you see the look on their faces? Those birds were a nice touch by the by."

Nicoletta looked puzzled. "I didn't call the birds," she said. "I have no idea how they manifested! I laid the runes to cast cyclokinesis but only at the lowest energy level to create the illusion, so I didn't have to clean up afterward. Sandstorms are so tiring to unwind. The mini cyclones chased them off, LOL. Wasn't it fun? I thought we might as well enjoy the fight.

"I tucked a note into Maleficent's collar and sent her to the stable boys at Trove and asked them for two horses to meet us, and fortunately, they got my message because here are our horses right now."

Two ginger geldings galloped up.

"Hello, boys, aren't you fine." Nicoletta swung her leg up over the closest horse and mounted. "We have no tack, but that's okay. We'll just ride bareback, probably chased on foot by these incompetents

217

that Carlotta has called on us. I'll just get our boys names." Nicoletta concentrated. "Okay. I'm sitting on Gingerbread, and you have Sarsaparilla."

"I wish you a safe trip," said Stubby, and he scratched his head. "A hippogriff—well, I never…"

"You forgot something," said Tan. "Take all these feathers. Either the owners will come looking for their feathers at some stage, or you can get your mom to make a feather duster. Tell your mom I said hi, and she owes me a lasagna for cleaning out Polly, the Labrador's ears. You've become an unlikely hero, Stubby. The best kind."

Stubby grimaced, but he took the feathers proffered by Tan.

With the wind on their backs, Nicoletta and Tan turned to the road.

"Giddy up," said Nicoletta, and away she went on Gingerbread, Sarsaparilla following with Tan.

HERBERT

"You look quite delightful in that outfit, my dear," said Herbert to his adjutant.

She blushed and tucked a curl behind her ear.

"Hold all my meetings. I'll be in my office." *Like hell he was going to be in a meeting*, he thought.

He needed an infusion. He went through the ritual of having his thumb pricked and got in his private elevator with his blood analytics and sample for the augments. He had requested that a car be available for his use for an hour.

He arrived at one of the many clinics he had come to be acquainted with after his investiture.

"It's quite calming here," he said to the nurse assistant.

"We're doing a public service," she said. "No one wants these animals. We send them back to the source. You'll get a serum to enhance your abilities to contribute to the construction of Phoenix City."

"Where is Phoenix City?" Herbert asked.

"Where's your knife?" the nurse said in response.

Herbert slid it from his pocket and withdrew it. There was a sheep in a cage, he noted.

The nurse met his gaze and snicked a drop of blood from the sheep.

"I'm not going to auto-infuse you today. Today is a sacrifice day."

Herbert shrugged.

She continued, "By the way, two sacrifices today. We have another initiative, one for you to carry out and one for the initiate."

Herbert shrugged again. "That's the drill," he said. "I want to have lunch afterward. Who's here? Andrew and Sophia? I know they're in your division." He leaned forward to take the knife from the nurse.

Andrew and Sophia seemed somewhat agitated. Herbert sat down at the table and leaned into the discussion.

"We've extended our lives individually. But as a whole, as a community, there is no hunger for taking the next step and wielding power!" Sophia exclaimed with frustration.

"More power?" said Herbert with a question mark in his voice. "What more power do we want? I mean, Andrew, you're a city father and, Sophia, you're a scientist!"

"Oh, Herbert," said Sophia. "You're such a noob."

"Ouch," said Herbert. "That hurts."

"Okay," Sophia conceded. "You're an innocent. You've been stuck on the lower levels of the city wheel for too long with the rest of the carrots (the term commonly used by them to describe the population they would have to guide). Think big, Herbert. Yes, we can push the parameters here in the city and insert ourselves in the guidance of the city affairs, but that's what? Five million people! Imagine ruling other cities! Other people!"

"Are they people?" said Andrew cryptically.

"I'm happy the way I am now," said Herbert.

A waitress wheeled up on roller skates and passed Herbert a baton.

"What's this?" said Herbert.

Sophia smiled. "You remember the concert you went to at the age of twelve? You were having piano lessons, and your mom sent you to the concert with your uncle right before he passed? You were quite inspired by that experience. You wanted for a while to become a musical engineer for the city and compose pieces of music that get piped into the open spaces and maybe one day become a conductor for that very same orchestra."

"How did you know that?" asked Herbert, honestly baffled.

Sophia looked at Andrew and tapped one long manicured fingernail on another. "That office that you were so delighted to find out had a hidden passageway or two."

Andrew laughed until he snorted.

Herbert looked from one to the other.

Sophia explained, "The purpose of the elevator is to keep you in place while we scan your memories. It's really not a very complex machine. Once we knew you were friendly, we drew you in. And then we realized you are more than friendly, you're a visionary, one with sight. The one we've been waiting for. No ordinary carrot, your dreams showed us. We analyzed your memories and your dreams. That's the only way we could know what your heart's desire was for sure."

"I feel quite different about things now," said Herbert. Do you think there's still time? To realize a dream?"

Sophia said, "Maybe not in music, but you could feel like this. Here, watch." She drew a stage floating in space.

Herbert saw the orchestra pit, and he saw himself conducting with a mini baton. Then she tripled and quadrupled the stages and, likewise, the mini Herberts and filled the room behind him with the virtual spectacle.

"Do I have to explain it any further?" said LaVey, walking up behind Andrew. She put a hand on Andrew's shoulder, and he reciprocated by putting his hand on hers. "It's absolute power. There are heights we can attain, but most of us are asleep. We think, 'Maybe that is enough,' and we return to our slumber. But is it really enough? Or can we be visionaries and rise to greater heights. Some of us are visionaries. You're a visionary, Herbert!"

Herbert stared at LaVey standing behind Andrew. Amazed how he was having lunch with an esteemed city father.

LaVey continued, "You were a visionary at the age of twelve and saw where life could take you. And then something happened. Your mom regretted her choices even though there are no real choices in the city, and you were pushed on one hand and neglected on the other. It broke your mom, but not you. Underneath you're still the same boy, a believer."

Herbert felt angry.

"You're angry," said LaVey. "You watched your mom lose her battle to believe, and it broke your heart. Being angry can be a motivator. Yes, you could have been a conductor, but your experience can take you to even greater heights. You're still a visionary, and with that vision, you could rule an empire."

"What do you mean?" asked Herbert.

LaVey stared at him. "There's more of us augments than there are of you visionaries. We're a big part of existence. We could rule the world by numbers, but people need someone to believe in, Herbert, and they could believe in somebody like you!"

Herberts heart started to beat faster.

"The city fathers—that is, the augmented fathers—want to make a pact with other cities to go out and explore Asperia and the unconsolidated territories and acquire new technologies, Herbert! To bring the fearful and the lost under our leadership! Isn't that a noble cause?"

Spearing a sardine, LaVey continued, "Not all the city fathers are believers, Herbert, and elections are coming up. So it's important that we have representative who's placed to expand a bold new vision for Diaspora—a person like you, Herbert!"

Herbert's mind turned upside down. He never thought of himself politically minded, but indeed, somebody had to run the city. Somebody had to oversee the people, the city mind, the culture and make sure the walls weren't breached, both literally and figuratively. If he, Herbert, could work in with these people and ensure new technological gains and trade with other bound cities, then that would be a magnificent legacy for himself and the people he worked with. And his mom would be so proud. He just had one vague feeling of discomfort.

"Not everybody's right with what we do though, Sophia, Andrew," vocalized Herbert.

"Oh, that," said Andrew. "The important thing is that you're all right with your actions. It really is neither here nor there, the spilling of animal blood. We're not committing any crimes. It is just a technological advancement, and furthermore, we're taking on all the risk by experimenting on ourselves. It demonstrates our love for humanity and for you, Herbert. Now will you show your love for us by standing with us?"

"Of course," said Herbert, blinking and looking at the three of them in turn—up at LaVey, who grinned back at him and across to Andrew with his year-round tan. And boldly, he leaned over and gave Sophia a peck of a kiss on her cheek.

"Ooh, Herbert," she said, reciprocating with more than just a peck on his lips. "You cheeky thing."

—⁄⁄⁄—

"He's perfect," said LaVey to Sophia in the woman's bathrooms. "He's so dull. He's like a blank canvas."

"He's more like a sculpture," said Sophia. "Of poop."

"Regardless of what you call it, we can shape him into whatever we like, and he can spearhead our vision for a city that's a refuge for our kind. A city to control all the bound cities—Phoenix City. And we will be immortalized as the ones who made a haven for our kind. I have spent hours poring over books from before the reawakening, and we were hunted, called vampires." Sophia made a moue of disgust.

LaVey coughed. "Can you not say that word? It's cartoonish, heretical. We're augments. Blood and steel. Strength meets purity! Steel."

"Well, you know, LaVey, we will need to sanitize the matter," Sophia mused. "People are so judgmental about killing animals unless they kill them to eat them. They would judge us for advancing the cause of science by disposing of the sick and unwanted, yet they bypass lab grown meat and eat healthy animals. It is double standards, LaVey!"

"Hush, Sophia," said LaVey, putting her hand on Sophia's inner thigh. "I understand your anxiety, but we're ushering in a new age for our kind who will thrive free of judgment from now on. We will take the city and unite our kind with those in other bound cities!"

"I feel elevated to half…woman." Sophia laughed. She unwrapped a bandage from her waist, and a snake's head leisurely slithered to her breast and started suckling.

"They'll feel honored to be ruled by us," agreed LaVey. "The weaker will protest. If they get in our way, we will run them down, like a field of carrots."

CARLOTTA

Carlotta was exasperated. She stared at the chief guardsman.

"How on Earth could you let them get away? I specifically said that there would be two individuals traveling out of town who fit the description, who were armed and dangerous and the weapons may not be visible to the human eye. There were forty of you and two of them. How did they get away?"

The chief guardsman started, "We were attacked. It was an aerial attack." All of a sudden, he felt his knees grow weak.

"You won't make that mistake again, will you?" said Carlotta thoughtfully, her head on her hand as she watched him with a piercing gaze.

"Aarrgh," cried the guardsmen, his eyes widening. "Can you see them, Miss Carlotta?" He stabbed at the air in front of him. "I'm surrounded by them!"

Carlotta sent a message to the front desk.

"The chief guardsman appears to be hallucinating."

"No!" said the guardsman. "No, we're under attack, but I can take them. I can force a retreat."

Carlotta twirled a curl with her finger and tapped a pen on the desk.

"Are you sure you're okay, Milton? Can you see something I can't?"

To his surprise, the guardsman felt his knees give way, and he collapsed as the swarm of wasps pullulated. Council security crashed through the double doors into the chambers where Carlotta was sitting at the mayor's table.

"Take him away," she said distastefully, pointing to where Milton was writhing on the floor. "I think he's fouled himself, and he was babbling about seeing things. He said he saw things while patrolling and then again in here. I do hope he isn't sick with something."

Milton writhed and babbled and struck at things in the air only he could see. The three council security guards started to drag him out. One was holding his nose. Another was holding his forefinger up and twirling it against his head to the third to make the universal sign of loco or mentally ill. Carlotta smiled. She stretched one foot out lazily and observed her latest pedicure. She did hope at the very least she had slowed those goodhearted fools down, and if they ever came back!

THEMYSTRICHYR

"Look at these fools," said Despoina. "Come up here, Athena."

Athena stepped up beside her sister, and they surveyed the ocean. A sloop pitched and yawed in the shallow waters off the sandbar aft of the island lookout. It wasn't unheard of to see a ship approach the island, but it was a rare occurrence. The barbarous reputation of the inhabitants of the island of Themystrichyr had long spread to the lands beyond. Most outsiders kept a wide berth, lest they run afoul of the women's changeable tempers.

Athena laughed. "How close should we let them get? However, it doesn't look like we'll have to intervene. They're just about to run up on that sandbar."

And indeed, two scrambling figures on the sloop realized they were in a unavoidable predicament and frantically started moving the sail to avoid the inevitable. The sloop lurched and inexplicably found a swell and shot a gap through to safer harbors.

On the boat, Alex scrambled to trim the sail aft, then he threw the mainsail halyard to a green and groaning Terry.

Terry yelled out, "How did you talk me into this again?"

A swell pitched the boat slightly sideways. A scavenging of seagulls overhead mocked the two boys, adding to their increasing distress.

"No time to talk," said Alex. "We're going to fetch up on that island any minute now."

"Jason from the desert said if a woman's disappeared in these parts, she may have been kidnapped by a group of savages who have regressed and live without men!" Terry said this, swaying. "Will they eat us?"

Alex, as he traversed the beleaguered boat, replied, "Terry! You're not helping. Of course, not. We'll appeal to their better selves."

And as he spoke, the boys heard a "thunk" and an arrow ricocheted off the deck just in front of the main sail.

"Holy smokes, we're not even there, and they're trying to kill us," said Terry.

He pulled out a stick of gum from his breast pocket, and a little white mouse head popped up hoping for an offcut. Terry scratched it absentmindedly.

"It didn't go too well for us last time if they're the same women," Terry commented.

Some more seagulls circled in, and then the whole school hove off into the direction that they were sailing into.

"Have you got anything to stop those arrows?" Terry asked. "Alex, I need land. Mist is not so effective on arrows. But let me see what I can do to try and keep the boat off the sandbar as long as possible. And when we wash up on dry land, I'm going to count on them eating the meatiest of us, which is you."

Alex watched disbelievingly as Falcon, the little white mouse, ran from Terry's hand to his neck and back down the other hand.

Terry said to the mouse, "This is true. Where men cannot go, animals do." He lifted his left hand to his mouth and placed two fingers into his mouth to let out a loud whistle.

A shadow appeared in the sky from just above the island that they were approaching. The boat was fast taking on water now, and Alex was busy bailing it back out with the with the bucket. Terry was seemingly unconcerned.

"Ease out the mainsheet," hollered Alex. "Stop talking to vermin and get busy helping me. We're about to run aground, you plebinous oaf!"

The shadow flew closer and closer and circled above the sloop. Fighting to keep the boat afloat, though he was, Alex tried to make out the shape of the winged apparition.

"Duck!" yelled Alex.

As angry as he was at his sailing mate, he was compelled to give warning.

"It's a flying seahorse!"

And indeed it was, an enormous fire-manned ursine apparition circled the small boat as if sizing up its prey. It stopped two lengths out and, without much ado, made a beeline for Alex.

"No!" yelled Alex as the seahorse's protruding chest knocked him over the prow of the boat. Alex fell into the surging surf.

Terry could see Alex bobbing in the surf. Terry shrugged back as if to say, "Sorry, mate."

Alex bobbed and glubbed helplessly as the seahorse hovered inches from Terry's nose.

Terry stared back the seahorse, who appeared to get a clear line to take aim at Terry. And then the mouse ran from Terry's cuff to his nose; hopped to the seahorse's nose, who promptly rose and hovered above the boat; paused; turned around; and ran into Terry's chest, knocking him into the water. Then the boat started to sink, leaving the two boys both bobbing in the sea. Terry shook his fist at the disappearing seahorse, which was most unlike him.

Terry took some strokes to lessen the distance between him and Alex.

"What's the backup plan, mate?" he yelled.

Alex appeared to be having some kind of internal struggle.

"Why the hell did I get on a dinghy with you, Terry? Is it raining now?" he said finally. "We were pretty comfortable in Trove. But no! I had to play Captain Asperia, and I picked the wrong damn companion to accompany me!"

As Terry stroked his way toward Alex, Alex continued to stare off into the distance. Terry swam up alongside Alex and got the gist of Alex's angry monologue. Terry lifted a sodden sleeve to wave to get Alex's attention.

"You had to go after Eliza, you daft wagon, Alex. It was the next adventure."

"It was the road calling, you idiot," said Alex, spiraling into despair. "The one person I picked, the most useless person I could have picked to go with me to rescue Eliza, and I chose you, you lazy squirrel chaser."

"Don't over egg it," said Terry.

"You bleeding well hang out with vermin!" continued Alex. "And you have no spine, no drive. Those girls carry you through the days at the apothecary. I need muscle. I need someone to help me get there."

"Where?" asked Terry, pulling some seaweed between his teeth, completely unfazed.

"To where Eliza is," said Alex, swinging himself around to point in the direction of the island and subsequently and unexpectedly hitting his hand on the shoulder of a naked woman. A bronzed goddess of a woman, he noticed, while in his abject despair.

She smiled sweetly, and it was the last thing he remembered. Then something flew out of the sky and hit him on the head.

EVA AND HANNAH

"It's my fault," said Eva. "I should have realized how distraught Alex was to lose one of the group, Hannah. Did you know Alex once trained to be a firefighter? I heard him muttering, 'No one left behind,' to the horses. Then he told me how he came to be a bounty hunter after he got rejected from the fire service. This is dreadful!" Eva exclaimed, striding around the stables. "I've managed to…I've lost all that we stood for. Everything's gone, Hannah."

Hannah, knowing she couldn't calm Eva's distress, rocked from one foot to the other, trying to match her mood and watching her pound around the stable walls in abject distress. Mirabelle, a nearby roan mare snickered in the stalls, picking up on Eva's energy. Berit, the stable hand, hurried to calm her. As Eva passed Hannah for the third time, she raised her head to Hannah, tears streaming down her face.

"Everything our family has worked for—it's all gone Hannah, gone like sandcastles washed away by the tide. There's no one behind left to rebuild. It's my fault, Hannah There is no one to come after us. And everyone who came before us is as helpless as we are. The continuation of the Ventura line depends on me. I'm the Ankh, the anchor of the House Ventura, sworn to protect, serve, and act as a sentinel so that others may come after. That is my duty and all I have ever known. To swear, protect, and serve and, in turn, swear in others to defend and serve."

Hannah grabbed Eva and folded her in her arms like a small child.

Eva heaved and sobbed. "I can't bear it! I can't bear it, Hannah."

Hannah used a thumb to soothingly rub each of Eva's eyebrows in turn.

"I've betrayed everybody's trust," Eva continued. "It feels like a knife stabbing, stabbing through my rib cage. It's twisting in my heart, and that's not the worst. I can't stop thinking, where did I go wrong, Hannah? Where did I go wrong, by all the powers invested in me. I was strong enough, alert enough. I had so much family support. Where did I go wrong?" Eva heaved.

Hannah interjected, one tear lacing its way down her check from her green eye as she felt her daughter's pain, "Listen, darling, if we were that lost, your leadership wouldn't have bought us here. You've just got to trust and have faith. We're all still here, and we will find our way back— together. With you to guide us. Sometimes pain is just pain. It hurts, but it's not the weapon. However, it sharpens the blade."

Folding the girl in her arms and massaging her scalp with one hand, Hannah continued, "From when we are kids, we learn from pain. That is how we grow. We touch hot plates on the range, and we recoil. Feedback from our extremities advises us to tend and be careful with them. Later, on we nurture them with lotions and polish, and we attract like-minded friends to ease the pain of growing up. Upsetting our friends on the playground wins us a thumping and puts us in coventry."

Eva almost smiled at this centuries-old term for when your friends refused to speak to you for a period of time.

"We must learn this lesson that pain brings growth. We must or we become Anti'Jhinii!" Hannah said, invoking the mythical half witch/half beast that Asperian parents frightened their kids with to get them to stay in their bedrooms at night.

"It hurts. It hurts so bad," Eva keened.

Hannah was worried though she was outwardly calm. Eva's distress was disturbing the animals. And she could feel a slight rise in Eva's temperature. Outside the sun was rising, and geese were honking and making their presence known, as they rose and circled into the horizon. Mirabelle whinnied and slung her head over the stall. Eva allowed herself to be led over to Mirabelle. Hannah uncurled Eva's clenched hand and held it out to a curious Mirabelle, who snuffled into it, and gradually Eva's tense frame relaxed.

Hannah wished she could do more to relieve the stress of her beautiful daughter. The big oak doors at the end of the stable creaked and opened.

"Look, Eva!" exclaimed Hannah. "Company!"

Two stable hands rushed up and tugged at the leather straps tied to handles of the weathered oak doors. The doors open wide to admit Nicoletta and Tan! They were each sitting astride two weary-looking sweat-drenched chestnut horses. Tan's face lit up, and a big smile spread across his face as he trotted Sarsaparilla up to Hannah and Eva.

Seeing Eva's face, he said, "Hey, cheer up, love. We're here now. Whatever we've got to face, we'll face together."

"Oh, Tan," sighed Eva. "We lost everything."

"Oh no, we haven't," said Nicoletta, coming to join them. "Hey, there's a good girl, Eva." She spoke to Eva as though she were a horse. "I hear there is a good cafe down the street. Would you like to take us there for breakfast?"

Relieved, Hannah knelt down and put two hands out so Eva could swing herself up behind Tan, and then Hannah swung herself up behind Nicoletta.

At Clifford's Keen Ear Café, they dismounted and pushed through the swing doors. Eva had some trouble getting to the seat the waitress gestured to as the kids all pushed up at the counter, who said in unison.

"Hey, Eva!"

"Hey, Eva, sign my yearbook."

"Eva, can you make my parrot say 'hello' in Spanish."

A little red-cheeked girl put her hand right in Eva's pocket and wouldn't take it out.

"Where's your mom, honey?" Nicoletta said.

"I don't have one," said the girl.

The waitress handed the group the Sunny Hope menu with the breakfast options. The table placed their order, Eva ordering strawberry pancakes and cream for the little redhead stowaway with her hand still in Eva's pocket. Then again, she started voicing her regrets out loud. Everything was coming apart. Just as she started getting into how it was all her fault, and everything was lost, Nicoletta stopped her and glanced at Tan.

"Eva, sweetie, a house isn't just built on one pillar. Or if it is, it's not going to last very long in bad weather. It has many pillars, darling. Yes, you're our Ankh, our once-in-a-generation source of ascension power, but the renewal and health of the Ventura line depends on many people."

Eva stared at Nicoletta unblinkingly, feeling hope for the first time in a week.

Nicoletta carved out a good amount of her breakfast and proceeded to spear it with her fork. Contemplating the full situation at hand, she said, "What did you say, those fools raced off to find Eliza?"

Hannah said, raising her hand, "We woke one morning to find a note under our door, I mean how juvenile is that, and two pillows also with notes stuffed in the bed saying, 'We're going to get Eliza. We'll be back tonight.'"

Nicoletta clapped her hand to her forehead. "That sounds like Terry. Obviously, Alex supplied the passion for the impromptu mission, and Terry percolated over it and thought up the ruse. Do they really think they could extract our companion from…" She sniggered and stopped talking at this last.

Hannah looked at her. "Uhh, Mom, what do you know that we don't know."

Either put one hand on top of Hannah's, and Eva leaned in and said, "Grandma, Grandma, you laughing?"

Nicoletta was sporting the biggest smile the girls had ever seen her wear.

"Good luck to those two boobs," she said. "I sent my fastest falcon, Maleficent, over to the shoreline and some nesting eagles relayed to her the news confirming Eliza is safe and well but those boys are not. It would seem they've been taken captive by the wild women of Themystrichyr!"

ALEX

Alex drifted in and out of consciousness, memory and dream mixing together to create a confused pastiche of an internal landscape. He opened them then attempted to focus his eyes.

"Oh, dearie, I wouldn't do that," said a husky voice that dripped butter and venom at the same time.

"Where am I?" stuttered Alex. He tried to raise his head and felt a sense of vertigo and a rush of nausea following the unpleasant disorienting sensation.

"Well, if you must know," said the beguiling and slippery but gravelly voice, "you're in a place that's not a location. It's both a test and a quest, and it's named the Apostle's Revenge."

"What's your name?" Alex asked the husky voice. He raised his head jerkily and was displeased to see a pool of vomit just where his head had been. Trying to fix on where the voice was coming from, Alex retched and jerked miserably without seeing anything. His memory was no help. His last memory was of swimming over a sandbar for shore.

"I see nothing. I mean nothing. But I have a name. My name is Serpentine," the disembodied voice replied.

Alex was confused. He realized he was befuddled more than the situation warranted, even though he'd obviously received some kind of head injury. Not enough to fully disable him, a mild concussion perhaps accounted for the vomiting and vertigo. But a contusion didn't account for what his senses were receiving and not receiving. He could see he was on a platform. And it was stable and not moving, but it didn't appear to be grounded to anything. It wasn't suspended either. It had four corners, but each time he tried to focus on the perimeter, he found himself looking beyond or inside the platform. Beyond was velvet nothing.

"You'll start seeing things out there soon," said the voice, not at all comforting. "Once your senses are deprived for long enough. You would think, wouldn't you, that you would see stars in the velvet nothingness? That your brain would recreate what you might see, looking up at the night sky? But no, just as despair sets in, you'll start seeing a movie reel of your life in front of your eyes. It's created by your brain chemistry to keep you sane. Similar to what they called Technicolor in the old days. Oh, I miss Technicolor!"

Serpentine continued animatedly, "It was before the reawakening. It was before technology. Modern technology that led to the misuse and misappropriation of technology. Technicolor was like chalk. Bright colors that filled a screen. They made stories about animals. Each episode had a moral lesson. They were very funny. My favorite was a character called Scrooge McDuck. Then they made a cartoon of an actual historical event called the Titanic. Do you want to know what happened to the Titanic?"

Alex felt his sinuses revolt, and he muttered a curt, "Sure."

"When humanity was both lovable and innocent, they used to go around the Earth in massive ships. Can you imagine, Alex? Titanic was one such ship."

Alex convulsed at the taste of his name in the mouth of the invisible entity. He struggled for a word to define the entity that droned on in the absence of everything or anything.

"Serpentine," said the incorporeal voice.

"Don't say my name," Alex said, choking, feeling revolted.

"Yes, I do have that effect on men," said Serpentine with a tinge of regret in its voice. "Where was I? Oh yes, back in more innocent days when people reigned and made wondrous invention. Before the other species came to infest the Earth. Mostly pests. Machines with minds and flying hybrids and augments and the Void knows what else. But anyway, I digress again. I do that, I'm the only being, the only super, all-seeing Serpentine. Before the breaching, humans used to go on big boats in seas, around shores and islands, and even into the vast oceans."

Alex wished it would get to the point so he could get a handle on the situation.

"Anywaaay," it droned, "this ship, this one ship, the biggest ever made, it lost its bearings and crashed into an iceberg. A big lump of frozen ice carved off from a frozen continent. And there were these two lovers, and right up to the last moment you thought they would get rescued…"

"Yes," said Alex tightly.

"And they died," said Serpentine.

"Thanks for the blow by blow," said Alex wearily. "Can I go now?"

EVA

After dropping the mic with regards to the boys whereabouts, Nicoletta hurried to qualify her words.

"If Alex and Terry took the most direct route and took a boat off the eastern shore to traverse the Strait of Verdant to get to the island of Themystrichyr, they may have encountered any number of obstacles. But it is a relatively calm, windless strait. Assuming they got to the island, the women of Themystrichyr are very protective of their privacy. They will not negotiate free passage with any hapless explorers or travelers. The parvenus get taken hostage and are only released after some rather ticklish encounters and displays of strength both physical and mental, solving riddles, etc., etc. There's no indication that any outsiders are harmed in the making of the legend of the woman of Themystrichyr, but those who have experienced their hospitality look quite shaken afterward. Eliza will have fared better and may even be experiencing some good cheer and cordiality. We don't need to worry about her for the time being. Now we need to make our own plans to go forward. It will all come out in the wash, you will see, and I absolutely expect those boys to wash up back in Trove, or at least on the eastern shores!"

"It's still awful," Eva said soberly. "There are soldiers garrisoned at the apothecary. We're a company torn asunder! Guardians know what other forces we are up against!"

Tan, turning food over with across the table, his eyes dark as hematite stone, spoke up.

"We need to define our mission properly. It's not good enough to wander around in the dark without a goal. Currently, we don't know where we're going, what information we seek, and what direction the danger is coming from."

"The mission, it's too big," cried Eva desperately.

"Originally, we said we'd find out new information and take back the apothecary," said Hannah. "Only now we've lost some of our party."

"We've spoken to everyone who has any insight and haven't identified why the council of Destin turned its focus to warmongering and why the bound cities couldn't stop Eliza escaping. I fear they may take an interest in the business of our peaceful Asperian towns. Doug and May are very faint and can't give insight," said Nicoletta.

"Stop!" yelled Eva. "I can't take it anymore. It's getting worse. It's like a hurricane spiraling out of control."

The whole room stopped and looked at Eva. She was yelling louder and louder without realizing it.

"I like you," said, Terry wandering in through the cafe door.

Eva ignored his sudden appearance and continued her monologue.

"First, we lose the apothecary, then we start losing people! More and more people. And now you're telling me that we cannot see Doug and May in Ascension! Our very ascendants are fading away. Something is really f—— wrong here! Wrong all throughout Asperia and wrong with ascension! It's almost as though a taint has developed here that's hurting our ascendants!" Eva paused, took a breath and straightened up. She walked over to the front of the café and hugged Terry.

Folks being folks had a variety of responses to Eva's very public outburst. Some families stayed to see what this authoritative and passionate young woman had to say next. One man started playing a banjo in the corner, muffled, his companion marking the beat with a small percussion instrument. Some café goers lifted their noses and pushed their chairs in as if to say, "How dare you spoil the peace and talk such foolish notions." Yet a notable number of them who had heard the context of Eva's eruption shortly rushed home to ensure they could touch their ancestors in ascension.

Eva walked back over to the table where her family were all looking at her searchingly, waiting to see what was coming next, waiting to take her lead—all except for Nicoletta, who was examining the end of her long locks of black hair.

"We can all feel it," said Eva. "A contamination. From several sources. The councils. The bound cities perhaps? And I am coming to the understanding it comes from me. If I hadn't been so prideful, I would have foreseen this chain of events earlier, the threat to the apothecary. The decimation of our numbers. Know this, I am the Ankh. I am Eva of the line Ventura. I am responsible for the well-being and health of animals and gifted with the blessing of bestowing life-force through herbal care and love made manifest and lore. I have missed important details because I was so busy playing the big-shot warrior. When you're too strong, your strength can eclipse you, overshadow your inner core and values. It brings you to your knees and humbles you. Now I'm too weak to draw on my wisdom. Anything I do or say now I may not help. I cannot see! Please, Guardians, give me back my powers. Bring me back my sight!" Eva collapsed to her knees.

"It's not you," said the red-cheeked little girl, suddenly appearing at her side.

Eva was startled. She had all but forgotten the little girl who had entrusted her hand to Eva's pocket earlier.

"Oh, it is me," said Eva, bedeviled enough to engage with a child less than half her age. "I have certain special abilities to hear and see when people need help or when people are hurting other people. It's a constant thrum of voices in need. And I see my way to them. It's not with me anymore. There is something wrong with me. I cannot hear, and I cannot see!"

A mist arose around them. Emerald-green flecks coruscated in the nebulous cloud.

"What is your name?" asked Eva. "I cannot keep calling you little girl in my mind." To her own ears, Eva's voice did not sound like her own. It sounded plaintive, young.

"Come see," said the little girl. "Hold my hand. My name is Chyra."

Eva looked to Hannah for guidance.

Hannah looked at her distantly with her green eye shining. Abstractly, Hannah gave her some guidance.

"Go, Eva, go. I am drawing down, hoping to find Doug and May. Something tells me you need to find your way forward free of us to distract you. Perhaps Chyra can help."

Terry was sitting on the bench looking jovial. He smiled at Nicoletta. "There is no time to waste. The state of affairs is getting worse, but fear not, the young 'uns seem to have the run of the roost and have the measure of things."

The mist dissipated.

"Did you not hear what your friend said?" Chyra tugged at Eva. "Things are getting worse. Come, sister. Come, we'll be there by nightfall."

"What do you mean?" countered Eva. "Am I going mad?"

The sun just came up.

"We just came here for a peaceful breakfast and to regroup. Where are you taking me, little girl, I mean, Chyra. And what do you mean 'pack'? Are you taking me to see your parents?"

Chyra put one finger on the side of her nose, shook her head, and said, "Let's take a walk in the forest. I have echinacea and rhodiola root that will take your temperature down."

Eva replied quickly, "Echinacea can raise your temperature. I need fever few or catnip. Preferably fever few as I am starting to get a headache."

"You are very good with your herbs. I love you, sister," Chyra said quickly and appeared to grow before Eva's eyes.

"All right, let's go for a walk," Eva said, trying to sound a little authoritative.

RAVENNA

There was not a day that Ravenna didn't regret in the last twenty days of leaving Kingdom Ridich and coming to the Kolkhoz. It was like a boot camp. In fact, it was a boot camp! That's all it was! Discipline. Endless freaking discipline. She awoke in the morning, made her bed, or as she tried to do on the first morning but failed, and then she had to shower naked in an outdoor shower positioned by everyone lining up for breakfast. She had to though there was no overt compulsion. No one yelled or enforced rules like in her father's army. It was strange. She didn't want to, but the night before a strange little woman with a worn face said, "There's no false humility around here, girl! In the morning you're up! Clothes on, bed made, or you shower naked. You'll only do it once."

Sure enough, Ravenna had suffered for the consequence when her bed was checked the next day, her first morning. She had quickly tried to explain she didn't know the technique for making a bed. It was, in fact, her maidservant Brynn's fault.

The woman had raised one eyebrows and pointed her head in the direction of the shower; and Ravenna, hot with anger, had walked over, stripped off, and suds up under the shower head in full view. She hadn't kicked or screamed or made false threats of leaving in days.

I should shower butt naked in front of everyone, she thought. She, Princess Ravenna. While everyone ignored her. Everything was in the open from the shower to the breakfast line.

Oh, they had some interesting ways here in the Kolkhoz, but it wasn't awful. There was plenty to eat and camaraderie abounded. There was especially humor in the older hands teaching the ropes to the newer

241

arrivals, or tenderfeet as they were called. But it was humiliating being here going from luxury where her every wish was met to indenture, and she was reminded periodically, when she complained.

"It was your choice to be here, you're quite welcome to go."

But she stayed. Even though her surroundings were more spartan than the palace, it was more attractive in its homespun simplicity.

And even though the population meditated for two hours every morning following breakfast, somehow, Ravenna endured it. Even though following the meditation she had to clean s—— out of the pig stalls, and her efforts were quite often derided, or under appreciated. She didn't actually mind s——, and she was a damn good s—— shoveller, she thought, and she was saving everybody else from shoveling s——. She was stronger than most of the other girls who came in with her clutch, but not stronger than the sherangs. They always came along and gave her a hard time.

"What's happened to your wrists today, Ravenna?"

"Lost some strength there, Ravenna?"

But eventually, she got her lunch, and it was so good! And at night, they played cards, tenderfeet and sherangs alike. That was fun too. Fun! She was having fun for the first time in a long time.

Caryn, the head sherang, clapped Ravenna on the back as she walked in for lunch.

"This is humiliating," said Ravenna, glowering back at her.

"Humiliating or humbling," replied Caryn, not missing a beat.

Ravenna considered this while scraping the lump of pig shit off her shoe on the nearest rock. She was smart enough to realize when she had just heard true wisdom.

"Guess what, girl?" Caryn said, her face shining.

"What's up?" said Ravenna, baffled by the older girl's sunny demeanor.

"You're the newest sherang," said Caryn.

"Really? Who said so?" asked Ravenna, acting flippant but wondering if it could possibly be true. "And didn't you just call me lazy?"

"Aw, sweetie," said Caryn, "that was affection. We know you're from nobility. Gotta take you down a peg or two, especially when you walked in here acting like you own the place."

"Technically, I do, if you're in my father's kingdom!" said Ravenna. Then she couldn't stop grinning. She had just made a joke.

Caryn slapped Ravenna on the back again and said, "You can pick up your leather chaps and gloves from the store after lunch, and there are some novices to orient after. You're no longer a newbie, Ravenna! And a man that came in today on horseback was asking after you! I thought you said you didn't know anyone."

Ravenna's cheeks flushed. "I don't, but you meet people on the road. Make their acquaintance."

Caryn continued, looking at Ravenna with interest, "He said to give you a message. He said he's waiting for you."

Ravenna blushed and shrugged.

"It's a mystery then," said Caryn, still watching her. "Shall we go and eat?"

BRYNN

"Come with me, girl," hollered King Ridich.

Brynn tottered as she attempted to retreat to the scullery from the direction of the oncoming figure. It didn't help that she was nursing her arm with the injured finger. It impeded her progress and the vibrations from his booming voice moved through her, and the force of his voice almost knocked her off balance.

"Hey, you! Brynn, is it? I want you in my bedchambers tonight."

Brynn sighed. She had been hoping to go to the castle scullery and get some antiseptic herbs and bandages to dress her wounded figure and the dismembered tip. After the show, Brynn had dressed the wound temporarily and tried to press the tip back on with an old bandage and some chicory root, but now she needed access to the cook's arsenal before infection set in. She would like to keep the tip if she could.

"Yes, Your Majesty." Brynn curtsied as he approached closer. "As it pleases you, Majesty."

Brynn had some shantung silk gloves her last mistress had given her. That would cover her wounded hand. She could alternately give him a massage and caress him.

Perhaps he would be satisfied with that, thought Brynn wearily.

EVA

Eva was struggling to keep up with Chyra as they walked through Trove toward the outskirts. The girl was so fast she loped. To the left was desert and to the right where they were heading, and into the direction of the sun setting was a caravan of people walking toward the forest.

"Hey, Chyra, why are they all walking?" asked Eva of her diminutive companion.

Chyra looked back. And all of a sudden, her face changed. Eva heard her snarl. A cloud moved across the sun.

"Why?"

The caravan moved along. The procession had people of differing heights with different color skins. Children were holding adults hands and each other hands.

The sun was in a different place. Eva drew her maps into her vision. It was later than she thought. It was now midafternoon, though it felt like they had only been jogging for an hour.

"Are you sick?" Eva inquired of Chyra, who was now doubled over.

"Raaarrl," came the reply.

Eva stopped, concerned. Eva stood there helplessly looking around. She didn't have her medicinal pouch on her, and she was lost. She scanned for her companion and then felt Chyra's hot breath on her legs. Chyra growled…barked (?) exasperatedly and turned her face up.

Eva gasped.

The face was all hairy. Chyra smiled. Two fangs gleamed.

"You'd best go with her," said a woman from the caravan, passing. "Skinwalkers never take no for an answer."

Eva clapped her head. The little girl! Only she wasn't a little girl. Hadn't Hannah just been teasing her about the Anti'Jhinii? Shapeshifters or skinwalkers, various cultures called them. And now she was in the company of one! She didn't feel equipped to continue in this one's company. Just as she thought of turning back to Trove, the Anti'Jhinii opened its fanged mouth and made it perfectly clear that it did not approve. No longer a little girl then, the Anti'Jhinii rose to Eva's waist with head and fanged face upturned to Eva. The menacing aura was not lost on Eva or the people of the caravan who had stopped to watch the encounter. Women clutched their children close.

"So you see," the woman said, "you must go with her."

Eva searched her memory banks about the legends associated with the beasts. This might equip her with the knowledge and mindset she needed to continue. Until today, Eva had thought the existence of such beasts to be mythical. The woman stopped seemingly waiting for Eva to ask questions. As the legends of the Anti'Jhinii came to her, from deep within her memory banks, she grew more and more horrified. She slipped out with, "They eat babies!"

The woman said, "That is not completely accurate. There is a pact between the Anti'Jhinii and the villages that surround the Taiga, the forest they live in. The pact is thus—if the Anti'Jhinii request, woman must go have their audience, and it will be decided who will bear a child for them. This occurs annually. Or theAnti'Jhinii will take the weakest of the children to be sacrificed or raised as one of them!"

The caravan looked as one at Eva, awaiting her response.

"I will go," she said, horrified at the thought that the beast in front of her must have once indeed been a little girl.

She had come into Eva's company and shapeshifted specifically to make Eva's acquaintance. Eva supposed she would have to see out the beast/little girl's scheme according to this woman acting as an advisor. But first, she would see if she had any more information.

"What are you doing? Where are you going as part of this great caravan? And what is your name?"

"My name is Haarlem. I am a Fauna Adept. We all are, despite our physical differences. We must go into the Taiga, the great forest, to mourn our dead in the upcoming war! We know there will be a great war as the forest has told us. Many will die."

The crowd nodded and shifted.

"Go," said the woman. "We must go, make peace with our forests. You ought to go right away to talk with the spirit animals. And do what they say. They will chide you if you don't. And they are very much incarnate, with poison-tipped fangs. A word to the wise—you may have to do battle to prove your worth."

Chyra gave Eva the once over with one more upturned glance, licking her unsavory, green-tipped fangs. Eva was unfazed by the talk of poison-tipped fangs. She had poison immunity. She refrained from asking Haarlem any more questions about the war the woman had referred to in the future tense. As far as Eva knew, no one outside the apothecary, or the line Ventura could see into the future, but until today, Eva had not really believed in skinwalkers. As knowledgeable and practical she thought herself to be, there were gaps in her body of learning.

"That's where arrogance takes you," she muttered to herself.

Chyra growled and started walking into the setting sun.

Eva followed wearily.

ALEX

Serpentine had indeed accurately described the phenomenon of what Alex was starting to experience. It was so black, and Alex was so sensory deprived he was starting to have visions. People and animals played out distorted tableaus in front of his (closed) eyes. The disembodied voice of Serpentine had stopped talking after what Alex had presumed had been his noxious orientation to wherever he was, and he still had no idea why he was there. He had no idea how much time had passed. He was in a Neverland, devoid of sensory input, other than hearing; and even that was dubious. Serpentine could easily have been a projection of his own mind!

"I am not, you know!" said the voice. "You must be wondering how you get out of here."

Alex felt his head start to roll again. He wondered why he couldn't smell anything, not even his own vomit.

"The answer to that question," said Serpentine, "is you won't. And I'm not going to tell you where you are either!"

"Don't tell me then," said Alex warily, trying to turn his head to sniff at his vomit. It had no scent.

"Oh, don't be like that," said Serpentine. "Since we're going to be here for all of eternity, we may as well be friends."

"Eternity," repeated Alex miserably.

"Yes, when I was created, I was told that I could keep whatever I found." Serpentine chuckled jarringly. "That includes you. There was a man and a woman once. I got sick of them," offered Serpentine.

"Do go on," said Alex.

"I offered to become them. They could stay the same and become me, and they would never die. Do you know what they chose?" said Serpentine.

"Surprise me," said Alex.

"They chose each other. Spoiler, true love. So I turned them mortal and gave them food and clothes for when they got sick of looking at each other's bare-ass naked bodies, which wasn't often, by the way. They proceeded to clamber all over each other and make babies. Eventually, they grew older, and they died! But here you are!" Serpentine finished brightly.

"Yes, here I am," said Alex thinly.

"Oh, you're no fun," said Serpentine. "Doesn't it intrigue you that there's at least one way out of here?"

"You just said I'm here with you for all of eternity," Alex said.

"I can wait some time before we start playing mind games. Yes, but I'm going to drive you mad too," said Serpentine luxuriously. "And it will be drab while I wait for you to recover. Did you know there have been others before you? Some died. Some got out, but they were much cleverer than you. Probably weren't as fat either. Did you know you were carrying extra weight? Now guess how they got out of here!"

"No, first you tell me how I got in here!" said Alex.

"That's the first bit of spirit you've shown. Guess what! The answer is the same for both questions." The serpent laughed!

"Will you let me out of here if I guess correctly?" asked Alex, grasping at straws.

"No," said Serpentine "I can't. You have to guess the answer to another riddle. I didn't make the rules. I just found myself here too, but you can find the answer, and then I can tell you the one other way out. I ask you a question, and you have to give me an answer!" Serpentine was excited by the tone of his own voice.

Alex replied impatiently, "I didn't do anything to get here! I was in the water, bailing out, and I got knocked into the water by a man-sized flying seahorse. I saw a goddess walk up to me, then all of a sudden, I ended up in this in-between place with a madman! Or madwoman thing (It's hard to tell) with no proper name!"

"Hold that thought!" said Serpentine, audibly excited. "Let's do this together. After all, we have time! So I'm the most precious commodity that anybody can have. I'm more precious than money, and I'm what the couple had. And I had to let them go, though I offered them me and all my properties, and they could have had anything they desired through me, including immortality."

"What did they have?" Alex played along. "Gold or diamonds?"

"No, dummy. Try harder. I'm more precious than any jewels, and you can't see me!"

I might not be able to see you, but you sure can talk, thought Alex, but his attention was now grabbed by the riddle. He gave it some thought.

Serpentine said, "And why were you in the sea?"

"I was trying to rescue someone!" said Alex.

"Why?" asked Serpentine coyly.

Alex was now very tired, and that damn snake thing wouldn't shut up.

This is ridiculous. I must be in a coma, came the comforting thought to Alex. "The couple had it, and it was more precious than jewels," Alex muttered. "I'm going to sleep." He said to himself, "You can't see me. Between a man and a woman?" He went slightly further. "Could it be true love, Turpentine?" he sassed.

"Bingo! We have a winner!" exclaimed the exuberant disembodied voice. "Yes! True love! They chose to turn away my generous offer, *moi*, for each other. Suckers. And by the by, you would have died if you had slept. Not my rules!"

"It still doesn't make any sense. I was just going to rescue her," Alex said, exasperated.

"And by the by, what are you? Boring," boomed Serpentine. "Want to make a real effort to try to get out of here?"

"I thought you said I was stuck here," said Alex.

"Yes, I know, eternity, yada yada yada." Serpentine continued, "But even eternity gets sick of itself. And I'll get sick of you eventually. Do you want to have a go?"

"Are you saying I ended up here because of true love?" asked Alex. "Did I?"

"Boy, you're slow," said Serpentine. "I really hope you don't get this, because, you know, you're so slow. You're quite the entertainment. We could talk about cartoons forever!" It said this last word with relish. "True love bought you in, and true love will find you a way out. Here's the main riddle—Serpentine needs a new name for his next home. If you find my new name, and it's the correct one. *Poof*, I'm outta here, and so are you!"

Whatever did I do to deserve this? thought Alex. He supposed he did quite like Eliza. At least he felt quite protective of her. He was curious to know more about her background. They were two lost souls it would seem, and now he would never truly know her unless he guessed this darned creature's name.

"What did he ever do in a previous life to deserve this?"

A jolt shot through him.

Karma!

"Your new name is Karma," said Alex.

The platform suddenly lurched and moved from beneath him. He felt himself falling as a silvery laugh disappeared into the distance. An apparition came toward him, and he was looking up at the same halo of curls that had whupped him and taken his Eliza on the road. He vomited sand and water into the face.

MAKING SONIA'S ACQUAINTANCE

"Where am I?" stuttered Alex, spitting out a bit of conch shell that he dislodged from behind his tonsils.

"You were in a Rebus Cube," said the face. "We put you there. Ha ha ha," it cackled.

"Who are you?" said another body joining the first woman.

Alex waited.

"Oh, don't be so coy," said halo face. "You remember me, I'm Sonia, and I kicked your ass in the road."

Alex lifted himself up onto his elbows, annoyed how much time had passed, he thought. It felt like weeks, but maybe it was just a few days. Maybe he'd been sick for a month.

"Half an hour," said Sonya. "Half an hour. You passed the test. If you hadn't, you wouldn't be here."

"What do you mean passed the test?" quizzed Alex.

Sonia sat down now. She was sitting cross-legged, and Alex was stretched out, leaning back on his elbows, feeling remarkably unbothered despite the near drowning and, he assumed, being in a coma. Despite what this freckled freak was telling him, he must have been out for longer than half an hour.

He asked, "Am I back on the mainland? Where am I?"

"You're on an island, and right now we're deciding what to do with you. To send you back from when she came or, well, there aren't a lot of options here. We can harvest you for children. Girls, that is. We can put you in arena with fearsome beasts and keep you alive until you are dead of injuries or gray and old. But you wouldn't last long! Alex, can I call you Alex," she said.

Then Alex remembered his mission with some urgency. He snapped to and demanded of the face of the savage facing him.

"Now I remember! What have you done with her?"

Exhaustion, hunger, fear, and adrenaline awoke in him all at the same time.

Sonia looked back at him, half sad and half serious. She clasped her hands and cracked her knuckles.

"We've treated her very well," she said. "The way she should have been treated from the day she was born. She will come to know that without us, she was in grave danger, so we had to remove her from the stream of time, and now here you are, and what do we do with you, I wonder."

Alex observed the waves lapping on the shore and the seagulls circling above. The seahorse flying just above the sandbar. Alex considered Sonia's words and conceded that, indeed, he must be on the island; and therefore, his immediate fate was in these women's hands.

Sonia, seeming to have the power to read his mind, said. "Come. You will eat and rest now. You will see her before nightfall. It will be hard. You love her, or you wouldn't be here. But you must leave her with us. She cannot know yet if she loves you. And you must go back and lead an army into battle."

"Have you given me a drug?" asked Alex, feeling totally crazy. "Acid? It feels a little like lysergic acid, the rye bread drug." Alex glared at Sonia.

She met his eyes with a cool stare.

"You cannot possibly know how I feel about another person. What I know is that you and your pack of werewoman..."

Sonia raised an eyebrow at this.

Alex continued, "You and your pack of werewomen ambushed us! Kidnapped a defenseless girl who had, has no knowledge of how the world operates. You frightened her senseless and put me into a coma."

"No coma and no drugs," said Sonia, standing and extending her hand to him once again. "And definitely no lycanthropy. Shapeshifting into wolves. I never. The time effect is due to the presence of a calypso machine. Stop talking and come now."

ELIZA

Eliza was royally sick of the fawning and the attention paid to her by a series of woman who would enter into her room and ask her if there was anything that she required and were met with Eliza's standard response of, "No, I'm just fine. I'm ready to return home now."

The women would place their palms on their knees outward and say nothing and back out deferentially.

Why was she still here? She knew and accepted on one level that she was a prisoner. Maybe not a prisoner as the surroundings gave to a higher status, but she was being hosted indefinitely and was being given no further information. She supposed she was if not happy, she was cared for, but she was powerless to do anything but go along with the woman's plans. In her heart of hearts, she knew they meant her no physical or emotional harm, but she hated not having an escape plan for the first time in her life, a back-up plan to keep her safe. Eliza smiled at the thought of the lightning striking the ground behind Sonia the day they woke her up.

Maybe if she stayed here a day or so longer, she could seek to find that power within her to command. Well then, maybe she could start thinking seriously about escaping! Sure, she liked it here. It was very flattering to have all the favorable attention heaped on her and the meals served to her on fine china, and numerous companions to chat to. But she really wanted to be back with her friends from the apothecary—her gutsy, fighting travelling companions and Foxy. She hoped Foxy was safe.

The latest woman, or as they called themselves a lady-in-waiting, crept to her room backward. Her room was really nice. It had a four-poster bed, a writing desk, a case with a musical instrument in. What instrument, she wasn't sure as she didn't want to look. Every time she touched the case, she felt a sense of terror. The room also had a basin to wash her hands in with fresh flowers on an accent table besides rectangular windows that looked into a conservatory. She knew from entering and exiting the room for her audiences with Katalanta and Sonia that two cycads or common palms stood outside her door like sentinels. An uncomfortable emotion rose to the surface. Eliza had never experienced such luxury, and she could bear it for a day or two she supposed, but the one thing she couldn't bear was not being able to tell her friends what was happening. Her new friends that she'd assumed her fortunes were tied up with. Eliza looked around the room. Finally, there was an emotion she could identify, a familiar emotion. She had left her old city because she was useless in that setting, and now here she was, useless again. She passed the bed and, acting on an impulse, kicked one leg.

"Careful," said Sonia through the door, "you'll break your toe before you break that leg."

"I'm bored, I guess. Can I do something to assist?" said Eliza.

"I thought you'd never ask," Sonia said. "Ask and you shall receive. As a matter of fact, you have a visitor."

"What!" said Eliza.

"Someone's come quite a long way to see you, dearie. Follow me."

"But who?" asked Eliza, dutifully following Sonia. She walked out the door of her boudoir and followed behind Sonia down the hallway. Looking into the small room that that Sonia walked into five doors down, she saw a familiar face, and her heart skipped a beat. She watched as Alex rose to his feet, a cautious smile crossing his face.

"Alex!" cried Eliza.

Sonia closed the door and turned to Eliza, and knowing the answer, she asked, "You know this young man?"

Awkwardly, Eliza shuffled her feet. "Yes, no, I mean, well, we just met really, you know. It's Alex!"

"You'll have to explain yourself a bit more clearly, dearie," Sonia said, the chair in one hand, her chin in the other.

Eliza started, "Well, when I left Diaspora, he was there, and so was Eva, and I stayed with them for a few days. Then we left on an adventure to find answers..." She trailed off miserably. "You know what happened then. You stole me from them." Eliza could tell she was not making too much sense.

Sonia said, "You're not making sense, Eliza."

"Alex, how do you know Eliza?"

"I found her," said Alex. "I found her, and she was in need." Alex looked from Eliza to Sonia in the small room. Had he been looking for her? He had almost forgotten why he was looking for her in the first place.

Sonya bounced on her feet. "Let's go back a step. Why were you looking for her?"

Alex thought he couldn't remember, and then he did. But he wasn't going to disclose all the details to this audience he didn't entirely trust.

"Because she needed to be found," he said finally.

"Ha-ha!" said the shrewd Sonia, not fooled. "Hold that thought. It's as valid an interpretation as any." She turned to Eliza. "Why did you trust him?"

Eliza thought about it and struggled to find any concrete reason. He had just been part of her life ever since her exit from Diaspora.

"I know!" she exclaimed. "He was kind. He explained things to me."

Sonya tapped her nose and said, "And how do you feel now?"

"I'm glad to see him," said Eliza.

"I'm glad to see her," said Alex.

They both said at the same time.

"Why are we both here?" they said in unison.

Sonia said bluntly, "Alex, you're here to visit Eliza, and you need to approve her new name, and then you can go." Checking that Alex had heard her, she looked at Eliza. "Eliza, you are less sure why you are here than Alex, who's still a little confused but passed his test."

Alex pretended as though he didn't hear Sonia and muttered peevishly, "There sure seems to be a lot of renaming today. First, a hoary old snake and now a friend." The words "friend" or "my love" entered his mind.

Sonia ignored this and took Eliza's hands in hers.

"Honey," she said to Eliza, "stay with us. There is much we can teach you."

"Do I have a choice?" said Eliza, not best pleased.

"No," said Sonia. "You will stay and be made anew. First, we give you a new name." She turned to Alex. "You," she barked at Alex, who jumped and glared at her. "Give me your hand."

Alex, who had been wondering exactly what drug they had given him and for what purpose, nevertheless meekly gave Sonya his hand.

Sonia took Eliza's hand and put in on Alex's.

Soft, thought Alex.

"I, in agreement with the Council of Themystrichyr and being a direct descendant of Apollo who fell from the sky, present this battle-scarred innocent a new name in the presence of her lover," pronounced Sonia.

"What!" yelled Eliza.

Alex examined the tips of his fingers, all of a sudden very interested in the state of his fingernails, his mind drifting to the softness of Eliza's skin. *Was it that soft everywhere?*

Sonia tickled him under the chin. Slightly aglow, he did not mind.

"Aren't you going to ask what your new name is?" asked Sonia, positively enraptured.

"No," said Eliza. "I have a perfectly good name, and you're all nuts."

"You've been renamed," Sonia said. "'Eliza is a beautiful name, worthy of an artisan but not a warrior."

Eliza felt her eyes well with tears as she remembered her ambitions to make jewelry. She looked to Alex for strength.

He gripped her hand and squeezed and looked back at her steadfast.

Sonia continued, "Eliza, you must be free of both of your birth names. You are no longer tethered to the bone-shackling name Cruikshank! No more hideous moniker! Dance out of here on the wings of fortune and grace. You shall henceforth be known as Vega of the Flameborn! She who flies and sends arrows of flames to the skies!"

Then Sonia shrank back into herself, and turning to Alex, she took his hand out of Eliza's hand and said, "You can go now. You have seen Vega's rebirth. Despoina will take you down to the dock, and you'll be ferried over to the mainland, and there you can rejoin your companions."

Alex raised his eyebrows, then he glared at Sonia. "Whatever you think is happening here, I am not going anywhere without Eliza." He put his left hand on his right wrist and made a fist with his right hand, his eyes not leaving Sonia's. "I'm taking her with me," he said.

A wave of nausea washed through him. Sonia moved quickly as if to step in the gap between him and Eliza. Alex moved quicker to protectively stand beside Eliza.

Sonia stopped and waited patiently. Alex turned to check the door that they had come through. He unclenched his right wrist, feeling he no longer had the need to parry and grabbed Eliza's left hand. With his free hand, he attempted to turn the knob of the door, but something restrained his hand. It wasn't Sonia. But what?

"Now what?" said Sonia. "If you have no idea of where she came from or of who you are and where to go once you sally forth, how will your love survive and thrive? What drives you Alex? What are your goals? Your compacts with your ascendants, Alex?" She pushed some curls away from her forehead, which creased as she examined him closely.

Eliza stood there looking from Sonia to Alex.

"What's got my hand?" snapped Alex, his arm on an awkward angle. His shoulders ached and burned.

"Griffin grips," said Sonia joyously. She looked at Alex as he resurveyed the room and took stock.

The walls were not square to the ceiling, he noticed. And the floor? He felt like he was standing straight, but he estimated the floor was not level. The angles to the walls were off, and the bookshelf in the corner was leaning.

"Where are we?" he asked, feeling both subdued and irritated.

Eliza was silent, waiting for the unexpected tableau to play out.

Alex drew on his hot temper to get things moving. "Let me out of here. Let us out of here!" He went to smack his head, thinking, *How could I be in the same situation twice in one day!* But, of course, he couldn't move his hand. Whatever held him, held him fast. *Ugh. This should not be happening*, thought Alex. He was used to getting what he wanted by force if necessary. *Think.* Gathering his thoughts, Alex said calmly as though he were reasoning with a mad woman, "Eliza, Vega, whatever.

She and I were with our fellows, the apothecarians, on a quest to find what endangered their home and the township of Destin and things got a little gnarly. Thanks for your hospitality, but we need to get back together!"

Sonia said, assuming with all the delicacy she could muster, "Then whatever held you together until then can't have been very compelling or stable then, could it?"

"Or you wouldn't be here?" Alex asked exasperatedly.

Sonia filled the gap in discourse and continued, "Relax, Alex. You're on the defensive and too busy looking for patterns in people's behavior to confirm your belief that people will always let you down. You need to relax if you ever want to know the glory of enduring lore."

"Magnificent words," said Alex tiring of the tête-à-tête. He said again, "Where are we? This is not a normal room."

"Alex," said Eliza, feeling the need to contribute. "It's different from all the other rooms. I haven't been in here before."

"Hang on, darling," said Sonia "What are you thinking, Alex?"

Alex was finding it hard to verbalize his thoughts. His training was telling him, "Don't negotiate with a mad woman," but he was unable to draw on his recourse to clear his mind. Movement and action escaped him, as he was immobile from the neck down. Something unseen had his shoulders now, and a force was gripping his arm.

"Look at your hand," said Sonia. "Then look at your other arm."

"I can't see anything," said Alex, then he made out translucent vines.

"This room," said Sonia, "is a room where the impossible becomes possible based on your attitude and hubris. You were in such a one after your boat sank. A Calypso machine. The function of a Calypso machine is to examine someone's character. What you're experiencing is an extension of your own pride and hubris. Let me ask you, Alex. Are you really concerned for Vega's well-being, or are you intent on playing the part of the returning hero, having rescued the damsel in distress. How do you know you've adopted the truest most faithful path? Are you on the right mission? Are you strong enough to complete the mission the Guardians have given you? Have you spoken to the Guardians, through dreams; visions; or their agents, the forests?"

Alex started at this. He had come to rescue Eliza, dammit, Vega, because she had been taken from their party. And he had missed her unbearably. He was strong, and he was certain of his mind!

"But are you?" said Sonia. "You just look for the familiar, the most comfortable path in life, like a moth beating on a flame. A moth is entapped in the initial instance because it knows not better than to fly toward the light. It is the only passion they are familiar with. That drive that excites within them the urge to go to that light brings the next preprogrammed act that runs counter to its survival instincts, and nonetheless, leads to its death. Alex, look beyond the light, beyond Vega's light, to see beyond the light. You must reach beyond familiar patterns and learn to trust people. You must! Anyway, you will know this in yourself by the end."

Alex shifted from foot to foot, his shoulders heavy and his hand restrained.

Sonia continued, "I will tell you that as soon as you are clear on your next mission, you will leave the room. When your focus and true concern for another returns, you will go and a star will point your way on your departure from the dock. Lastly, Alex, a Calypso machine can also highlight other aspects of your character. It will show the truth about your intentions and highlight your pride and hubris. It will also show you where your strength lies. For you, Alex, your strength lies in your shoulders and your mind. You display great mental strength. Once you find your focus, you will be a great leader."

Alex was tiring. He needed to wind this up.

"Keep her safe until I come back for her," he said gruffly.

"Very well," said Sonia.

Alex realized he had lost the chance of returning with Eliza, who was now Vega. Did he really know her? He thought of what a soft bed, what a hot meal, and a bed could do to clear his mind. The vine loosened and fell from his hand, the door handle turned, and Despoina's aged cheerful face peered in.

"Have we finished in here," she said, casually reaching an arm to rest on Alex's shoulders.

He said, "Yes," and sullenly withdrew.

Sonya threw her arm around Eliza. "Vega, you have to start thinking of yourself before you can be part of a group or one with another. That was your first taste. Right you…" She directed this to Alex, then looking at the door. "Off to the dock you go. Vega, we have work to do."

EVA

Eva and Chyra came to a river with an aged wooden bridge.

"You stay here," came an order.

Eva looked around, but she couldn't see anybody else. She looked back; and Chyra, the half girl/half beast, had disappeared. Eva took a few steps onto the bridge and waited. Beneath her feet, the water rushed, and she could make out an urgent sound of drum beats in the distance.

Approximately, fifteen minutes later, the drum beats got louder.

"Didn't you hear my whistle?" came a familiar voice, and Chyra appeared on the other end of the bridge.

Eva had been looking into the water staring at the swirling patterns.

"Come on, putz," called Chyra.

She most definitely had grown taller, and older. Trousers now rode over her footwear, but Eva couldn't be sure of her age. She looked for more clues at Chyra's identity even while raising an eyebrow at the precocious insult.

"Why 'putz,'" she queried, painstakingly taking notes of Chyra's new appearance and her surrounds. If she humored the half girl/beast, she could hopefully take her leave and be back to Trove by midnight.

"You're cleverer than most," replied Chyra, "but you need to go faster. The Clarion pack has convened, and the Regis is in session. Tomorrow will bring horror and revelation. We need you. So come on, dummy."

You need me? thought Eva, bewildered.

"You and the rest of your family. We didn't realize war would come so quickly. Your ride is right here. No time for questions," said Chyra, who was now all of the age of thirteen to Eva's experienced eyes.

Chyra gestured with a hairy hand to a copse of trees, and out from behind it trotted an animal that was half black big cat and half bear! It trotted up to the two females and knelt down, one shoulder resting on the ground, obviously looking for one of the two females to mount it.

"Go on, get on," said Chyra.

Eva, thinking furiously how she had never have come across such an animal in her training, did as she was bid. Another of the beasts came out of the shadows, and Chyra mounted the second. Then she pulled a riding crop from behind her back and switched the animal, and without warning, the pair of mounts was on the move, Eva following Chyra and doing her best to find purchase on the back of the animal with her knees. She slipped, and she slid, but thankfully, it wasn't a long journey until the beasts came to a halt in a clearing. Fireflies circled the edges, giving light to the otherwise lightless glade.

"Where are we?" asked Eva.

Chyra said, "Look to the right, there to the side was a bamboo curtain." Chyra dismounted and pushed through and beckoned.

Eva followed and found herself looking down a sheer drop to a platform on which hundreds, if not thousands, of wolves and creatures like Chyra were milling around. Burning torches threw light everywhere. In the middle was one of the beasts like that that had carried Eva to the mountaintop, standing on its hindquarters.

Eva looked around, and the two that had carried them were also standing, backs to the bamboo curtain.

Like silent sentinels, thought Eva. *What were they guarding. Or were they preventing her from leaving?*

Fear gripped Eva.

A man standing down below yelled up to the night, up to the top of the mountain where the girls stood.

"What have you there, my sister?"

Chyra leaned forward and shouted down, "I've bought the sacrifice, my brother!"

This got Eva's attention. She assumed a guard position, and out of the corner of her eye, she saw Chyra nodding and gesturing downward to the milling throng. Momentarily, she turned quickly to face Eva and came toward her, chin jutting forward, her eyes hot and glowing embers. Eva had no doubt about her intentions. There was no trace left of the helpless young girl about Chyra. She was all animal, and she was coming straight for Eva.

Flexing and tuning from her hourglass position, Eva blocked the approach with her left shoulder and shot her right palm forward, meeting the beast's jutting chin. The forest floor let out a roar. It appeared she was in a fight to the death. She could not afford to debate the morals of fighting a child. She put her overprotective frame set aside to preserve her own life. A mist went briefly over her central vision, and her periphery sharpened. Bloodlust unleashed within her consciousness. Eva rocked back and forward on her heels in a taut hourglass pose, all steel and sinew.

The beast slavered. Stepping back and sizing Eva up, it then let forth a flurry of attacks that Eva easily parried. First, she identified the beast's plan of attack. It was trying to get to her neck and disable her. Eva easily parried the attacks, being a whole head taller than Chyra, but she wasn't fooled that the match would end quickly. Its tactic would be to wear her down, and then land a blow. Frustratingly, Eva could not get in and land an offensive blow. She was in a holding pattern of defend and parry until she started to tire. How was she going to break the beast's attack? The transformed Chyra was astonishingly nimble and rhythmic. She/It did not miss a beat.

Drawing on extra reserves of energy, Eva somersaulted back, landing into a crouch position, and swept one leg under the beast. This gave her time to get further out of the way of Chyra's reach and allow her to retrieve some tools of trade. Alex wasn't the only one who was skilled in throwing weapons. Despite the hurry in packing to get away, Eva herself had foreseen potential trouble on the road and had tucked into her traveling jodhpurs, a number of darts tipped with sumac flower and hogweed sap. She snapped a vial from her belt and sitting it on the ground in front of her opponent flung the tipped darts at the beast.

Sssht…sssht. The first two flew past its head. Then the third pierced the beast in the right eyeball. The vile released its contents. Small hairs floated up, causing the beast to collapse to the ground, clutching its face.

Eva glanced around. The two bear/cats were standing motionless, one to each side of the bamboo curtain. The crowd milling below was waiting to see what would happen next. Eva, knowing her life was still in danger, endeavored to finish off the fight, getting ready to parry should the beast jump up and attack her again. It lay motionless, a paw pressed to the forehead. One bear/cat moaned, and the other purred, and the beast stopped moving.

Eva glanced to the left, then to the right, looked down, and a great cheer rose to the sky. It appeared Chyra the half girl/beast was dead. The bloodlust left Eva, ebbing away, leaving her in a state of confusion and self-doubt. What could she have done differently to preserve Chyra's life while not losing her own? Its chest rattled, and it collapsed on itself, and the death rattle came forth from cavernous lungs. Again, a chant rose from the forest floor.

A bear/wolf/man in the middle shouted, "The sacrifice has been made. We are now ready for the war of beast versus men. Pack Clarion calls on all allies to defend against the creeping madness and ink-eyed spawn of darkness."

The sentinel half bears finally moved, dropping on all fours. Eva pulled another defensive stance with a pang of desperation. There was no way she could get out of here alive. Was this how it was to end? Torn apart without ever being given a chance to redeem herself, to take care of the people she loved. Giving up, she put her head in her hand.

"Don't disappear," said a voice soothingly. A male voice said, "The fight is over, at least temporarily."

Eva raised her head to see one of the half beasts transform into Basil, the foundry man. Eva felt shaky, disturbed, and tearful. The other half bear dropped to all fours.

"What in the nine circles are you doing here?" she said in a surly voice.

"Nice to see you too," he joked.

It was a quip that was so unexpected and so out of place that Eva gave a wonky smile in return. Basil held out his hands and gestured for Eva to mount the other half beast. Eva was still reconciling within herself the drive to nurture and protect with the way she had dispatched the Anti'Jhinii.

Child, her conscience whispered to her.

"Don't second guess yourself," said Basil. "It's done." He waved at the corpse.

Before her eyes, it started to smoke. Smoke curled above the corpse, then dissipated, leaving purple crystals in the clearing.

A salt, she thought, *and some dried leaves*. There were no clothes, no bones, nothing. Eva was left with no choice but to use Basil's hand as a stirrup and mount the half beast. Basil mounted behind her, and then they were moving.

"What is it?" asked Eva of her companion to the rear. "What are we riding?"

"A pentarian," said Basil. "A hybrid. We're more familiar with hybrids here, where the desert meets the Taiga on the border of Asperia. Many of us also are hybrids."

Eliza sneezed, and with the involuntary expungement, she realized her new friend, Basil of the Forge, was one of those baying beasts, a hybrid!

"Hold on," he warned.

With that warning, Eva found herself looking down at the forest floor as the Pentarian went over the cliff on a vertical lean, and she realized they were clambering their way down the cliff face. The half beast/half man in the center of the clearing gestured them to come forward, and the Pentarian carried them to him, it.

"The sacrifice to the Guardians cleansed the way for a worthy battle," said the beast. He addressed the two, who were still mounted. "Hello, dear," he said to Eva, and the crowd cheered. "Eva," he continued, "fate dictated you weren't to be today's sacrifice. Had you not been such a good fighter, you would have been. But you are preserved because you embody strength and are the embodiment of the feminine force to lead us into the war."

"I don't fight," said Eva. "I heal and preserve."

The beast, Chyra's brother, replied. "You've never been in a war before. There has been times of peace until now. This has all changed.

You're a strong fighter, Eva. You fight to preserve life, and you must learn to attack those who would take life frivolously, without regard for ritual or custom." The beast shifted gears. "Today's sacrifice was made by one who had studied and taken in the veniality of the enemy. She gave her own life via the aegis of an honorable fight. Her doing so was the right sacrifice and the true embodiment of selfless love. Today's sacrifice has been made, Eva. Henceforth, you are asked only to stand for your values so the fight to preserve everyone's way of life and customs may be fought again and the sanctity of life will be valued for evermore! Don't say you're not capable Eva, or willing! These are the very qualities you embody. You put your life on the line for life. Don't waste time on negative thoughts. You're not compromising your values. You're a pure, wholesome forger, just like our Basil here."

Basil looked down at Eva and winked. Eva was now in an after-fighting glow, and she was feeling quite pleasant from the close proximity of Basil, so she decided that she would give this unnatural pageant the time of day. Speaking of which, was that streaks of dawn breaking over the field? And what did he mean by "forger," this man/beast? She did not know how to work metal like Basil.

"Hang on," said Eva plaintively. "There is no war. We came here to seek help!"

The beast changed his tone of voice and said, raising to the voice to the skies, "The war has started. It started a long time ago. Now it reaches the pinnacle of fighting, in the heart of the Taiga. Lead us into battle, Eva. Be our figurehead. Let us put all our hopes on you, our hopes of glory, of victory, of vanquishing the ink-eyed soul that devours, that would enslave our kind. It is done. The compact is forged." He raised the gnarled staff passed to him by another of his kind. He raised it and then struck it on the ground: one two three. "They have taken our blood. We have taken their shadows and distilled as an honorable sacrifice unto one of us, who received them gratefully. They can do us no harm. But we, we will seek and destroy."

A chant grew in volume, rising up from the forest floor.

"Seek and destroy! Seek and destroy. My name is Gambit," he said to Eva. "You will go ahead now, and you will know what to do. You have performed the required sacrifice to animate and rouse our people. We will fight, and at the end of the war, we will go home weary with spoils, replete with the rewards of victory. On our return to our hearths, cries will rise into the air, telling of our majestic feats. Our womenfolk will embrace those that are still standing, and we will dandy our children on our shoulders and our laps, and we will all know we have given everything to keep the Taiga free. Join us, Eva. Be part of our great clan."

Eva desperately needed to sleep. She looked at Basil for help.

"Come, let us go rest," he said. "We will ride back to Trove and await the drums of war."

CARLOTTA

Her irritation had risen to a crescendo of anger. Carlota was in desperate need of distraction when a guard tentatively approached her.

"The mayor has been asked for an urgent audience."

"With who?" snapped Carlotta.

"With the proctors of Diaspora," said the guard.

"The mayor is indisposed," replied Carlotta.

That was the source of her irritation. When the mayor made proclamations from his chambers, she was able to decipher them and tweak policy as she so desired.

It wasn't so easy when he retired to his homestead on his annual vacation or when he was on sick leave, as he was now with a flare up of chlamydia. He tended to shutter council business until his return, which might not be for weeks given the nature of his illness.

Carlotta was the only one who knew he had contracted a sexually transmitted disease. She had sympathy. She had once contracted gonorrhea throat. The kidney-bean shaped bacteria had made her miserable for weeks. The merchant she'd contracted it from got a secondary infection from her as a token of her appreciation. She smiled. It had been rigorous sleeping with him that second time, but it was worth it knowing he had later died of heat stroke in the desert. Regarding the mayor's illness, she'd hacked into Betty's, the nurse assistant's notes and erased them. She gave Betty mono while inquiring after her grandmother so she wouldn't be back to work for a while, then spread it around that the mayor had influenza. Eric, the mayor, was very grateful when she let him know that gossip wouldn't spread the true nature of his infection. Not grateful enough to fully hand over the reins of power but Carlotta still knew she had a favor to call on there. And Eric would henceforth be wary of her and her abilities.

She employed an imperious tone with the guard.

"We are not to bother the mayor," she stated.

The guard, anticipating this, said, "Ignoring their request would be a serious mistake. Diaspora is our largest non-Asperian neighbor. As a city, it has many ways to make its displeasure known. In all likelihood the city's chagrin would be felt via tightened trade."

"I cannot understand why they want to speak with us," responded Carlotta.

She actually had an idea forming, but she was buying time thinking what she might gain from officially forming an alliance with Diaspora, rather, the real power behind the city engine of Diaspora. Perhaps time had run out, she thought. She had supposed she might have longer before she disposed of the mayor, but maybe, just maybe, everything was in place.

"Listen, Lawrence," said Carlotta. "The mayor is not here, and he's not due back until next week at the earliest. You look like a capable man, so you and I are going to meet with the proctors. We'll see what they have to say."

Lawrence shuffled nervously. He supposed this would be within his dominion. The Nine Circles take him. *Two months on the job, and now he had an extra fifty thousand men to feed and clothe with nothing much to do. And now, dammit, this. Where is the mayor? However, the mayor's assistant seemed authoritative.*

Carlotta discerned the thoughts running through his head.

"Lawrence, listen to me." She drew up a screen. "The mayor is not here. In his absence, I translate and determine his decrees. I execute (this said with relish) his operational decisions. I understand you're the commander general of the troops, I mean, the guards."

Carlotta dotted the location of the men in her de facto army on the screen and flattered him.

"Lawrence, you already have a lot of responsibly. You don't want the added stress of a possible dispute with a bound city—or aggravating the mayor who is quite quick to anger, or so I have heard. He's always been level tempered and pleasant with me. All we have to do is hear what the proctors have to say, and then we can discuss it with a mayor on his return. Really, we're just carrying out our duties in absence of the mayor, and you look like the most capable and intelligent man to do so."

Lawrence shifted from foot to foot. He supposed he was.

Carlotta dispatched her personal screen.

"I presume the meeting is virtual and it's urgent? Can you draw up a sister city screen?" She directed Lawrence, referring to the intercity neural links that trade and official business were conducted through.

"Yes," he said hurriedly and grabbed up the stylus from the mayor's desk. Drawing up the screen in the space above the desk at head height, he handed the stylus to Carlotta, wishing he was already off work so he could go and complete the roster and next week's reconnaissance time-table for what he supposed was now an army.

The Diaspora seal, an ornate *D* and a feather in a circle, flashed up on the screen and was replaced by the pleasant featureless face of a proctor that Carlotta had never met.

"Good morning, whose acquaintance do I have the pleasure of making?" she asked.

"Proctor Herbert," Herbert replied evenly. "I'm in charge of Deployment and Emergent threats."

Carlotta's heart started to beat faster. Those were words that got her blood stirring. They sounded like fighting words: "Deployment" and "threats."

Any person of influence knew full well that you couldn't gain power, title, or money without fighting battles.

"What's the Department of Emergent Threats?" Carlotta asked.

"You're not the mayor," Herbert countered.

"Yes," she said. "I am Carlotta, the mayor's entrusted subalternate."

That sounds made up, thought Herbert, but he wasn't one to challenge his audience or consult another proctor on protocol. He himself had been thrust in the role he was in only a few days earlier.

"Have a conversation. Get this done and form the alliance," he had been instructed.

Once he was done, he would get his fix and attend a dance party that evening.

"You're a subalternate," parroted Herbert, and Carlotta waved the words away with a flick of her hand.

"We passed it at the last council meeting," said Carlotta. "When the mayor is away, the person who had executed the most orders for the mayor in the previous period would become the subalternate voice for the mayor, effectively the mayor's voice."

Oh, she was good at making this stuff up off the cuff, and she would make damn sure these rules would be buried in the recent clauses that were passed to approve additional infrastructure, passed at the last council meeting. Carlotta smiled grimly.

"We anticipated if he would be away there would be a need for a spokesperson in case of emergency. And lo, he has been stricken ill, and I am the only person here who can speak for him." Carlotta was doubling down on her story, the series of lies tripping easily from her mouth.

Herbert leaned forward. He was bored now and had no need for any further explanations as long as they could both conduct the business that he needed to push through.

"Very well, Carlotta. Today is a day we're calling on you to assist us meet the latest emerging threats."

"What threats do you speak of?" asked Carlotta.

"We have information that traditional denizens of the forest, bound city fugitives, and the odd peripatetic desert goer have organized themselves into regiments deep within the oldest forest, within the Taiga, and they have formed unnatural bonds over generations with the beasts within. They've turned large beasts into steeds to attack our walls and bred with other species to trick us and entice us, to look like us, to become us, to infiltrate us. There are those who would walk among us, masquerade as us, and attack our cities from within! They live in close proximity to my very own bound city, Diaspora, and they are planning to group up as regiments and attack us with new technology and strike our food supply, our farms. You in Destin are further away from danger than us, but you should take an interest in our affairs! If they attack us, it may be that they turn their claws and their weapons on your town next!"

"I had not heard of such an emergent threat," said Carlotta, trying to match his lingo.

Now it was Herbert's turn to lie. There was no such threat, of course. Diaspora was easily able to see off any threat from the outside. The city had sufficient defenses and was quite self-contained, growing what it needed without farming, which perhaps explained the hunger for the strange animals that so satisfied Herbert's needs, his and that of his new acquaintances.

"Yes, we have a technology that allows us to detect heat emissions. We are willing to share it with you and show you our heat maps if you commit to assist us meeting the threat and sharing with us any technologies we may not have."

Carlotta, feeling like she had to start steering the conversation and demonstrate authority said, "I must understand the threat, Proctor. The mayor will demand a full explanation on his return."

"I understand," said Herbert. "The heat maps show that there is a large mass, practically an army forming and oscillating in the middle of the Taiga. It has been extremely active, and the pattern formations indicate a military intent. We proctors and fathers fear it may launch from the jungle and attempt to breach the city walls."

Herbert was also lying easily.

"There was no way that even the complete mobilization of, say, the entire upgraded forces of Destin could get close to the boundary of Diaspora."

Herbert had not been charged with detailing the truth to the leaders of Destin. He had been instructed to develop and execute a plan to flush out enough of the animals from the forest so that they may drain the essence of the inhabitants en masse—for science, for their benefit.

Herbert continued, "There is nothing in the forest apart from rotting trees and hybrids. Monsters that changed into beasts and sired more half beast/half men interbred abominations. And really, the whole forest needed to be burned down, which they would do after it was purged. Only this measure will save the animals that are fit and healthy."

Sophia had assured him that they would have enough of a supply of bioplasm to become elevated.

"Herbert," she'd said, "we may even be able to command the skies again."

Herbert didn't have a full grasp of the technology. He was just an administrator, though he was quite pleased with himself having negotiated thus far though the city ranks. He was not a technologist, but that was okay, he was advised. LaVey had wondered out loud that if his plan worked. He and certain other proctors might even have control of the skies again. Who would not want to both fly and stay young? Both were out of reach of the dreams of human. Or were they? He could feel them both within his grasp. If he could stay young, he could command respect. Who was he to argue with LaVey and her friends' vision? He was not a technologist. Knowing how things worked was not his forte, but he did know that it took special people to come up with effective and original solutions. He was one of those special people. Just look at how he had come up with a tailor-made plan to meet the augments' objectives. Thank the Guardians he saw the potential in LaVey and let her into his life.

"What do you expect us to do?" snapped Carlotta, bringing Herbert back to attention.

"As it so happens," said Herbert. "We have foreseen this threat develop for some time." He droned on, now reading from a prepared script. "We have a custom military drill making a foray into the Turing Turnpike, the entrance into the Taiga where the desert meets the forest, and both meet Asperia."

"Yes, I know where Turing is! When is this happening?" asked Carlotta, inspecting her fingernails as she elbowed the new chief of guards, who was nodding off.

"In three hours. We will be deploying five regiments to the extent of the boundary sickness zone, fifty thousand men in total. Do you have any military cover that you could provide in the event we are met with greater force than we anticipated?" asked Herbert, quite proud of his delivery.

"Of course!" said Carlotta with vigor, sitting up straight. "It so happens that I anticipated recently that our proud town of Destin might become the target of unfriendly outside forces, and I increased our training numbers and military barracks, and I can indeed provide some trained and armed soldiers to deal with the threats you say may be imminent! I can meet Diaspora's fifty thousand with an additional twenty-five thousand troops."

The chief of the guards snored and fell off his chair. Carlotta scooped a tarantula from the underside of the mayor's table, muttering to the prone body, "Goodbye, you idiot. I'll go and give the orders to the troops. No reason to trouble the mayor with a welcoming party." She curled the corner of her mouth down into a moue of discontent.

THE STABLES

The pounding awoke Eva first thing and the whinnies of unsettled horses. She heard the tinny sound of metal against metal and popped her eyes open to see Terry nonchalantly leaning against a bale of hay and spooning food from a flask. Clearly, Eva had been offloaded from the Pentarian and into the stables with no memory of dismounting.

Eva raised herself up onto her elbows, pushed her bangs out of her eyes and said to Nicoletta and Tan who were sitting cross-legged in the opposite stall playing out a hand of cards.

"What is your account of yesterday's events? Alex arrived home," announced Terry, unasked. "Totally sodden, wet as a muskrat, limping home from the dock, complaining about devilry and women who enjoyed wielding power over men, subjugating them. I almost wish I'd been there! And what an appetite he had! Basil took him back to the forge so he could have a decent rest in a proper bed. Nothing wrong with these digs though!"

Terry smiled and looked around at the stables, taking in the high-pitched roof, and the horses pawing at their beds of hay.

"Who would have thought that a stable could be so comfortable, be a home? This is the favorite place I have ever slept in, always somebody to talk to."

He blew gently on a gerbil that was nesting on the back of his hand. He put his hand down on the table and let the gerbil scamper off.

"Other than the apothecary," he added glumly. "And, oh, Alex got to talk to Eliza!"

—◊—

Eva startled. The events of yesterday coalesced in her mind. All the memories racing in and overwhelming her like water cascading off a tremendous drop, resulting in a unsettled turbulence.

"War!" she shouted.

—⁓—

Nicoletta and Tan leisurely finished out their hand of cards and strode out the stable doors, to check on the pounding from outside. The horses neighed and moved restlessly, and one horse kicked at its stall. A black stallion called Blackfish reared on its hind legs.

"We haven't got long, if so," said Terry reflectively. "I don't yet know what happened after we parted company yesterday. But I can see you're covered in bruises and scratches. So by my guess, we're now out of out of the frying pan and into the volcano, I mean, fire." And he winked.

"Stop speaking in riddles," cried Eva, frustrated.

"Obviously, we're on a new mission," said Terry. "We're on a new mission, but it's the same old mission. We go to save animals, as many as we can and find and defeat the—"

"Hear, hear!"

Tan pushed open the doors and strode into the stable, Nicoletta followed close behind, crackling with barely suppressed energy.

"Old words from a wise mind," said Tan, twinkling at Terry.

Foxy scampered past Tan's legs to sniff at Terry's ankles and lick his outstretched hand.

"You heard me," said Terry, trying to assume a dignified stance as befitting a wise person.

"Saving animals! Not taking anything too seriously. Ahem." Nicoletta coughed. She looked serious, and in the background the drumming of the big war drums sounded, and the beats got closer together.

Nicoletta crouched, launched into the air, and landed on her feet on the back of the Appaloosa filly behind her. She took two steps toward the horse's tail, bent backward, and somersaulted forward, arriving on a rather surprised Sarsaparilla. Tan watched admiringly as Nicoletta stood up straight; saluted to the other three; looked and counted off all the horses in the stables, naming them one by one. Then she tumbled and dove, jumping from post to horse to column to horse and then landed in front in front of her admiring company.

"I've been practicing formation and tumbling with my marching team during the quiet years. Yesterday, I got word from my marching team from Destin with fresh news. The girls told me, the men have all been called up into something called the Destin reservists. All the men, all the husbands, all the male grandparents. No one spends any time in ascension because the menfolk are all seconded into this training, full time. Eventually, they stop seeing the faces of their elders. It's forced and unnatural. There have been consequences. The rebirth equilibrium is out the window, and that is part of what bought us here. One piece of the puzzle. The drumming you can hear is the sound of war drums echoing through Asperia. The men were reluctant to participate originally, but now they are on the move they have been told to defend the towns against a hostile threat. A threat that might bring harm to the women and children," said Nicoletta, shifting from one foot to another. "They must be being lied to! You and I, our entire family having been entrusted with the noble preservation of life by way of the of the healing professions. Know that that is not the case. There is no outside threats to Destin, to any of the towns in Asperia. Not from any other human source, as our settlements have coexisted thus far for hundreds of years with the assistance of our forebears in ascension. And animals have not the drive or the capacity to cause the harm humans have done in the past. The threat must be coming from within. This threat started out as a dust storm. Some vague challenges to our birthright from within the town council. The threat of a dust storm has now grown into a tornado, and today we must lean into the storm.

NICOLETTA

Hannah finally found Doug and May in ascension. She partook of her special mushroom broth,and St. Anthony guided her to them. They were faint, she said, like outlines with the color fading out; but they were able to exchange information. And Maleficent took a flight around the border of Trove.

"I viewed it myself," she crooned. "It is seen that today great tranches of soldiers will fall on the Turing Turnpike, the trading post where desert meets Taiga meets Asperia. Soon we will see our enemies' faces. See their shadows fall long, over commingling domain. And we must fight this first battle to preserve our credo. Venturians will not be banished, smitten or defeated! We must fight today. Not to preserve but to kill. To dispatch every last hostile, and then we must vanquish their shadows, lest they come after us and extinguish our light. Then we will see our enemies' faces proper. We will reason with our loved ones to return to peace and not go to war with the forest, which is what I fear it has come to. There is a large army exiting the bounds of Diaspora and regiments of soldiers coming from Destin.

BASIL

The front of the forge was packed with men with concerned upturned faces. A Sovran schoolteacher, Drew, stepped forward. Instead of the usual Sunday morning sounds, the ever-present drumming noise reverberated plaintively in the distance. The atmosphere was pent, strained, and suppressed. Drew spoke clearly, enunciating each word.

"Catastrophe is about to fall upon us. We have friends and relatives in Destin. Our quandary is of how our blood came to take up arms and sally forth with the intent of causing mayhem and potentially turning on Trove. We have brethren in the desert and the forest. We cannot allow this travesty to happen."

Basil's eyes conveyed compassion and iron to the throng of men gathered around the forge.

"Horses are made for riding in times of peace and also for bearing men who wield arms," Basil said. "That way you can find two ways out of the jungle. The quickest way is to outrun the enemy". "You can rain blows on the enemy" "Or you can hack your way through the vines that threaten to strangle you and take you away from your woman and children." His eyes turned cold. "I have kept the fire in the forge burning for a long time, seeing generations come and go. The flame did not go out between generations—my father, his father, and I. The fire stays alive to this day though I travel hither and yonder. I wear many cloaks and go many places, but the important thing today is the fire still burns."

Basil assumed a somber demeanor and, looking Drew straight in the eyes, said, "I cannot predict what's going to happen today just know this—we must dress for speed, and we must be very prepared to hack our way through the tracking vines and the clumping underbrush. We must fight to win, to protect and preserve the flame of the forge. The individual struggle is not as critical in this battle though you are all uniquely important. What is important is making a united stand to keep the flame burning to keep all the woman and children safe on our return. You will see, each of you will have a light to return by."

Drew turned to the crowd.

"Keep our flame safe," he said to the crowd. "Preserve the forge at all costs." Then he instructed the crowd, "Help yourself to my armory."

And throwing the doors wide open, he strode back inside. The crown bustled and jostled and murmured approval and followed the swarthy forger inside.

TURING TURNPIKE

High above the turnpike, Maleficent soared. Nicoletta was receiving the impressions of the three roads into the turnpike and saw all three roads full of lively military activity. Her heart ached at the sight. On the ground beside Nicoletta, Tan put his hand on her elbow.

"Give me your hand," he said as he steadied her.

Together they watched as a man from Destin in a military tunic rushed past them; recognizable as such with the town insignia, a heliotrope flower embroidered on his breast pocket. He roped together a string of horses and pushed through, pulling at the rope with one hand and admonishing a recalcitrant stud with a pull on the rope with the other. Occasional military vehicles rumbled in another feeder road into the turnpike reminding them how quickly the situation could escalate.

"Combat cars," said Tan.

"Mmmm," said Nicoletta distracted.

"That's what those vehicles are. Weaponized vans disguised with vines and canvas drapes. Could be worse," said Tan. "I can't see any heavily armored trucks."

—⁊⁊—

Gingerbread and Sarsaparilla were nuzzling over the top of the stalls they were in.

"Hey, boys," said Eva, scratching them each in turn.

They neighed their appreciation as Basil arrived at the door of the stable.

"You and I are going to the foot of Mama Mountain." said Basil to Eva. "Otherwise known as Mont Marguerite."

Eva looked at Hannah, who was looking skyward, green eye tilted up, as though she was communicating, though Eva could see she was not in ascension. Hannah shook, and then she smiled and wrapped her arms around herself.

"I'll see you at the end of the battle, Eva dear," she said.

She looked down at the ground, her blue eye watering the parched earth.

"Follow your heart and be a defender of Guardians," intoned Hannah. "You will need to bury the dead after. We will both mourn the loss, and each passing hour gives the advantage to our enemy."

Hannah stopped talking.

Eva tried to reply and ask her earth mother where she would be and why Hannah wouldn't be accompanying them, but the words kept slipping away. Her mind was foggy momentarily, her knees weak, and she trembled. Another member of the company, her very own Hannah was now travelling separately?

Basil slipped his arm around Eva's waist to steady her and said, "Your ride is here, Eva."

She looked up at Basil to see clouds passing in his eyes as he considered his words carefully.

"The queen doesn't go to battlefront on a horse or in a mere functional van."

He opened the stable door and ushered Eva out.

"The queen?" said Eva. "What on Panacea do you mean by the queen? I'm a healer, not at all royal. And I don't know what is going on."

"Again, the forest needs you," said Basil. "The forest requests your assistance from the old Guardian trees, the towering canopy to the underbrush. The animals and other sentients anticipate your arrival, as does the underground city of life. Your warrior spirit is needed at the Taiga, today. Your presence is required at Cleft's Severance."

Basil was speaking in tongues as far as Eva was concerned.

"And you're right here, so we haven't got time to argue."

Eva decided not to point out the lack of logic in his last sentence. She followed his eyes to see a Pentarian beside her. Slinking along the path Basil had deftly distracted her into walking along with his arm around her waist.

She sucked in her breath sharply and let out a small whoop as Basil reached down and slipped her legs out from under her. Using his arm around her waist, he maneuvered her onto the back of the nearby Pentarian, and then he was on its running mate that had appeared from the left, and suddenly, they were speeding toward the mountainous ranges. It was all she could do not to throw up as her ears started to thrum as the drum beats got louder. She presumed they were approaching the Turing Turnpike. An alert on her maps sent to her inner ear told her that Nicoletta and Tan were also near.

They thundered for another half a mile, and here came to a sudden halt.

"Here we are," said Basil. "The foothills had given away to the massive three-way waypoint that routed travelers into Asperia from the Taiga and the desert."

He jumped off the Pentarian and helped Eva dismount.

She bent down to tie a lace that had come undone on the race to the Turnpike, and as she stood, she looked to see if anyone had noticed the Pentarians. Surely, they would draw attention to them. They were not where she had dismounted. Instead, Basil was leaning into a booth that sold straw hats and flasks and chatting animatedly with two other men Eva recognized from her short time in Trove.

Could it be Robert's dad? she wondered.

The other, Alan Benton, clapped Basil on the shoulder and bade him a good day.

"Look after our princess," he said, his voice carrying to Eva.

She looked around to see who they were talking about, and when she looked back, the two men were skipping away jauntily in the direction of the oncoming crowd.

ROSELLE

Roselle in the toll booth of the Turning Turnpike was struggling to hold back tears. As far as the eyes could see, she saw a longer line than usual of travelers to process. She was the only checker on the Trove feeder lane, and she had a burning finger from a rat bite that she received when she got to work earlier. There was never any warning from management when there was a surge in traffic. And this was possibly the most people she had ever seen since she started working here ten years ago.

Looking down at her feet, distracted by the discomfort of her swollen ankles, she saw a small dog in the booth with her! But when she reached down to say, "Heya, fella, what are you doing down there," her hand passed right through him. She shrugged. Occasionally, there was a remnant that came through from ascension. She hoped the fella had had a good life. Looking back up over her booth, she sighed and waited for the questions to start. Though no one paid for passage through the crossing with physical money, there were always questions!

"How far till the next turnpike?"

"Where can I enter the desert?"

Roselle almost missed the falcon coming out of the sky and crashing into the glass face of the booth. It made a "corumphf" sound that caught her attention, and its feathers splayed out across the glass of the booth window then it fell to the ground. Turning to check on the welfare of the bird, she missed entirely the woman putting the hand into the booth with an egg shape. The woman quickly placed the object on the shelf in front of Roselle as she turned back around and noticed the object.

"What's that there now? First, a bird and now an egg?" She laughed at herself as she said out loud, "Which came first the chicken or the egg?"

Picking it up, her finger went right through the shell, and all of a sudden, a smokey mist filled the air. Roselle started to cough. Her throat caught, and she felt as though there was something in it: a lump. The lump started to expand. Now she was feeling a little scared.

What's happening? she thought.

It turned one in the afternoon. The sun was just past its zenith as the first traveler in line rapped on the glass. Roselle implored him with her eyes plaintively, helplessly.

Thornton had decided not to head back to the desert that day. He had plenty of herbs to sell to the desert nomads, the herbs he had purchased from the Uyghurs and the Tzigane. But the cacophony at the turnpike! The whole pressing mass of people around him made him want to head back into the desert and let go his day-to-day affairs go unattended while he bartered and ate with the desert tribes. Instead, he was first in line. All the better to get into the forest and up to the mountains where his lady awaited with a pot of partridge broth and heavy blankets he could slumber under for a week and rest and fast before news of his presence got around, and he was inundated for requests for remedies and was denuded of the trinkets and bagatelles he'd accumulated.

At the toll booth window, the woman inside the booth turned around, and Thornton gasped! She was in obvious pain and trying to claw something from her mouth. As she withdrew her hand from her face, she left rake marks down her face and grabbed at the window, her eyes pleading, "Help," to Thornton. He watched helplessly as she left bloody streaks on the glass and disappeared from sight. Instinctively, he moved behind the booth to help and found her on thefloor straining to breathe. Grabbing her wrist, he felt a soft flutter of a pulse that abruptly disappeared. Putting her arms gently on her chest, Thorton rose to look for somebody who could help. Outside the booth, a woman was standing there, sharply outlined in the afternoon sun and against the backdrop of his state of shock. She looked from him to the body, obviously shocked, and then she backed off, looking horrified.

"No!" she said. "No," she said again, obviously distressed.

Thorton put out his hands, facing outwards, to show he had nothing to hide.

The woman backed away and let out a scream.

"This man killed someone! He killed her."

The pushing and shoving started almost immediately as the words sank into the crowd's ears. It was almost an afterthought that a man nearby grabbed Thorton's wrist as he tried to leave the scene. The man held Thornton's wrist up.

"I have him! The killer."

The woman put two laurel leaves over Roselle's eyes and drew up a map to call emergency services. Maleficent swooped over the scene. Nicoletta surveyed as the pushing and the shoveling turned into fists slamming into faces and the normally peaceful folk of Turnpike started using whatever came to hand as weaponry: studded rings and belts, scissors, and knives, and nunchakus all came out.

LaVey eased back into the crowd, pleased. Her work here was done. It took a surprisingly short time to raze the Turnpike and dismantle its few civic structures. Thornton was running as if the hounds of the seven outer rings were after him. Once the buildings had been smashed to bits, the fighting had calmed down. A massive non Diasporian Army was now drawing power from the grid for idle games, playing clicker games on maps, or street poker among themselves or most were just sitting in the sacked wreckage waiting for instruction.

Gilbert, Destin's latest chief of guards, pushed through the melee to locate the commander from Diaspora. Carlotta's latest message flashed up on his maps augment so he could hardly ignore her. He could just see her in his mind's eye: peremptory, bossy, and dismissive.

"Make sure you offer the commander any assistance needed to approach the Taiga. If the southwestern interests are not secured by nightfall then, well, our families will not be safe. And I know you have another child on the way."

Gilbert sucked his breath in remembering the implicit threat. Carlotta was venal certainly. He'd known that ever since she had offered him a gift of money and dangled the promise of a promotion in front of him if he filmed Milton's suffering in the council chambers and eventual demise. After that she had told him to keep quiet about the events in the chambers or she would let it be known he was guilty of taking bribes. Was she thinking of usurping the mayor? He had pointed out her simony to her and nothing more was said, though a cold glint in her eye had unnerved him. Had she caused Milton's suffering? He couldn't imagine a woman to be capable of a cruel act. Certainly not barbary, this long after the reawakening. But that was a very pointed comment considering his wife, Stella, worked for her.

—⟋⟍—

Gilbert walked reluctantly past three nineteen-year-old youths smoking rolled up tobacco while they waited. He used to be partial to baccy himself. He would only partake after hunting opossums and finn raccoon for the fur trade as a youngster. Now he was a husband, his days were spent overseeing Destin's guards and his nights with his young family. The Diaspora commander was tapping a paper map on a table, a relic removed from one of the demolished civic buildings and gesturing to Gilbert.

Impressive boiler plate garb, thought Gilbert looking at all the men dressed the same as the commander, Oleeve. His own men were dressed in leather pants and linen tunics. General Oleeve was wearing a breastplate over a tunic, chain mail pants, and rucking boots with steel caps, as were the team of six men he had with him.

"Right here," said the commander, tapping the map of isolated areas of low-density bush. "Right here," he repeated, tapping the map again. "I have located three areas of low-density bush that could be defended. In two of these clearings, our men could get ambushed from nearby features on higher land. We need to take two platoons to each of these clearings, securing them from the higher ground, clearing the land of hostiles as they advance. This leaves one entrance into the forest we can be comfortable of securing in the initial incursion."

Gilbert didn't like the aggressive tone in Oleeve's voice and interrupted, "Our instructions were to ensure that we meet any hostile forces coming out of the forest, at what point do we enter the forest? It's a terrain we're not used to skirmishing in. We were only to fight if we're attacked! We don't know what or who we'd be fighting."

The commander stuck his big glossy nose out and, looking down it, stared upward examining Gilbert's forehead.

"Do you think that we wait for our enemy to come to us?" He didn't wait for Gilbert to answer. "No! We're going in, sonny."

Gilbert scratched at his stubble, turning this over in his mind. The commander outranked him was all he knew.

"I understand," Gilbert volunteered.

"Can you neutralize any forces in these clearings?" said Olceve peremptorily, turning back to rap on the on the map.

"I know there are all sorts of beasts in there. I have seen the heat images. We must keep Diaspora safe, productive, and sound. Safe from threats. My army is in a greater state of readiness than yours, so we will lead. We were told to move out yesterday morning, so our levels of preparation are greater, more sophisticated."

Commander Oleeve waved this unfortunate detail away with a swift movement of his hand.

"That's fine for now. Your forces are far less than ours. So we will enter here!" "Bang" on the map on the table on the third clearing. "And your men will form two flanks to catch any threats to civilization that escape afterward. Then we're all going to have to go into the forest because there will be nests of these vermin that we have to find and burn."

Confused and worried, Gilbert searched in his mind for an adequate response, maybe even a rebuttal of Oleeve's instructions. But Oleeve got in ahead of any protest.

"You've got it, right! We're leaving in thirty minutes as soon as our last squad has left Turing. You follow and send your men into those clearings then out to flank us. Okay! You've got this." And Oleeve started walking away.

THE TAIGA

Alicia had only meant to play in the stream until lunchtime but the patterns of bubbles and the water skaters were so captivating she lost track of time. A piece of wood shaped like a scoop had been used to carve out a moat on the sandbank.

If I go back now, the moat will wash away, she thought, tucking her forefinger in her blouse. *And if I go back now, my older sister Gilly would tell me off and point out my skinny shoulders.*

"Skinny shoulders," she would say. "You don't eat, skinny Minnie. And, Alicia, you're short!" She would finish up tugging Alicia's braids while Alicia squirmed to get away.

Alicia didn't want to be the brunt of Gilly's teasing today. She wanted to stay right here in nature. And Elk might think to come and find her. Elk was from next door who was the same age as her. He never teased her. He had kind eyes and would join in many of Alicia's games, like hunting for treasure. There was always treasure to be found here in the river. Flotsam washed down from upstream. Buried metal objects and shells. Old ancient debris trapped by volcanic action, stuck in time, then finally released by the force of erosion.

Why the beat of drums and the staccato of heavy traffic? wondered Alicia. *It was quite distracting. Why today? Adults never said anything about why anything ever happened. Not that anything did happen in Trove.*

So she came here to explore. Alicia dug at a patch of clay and uncovered a block of amber. She gasped and added it to the pile of treasures on the bank: a huge eagle feather, the flower spike of a salamander plant leaked a milky sap but would burn all night if lit so she could stay up reading, and a coin of the old currency that was covered in green moss. She liked it though it was useless. The coin had a head on one side. Maybe a hero from the old days? Or maybe anybody could print their likeness onto useless alloys.

Thunk! A blow to the side of her head took Alicia her out of her reverie. She began to wail. It was such a beautiful day and now! A giant pushed her out of the way, and another grabbed her arm. She felt a crack. How could that be? You hear something crack not feel it. And then a burning pain in her arm to match the pain in the side of her head as her body met the ground, Lying on her side and through blurry vision, Alicia saw a stream of giants running single file, kicking her treasures aside.

"No!" she breathed futilely. "No!" She breathed, witnessing holstered weapons on their hips, and then she saw black. "Guns," she said with her final breath. "Guns."

GUNS

Eva found herself staring at a rock face while her Pentarian sniffed its fellow, and Basil walked around tapping on his thigh as the staccato of the drums rolled on.

"Guns," he said after a while. "Guns! Before the reawakening, people used to take them in flying machines and shoot their enemy on the ground without engaging them. Can you imagine a greater evil then killing someone without seeing their face?"

"I hadn't thought about it," said Eva.

"It's not easy to reconstruct that diegesis, admittedly," remarked Basil thoughtfully. "We have no flying machines. Then we stopped using pump and sump guns without the flying machines. Rifles to hunt for food are all we've known for generations. There are two things that worry me—the forest defending itself against an enemy with rifles and if we should ever get to the air again, would bad men take to air with guns?"

Eva waited for Basil to finish. "Even if so, it is not so easy to shoot low and true in the jungle and find your mark," said Eva.

"Today will be a day of heartbreak and sorrow, regardless," said Basil.

"Perhaps it is cleaner this way. The enemy out in the open. We will know the faces of our enemy who seek to destroy us."

"Yes," said Basil, standing taller. "It is easy to address the punctures of a hundred small basket snakes than find yourself in the grip of a ravenous boa constrictor. But both types of snake attack are unpleasant. Today I fear we may find ourselves encircled by a ravenous serpent. He slapped his thigh. Today we will see the faces of our enemy, and we will prevail."

Hearing leaves crunching underfoot, they both turned to see Nicoletta and Tan crossing from behind an ancient oak tree to stand in front of Eva and Basil.

"Come, grab my hands," said Nicoletta to Eva. She took Eva's right hand and grabbed Basil's hand with her left.

Tan took ahold of Eva's other hand, and a dirge started to play from an unknown source. The four sang and hummed along.

> "Oh, bright maidens. Oh, fair sons. Hail ancestors. Drawn in time, history written. By the stars crying secrets for the kingdom's long past. For the kings and his fief so loyal. We rise to meet the scars and the boils of the battles of war. Bought by an enemy thought long vanquished."

"I thought it was just a nursery rhyme," said Eva, her blood thrilling and her neck goosing.

"Nay," said Tan. "It's perfectly fitting. What is the enemy that pits man against species even as ages have passed and we lived in peace for so long. Man confronts a paradox."

"Quack," Terry said, appearing out of nowhere.

"No, not a pair of ducks!" said Basil, exasperated. "It's a discrepancy between reality and an underlying truth. I'm glad you're here, Terry. I want you to stay with Eva. I need to be in a position to negotiate with the incoming battalions."

As he spoke all sound suddenly stopped—the war drums, the piping flutes, the dirges.

"C'est commence," said Tan. "It's started."

—⁂—

Oleeve stood, told Gilbert to hurry, and gifted his team ten camels and officers to ride them.

"We enter here and at least ten miles in there is serious evidence to suggest a hideous no-formed race of beasts. Abominations that are part man and part beast that have made the forest interior their home.

Over here toward the eastern edge of the forest. You must pass by the outskirts. We don't want to give ourselves a bad reputation to the villages living here. They call themselves the Fellows, but if you see anything disturbing feel free to investigate once we've rooted out the evil. Once we have beaten a path back towards the falls on horses and cleared the forest, we will meet on the beaches. The Badgers; the river dwellers will take us down the coast, and there we will move back to Diaspora. Now who will save the day?" he yelled.

"We will! Oleeve!" The men punched their fists into the air.

"Oh, it's a grand sight, different than it was in my day," said another man to a Diasporian soldier. "You young men haven't seen any fighting!"

"Just the old scuffle in the city walls," replied the soldier. "The prisons are always empty."

"You'll be seeking blood, feeling for and digging deep in enemy necks to feel the veins come loose in your hands!" interrupted the old man with relish.

"Quiet, you old fool," said the soldier, and he went to clap the old man on the head to sit him down and get him out of the way, but somehow his fist went past him.

Another man offered, "Hear, hear!"

Albion skipped past the old man, who was looking absentmindedly to the horizon.

MALEFICENT

Maleficent had been awake all night but her loyalty and her hunger to be with her owner drove her on. She needed to return to her handler with the sugary voice and the surety of presence. Through their shared bond, Nicoletta was winging alongside with Maleficent, and they both watched from the falcon's eyes. But Maleficent needed succor, the physical presence and calming voice of her mistress. She needed to curl her claws around gloved hands and dig them into leather. Alongside her, the five other released falcons made a lazy kettle of eyes in the sky. It had taken Maleficent all night to pick at the leather straps and weaken the binding on the falcon hutch with Nicoletta crooningto her from afar and encouraging her on. But she'd done it, freed her companion birds of prey. Maleficent stretched her neck out, and the falcons winged and formed and glided—home to their mistress.

NICOLETTA

Nicoletta watched with horror through the falcon's eyes as platoons of Oleeve's men ran toward the forest clearing. The first wave of men carried rifles with the rear tranche following behind them with dual wield axes.

"And in ancient wars," said Basil, reading out of his ancient history resource on his maps. "They could be used to attack, and they also could be used for butchery or dismemberment for attacking from the rear."

Terry twiddled a stick in the ear and looked tortured.

Basil remembered where he was and who his audience was.

"Sorry," he mumbled. "This was my birthright—keep the foundry glowing should war come back to the land. In case we need to take up weapons to defend ourselves and our community." *One day*, thought Basil, *we shall find the source of the corruption. I know by the insight invested in me by my forefather, evil comes not from the forest. It comes from elsewhere. It comes forth and manifests in men's hierarchical nature, and it pulls and pulls at the men's chests. It calluses their responses to their customers. Eventually, to the rest of their fellow men down to the children and finally to their wives, and that's when we all turn on one another. Why do they not realize that turning on the forest is turning on ourselves?* He slapped his forehead and strode around the perimeter of the makeshift encampment.

"Where are we?" asked Eva as an afterthought.

"This is Cleft's Severance," said Basil.

Noise levels were climbing up in the background. The sound of instruments replaced by the disturbing sound of war cries and baying and howling and crushing. Eva waited for Basil's explanation.

"See the face of the rock there?" said Basil.

Eva turned her eyes to the cliff face.

"There are speckles. Look closely."

Eva looked and could see the grainy rock was indeed speckled with little flicks of lighter crystal.

"There is a legend or a child's fable that rock like that is Earth wings," said Basil. "Where they come close, and there is a *V* or a cleft, you will see two formation joined together. They looked like wings from above. Legend says if the Earth gets too disturbed, she will move her wings. The wings will open and discharge a horde of mechanical insects, belch fire, and after she is finished, she will stop, and all those speckles are fireflies trapped from the last time she was forced to defend herself. Another legend says that where the two wings meet is an old path to underground caverns; great underground caverns with lakes bigger than any on Panacea, where they have metal fireflies and they also still have bees and butterflies and hummingbirds. And there are trees and ancient folks, and we're not allowed to know if they're present until they are sure that we will never take up arms against each other again."

Eva guessed Basil was telling her the story mostly to overcome his sense of disquiet and trepidation. The two stood silent as a platoons continued marching into the jungle slashing at anything and anyone and any beast in their way.

EVA

"Nooo!" yelled Eva.

She broke past the Pentarians standing sentry in the clearing and, pushing through brush, forced her way past Nicoletta, who would go to stand in between her and the fray.

"Nooo," she yelled. "We don't want this! We don't want harm. We don't want violence. We don't want killings, and we don't want maces harming the old forest!"

Panic drove her feet. From the clearing toward the noises, the air imposing drag on her progress, she ran and ran faster. She jumped logs, and her heart beat faster, and her panic got greater. What would happen to Asperia if an army could just be called up on the spot and without warning? Without any threat, it could be dispatched to take down all that was near and dear. The Ventura's treated life. They did not destroy it! And now she must call on her long dormant powers and fight!

"Where did this desire to hurt, to harm, to destroy, come from?" Eva despaired inwardly as she ran.

All the sound from the forest drained away, and she focused on running and clearing any obstacles. A tree trunk in the distance came crashing down and pulled her back just in time as she just missed catching herself on thorn creepers. A madrick ball exploded off another trunk and puffed tiny vectors of crim spore into her eyes. She blinked away the stings as they burst. She would look like a fright as the spores dyed her tears for twenty-four hours. The forest too then was panicked and unleashing its defenses. Turning past an old dugout, she hurdled a felled beech log with a family of skunks crouching underneath. Sucking in hot furious breath and taking another sharp turn with a round off into a handspring, she landed in the middle just outside a clearing where furious activity was taking place centered around one of the old trees—the Guardians.

She watched, hidden by the underbrush. There was one man, then five, then twenty, then fifty, each dragged in a body smaller than themselves and proceeded to throw the furry corpses in a pile by the old Guardian tree. One or two bodies were still moving. One screamed, and a soldier kicked it into the pile. She couldn't make out if it was skinwalkers or if it was defenseless spider monkeys. She looked with horror. Her heart drummed.

Eva stood and danced from foot to foot, not worried the snapping of the branches that she was dancing on would identify her location and ignoring the soldiers' movements. She concentrated on her level of panic at the destruction of life all around her, trying to become fully aware before bringing it to her good use.

Just as she felt she was going to splinter into parts and energy, she tempered the flame of fury down to make it cold. It would do no good for her energy to diffuse and dissipate into her surroundings. Just then she was noticed.

"Hey, girl," said a soldier, "Get out and stand back." He noticed her hair sticking up. "Hey, we've got an undead right here. Skinwalker!"

Eva ignored him, throwing her arms back, taking a deep breath as two soldiers moved toward her position. She had pockets full of poison-tipped shuriken, but that would only cause trouble for the three men heading straight for her. Then she was potentially trapped by greater numbers. This was not fighting in the open. What was she going to do? A vine dropped down at her feet. A stag weed vine with grooves and notches. Without looking upwards, she grabbed and made purchase, hauling herself upward. And reaching down to the bottom of the vine and giving it a shake to anger it, Eva pulled out her step knife and cut the length of vine beneath her.

"Fssst," it said as is it dropped to the ground and attacked the nearest soldier.

She felt badly for cutting an arm of the vine. *To cut, to save,* she thought. "It wasn't as though the vine couldn't regrow, and boy, wouldn't those three soldiers get a fright," she told herself. She climbed up higher until she crested the forest canopy and grabbed a thick branch, swinging herself up to watch the action below. The Guardian who dropped the vine, thank the Nine Circles!

Eva gave out a howl, and hooked her knee over the branch and swung herself up with no branches above her. She danced along branches until she had a bird's eye view of the clearing below. Sadness tugged her heart as the three soldiers she had left on the ground were pulling at the ankles of a motionless baby. Fresh regrowth from the vine she'd cut would encircle their ankles and pin them to the ground, so they weren't a problem, but there were so many more men rushing in to take their place. She pulled out her stack of shuriken. She was only one female, one leader, but she could do what she could do to stop what was happening to the innocent forest folk and make a stand to preserve their innocence. Hooking her finger under her ringfold of shuriken and taking one off, she sliced it with a clean movement of her arm. Her mark a soldier below, hitting him cleanly. He fell to the ground, scrabbling for his nose. She kept on throwing and breathing and throwing as the soldiers looked around for the volley of missiles launched upon them from the sky. And calm had descended on her heart. She was a weapon herself, now defending the weaker, and she could not afford the emotion she knew was behind the walls of her heart coming forth and unravelling her control at the sight of so many faint bodies, helpless bodies piled up lying in the ground. Later, she would think about how it had come to this, what could be done to prevent it in the future. Right now, she had to be merciless in stopping the pointless brutal killing, stop the intrusion into the old forest.

Halfway down the chain that held her shuriken, she realized it wouldn't be enough. For every soldier she distracted with a carefully aimed shuriken, there was another to take his place. There was now a crush in the clearing below. Someone had spotted here and was pointing upward.

"Verbalinae! Skywitch," he cried.

Trying to dodge the falling missiles, the men did not see a vine arm snake around one of their number's throat and clap a furry hand over the soldier's bloody mouth. Most of the men were looking upwards by now and pointing up, alarmed.

BASIL

"How could you lose her?" said Basil to Terry. "I asked you to watch Eva for a moment while I circled the fray. As the Ankh, she has a specific role to play in this most dangerous of times. And the forest may lose this battle, but we need her for the war. I know she is still alive. I feel the Nine Circles would be mourning if she wasn't, but she is in great danger, Terry."

Terry kicked the ground desolately. "She was just here," he said. "I was with her. The noises, well, it was very loud. And maybe I was trying to block it out." He scuffed his hunger along the neck of Falcon that was poking his head out from Terry's sleeve. "Basil, I'm sorry. What can I do?"

"Well, there's nothing you can do," replied Basil. "Ride with me, Nicoletta. Tan, ride with me. Knowing Eva, she's gone closer to ease suffering."

"We can only hope she's not too close to the fighting or in the middle of the fray," said Tan, placing his forehead into his calloused hand.

"She's an adult. We have to trust she made sensible decisions. We're all adults, and we all need each other. Let's go rescue our family member. Terry, wait here," Nicoletta said, echoing Basil's words.

Tan and Basil, looking older and with knotted forehead and glancing to the glowing skies reflecting the fires of fighting, nodded.

The trio mounted three of the Pentarians and disappeared into the brush toward the noise. Terry sank back on his heels feeling helpless, wondering what he could do. Not an idea came to him.

—ɯ—

Eva was tiring, and she was out of shurikens. An officer below was retrieving some kind of crossbow or missile launcher from a wagon, and they looked as though they were having discussions about how to dislodge her. Eva from the tree considered her options, and it was all looking pretty grim when Tan and Nicoletta and Basil appeared in the clearing, three of them making a triangle, avoiding the bodies. Eva stopped overthinking. Now it was time for listening.

Eva, you brave thing, she heard Nicoletta's end. *Eva, Basil has an idea but can't do this without you. He needs you to find a spark or two.*

It was too dangerous to light a spark up here, and she could only find spots of glowing embers on the ground despite the fury that fired the missiles from her hand.

Eva sent back; *I risk setting the whole forest on fire. I cannot risk a spark.*

Nicoletta sent back: Eva, concentrate here. Anchor into the sparks so that you might find space in the air to coax the sparks to do your bidding. Do not use the air to create a fire. Use your fury". "We need your fury. We need to hone our craft so the fire gathers to itself and passes through us, and we can use it to dispatch these men", "Yes, some of them will die".

Eva said, "No, I'm standing on a Guardian. The Guardian crown was fine.

Niccoletta sent: *Trust me, trust me, trust me.*

Eva looks down between her feet, and all she could see was piles of bodies that are stacked against the tree's sturdy trunk. Blood was running from the foot of the old Guardian to the edge of the forest. She started to sob. She's rising and falling. Tan's voice was there. He was like the sound of rocks and a seabed.

"Hold your grief. Hold it fast. Don't let it sink you. This is not the time for watery feelings. This is a time for fire. We need fire to stop this travesty today."

"Yes, Tan, my father. "Yes, Grandfather," said Eva as the ocean of her emotions receded.

She saw between her feet a dress, a little girl, whole. She was angry now. Oh, she was so angry. She held her hands out in front of her. Examining her fingernails, that's where she could start. She examined her fingers. A little girl, whether she was human or Skinwalker. She could be a Fellow, breathing. She was human. She was not hate. She was not sick, twisted perversion taking over and home for somebody else's twisted perverted ideals. Today she was innocence lost. Eva's eyes focused on her two hands, and the horizon came and went in the distance. Her fingernails got sharper and sharper, and then they were tiny prints of light and then dancing front fire dancing fire flames on the end of her hands.

So pretty, she thought.

And she rested, and she resisted the urge to get lost in the pretty of the flame.

"It's just the pretty in the pent", said Nicoletta. *"But don't stay there. Fury now. We need fury to make a weapon for human flesh only. "*.

Lazily, Eva pointed her hands down toward the clearing. She pointed one hand down and toward Tan who reached his left hand up and his right toward Basil. Eva pointed her right hand toward Nicoletta who caught the flames dancing out from Eva. The energy passed through her and a Penterian came to stand between Nicoletta and Basil. He and Basil stretched out hands to each other, to make a five-sided flame shape around and above the clearing.

HATE

Clamor. Heat. Burning. Men realized too late what was happening. Some were running, terrified, did not look to see where they were going and crashed into others. They grabbed and writhed in each other's arms. Their clothes started smoking and turning to ash.

Eva pulled down and drew on all the sadness held in the Unriven, the blackness in men and woman's hearts that could drive fear and hurt and hate, all the accumulated sadness and suffering and uncertainty around her and channeled it into the fire that braided between the apothecarists. Eva had so much fear, herself, for the future, but she had to stay in the present and stop this atrocity where the unthinkable was happening. Marauding troops had come to destroy her beloved forest. Had to stop it now! Her feet trembled against the Guardian's branch, and she felt its life, felt its entire essence, innate goodness, its desire for all things living to flourish. Tears decorated her face, and she felt the current of life run all the way down into the Earth until through its tap root into the advanced network of fungi and living organisms that depended on the Mother Guardian.

Eva channeled and pumped up the fire, which streamed between her and Basil and Tan and Nicoletta and the Pentaria, stopping only to lift her hands above her head and exaltation and send a stream of fire to the sky. The fire streamed and centered through her chest. Eva shrieked with lust. She shrieked with anger, for lost truth and the thirst for vengeance and the need to protect her own, to protect those who came before and who stood to come in her stead.

And around the clearing the fire raged, and the men died. Several of them turned the wrong way; saw Eva; and found themselves confronted by the piles of men, children, and no more than babies stacked at the foot of the great Guardian tree. With nowhere else to go but to fall over and die on top of corpses, the confused pain ravaged men thought, *Why did we come here and take up arms? Were we used?* as the pain ransacked and ravaged their bones and skin and contracted their hands into wizened gripping claws. At the last, they were puzzled to the last agonizing breath as to why they had taken up arms.

Others, hearing Eva's shriek, shrieked back to her. Some so besides themselves with bloodlust that they shrieked off a promise to dismember her from limb to limb, to rip one leg off and then the other. They also died writhing in pain.

Eva, feeling the savageness of their thoughts, glance off her, noticed their passing with satisfaction. Others beseeched Eva to the skies and threw out a promise to her to forsake their tainted guns and arms that should never have been bought into the forest in the first place and promised to join her to follow her, if only she would take away the pain. They died too, and they died a slower more agonizing pain with feet jerking and kicking helplessly. A few lucky ones stumbled free, with their memories wiped clean, as they sobbed and stumbled free, making it clear of the burning pyre; and its great silent tree remaining as yet untouched by the inferno that consumed and burned all the flesh within.

Eva, on her and unharmed by the fire, now drained of rage and passion, felt the fury and the flame. Either way she felt desolate now and very scared. Familiar with the cycle of nature and the law of the Guardians, that all great things and those with power must shelter all that that was smaller and weaker, she knew she must bear responsibility for what was to come. And with pain and sadness, gripping her toes around the great branch, asked the Guardian, sending, Great Mother, must I really?"

"Yes, child, it is time," said the wondrous oak. "It is done, I must perish to allow a new mighty oak to thrust skyward."

"But, Mother, I can't," said Eva.

The Guardian tree responded, "You are a tool. The machete that cleaves the mature tree for heat for two legged ones and in place plants seedlings afresh. Wildfire that races past the hills to prepare the seed for a new generation. Release me, Eva. It will clean the land of the evil below."

Eva, using the last of her fury, picked up a seed dropped by the Mother last season and sent a stream of fire to the crown of the tree. The top of the tree started burning.

Hugging herself, Eva advised Nicoletta and Tan and Basil the job was done and swung herself down a branch and down another one, and nimbly deeply racing ahead of the fire. Down the tree, she grabbed on to Basil.

"Oh, Basil," she said with the stench of human flesh rising up around her. "Basil, what have I done! We are caregivers, and I have wrought great destruction on a Mother, a Guardian."

She shrugged as she looked at the carcasses of soldiers piled up and looked back to the furry innocent bodies and the dying Guardian tree.

"For is the mighty mother who would protect all!" And as the flames crowned the mighty tree, Eva sobbed and heaved, falling into Basil's arms.

He gently led her from the scene of the destruction.

Nicoletta and Tan followed close behind them.

TERRY

The burning continued and eventually the smell reached Terry.

"Oh s——," he said helplessly, then feeling horror, realizing the smell was burning flesh.

The Pentarians walked in a circle around him, prowling, and one of them disrupted his stride and streaked out of line and knocked Terry over.

Terry sprung to his feet, and the Pentarians dropped to their haunches :Terry turned and looked at the Pentarian gazing into its green eyes as smoke carrying the smell of child remains, drifted toward them.

They held each other's gaze, and Terry said, "What now?" He received a helpless nod in return.

Not being a fighter, he felt hopeless, lost, and defeated.

"How could he make an impact? Where were the others?" He ran through his skills as an apothecarist. Of his skills, the most useful skills he possessed was to manipulate smoke and neutralize most poisons. Useless in battle! He had no elemental skills, as Eva did with fire.

Little Falcon shot up off the Pentarians back and onto his hand and ran up his shoulder to Terry's head. Terry heard a sound like a loud swooping eagle, sound up above him. A huge flying (thing) hurtled out of the sky and suddenly, terrifyingly, Terry felt Falcon's tiny claws gripping into his head and then...nothing. Terry had been knocked off his feet by the blow of an impact and felt some of his hair and tear away with Falcon's claws. Appalled, he looked up as the very devil itself (herself), with its painted lips and long red talons on the end of some kind of synthetic wings, thrashed off into the hazy smoke and the glow of the horizon from the setting sun, winging south. Terry cupped his hands to the sky, and silent tears started running down his cheeks. This was how Eva, Nicoletta, and Tan found him on their return to Clefts Severance. The three Pentarians keeping a silent vigil around a sobbing Terry in the setting sun.

THE ENDING

A man pinned to the great burned Guardian was barely recognizable as such. His head was fastened by a spike to the tree. His tunic rendered to shreds, sliced leather pants swinging off his hips barely kept his dignity intact in death. Rucking boots placed carefully to one side of his corpse. Both his corpse and his boots already bore signs of having been assailed by wildlife.

"This is not good," said Despoina, scratching her head, stepping through the curtain of vines into the clearing around the still-warm Guardian. *This does not conclude the matter here*, thought Despoina, scratching her head. The cities will not let the species stay free without an act of retribution. This marks the start of the next great war, a war between man and species.